AF263255

ROYAL VENGEANCE

ALSO BY AIMÉE CARTER

Royal Blood

Royal Scandal

ROYAL VENGEANCE

AIMÉE CARTER

DELACORTE PRESS

Delacorte Press
An imprint of Random House Children's Books
A division of Penguin Random House LLC
1745 Broadway, New York, NY 10019
penguinrandomhouse.com
getunderlined.com

Editor: Kelsey Horton
Cover Designer: Ray Shappell
Interior Designer: Michelle Gengaro-Kokmen
Production Editor: Colleen Fellingham
Managing Editor: Tamar Schwartz
Production Manager: Shameiza Ally

Library of Congress Cataloging-in-Publication Data is available upon request.
ISBN 978-0-593-48597-2 (hardcover) — ISBN 978-0-593-48599-6 (ebook)

The text of this book is set in 11.5-point Adobe Garamond.

Manufactured in the United States of America
1st Printing

The authorized representative in the EU for product safety and compliance is Penguin Random House Ireland, Morrison Chambers, 32 Nassau Street, Dublin D02 YH68, Ireland, https://eu-contact.penguin.ie.

TO SARA HODGKINSON

And in memory of my dad, Richard Carter,
who loved this series. I hope you still get
to find out how the story ended.

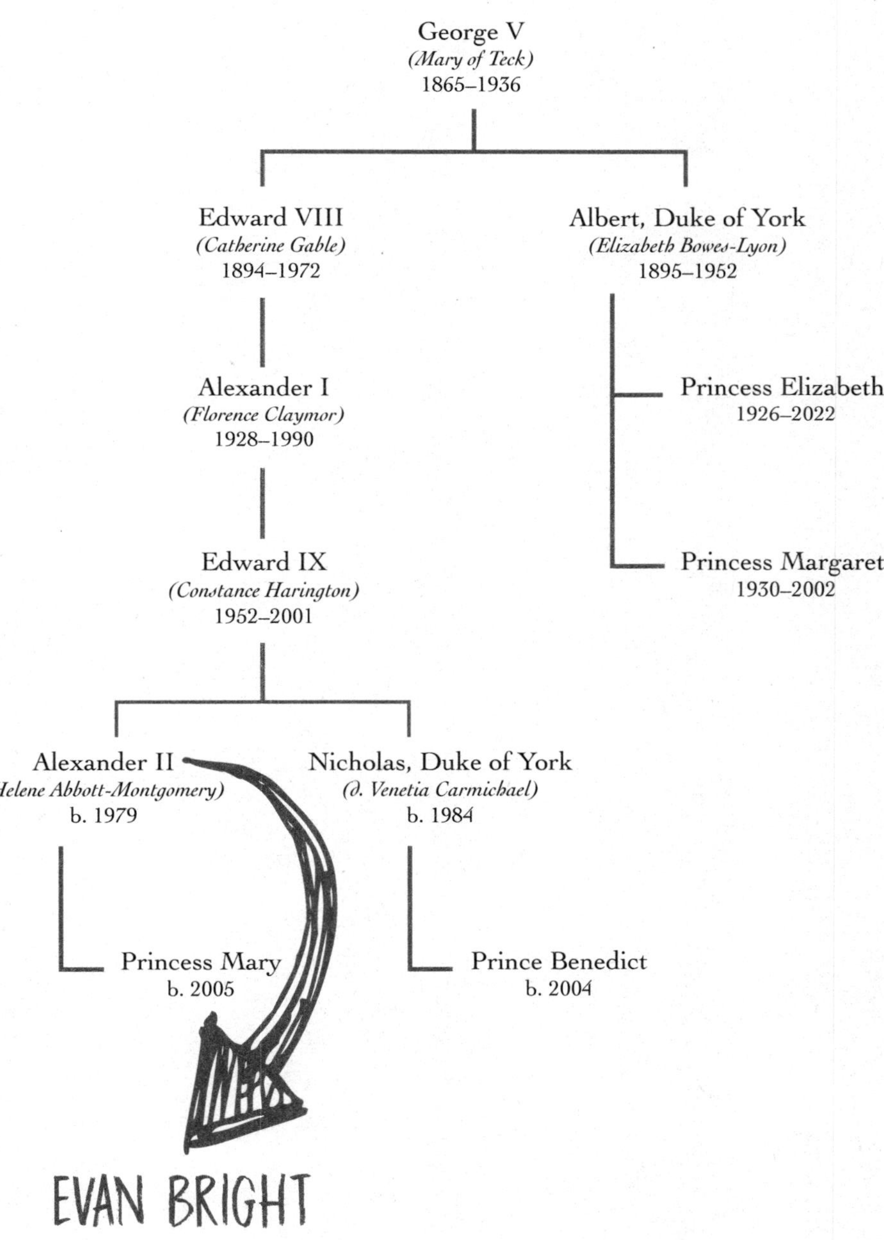
George V
(Mary of Teck)
1865–1936
Edward VIII
(Catherine Gable)
1894–1972
Albert, Duke of York
(Elizabeth Bowes-Lyon)
1895–1952
Alexander I
(Florence Claymor)
1928–1990
Princess Elizabeth
1926–2022
Edward IX
(Constance Harington)
1952–2001
Princess Margaret
1930–2002
Alexander II
(Helene Abbott-Montgomery)
b. 1979
Nicholas, Duke of York
(d. Venetia Carmichael)
b. 1984
Princess Mary
b. 2005
Prince Benedict
b. 2004
EVAN BRIGHT

CHAPTER ONE

RAVENS MISSING FROM THE TOWER

Three of the seven ravens residing at the Tower of London have mysteriously vanished, leaving fewer than the six required ravens inside the historic fortress.

Ravens Bronwen, Chester, and Phillip never returned to their aviary last night, according to Jacob Johnston, Ravenmaster of the Yeomen Warders, and after an exhaustive search of the grounds, the birds are presumed missing. While this isn't Phillip's first taste of freedom—he famously disappeared from the Tower in May 2018, only to be found a week later perched atop a pub a quarter mile away—mated pair Bronwen and Chester aren't known for their wanderlust.

"It's ominous, isn't it?" says Katie Mayburn, owner of the nearby Teapots and Treason Café. "Everyone here knows the legend—that if the ravens ever leave the Tower, both Great Britain and the Crown will fall. And with His Majesty in a state and the entire royal family hiding in Scotland . . . well, we can't blame the ravens for seeing the signs, can we?"

One might agree that it is indeed yet another blow to both country and monarchy, after the 12 January bombing of the Modern Music Museum in London that killed eight and critically injured His Majesty King Alexander. Though MI5 has arrested several alleged members of the Army of the British Republic, the antimonarchist group claiming responsibility for the terrorist attack, the royal family, including heir apparent Crown Princess Mary; Queen Helene; Prince Nicholas, the Duke of York; Prince Benedict of York; and the Queen Mother, have all reportedly taken refuge at Balmoral Castle until ABR leadership has been apprehended.

One royal-adjacent notably missing from Scotland is Evangeline Bright, the eighteen-year-old illegitimate daughter of His Majesty and American artist Laura Bright. Evangeline, who was named a co-conspirator in the bombing by the unknown head of the ABR shortly after the attack, was reportedly not invited to Balmoral due to security concerns. She and her boyfriend of seven months, Christopher Abbott-Montgomery, Earl of Clarence and nephew of the Queen, were also photographed with a suspected member of the ABR in the weeks leading up to the attack, lending credibility to what royal insiders have attempted to dismiss as a preposterous claim. Though Bright has yet to be arrested or charged, she is allegedly under investigation by MI5 for her suspected involvement in the attack.

While Lord Clarence has returned to Oxford for the new term, Evangeline, who has spent the past eight months straddling the line between commoner and royal, hasn't been seen in public since the bombing. Sources within the palace report that she has fled to the United States, and after the endless trail of trouble she has caused in her short time in Britain, no one expects her to return, even as His Majesty's life continues to hang in the balance.

The Ravenmaster has offered a substantial reward for the safe return of the missing ravens.

—*The Daily Sun*, 31 January 2024

SOMEONE IS FOLLOWING ME.

The steady thud of their footsteps echoes against the cobblestones, and I shove my hands deeper in my coat pockets as I hurry through the tunnel. My knit hat is pulled down to my brows, and my scarf is wrapped around the bottom half of my face, leaving only my eyes exposed to the January chill. No one should be able to recognize me. And yet—

Thud, thud, thud.

Maybe I'm imagining things. I have plenty of reasons to be paranoid, after all, and Oxford isn't exactly a ghost town in the middle of term. Maybe we're just headed in the same direction. Maybe—

"Oi!" calls a deep male voice, and the footsteps grow louder. "Wait!"

My stomach sinks, and I rest my finger against the panic button sewn into the lining of my pocket, but I don't press it yet. If I do, any number of MI5 agents and personal protection officers will descend on this walkway, and everything I've been working toward—everything we've all been working toward these past weeks—will be ruined.

I could whirl around and confront him, but if he's one of the dozen paparazzi staked out on the other side of the building, where Kit's last lecture of the day lets out soon, I'll only be blowing my cover. And in the time it takes to upload a photograph and write an attention-grabbing headline, the entire world will know that I'm not in the US, like everyone thinks I am.

And if he isn't a paparazzo . . . if he's someone much, much worse . . .

My heart is in my throat now, and I focus on the courtyard ahead, resisting the urge to break into a run.

"Oi!" he calls again, panting now. "Bloody hell, I'm not going to hurt you. You dropped your keys."

I should keep moving. It could be a trick, but my hands grope around in my pockets anyway. Wallet. Defense spray. Phone. Tissues. Tracker. Everything's here, except—

He's right. I've dropped my damn keys.

My boots root themselves to the ground. Those keys are my only way into the flat I share with Kit, the singular safe harbor in the shitstorm that is my life, and something primal within me refuses to take another step without them. But before I can think this through—obviously *someone* in my security detail must have a copy—a bulky man in his thirties steps in front of me, blocking my path. He's at least twice my size, with patchy stubble on his chin and watery eyes that rake over me, but if that wasn't enough to creep me out, he also has a camera hanging from his neck.

Shit.

"Here." He dangles my key chain in front of me, and I snatch it from him, not caring that I'm being rude. He's the one following me into an empty part of university grounds, after all. And he's the one trying to profit from Kit's supposed misery.

"Cheers, mate," I mutter, and to my horror, it comes out in more of an Australian accent than an English one. He studies me closer now, and even though I'm wearing color contacts, I avert my eyes.

"Me mum's from Brisbane," he says, as if this is supposed to endear him to me. "Where—"

"Gotta go," I mumble, and this time I sound Scottish. Without giving him a chance to tell me his dad's from Edinburgh, I dart past him, no longer bothering to disguise my fear.

Please don't recognize me. Please *don't recognize me,* I silently beg as I hurry toward the courtyard beyond. But while I'm sure he watches me for several beats too long, at last I hear a low grumble and the shuffle of footsteps as he finally leaves me in peace.

That was close—too close. And as I burst into the courtyard, my pulse is racing and my scarf has come undone, leaving my nose and mouth exposed. I pause to fix it, my gaze sweeping across the dormant lawn, but no one else is here, and—

"You're late."

I whirl around and bite back a curse. Lady Tabitha Finch-Parker-Covington-Boyle stands directly behind me, her designer coat belted at the waist and her black pixie cut hidden by a hat with a sparkly pom-pom. Her expression is dangerously neutral, and she holds two thermoses of what I suspect is coffee.

"Did you not see the paparazzo following me?" I say, glancing once more into the tunnel. Part of me expects him to double back, but he's gone now, disappeared onto the busy road. "I thought he—you know."

"Recognized you?" Tibby raises a single perfectly plucked eyebrow. "Did he?"

I shake my head. "Pretty sure he thinks I'm Australian. Is one of those for me?"

She offers me a thermos with a sniff, and I take it gratefully as we make our way to a nearby bench. English winters have nothing on the icy air in Vermont, or Michigan, or any of the other states where I spent almost seven years of my life being expelled from various boarding schools. But it's perpetually damp here in a way that seeps into my bones, and I've all but forgotten what it feels like to be warm and dry.

As Tibby and I sit side by side, a nearby clock tower starts to chime. Kit's final lecture of the day is letting out, and by now the paparazzo who returned my keys has undoubtedly rejoined the other so-called photographers, camera at the ready. But just like yesterday—just like every day these past weeks—Kit will take their shouts and insults and leading questions on the chin without comment, his silence the only answer guaranteed to leave them frustrated. Anything else—a smirk, a wink, or even a glance in the wrong direction—and they'll happily turn it into a scathing headline. Which will only bring more vultures to the perch for tomorrow's encore.

A pang of guilt cuts through me, and I disguise my grimace with a sip of mocha from the thermos. Kit's here in Oxford because of me. He's enduring their abuse—the abuse of the entire world—so I don't have to do this alone. And I will never, ever be able to repay him.

"We haven't got much time," says Tibby, and her tone makes it clear that she blames me entirely. "Have you made any progress?"

"You know I can't tell you that," I say, and she gives me a withering look. Technically this is true—Tibby isn't part of this operation, and she has no business knowing what's going on. But she somehow has all the details anyway, and I sigh. "I completed my cybersecurity course."

"Wasn't that supposed to take you two months?" she says, and I shrug.

"I don't exactly have much to keep me busy right now. Might as well learn how to hack properly."

"Inspiring," deadpans Tibby. "And Kit? Is he also learning how to lead a life of crime?"

I shake my head. There's no use explaining to Tibby the difference between a white hat and a black hat hacker, or any of the colors in between. "He's trying to reestablish his connections to Fox Rex, but he's worried they don't trust him anymore."

Tibby's expression flickers with barely disguised disapproval. "Have you considered the possibility that they might bring him back into the fold, only to silence him for good?"

Suddenly the temperature in the courtyard seems to drop

twenty degrees. "That won't happen. He has his own security team, and Fox Rex isn't the problem—"

"Fox Rex feeds directly into the ABR," says Tibby. "They may fancy themselves a secret society, but they're terrorists in training, and you know it."

I grip my thermos tighter. "*They* don't, though. There's no evidence that any of the members of Fox Rex know they're connected to the ABR—"

"And what if it isn't Fox Rex that comes knocking?" says Tibby. "What if the ABR and this *Guy Fawkes* arsehole go after him instead? What if—"

"Would you please just *stop*?" I snap. "I know you and Jenkins don't want us here, but Kit and I have a real chance at finding the list—"

"You mean the list that may or may not even exist?" says Tibby, and I huff.

"Aoife Marsh said that Guy brags about their former members all the time. Doctors, lawyers, members of Parliament, nobility—even people working inside the palace. And MI5 is sure that means he has a list somewhere. Aoife agrees, and she hasn't steered us wrong yet."

"You are, as always, an excellent judge of character," mutters Tibby before taking a long drink. "And what happens when you find this supposed list?"

"Then MI5 will know who to investigate," I say stubbornly. "They'll know everyone who could possibly be associated with the ABR, and everyone who might've been involved in the bombing—"

"But you do realize Ben won't be on it, yes?"

I blink. "Of course he won't. He doesn't even go to Oxford—"

"So you're doing this out of the goodness of your own heart, then?" she says. "You're risking your life—you're risking *Kit's* life—to simply give MI5 a hand?"

Our eyes meet, and I grit my teeth. "If the ABR finds out that MI5 knows about their connection to Fox Rex, they'll burn any evidence, including—"

"That list of names. Yes, I'm aware," says Tibby.

"And . . . any proof that Ben's involved in the ABR, too," I mutter. Because she's right. I'm not just here for that list. And I can't go home—wherever that is these days—until I've done everything I can to make sure the monster trying to kill my family pays for it.

"Evan," she says with a sigh, as if I'm a misbehaving child who needs to hear the rules one more time before they stick. "That's not on you."

"No one else is looking," I protest. "No one else believes Ben is part of this—"

"Plenty of people believe you," she says. "He can't go anywhere in Balmoral without being tailed by half a dozen protection officers, and *he's* not the one they're protecting."

I clench my jaw. "If I'm going to accuse the third in line to the throne of treason and terrorism, then I need enough evidence to nail him to the damn wall. It can't be hunches, or coincidences, or the looks he gives me when no one else is watching. It has to be concrete. It has to be *enough.* And this is the only way, okay? Ben's too smart to leave a trail, but maybe the ABR slipped up."

"And if they haven't?" says Tibby, softer this time. I swallow hard.

"Then he's going to kill everyone who stands between him and the throne until it's finally his."

This isn't an exaggeration—I have the bullet wound to prove it, still healing and too close to my heart for anyone's comfort. My father will always bear the scars that prove it, too, if he ever wakes up. And it's only by sheer luck that my mother wasn't caught in a fire that could have—*would* have—killed her.

Because we're the ones in Ben's way now. And there is nothing Prince Benedict of York is more afraid of than the simple fact that if my parents ever decide to marry, I'll be legitimized, and the crown that was once all but guaranteed to be his will fall to my potential heirs instead.

"How's my dad?" I say as I trace the logo on the thermos with my bare fingers.

Tibby purses her lips. "His Majesty is showing signs of regaining consciousness, but it's slower than his doctors would prefer."

I bite my lip. It's been almost three weeks since the bombing that nearly stole Alexander's life, and with every day that passes, I know the hope of a full recovery—or any kind of significant recovery at all—dwindles. "Is my mom still with him?"

"According to Jenkins, she doesn't leave his side," she says. "He also told me to tell you that should His Majesty grow aware of his surroundings and ask after you—"

"He'll tell Alexander where I am," I mumble. "I know."

"And frankly," says Tibby, "if this little sojourn of yours goes on much longer without any progress, I wouldn't put it past Jenkins to go to Her Royal Highness and have her pull the plug."

I shudder at the thought of what Maisie, my half sister,

would say if she knew what I've been up to while she's been stuck in Balmoral, but there's also a distinct possibility she wouldn't care. As the heir to the throne, she and the other Counsellors of State have their hands full trying to keep the monarchy from collapsing, and considering how furious she was with me for my evasiveness during our last phone call, I wouldn't be surprised if she's all but banished me from her mind out of sheer spite.

"We just—need more time," I say, my voice cracking. "Please, Tibby. Whatever you can do to convince Jenkins—"

"And if I don't want to?" she says, but when I give her a pleading look, she sniffs. "This is reckless, Evan."

"I know. But so is doing nothing and letting Ben get away with it."

A muscle in her jaw twitches. "No matter how deep you dig, you might never find what you're looking for."

"At least I'll know I tried," I manage, and she holds my gaze for another long moment before finally rising to her feet.

"Don't die," she says simply. And with that, Lady Tabitha Finch-Parker-Covington-Boyle strides away, leaving me with my thermos in hand and the weight of the monarchy's survival on my shoulders.

CHAPTER TWO

Christopher Abbott-Montgomery, Earl of Clarence and one half of the most hated couple in the world, was spotted leaving the college of Christ Church this afternoon, where he was accompanied by a leggy blond who is most certainly *not* the Bonnie to his Clyde.

The pair was seen making their way down High Street together before parting ways inside their student accommodations with a *lingering* goodbye. The nephew of the Queen was, according to an eyewitness, eager to escort his companion to her dormitory for some time away from the limelight, but she coyly fended him off, no doubt unwilling to get entangled with a suspected terrorist.

While the whereabouts of Evangeline Bright remain unknown, the trusty hounds of Fleet Street have been dogging Lord Clarence's every step as he joins the new term at Oxford University after his *alleged* participation in the bombing of the Modern Music Museum in London. Suffice to say, when his lesser half gets ahold of him, no doubt she'll have as many questions as we do about his chosen company as of late. Will he follow his ball and chain all the way behind bars? Or has Lord Clarence finally seen the light and distanced himself from His Majesty's illegitimate—and degenerate—offspring?

Click below for a gallery of Lord Clarence's former flames, and check back in tomorrow, when we'll have an exclusive interview with Jasmine Jay, with whom he had a whirlwind romance in the days before Evangeline's arrival in England last year.

—*The Regal Record*, 31 January 2024

I'VE BEEN BACK IN THE flat for five minutes when a key jangles in the lock, and I watch from the dining table as the door swings open and a red-faced and breathless Kit trudges into the tiny foyer.

"Bloody parasites," he mutters, dropping his satchel on the ground and raking his fingers through his dark waves. "They tried to follow me inside the dormitory this time. Security got involved, and I had to slip out the back."

I frown. One of the many levels of subterfuge we've had to implement is the fiction that Kit is living in the dorms, when we're really staying half a mile away, in a building that's crawling with undercover agents and personal protection officers. "We should get you a coat that turns inside out," I say through a mouthful of cereal, because making light of the situation is our only real option anymore. "That way, if you ever need to make a quick escape, all you have to do is flip it around, pull a hat on, and no one will know it's you."

Kit joins me at the table and cups my face, his lips brushing mine. "Genius," he murmurs, and I can practically feel his bad mood melt away. "Though they'll still find me somehow. They always do. May I?"

I hand him my spoon, and he takes a giant bite of cereal with the kind of hunger that makes it clear he hasn't eaten since breakfast. Another wave of guilt washes over me. He should be able to buy a sandwich like any other student, but the few times he's tried have ended with a dozen cameras being shoved in his face—or worse, like when a barista refused to serve him, which made headlines around the world.

"Ben posted again," he says as he tries to hand the spoon back to me, but I offer him the rest of the bowl. "Apparently I'm cheating on you with a leggy blond."

"Are you?" I say with only mild interest, and once he takes the cereal, I pull out my phone—my real one, not the one MI5 gave me for emergencies—and navigate to the *Regal Record,* the royal gossip site Ben secretly runs, which is now solely dedicated to tearing me and Kit apart. It's surreal to see the pictures that Ben has somehow already posted of Kit's short walk between the college and his supposed dormitory, accompanied by a tall girl in full makeup. "She looks like Helene."

Kit wrinkles his nose at the mention of his aunt—or, more likely, at the insinuation that comes with their similar appearance. "She's in one of my lectures—Vivianne Blanc. She was waiting for me by the door."

In almost all the pictures, she's smiling and glancing at the cameras, clearly basking in the attention. "Maybe you should ask her which she thinks is more effective, TNT or dynamite."

"Don't be silly," he says. "Everyone knows it's C-4."

He presses his lips to my cheek in a milky kiss, and warmth spreads through me as I continue to swipe from one photo to the next. But without warning, that heat turns cold as the gallery of Kit's afternoon is replaced by pictures of him before we met, stumbling out of nightclubs with Ben or Maisie or a group of raucous aristocrats I don't recognize. And every single one features a different girl on his arm.

I've seen evidence of Kit's former flings before. He has a type—tall and willowy, with stunning bone structure and the kind of beauty only a life free of any real hardship can achieve. Ben has been posting batches of so-called throwbacks over the past few weeks, amplifying the cheating allegations and clearly determined to drive a wedge between us. And I refuse to let it work.

That doesn't mean seeing Kit with his eyes unfocused and his arm wrapped around a different girl each night isn't uncomfortable. But he didn't know me then. And I'm not about to hold his past against him, even though it's hard to ignore the part where I'm definitely the weed in the otherwise expensive bouquet that is Kit's love life.

Kit watches me closely now, cereal temporarily forgotten. "Do you want to talk about it?"

"Talk about what?" I say, exiting the site and setting my phone aside.

"The rubbish Ben is posting to get a rise out of both of us."

I shake my head. "I know what he's trying to do, too," I say, my voice a touch too tight.

Kit's gaze doesn't waver from mine, so intense that I have to fight the instinct to look away. "I remember every detail of the night we first met," he says. "I know you had other things on your mind—"

"Not really," I say, trying to lighten the mood. "Just, you know, getting hauled across an ocean to meet my deadbeat father, whose face happens to be on your money."

"Tale as old as time," says Kit, and the corner of his mouth twitches into a smile. "But the moment you looked at me, I felt like my entire world shifted off its axis, and it would never be the same again. And I didn't want it to be."

Heat rushes through me, and I hook my little finger with his.

"Is this your way of saying that you haven't thought about those other girls since?"

"Not even for a moment. I was in a dark place when those photos were taken, but you gave me a reason to fight my way out. And by loving me, you give me permission to love myself again, too. That's not something I'll ever find at the bottom of a glass or in a club surrounded by strangers. Nothing like it exists for me, except right here with you."

Before I know it, I'm kissing him again, slow and lingering this time. His fingers thread through my hair as he deepens the kiss, and I want to crawl into his lap, to wrap myself around him knowing I'll never be safer or happier or more loved than I am when I'm with him. But as I shift my weight, a sharp knock echoes through the room, and the front door bursts open.

"Shit." I pull away from Kit, nearly losing my balance as a tall man wearing a gray tailored suit strides into our flat. "Singh? What are you *doing*? We don't have a meeting until—"

"It was bumped up," says Agent Suraj Singh of MI5 on his way to the kitchen. While he must notice that we're both disheveled, he has the decency not to say anything. "Haven't you told her, Lord Clarence?"

"Told me what?" I say, glancing at Kit. He focuses on the cereal instead, his cheeks as red as mine feel.

"I received a . . . er, text this afternoon," says Kit, and he clears his throat. "From Dylan."

My nails dig into the edge of the table. Dylan is—*was*—one of Kit and Ben's friends from Eton, and when he ended up in the same course at Oxford alongside Kit, he and his girlfriend, Aoife Marsh, pressured Kit to join Fox Rex.

That alone is more than enough reason to want nothing to do with Dylan. But Dylan is also the one who, with Ben's help, sneaked onto Sandringham grounds on Christmas Eve and hunted Kit and me down like prey. Kit was grazed in the arm, and the same bullet hit me in the chest, barely missing my vital organs.

We should be dead. If Ben and Dylan had their way, we *would* be dead. And while Ben has never physically attacked me himself, I'm positive Dylan won't hesitate the first chance he gets.

"What—" My voice catches, and I try to adopt a casual tone. "What did he want?"

I can tell from the flicker in Kit's dark eyes that he isn't fooled, and he wordlessly hands me his phone. A text thread from an unsaved number is already on the screen, and I scan it, a knot of fear forming in my throat.

How does it feel to be a modern-day Prometheus, Kitters? Bring freedom to the people, and the gods will make sure you're punished for eternity.

Kit

You know I had nothing to do with the bombing, Dylan.

And yet your family has thrown you to the wolves.

Kit

What do you want?

The pleasure of your company.

Kit

No.

Are you really going to turn your back on the only friends you have left?

Kit

We have very different definitions of that word.

Aoife fooled us all, Kitters, including me. She took it too far, and she'll pay the price, but her choices aren't mine, and they aren't the club's.

Kit

Are you saying you had no idea you were dating a terrorist?

I had no idea the ABR existed until her arrest. She lied to us all.

Kit

And how can you be so sure that the accusations against me aren't true?

Because you and Evangeline were inside when the bombs went off, and you'd rather carve out your own heart than let anything hurt her.

Kit

Then how am I supposed to trust that you weren't part of it, too?

Let me prove it to you. Tonight, 8 o'clock. I'll send you the address.

Have you considered the possibility that they might bring him back into the fold, only to silence him for good?

I exhale, my heart pounding as Tibby's words echo through

my mind. "How—how did you know it was Dylan?" I say, grasping for something normal to ask.

"Only he and Aoife ever call me Kitters," mutters Kit, and he looks to Singh. "I'm not going. Dylan's too dangerous."

"Need I remind you that this is the reason you're here?" says Singh, digging through a carton of Thai leftovers with a plastic fork. "This is the opening we've been waiting for."

"We're *here* to find the names of current and former members of Fox Rex," says Kit. "Facing Dylan was never part of the deal. I thought he fled the country."

"Dylan Baxter is your main point of contact within Fox Rex—your only one, now that Aoife Marsh is in custody," says Singh. "We've been keeping tabs on him, but once we discovered he was in Oxford, we knew he was your best bet for returning to the club."

"You knew he was here, and you didn't tell us?" says Kit, his eyebrows climbing. "He tried to *murder* Evan—"

"Your protection officers are all well aware of the situation," says Singh. "Dylan hasn't tried to approach you, and he, like the rest of the world, has no idea Evangeline is here."

"If anyone can figure it out, it's him," growls Kit. "I agreed to this because I thought we had a chance of getting that damn list, but if Dylan's part of the equation, then I'm out."

Singh sighs, but as he sets the container down, no doubt to launch into a speech about why Kit's being unreasonable, I open my mouth.

"Then I'll go instead," I say, and while Kit turns to me like I've just announced I'm moving to Mars, Singh picks up the leftovers again and takes another bite. "It's a club meeting, right? There'll be other people there?"

"If you go anywhere near Dylan, he will try to kill you," says Kit, so bluntly that even though I know it's true, it still sends a shock wave through me.

"Not if there are witnesses," I counter. "If we turn this down—"

"If *I* turn this down," corrects Kit. "Dylan doesn't know you're here."

"Then he won't be prepared to get away with murder," I say, sounding more confident than I feel. I've only met him once, but I'm pretty sure Dylan isn't the type to let something as fickle as the element of surprise get in the way of putting me in my grave.

"Evan . . ." Kit takes my hand—the one that isn't still clutching his mobile. "You know as well as I do how dangerous Dylan is. If I go on my own, it'll be a risk, but if you come with me, your protection officers will be forced to interfere, if they can even get there quick enough to stop Dylan from . . . from . . ."

"He shot you, too," I say quietly as I glance at his sleeve, which hides the pink scar on his bicep. "For all we know, he could be after both of us."

Kit shakes his head, but I see a flicker of doubt in his eyes. "Maybe, but either way, we *do* know that if you go, this will all be for nothing. Either Dylan will kill you, or he'll force you to blow your cover, and neither outcome is an option."

"We can't walk away, either," I say. "You know we can't. If this is our only chance, we have to take it."

Kit closes his eyes briefly, and I know I've finally gotten

through to him. But as I part my lips to offer a few suggestions—a wig for me, maybe, or even a fake nose—Kit speaks.

"Then I'll go," he says. "But not with you, Ev."

I blink. "Kit—"

"I mean it," he says, first looking at me, and then at Singh. "I'll do it, but Evan stays here. It's too dangerous no matter what precautions we take."

Singh scrapes around the bottom of the takeaway container. "I agree," he says, and my mouth drops open. "Evan, you'll stay here. Kit, get that address from Dylan, and my team will draw up our plans."

I look between them both, slack-jawed. "That's it?" I say hoarsely. "You're going to send Kit straight into the lion's den, and I'm—what, grounded?"

"If that's how you'd like to look at it," says Singh with zero sympathy. Not that I expect any from him, but when I look at Kit, his lips are pursed, and he can't—won't—meet my eye.

"I'm sorry, Ev," he says. "But you're right. This is what we're here for. We can't let this opportunity slip away."

"Bullshit," I mutter. And though I want to fight—I want to argue them both into submission—my eyes are hot and prickling with unshed tears, and my limbs tremble as I stand and march to the bedroom. I don't understand my physical reaction at first, so strong that there's nothing I can do to stop it, and part of me worries that Maisie's temper tantrums are rubbing off on me. But as I close the door and lean against it, both grateful and wrecked when I don't hear anyone following, a cold fist wraps around my insides, and I recognize this feeling for what it is.

Panic.

With Dylan in play now, the game just became deadlier than either of us anticipated, and if anything else happens to Kit because of me . . .

Have you considered the possibility that they might bring him back into the fold, only to silence him for good?

CHAPTER THREE

You're sure?

Sure as I can be without dragging him there myself. Which I might.

Good. Deliver the package.

Tonight? In public?

Are you afraid?

No.

Then do it.

What does it mean?

That's above your pay grade.

—Text message exchange between two prepaid mobile numbers, 3:03 p.m., 31 January 2024

I SPEND THE REST OF the day locked in our bedroom, while Kit spends it with Singh's team, no doubt going over their plans for keeping him alive tonight.

At seven-thirty, just before Kit is due to head out, he knocks softly on the door. I'm curled up in our bed with a book in my lap, staring at the same page—the same paragraph—I have been for ages, and for a wild moment, I consider pretending to be asleep. I tell myself that I don't want to say anything that might distract him from his mission, but the cowardly truth is I'm not sure I can face him, either. Not when there's a real risk I might never see him again.

The seconds tick by in silence, and when I hear the floorboards creak, as if he's taken a single step away from the door, another wave of panic floods me like a dam has broken, and suddenly I can't breathe at the thought of not getting to hug him one last time. Flinging the book off my lap, I scramble to my feet and launch myself at the door, only to nearly hit myself in the face as I yank it open and—

There he is, standing a few steps away now, his dark eyes guarded and vulnerable. And I can't move another inch.

"I . . ." He clears his throat. "I'm about to head out. I just wanted to . . . to say goodbye."

I can feel the impact of the word between us, and something in my chest twists painfully, as if the bullet is still lodged inside and has decided to bury itself in my heart instead.

"It's a good plan, right?" I say, the words cracking. "Singh and MI5—they've got your back?"

"They've got my back," he confirms. "I wouldn't go if they didn't, Ev. I promise."

I don't want him to go at all, and I curse the version of me that ever thought this was a good idea—that Kit and I could ever bring down a terrorist organization, even with the entirety of MI5 behind us. "Please don't die," I manage, nearly choking on the words.

His arms are around me in an instant, and he buries his nose in my hair, even as I press my leaking eyes into his shoulder. He's wearing a black button-down and gray trousers, and idly I wonder if he'll change before he leaves, or if he'll carry my tears and snot with him to this meeting.

"Singh said you could watch the live feeds with him, if you want," he whispers, stroking my hair. "And there will be agents everywhere. If anything goes wrong, they'll be no more than fifteen seconds away at any given time, all right? They'll get me out of there."

I count to fifteen in my head. It might as well be infinity. "You don't have—a Kevlar vest on," I say, with a hiccup in between, and I run my fingers over his shirt. His chest is beneath, with nothing protecting him from a bullet.

"Singh thinks they'll search me, and a vest would give it away," he says quietly. "And I agree. Guns are illegal in the UK, and I doubt Dylan will be carrying around a hunting rifle."

Even though he's right, I can't help the extra layer of anxiety that wraps around me like insulation, muffling any sense. "How long?"

"A few hours, maybe," he says. "I'll be back as soon as I can."

A few hours. I have no idea what I'll do with myself, but I nod anyway and peer up at him. "I love you," I say, and it comes out as more of an accusation than a declaration. "Don't you dare die."

Kit smiles down at me, but I can see the sheen in his eyes, too. "I'll do my very best," he says, pressing a kiss to my forehead.

I walk him to the apartment door and watch him stride to the lift, accompanied by four guards in full-body armor. He glances over his shoulder and lifts his hand in a wave, and

I hold mine up in return, my vision blurring as the doors open and he steps inside. My last glimpse of him is of the back of his dark, wavy hair, and as the lift shuts behind him, I fill my lungs with air like I'm steeling myself against a storm, and I head toward Singh's makeshift command center at the end of the hallway.

I don't bother knocking. Singh barely glances up from the wall of monitors he and his tech geniuses have set up, and instantly I pick out the camera that they've managed to attach to Kit through what I quickly realize is a button on his shirt. Apparently he won't be changing after all.

That feed doesn't show him—it only shows the lift doors opening, revealing the lobby of our building, and I can see each step he takes. But there are other cameras on the guards that surround him, and with my eyes glued on the expression of neutrality Kit wears, masking his own fear, I settle into the seat Singh gestures for me to take. The one beside his.

"If you kill him," I say quietly, "I'll kill you. That's a promise."

"Noted," says Singh. And together we settle back to watch the single most terrifying night of my life.

THREE HOURS. THAT'S how long a glossy, charming, *posh* version of Kit I've never seen before is stuck holding court for dozens of preening sycophants who spend all night vying for his attention. Given his closeness to the crown, I half expect him to be shunned at this party full of antimonarchists, but instead he's center stage, by far the most interesting thing at an event supposedly dedicated to honoring the real Guy Fawkes's brutal death. A startling number of partygoers greet him like an old friend, and beside me, Singh scribbles names and descriptions as they come, noting who shows genuine concern for Kit's well-being and who praises him for his supposed role in the Modern Music Museum bombing.

Kit's reluctant to talk about it, but eventually the crowd convinces him to recount his own death-defying perspective of the terrorist attack—with made-up details, as far as I can tell, since I'm pretty sure there was no grand piano in the foyer that was crushed when the ceiling caved in on top of us—and the members of Fox Rex clap and cheer and gasp with delight.

"How *is* His Majesty doing, anyway?" says a smirking boy named Wesley. I want to reach through the screen and throttle him.

"I don't know," says Kit, and there's a strain in his voice that doesn't sound like he's pretending. "I wish I had better news for you, but . . ."

Someone giggles, and I'm immediately reminded of the fact that in this crowd, *better news* doesn't exactly equal the King of England's good health.

At long last, Dylan appears in Kit's feed. The crowd parts for him, revealing his dark outfit and stoic expression, and I immediately spot the odd bulge at his hip. "Singh . . ."

"I see it," he says, and he immediately presses a button and speaks into a mic he hasn't touched so far. "Alpha team, the suspect is in range with a potential firearm. Over."

There's a flurry of activity from half a dozen feeds that have shown nothing but darkness or dim lights so far, but I can't pull my eyes away from Kit's monitor. Dylan steps closer, and Kit rises to greet him.

"Dylan," he says. "It's about time."

"Lord Clarence," says Dylan in a tone that makes it clear he knows how much Kit hates his title. "I thought I'd give you the chance to speak with your fans before I cut in."

"And what a lovely conversation we've all had," says Kit, and I can hear his warm, insincere smile. A few people nearby giggle, and my nails dig so deeply into my palms that my skin throbs.

"Get out of there," I whisper. *"Run."*

"Guy sends his apologies," says Dylan. "He was hoping to be here, but I'm afraid something came up."

Singh snorts. "Of course it did. Best to send in the sacrificial lambs first to make sure no one gets arrested."

I ignore him. "Does Kit have an earpiece in? Can someone warn him about the gun?"

"We don't know it's a gun," Singh points out. "Take a deep breath, Evangeline. Alpha team is on it."

"You're really going to tell me to relax right now when I can see the cords in your neck?" I counter. Singh swallows, and the tension in his shoulders lessens only slightly. But at least he doesn't try to tell me to calm down again.

We've missed something, and now Kit is following Dylan away from the main party, his overcoat draped over his arm. My heart thuds against my ribs. "Where are they going?"

Singh presses the mic button again. "Suspect is on the move with asset. Alpha team, stay close. Beta team, get in position. No deadly force without my say."

"Yes, deadly force," I protest. "Dylan has a *gun*—"

"Evan," says Singh sharply, his stare fixed on the monitors. "If you can't handle this, then I'm going to have to ask you to leave."

I want to claw his eyes out. I want to reach across the space between us and do as much damage as I can to Singh's face with my bare hands, but instead I clamp my mouth shut and rise to my feet, as if that will help Kit somehow. But I don't move from my spot.

They end up in an empty room that looks like it might've been an old-fashioned parlor at one point, with mauve wallpaper and large dark spots on the sun-bleached floor where furniture must have once stood. Dylan leans against the wall, fully at ease, while Kit remains several feet away, his back to the door.

"Why am I here?" says Kit, and Dylan shrugs.

"Guy thinks you're useful to the club, and it's my neck on the line if I lose you. Besides, you're my mate, Kitters. And I'd hate for a misunderstanding to get in the way of years' worth of friendship."

A misunderstanding. He's calling the bombing and the deaths of eight people a *misunderstanding*. "That's it?" says Kit. "This was a test to see if I'd come?"

"It's an apology." Dylan reaches for the bulge on his hip, and I grip the back of my chair as Singh presses the mic button again.

"Hold—*hold* until I say so," he says with a note of anger in his voice, and I notice a high-powered rifle on a monitor in the corner, pointed through a window and aimed directly at Dylan.

"For you," says Dylan as he pulls something from its holster at his side. A strange buzzing fills my ears, and my brain goes wild trying to fill in the blank the camera hasn't caught yet. But when we finally get a good shot of the old-fashioned pistol in Dylan's hand, the first thing I notice is that it has a ribbon wrapped around the barrel. Which is pointed at the floor.

The gun is a gift.

"What the hell?" mutters Singh, and he presses the mic again. "Stay at the ready, but *do not engage.*"

Kit reaches for it, his hands shaking slightly. "An antique," he says, the words strained. "How thoughtful."

"From Guy himself," says Dylan, relinquishing the weapon. I almost melt with relief. "Your father collects them, doesn't he?"

"He used to," says Kit shortly. "Please thank Guy for me. I look forward to meeting him."

"Soon, I'm sure," says Dylan, and he offers him a terse nod. "Go back to your fan club, Kitters. I'll text you when Guy's ready to arrange a meeting."

Kit makes a vague sound and steps out of the room, turning his back to Dylan. Rather than returning to the relative safety of the party, like I expect, Kit pulls on his overcoat and heads straight for the side door, stepping out into the cold January night.

"That's enough," he says quietly. At first I don't understand, but when Singh exhales a sigh and presses the mic button, I realize Kit is finally, *finally* leaving the party.

"Alpha team, shadow the asset until he rendezvous with transportation," says Singh. "Beta team, keep an eye on the suspect until he's out of sight. Mind the exits until the asset is collected."

While he speaks, Kit takes off down the dark street at a hurried pace. As he buttons his coat, the camera catches sight of his hands, and my heart wrenches with dread.

There's nothing subtle about the way they tremble now.

CHAPTER FOUR

Did he like it?

You scared my prized blue blood away.

You were done with him anyway. Did he cry?

Dylan said he was stoic.

Pity. I would've liked the footage.

You'll have to find something else to wank to.

I have a few ideas.

—Text message exchange between two prepaid mobile numbers, 1:12 a.m., 1 February 2024

IT'S WELL PAST TWO IN the morning when, after a long debriefing with Singh, Kit finally unlocks the door to our flat and slips inside.

"There you are," he says tiredly, and I fly to my feet and fling my arms around him, hugging him as tightly as I dare. Like he's been injured, and I'm not sure where the open wounds are. Which isn't far from the truth, metaphorically.

"Are you okay?" I say. He nods against my hair, pulling me to him until my body molds perfectly to his.

"They didn't touch a hair on my head," he promises, and while he's trying to hide it, I can hear the weariness in his voice. It's not just exhaustion. It's something else, too—that same something that sparked into existence when Dylan gave him that *gift*. "Singh isn't thrilled about the lack of intel, but it's better than nothing."

I murmur my agreement into the soft shoulder of his undershirt, which smells faintly like his cologne. The button-down with the camera is gone. "Singh said something about Guy testing the waters. Waiting to see if Dylan was arrested before coming out of hiding."

"The whole party was a test, I think. A test for me." Kit sighs and rests his forehead against mine. "Singh also mentioned you watched the feeds with him."

The worry in his voice is obvious, as if I'm the one who risked my life tonight. "I've had better evenings," I admit, brushing my lips against his chapped ones. "Especially when Dylan showed up with that gun."

Kit tenses. I've hit a nerve. "MI5 took it as soon as I got in the car. I doubt it was loaded—Dylan isn't that stupid."

"And it's old, right? An antique?" I say, hoping this isn't too much to scare him off the topic. "It can't be all that deadly."

Something flickers in Kit's eyes—that same *something* as before. "Old, but likely still functioning," he admits. "My father used to own an identical model. It doesn't aim particularly well, but it'll get the job done at close range."

Close enough for Dylan to have been able to threaten Kit in that parlor. Close enough for Kit to have done the same. My realization must show on my face, because he tilts my chin upward, his deep brown eyes seeming to drink me in under the warm lamplight.

"Thank you for not coming tonight," he says. "For not forcing the issue. I'm sure it was incredibly difficult being left behind, but if you'd been there . . ."

"I want to help next time," I say, lacing our fingers together. "I want to be useful."

"I know. I'm sorry. For making you feel useless, I mean. But I'm not sorry you weren't there tonight, and I suppose I'm sorry for that—"

"Stop." I manage a wry smile. "We're a team, and I want to be part of that team with you. Not sidelined. That's all."

"Okay." He kisses me again. "I'm sor—"

"Stop!" I protest, laughing now. I can feel his grin against my mouth, and as I turn away in a mock huff, he drapes himself over me from behind.

"Remind me again why we agreed to this," he says, sounding more like himself than he has all evening.

"Because it would've taken MI5 months, maybe even years, to infiltrate Fox Rex," I say as we walk as one ambling creature toward the bedroom. "And by then, half the family would probably be dead."

"Right." He buries his nose in my hair, letting me lead him. "I suppose they're very, very lucky we love them."

"Very lucky," I agree, even though no one in the royal family knows we're here, or that we're doing this. And while it's impossible to keep them in the dark forever, I'm dreading the day we have to come clean.

Once we reach our room, Kit sinks onto the bed and peers up at me, the hollows beneath his eyes so purple that it looks like he hasn't slept in weeks. "You still have your makeup on," he murmurs, and I scowl.

"I probably look like a raccoon by now," I say, rubbing my eye, but Kit brushes my hand away.

"Let me."

He reaches toward my nightstand, where I keep a bottle of makeup remover and some cotton pads for the nights I'm too tired to wash my face. And while he's preparing, I climb into his lap, one leg on either side of him.

"It was a rented party house, right?" I say. "There has to be some kind of paper trail with the owners, or a money trail Singh can follow—"

"I mentioned that to him already," says Kit, soaking a cotton pad with some micellar water and gently wiping it across my cheek. "He's checking it out, but he isn't optimistic. It's unlikely Guy Fawkes would slip on something so easily traceable."

My shoulders slump as he dabs at my mascara. "They have to be based *somewhere,* right? Is it worth checking property records or . . . I don't know. Pinging phones—"

"Fox Rex was banned by Oxford ages ago," says Kit. "They haven't got an official location, and it's all cloak and dagger and word of mouth. No one knows who really runs it, and you can't simply ask to join. You have to be invited. They take their privacy *very* seriously."

"So you're saying they probably wouldn't have let me in even if I'd gone with you in disguise?" I say, deflating a little.

"*I* was questioned extensively, and my name was on the guest list. I doubt they would've taken kindly to anyone off the street trying to crash the party."

"Give me a little credit," I say, tucking a lock of his wavy hair behind his ear. "I wouldn't have been some random passerby—we would've met in a pub somewhere, or maybe in one of your classes, and I would've dazzled you with all of my witty banter and pointed political insights. And now that you're fresh off your breakup with that spoiled American brat, you'd be *desperate* to impress me so I'd offer you a distraction—"

"Oh?" says Kit, running the cotton pad over my jaw. "What sort of distraction?"

I lean forward until there's only an inch or two between our lips. "A really, *really* good one."

With one last gentle swipe down my neck, he sets the cotton pad aside, then brushes his lips against mine. "I'm afraid it doesn't matter how witty or insightful this supposed new girl is," he murmurs. "The only person capable of *distracting* me is you."

A wave of warmth runs through me, and I melt into him, capturing his mouth in a burning kiss. He meets me with every bit of intensity, as if he's been waiting for exactly the right moment to unleash a torrent of unspoken tension and relief, and I revel in every second.

When we finally part, we're both breathing heavily, and his fingers are tangled in my hair while mine are latched onto the front of his shirt. We stare at each other, both seemingly bewildered, before he inhales deeply, as if trying to lasso his own libido.

"I—" he begins, in what sounds an awful lot like the start of an apology, but I'm already speaking, too, and I refuse to let him take this moment from both of us.

"I want to," I say, and he blinks.

"Ev . . ." He swallows, as if it's taking every ounce of self-control he possesses to keep talking. "You've been through a lot lately. We've both been through a lot, and everything that happened last year—"

"If you're talking about Jasper," I say, and he visibly winces, "then stop. Please. He's done taking things from me—from us. Right now, tonight—this is just you and me, okay? No one else. And I want to. I've wanted to for a while. I love you," I say as he opens his mouth again. "And even if it's . . . weird or awkward or uncomfortable . . . I still want to try, okay? With you. And I want to keep trying until it's wonderful, because I know it will be. Because it's you, and even the weird and awkward and uncomfortable in my life is a damn good time when you're there with me."

Kit's Adam's apple bobs, and his thumb strokes my jaw as his gaze searches mine. "I want it to be perfect for you," he says softly. "Not some . . . adrenaline-induced whim after a rotten night."

"The only way it wouldn't be perfect," I say, in what might actually be the cheesiest true sentence to ever leave my lips, "is if you aren't there."

Kit swallows once more, but this time he rests his forehead against mine. "You're sure? You can't take it back."

"I won't want to," I promise. "Even if it's the worst thing about tonight—which it won't be—I just want to be with you."

Silence settles between us, heavy and heady, but at last Kit's hand slowly slides down to my shoulder, where my bra strap is peeking through the collar of my shirt. "All right," he says. "We can try. But if you have any . . . moments or flashbacks or . . ."

"I'll tell you," I promise, even though I meant what I said. I refuse to let Jasper Cunningham take this from us, too. "I think Tibby packed an entire pharmacy's supply of condoms in my duffel bag."

Kit clears his throat. "I have my own, if that's . . . ?"

"Yeah, of course," I say quickly. "Better to keep Tibby guessing anyway." The last thing I need is the third degree from her after she inevitably inspects the contents of my luggage. "You've, um . . . you've done this before, right?"

I expect him to squirm, or maybe dodge the question and go get his supply, wherever he's stashed it. But instead he stares directly into my eyes, no hint of embarrassment or uncertainty on his face.

"Yes," he says, his fingertips stilling against my skin. "Does that bother you?"

I think about it—about our conversation earlier that day, when I was looking through the gallery on the *Regal Record* of Kit and his old girlfriends, or one-night stands, or situationships I don't want to acknowledge. But he's with me now. And somewhere deep inside, I know he always will be, even if the part of me that's been disappointed and abandoned and heartbroken again and again can't admit it to myself yet. People may not be permanent, but Kit is.

"No," I finally say, and it's the truth. "I think I'm more relieved that at least one of us will know what they're doing."

Kit kisses me again, slow and warm and deep and everything we are. "Just tell me what feels good and what doesn't," he whispers against my mouth, even as his hand slides underneath the hem of my shirt, splaying over my lower back.

"Okay," I say with a shiver. "You do the same, all right?"

"I will," he promises. "We'll figure it out together."

His mouth moves from my lips to my jaw, finding a sweet spot on my neck and nurturing it long enough to help me out of my top entirely. I let out a soft sound that might actually be a moan, and he discards my shirt before pulling off his own.

"If you want to stop, all you have to do is say so," he whispers, his words warm and husky against my skin. "It doesn't matter what we're doing, or if we're already . . . It doesn't matter. We'll stop immediately, I swear."

But as his lips start a trail down my bra strap, past the healing red scar of the bullet wound that barely missed my heart, one thing quickly becomes clear: Despite the inevitable prickle of nerves and anticipation, despite the memories of unwelcomed hands on me that will always linger in the darkest parts of my mind, I don't want Kit to stop.

I don't ever want him to stop.

THAT AFTERNOON, WHILE Kit and I are still curled together, half-asleep and lost in our own world, my phone buzzes on the nightstand.

I ignore it at first, but then it buzzes again. And again. And again. There are only so many people I'm willing to talk to while we're in Oxford—even fewer who want anything to do with me—and the most important one is tracing invisible patterns on my stomach.

"Ignore it," I mumble as Kit shifts beside me, and even though my eyes are closed, I can feel him reaching for my phone.

"Could be important," he says, his voice thick with sleep. "Could be your mum."

"She doesn't use phones unless she has to," I say with a yawn, and only then do I open my eyes and take the offered mobile from him. I blink at the screen, then blink again as another message appears, and I sit straight up in bed.

"It's Tibby," I say, my heart racing as I scramble to untangle my limbs from both Kit and the sheets. "I need to go."

"What?" Kit rises beside me, his wavy hair sticking up at odd angles. "Why? What's happened?"

"I don't know." I stumble out of bed and run to the dresser, yanking out the first outfit I touch. "It's an emergency text. She wants to meet me now."

"She can't tell you what it is over the phone?" says Kit, baffled.

"Ben has this number," I point out as I dress faster than I ever have before. "Might be tapped."

Kit grimaces and pushes the covers away. "I'll go with you."

I shake my head, already bending down to pull on my socks. "It's too close to your lecture hall. The paparazzi might spot you. I'll be back as soon as I can, okay?"

Fear flickers in his eyes, but he stands and scoops my wild hair out from the collar of my sweatshirt. "Be safe," he says, and I pause long enough to give him a deep, lingering kiss.

"I will," I promise. And with my heart in my throat, I race out of our bedroom, knowing better than to expect anything but the worst.

* * *

I BURST INTO the familiar courtyard less than fifteen minutes later, my pulse racing and my oversized scarf unwinding from my neck, trailing after me in the dingy slush. Tibby is waiting on a bench with two thermoses, looking completely unbothered, and I'm so taken aback that I glance around, like there might be a second Tibby I'm missing who's tearing her own hair out with worry.

"What's wrong?" I blurt, hurrying toward her. "Is Alexander—is he—"

"Good afternoon to you, too," she says, offering me one of the thermoses. I take it, but only because it's blocking my view of her face.

"What's going on?" I press. "Why did you text me 9-9-9?"

She definitely doesn't look like she's had to rearrange her day for some kind of emergency, and she takes a sip of her drink before answering. "I thought you'd like to know that His Majesty is waking up."

My stomach does a strange somersault. "He is?" On one hand, this is what we've all been waiting and hoping for—for my father to finally regain consciousness after nearly dying in the bombing several weeks ago. On the other, as much as I even hate myself for thinking it . . .

"He is," says Tibby curtly. "Jenkins expects him to start asking about you in short order, and as soon as he does—"

"Jenkins will tell him the truth." Which means that our days in Oxford are numbered. I close my eyes and take a deep, steadying breath. "How is he? Can he speak? Does he recognize anyone? Are his eyes open? Has he had any more surgeries—"

Tibby sniffs. "I am not privy to His Majesty's medical status, nor should I be, considering I am not family."

"What is family, if not fifth or sixth cousins descended from one of the most inbred lines in Europe?" I say, and Tibby gives me a look that would make a mountain shudder. I, on the other hand, am immune. "Is that all? Because I need to get back—"

"To what, precisely?" says Tibby, eyebrow raised. "Have they finally given you something useful to do?"

I open and shut my mouth. "You know I can't talk about it."

"Of course not," she says in a tone that makes it clear she's humoring me. "Are you certain you're here to actually serve a purpose, or is it possible you're more like a team mascot?"

Her words sting like a slap to the face, and I have to bite my lip to keep from saying something I'll regret. "I'm here because I have to be. That's all you're allowed to know."

"Mm, of course," says Tibby, taking another sip from her thermos. "Do let me know when this is all declassified, will you? I'm very much looking forward to learning which Netflix series you're watching amidst . . . whatever it is you and Kit are supposedly doing."

I clench my jaw. "Tell Jenkins to delay for as long as he can. Please," I say tightly, and that's all I leave her with before I storm to the courtyard exit.

As soon as I'm on the other side of the stone tunnel, I slip into the crowd of students making their way to and from their afternoon lectures—which Kit decided to skip, no doubt to the disappointment of the paparazzi gathered to chronicle his daily walk of shame—and start back toward our flat building, ignoring the three personal protection officers tailing my every move.

Before I can take more than a few steps, however, goose bumps appear on my arms, and a prickling sensation spreads across my flushing skin, as if I've stuck a fork in an electrical socket.

Someone's watching me. Someone who isn't supposed to know I'm here.

I suppress the instinct to peek over my shoulder and tip off my voyeur. Instead, I use the windows and storefronts I pass to get a good look at my surroundings, and it's only when I pause to supposedly admire a display of books about Oxford's history do I spot a flash of a familiar teal scarf and maleficent stare.

The man who was protesting the monarchy outside of Sandringham at Christmas.

The man who was watching during the stampede outside the hospital when my sister and I were almost trampled.

The man who stood in the crowd of the Modern Music Museum opening, minutes before the bomb went off, watching me like he knew I wouldn't walk out of that building. Because he did.

Guy Fawkes. The leader of Fox Rex and the Army of the British Republic. The so-called mastermind behind the attack that murdered eight people and nearly assassinated my father. The terrorist who, along with Dylan, tried to kill me for over a month, only to publicly claim me as one of them so the entire world hates me as much as they do.

He's following me.

This time, I can't stop myself from whirling around, my heart pounding as I search the sidewalk opposite me. He was there—right between two groups of students, one clutching cups of coffee and the other laughing so loudly I can hear them over the traffic.

But he isn't anymore. He's gone.

I'm imagining things. I have to be. Fox Rex and the ABR have no idea where Kit and I live, so there's no way they could've followed me from the flat. And the chances of Guy or Dylan finding me in a city like Oxford, especially when there's nothing to differentiate me from the thousands of students wandering around—it's impossible. I'm being paranoid.

Taking a deep breath, I slow my pace to something leisurely and pretend I'm window-shopping. Books on the history of Oxford, handmade toys, colorful desserts that look like art—they're all suddenly fascinating to me as I use every reflection and break in the crowd to watch for Guy Fawkes, until—

He's there again, another flash of teal on the corner. And this time, when I look, he's staring directly at me, his features almost completely obscured by his telltale scarf. Except for those dark, gold-rimmed eyes I'd recognize anywhere.

Fury wells up inside me, shoving my fear aside. Fury for the people he killed. For what he did to my father, my family, to Kit—for what he's still trying to do to all of us. And when I run, it's not away from him. Instead, it's directly toward him.

I barely bother to look as I dart across the street, dodging traffic like a wild animal with no concept of my own mortality. Curiosity flickers across his face, and then, as quickly as he appeared, he's gone, ducking into a narrow alley. I reach it only seconds later, racing across the damp cobblestones, but when I emerge on the other side, he's vanished. Almost as if I imagined him.

But I know I didn't. And I keep running, up this busy road and the one beyond, through another side street and down the crowded pavement, until my clothes are damp with sweat and I've lost my way completely. There's no sign of him anywhere, but I can still feel his burning stare, as if he's watching me from the shadows and silently laughing. Or maybe, for the first time, he might finally be scared.

"Coward!" I shout, and the insult echoes off the old brick buildings. Several people nearby give me strange looks, but I don't care. Without glancing back, I shove my hands in my pockets and walk toward the only PPO who's managed to keep up with me, holding my head a little higher.

I'm done being afraid of him. It's time for him to be afraid of me.

CHAPTER FIVE

Tonight.

You're sure?

I don't remember asking you to second-guess me.

We need another few days, at least.

Get creative. I know you have it in you.

—Text message exchange between two prepaid mobiles, 1 February 2024

WHEN I STEP INSIDE THE flat thirty minutes later, after a car ride that took me and my PPOs through half of Oxford trying to shake any possible tail, Singh is perched on the edge of the dining table in his standard charcoal suit, looking annoyingly comfortable as he sips from my favorite pink mug.

"I hear you went on a little adventure," he says the moment I close the door.

"Nothing gets past MI5," I say, pulling off my sweaty layers before flopping down on the sofa, painfully aware that my deodorant isn't holding up its end of our bargain. "Where—"

"What do you mean, an adventure?" Kit steps out of our bedroom in a button-down and dark jeans, a pen tucked behind his ear and a paper map in hand. It might be the adrenaline still coursing through me, but he has never looked hotter. "Is everything all right? What did Tibby want?"

"My dad's waking up," I say as Singh takes a sip of whatever he's drinking. "She warned me that we don't have much time left. Why do you have a—"

"It seems Miss Bright believes she had an encounter with the man who calls himself Guy Fawkes," interrupts Singh, though he's already reaching for his mobile. "Did Lady Tabitha mention a specific timeline—"

"What?" Kit kneels beside me and cups my cheek. "You saw Guy? Are you all right? Did he say anything? Did he hurt—"

"I'm fine," I promise, ignoring Singh's question. "He didn't do anything. Just tried to look menacing. I have no idea how he found me, though."

"Your meeting place with Lady Tabitha is close enough to Lord Clarence's lectures that I expect the ABR is keeping tabs on the location," says Singh, typing into his phone. "You're certain it was him?"

I nod. "I recognized his scarf, and he was just . . . staring at me. I tried to chase him down, but he ran before—"

"You tried to chase him?" says Kit in a strangled voice. "Ev . . ."

"I had to do *something,*" I say, but now, looking at the fear and distress written plainly on his face, I start to regret it. "My protection officers were nearby. They wouldn't have let anything happen—"

Kit clasps my hand between his and bows his head. He isn't religious, as far as I know, beyond the god and pony show required of everyone even remotely adjacent to the crown, but it almost looks like he's praying. "Evan," he says as he once again meets my gaze, his voice so low that I can barely hear him over the *tap-tap-tap* of Singh's phone. "I am begging you. *Please* stop putting yourself in unnecessary danger. Chasing him down . . . running after him . . ." He shakes his head, and his eyes shine with unshed tears. "If something happens to you . . ."

"Nothing's going to happen to me," I say gently. "Kit, I swear, I wasn't in any danger—"

"You don't know that, Ev. Not for sure," he says, barely able to force the words out. "Every time something like this happens, all I can think is that this is really it, that I'm about to lose you forever, and I can't breathe—"

"Miss Bright is safe and sound, for now," says Singh, in a tone that makes it clear he has no patience for either Kit's panic or my shenanigans. "And with the timeline moving up, I'm afraid you have no choice but to go tonight, Lord Clarence. There's simply no way around it."

I snap my head up, confused. "Go where?"

Kit's jaw works for a moment before he sighs. "Dylan texted again," he admits. "He wants to meet me. He didn't say why, but he did offer to meet at a time and place of my choosing. Hence the map."

"We've narrowed it down to three pubs in the area," adds Singh. "I'll have agents on all of them, and we won't make a decision until Lord Clarence returns Mr. Baxter's text."

"Which will be no more than thirty minutes ahead of time," says Kit quickly, no doubt in response to the look on my face.

"Even if Dylan or the ABR are planning something, they won't have a chance to implement it. Not with agents and PPOs swarming the place. It's not foolproof, but we don't have a choice. Not if we want to find that list before your father is fully conscious."

My heart drops, which is a feat, considering it's beating so fast it's on the verge of taking flight. "I don't want you to go," I blurt as Tibby's warning once again echoes in my mind. "Whatever Dylan has to say—"

"Is the king waking up or not?" says Singh pointedly. "We've no time to waste waiting for the perfect opportunity. I would not approve this if I thought it posed any real threat to Lord Clarence—"

"Kit," I snap. "His name is Kit. And of course it poses a threat. Dylan almost killed us less than two months ago, and neither of us ever saw him coming. How do you know this isn't some kind of setup?"

"If Dylan or the ABR wanted to kill me, they would have done it already," says Kit quietly. "They know where I am most days, after all."

"We'll be doing a thorough sweep of the premises before the meeting place goes live," adds Singh, "and the rooftops and nearby buildings will also be secured. If anyone lifts a finger against Lord Clarence—Kit," he adds hastily at my deadly look, "they'll immediately be taken into custody. I assure you, Miss Bright—"

"If you do this," I say, looking straight at Kit, "then I'm going with you."

He blinks. "I—" begins Kit, but Singh cuts him off.

"Out of the question," he says, and Kit and I turn to him as one, my face heating with anger.

"I know what Guy looks like," I argue. "None of your agents or our PPOs do. I'm not saying I want to sit down at a table with Kit and Dylan—I want to be at the pub so I can watch his back—"

"Out," says Singh, slower this time, "of the question."

I stare at him, the edge of my vision red with fury. But Singh doesn't waver, and I sit up straight on the sofa, my feet hitting the floor.

"What am I even here for?" I snarl. "What's the point? I haven't done anything useful. I'm not allowed to go anywhere. No one even knew I was here until today—"

"Exactly," says Singh. "As far as we knew, Guy Fawkes had no idea you were even in the country. But now that we know for certain he does," he adds, bulldozing straight over my protest, "I refuse to put myself in a position where I have to explain to His Majesty why his daughter is dead."

I scoff, even as tears of frustration prickle my eyes. "I'm not quitting, if that's what you want. Not until we find the list." And proof that Ben is part of the ABR.

"On the contrary, I'd very much like for you to continue as part of this team, Miss Bright," says Singh. "Which is why I am asking you to trust that my agents will take every possible step to ensure Kit's safety tonight, and that includes ensuring yours so he can focus on the job at hand."

Once again, I look at Kit and thread my fingers through his, and his grimace deepens. "If I do this, I'll only go for a quick drink. No more than ten minutes," he says quietly. "Whatever Dylan wants, if he can't spit it out by then, I'm leaving. And I'll only go if you want me to, Ev," he adds. "Say the word, and I'll stay, all right?"

Our eyes meet again, and I can see everything he's thinking. All those horrors he's witnessed, all those times he's had to wait to find out if he'd ever see me again—he doesn't want to put me through even a moment of that. And somehow, despite my frustration and fury, I love him a little more than I did a heartbeat ago.

Singh sighs. "This may very well be our last chance with Mr. Baxter, particularly if His Majesty is well enough to demand your return," he says. And while his manipulation isn't subtle, his point is valid, and I chew on my lower lip.

"I need a shower. And a minute to think about this," I say, my gaze still on Kit's. But we both know what my answer will be. Whatever Dylan has to say, it could be the key to finding the list. To figuring out who Guy Fawkes is and taking down the Army of the British Republic.

It could be the key to finally unearthing the piece of the puzzle that proves beyond a doubt that Prince Benedict of York has been in on it the entire time, and that he, too, deserves to rot in prison for the rest of his miserable life.

"Very well," says Singh, and he continues to type furiously into his phone. "Lord Clarence—*Kit,* bring the map over here, and we'll sort out our final location."

Kit lingers beside me for a moment longer, his thumb stroking the back of my hand. "Do you want to talk about it?" he says, and I shake my head. If I speak now, I'm sure I'll ask him to stay, even though I know he can't. But after a beat, the words tumble out of me before I can stop them, my voice crackling.

"If something happens to you . . ." I clear my throat, tears leaking from the corners of my eyes. It's supposed to be me, not him. I'm the one who's supposed to be taking chances, and I can't stand the thought of him paying the price for my mistakes.

"It won't," he promises with good intentions, but it isn't a promise at all. Just hope. "I love you too much to ever leave you."

I want to believe him, but after the bombing, after seeing my father's broken body in the hospital bed and my mother sitting at his side day and night, waiting for him to return to her, I know that love and willpower alone aren't enough. He would never leave her, either, not if he had anything to say about it. But he didn't.

"Everything I am to you . . . you are to me," I whisper. And that's all I manage as I finally extract myself from him, our gazes locked until I pass into our bedroom.

I shower quickly, feeling like I'm racing against time. I wash the sweat away, but the helplessness remains no matter how hot the water is, and when I reemerge into the living room in my coziest sweats, my damp hair braided and thick socks over my cold feet, I feel like a ghost. But I know what I have to do—what we both have to do—and I glance around, searching the small space for Kit.

The lights are on, and the curtains are closed against the darkening sky. But the hook by the door, where Kit usually hangs his coat and keys, is bare, and Singh is nowhere in sight.

The flat is empty.

Kit left without saying goodbye.

I instinctively know why he did it—to spare me the burden of guilt and responsibility for whatever happens at this meeting—but that does nothing to take the edge off as I pace through the flat in a haze of fury and anxiety, itching to throttle something with my bare hands.

I text him fourteen times before I finally decide he's ignoring me on purpose. Or that something has gone horrifically wrong, and he's lying in the middle of the road outside a pub, bleeding from a bullet wound or a knife to the throat or—

I shove away that mental image and inhale deeply. He'll be okay. Singh will make sure of it. Except if they pushed the meeting up this quickly, did MI5 even have time to sweep the area? Do they know what Kit's walking into? What if the ABR planted someone in every pub within a two-mile radius of Christ Church, or—

Yet again, I stop that runaway train of thought with a sharp intake of breath. The PPOs stationed outside the flat would know if something bad was going down. They'd tell me. Except deep in my gut, I'm sure they wouldn't, because they know exactly what I would do—run right into danger as fast as I could, because that's what Kit would do for me. And because maybe, *maybe* there would be some way I could help him.

But if I follow him now, I'll only be putting him in more danger, especially if the ABR expects me to be there. If this is a trap, and Kit is the bait . . .

Have you considered the possibility that they might bring him back into the fold, only to silence him for good?

My phone vibrates in my hand, and I nearly drop it. A text.

My heart thuds against my ribs, and I tap the icon so aggressively that I have to try again. Finally my messages open, and—

It's not from Kit.

Instead, it's from an unknown number, one I texted with back in January. Ben—I thought it was Ben at the time, but it can't be now, can it? Frowning, I open the new message and suddenly feel like I've plunged straight into an icy lake.

It's a picture of Kit sitting alone in a cozy pub, taken through what looks like a long lens. Of a paparazzo's camera? From a phone zoomed in?

But then I see the thin black cross, and I know exactly what it is.

The scope of a rifle.

CHAPTER SIX

Evan

Don't hurt him

I have no intention, so long as you follow my instructions.

Evan

Which are?

Make your way to the west entrance of your building and wait. Bring nothing and no one with you.

Evan

I'm not where you think I am

I know exactly where you are.

Evan

I have guards

You're a smart girl. You have five minutes.

—Text message exchange between Evangeline Bright and a prepaid mobile number, 1 February 2024, 5:11 p.m.

MY PULSE IS RACING, AND I shove my phone in my pocket as I search the flat for an escape route. The usual pair of bodyguards are outside my door. Likely more throughout the floors we've taken over, and at least one lookout in the lobby. It takes two minutes to get from the flat to the west entrance of our building, which leaves me less than three to figure this out.

I spot the pink mug that Singh left on the counter, and suddenly I know what to do.

I step into a pair of sneakers, pull on one of Kit's cardigans, and scurry into the kitchen. While I leave the mug untouched, I hurl the dishes on the drying rack into the open living and dining area. A few bounce, but most shatter against the floor, scattering tiny slivers of glass everywhere.

"Miss Bright?" calls one of the PPOs from the hallway, and he knocks frantically. "Miss Bright, is everything—"

Before he can finish, I tuck myself into the small triangle of space behind the door, which can't fully swing open in the tiny foyer, and I let out a bloodcurdling scream.

My PPOs don't bother with their keys. Instead, as one calls for backup, the other kicks down the door in a single go, and it swings on its hinges, missing my face by half an inch. I flinch, squeezing my eyes shut as the PPOs rush past me and into the mess that is the living area, glass crunching beneath their shoes.

"Miss Bright?" one calls again. "Miss Bright!"

"Bedroom," grunts the other, and their footsteps grow muted. I have no way to tell whether they're still watching the entrance, but I take that risk and duck out from behind the door, darting into the hallway beyond.

It's empty, though it won't be for long. I sprint to the emergency stairwell and burst through the door, flying down the concrete steps so quickly that I'm vaguely surprised I don't actually take flight.

A few men in suits are rushing into the lift when I poke my head into the lobby, but thankfully no one's thought to check the stairwell yet. It's only a momentary oversight, and the clock is ticking as I slip across the hall, toward the rarely used west exit. They'll have this covered in a matter of minutes, too, if they don't already, but for now, my security seems convinced I'm still in the flat, and I seize advantage.

As I step out into the freezing evening air, my breath crystalizes, and I spot a black van idling near the curb. I inwardly curse myself, sure I've been caught by MI5, but then—

Then the door slides open, and a man wearing a black ski mask appears.

"Get in," he orders. Dylan. My throat tightens, and I know if I get in that van, there's a very good chance I'll never see Kit again. But if I don't, I *know* I never will, and that's the only reason I move forward.

Dylan grabs my elbow to haul me up, and the door shuts behind me as the van starts to move. Warm, pine-scented air blasts through the vents, and there must be some kind of partition between the front and the back of the van, because I can't see the driver or the windshield.

But I can feel Dylan's hands on me, searching my pockets and even my shoes. There's something detached and authoritative about it, like getting a thorough pat-down at an airport, but it still sends shivers through me. And in the darkness, I see the face of a dead boy named Jasper and hear his whispered crooning that everything's all right, and why don't I just relax?

When Dylan finds my phone in the pocket of my sweatpants, he pops open a tiny tray and removes my SIM card. With a muttered curse, he snaps it in half and shuts off my phone completely, then opens the side door only wide enough to toss both onto the dark street below.

"I told you not to bring anything," he growls, and I know I should be terrified. But now that I'm in this van with him, a strange sense of calm washes over me, and I refuse to let him see me fall apart.

"How else was I supposed to contact you if you didn't show?" I say with a shrug I hope is maddening.

He huffs and produces several zip ties from his pocket. "Hands."

I place my wrists together for him to secure, and he does so efficiently. Clearly this isn't his first time tying someone up. "Is that it?" I say, testing the plastic. It's tight, but not so tight that it'll cut off circulation.

Without replying, Dylan removes a black cloth bag from his pocket and pulls it over my head, effectively blindfolding me. A surge of adrenaline floods my veins, insisting I do *something* to save my own damn life, but I force myself to stay still. At least until I know Kit is safe.

"You're really going all out, aren't you?" I say as Dylan guides me onto the cold floor. "It's not like I can tell where we're headed anyway, you know."

"Shut up," he says in that same growly tone, and once again, his hands are on me. "Where's your panic button?" he adds as his fingers slip into the elastic band of my bra.

I jerk away, nauseated by his touch. "If you don't take your hands off me right now, I will shove my foot straight into your face, I swear to—"

He tugs off my shoe without warning, but at least he isn't touching me anymore. I hear him tear through the fabric, clearly looking for any hidden compartments that might hold a panic button, and I scowl.

"I just took a shower. I don't have anything except my phone, which is clearly not a problem anymore."

Still, Dylan doesn't say a word as he checks my other shoe, too, and then the waistband of my sweatpants, albeit with much more care than before. He finds nothing, like I knew he would, and at last he gives it a rest. "Secure," he calls to the driver, who grunts in return.

"Where's Kit?" I say. "You have to let him go—"

"Kit's safe," he says, which isn't at all reassuring. "Now shut your mouth before I shut it for you."

I snort. "What, did you read a list of kidnapper clichés before doing this? I'm not afraid of—"

His knuckles hit me square in the jaw despite the black bag covering my head, and pain explodes in the lower half of my face. My lip splits on something metal—a ring, I think—and I feel warm blood trickling down my chin, soaking into the fabric of the bag.

"I said," says Dylan in a deadly quiet voice, "shut your mouth."

I lick the blood from my lip, wishing I could spit it in his face. But even though there's a snarling animal inside me desperate to fight back, what few survival instincts I still have kick in, and I keep quiet for the rest of the ride, my mouth throbbing and my heart racing.

It isn't long before the van slows to a stop and the driver cuts the engine. The door opens, letting in the cold night air once more, and Dylan takes me by the elbow and roughly guides me down a stone path. I can see light through the bag, but only the vaguest of impressions as he tells me to climb a few steps, and we enter a building with a creaky hardwood floor. The smell of

Italian food hits me, and it feels almost homey as Dylan leads me through the depths of the building—house?—until we finally step inside a muffled room. The floor is carpeted, and it smells distinctly like—

Books.

Without warning, Dylan cuts through the zip tie on my wrists and yanks the bag off my head. He's not wearing his mask anymore, and he doesn't seem ruffled by the fact that I know exactly who he is, even though we've only met once. He does one more pat-down before finally stepping back toward the door, never turning away from me.

"None of this is personal," he says, and it sounds more like a threat than anything else he's said to me tonight. "Wait here."

And then he's gone, with the heavy door locked firmly behind him. My eyes slowly adjust to the warm yellow light as I touch my split lip gingerly, dabbing away what's left of the blood.

I'm in an old-fashioned study, with dark wood furniture and bronze fastenings, and floor-to-ceiling bookcases covering three of the four walls that overflow with books, papers, and dust. In the center of the room is a massive desk with lion head drawer pulls and a leather chair that's seen better days, and to my bewilderment, a state-of-the-art laptop stands open, the screen unlocked and open to its desktop.

What the hell is going on?

I stand frozen for what has to be a full minute, waiting for something to happen, but nothing does. There's no clock in the room ticking away, letting me know how much time has passed since I stepped into that van with Dylan, and no one comes through the door again, either to greet me or otherwise. Another minute passes as I count the seconds in my head, and I exhale, glancing around again.

This is a trap. It has to be. Or if not a trap, then what? A test?

As soon as the thought occurs to me, my skin erupts into goose bumps beneath the soft knit of Kit's cardigan, and I know I'm right. That's exactly what this is—a test to see . . . what? What I'll do when I'm left alone with a strange computer? A computer that's likely connected to Fox Rex and possibly even the ABR?

I don't look for the cameras that must be hidden around the room. Instead, I turn toward the bookshelves and scan the spines, some of which look like they haven't been handled in years. On the first wall, hundreds of spy novels are neatly arranged by author, and all have a thin layer of dust on their jackets. Nonfiction and textbooks take up the entire second wall, and they span decades. But while the variety of subjects on these shelves are fascinating, the third bookcase behind the desk is the real prize.

The lowest shelf boasts nothing but composition books—dozens of them, all crammed together so tightly that trying to remove one would undoubtedly result in an explosion of paper and dust. I leave those alone and move upward toward the collection of military history books, all about upheaval and revolutions throughout the western world. The English civil war in the sixteen hundreds, the Glorious Revolution that put Mary II and William III on the throne, the American and French Revolutions, the Scottish wars of independence and later Jacobite risings, the Cornish and Irish rebellions and Welsh revolt—

This isn't idle interest. This is a study. This is a master class on how to win a revolution against an enemy that seems unbeatable.

My mouth goes dry, and I brush my fingertips against their spines, like I'm reading the titles with breathless interest. In reality, however, I scan the shelf above, which is lined with more of the same. But crammed into the very end of the bookcase, almost indistinguishable from the texts of blood-soaked history, is a single leather-bound book. Unlike most of the others, it doesn't have a speck of dust on it, and there's no lettering on the spine. I shouldn't peek, not when I'm being watched, but—

"Ice?"

Cursing, I whirl around and face the man standing in the open doorway. He can't be older than twenty-five, with a face so painfully ordinary that I could have passed him on the street a million times and never thought twice about it. It's the kind of face that's invisible. Anonymous. The perfect mask for someone who wants to disappear into a crowd.

But his eyes are dark and rimmed with gold as they focus on me, piercing and unwavering, and I know exactly who he is.

The man who calls himself Guy Fawkes.

CHAPTER SEVEN

We're live.

I'll get the popcorn.

—Text message exchange between two prepaid mobiles,
1 February 2024, 5:53 p.m.

GUY FAWKES, THE SUPPOSED LEADER of Fox Rex and the Army of the British Republic, stands ten feet in front of me, holding a pack of frozen peas in one hand and a mug in the other.

The door closes behind him, and he steps toward me, his smile easy and unnerving in its almost-friendliness. "I'm sorry about that," he says, gesturing to my face. "Dylan was under strict orders not to harm you, but he's always been a bit of a wild card."

He holds out the frozen peas, and I hesitate. But only for a moment. "Lucky me," I mutter, taking them and pressing the cold bag to my jaw. It feels good against what must be some significant swelling, and I touch the corner to my split lip. "Where's Kit? Is he safe?"

"Perfectly," he assures me, producing a damp paper towel

seemingly out of nowhere. "He left the Flea and Hound of his own accord fifteen minutes ago, alive and well."

"Prove it."

"And how do you expect me to do that?" Guy steps closer to me now, so close I can smell his soap, and holds the paper towel near my lip. "Allow me."

This is such a wild about-face from the figure who's been stalking me since Christmas that I briefly consider the possibility that he's an identical twin. But no—this is all to make me putty in his hands. Good terrorist, bad terrorist, and he's cast himself as the golden boy.

"You have eyes on him," I say, inching the frozen peas away from my mouth. "You must, if you know he left."

Guy dabs the paper towel against my lip with surprising care, and only when he's finished does he drop the bloody towel in the trash bin and pull out his mobile. "Courtesy of the *Regal Record,*" he says, showing me the screen. I only have enough time to think that of course Ben has a hand in this—he has a hand in everything—before a video starts to play.

It's of the sidewalk outside the Flea and Hound, right on the precipice of twilight, with two girls announcing that 'Lord Christopher' is inside and debating whether to try to coax him into a threesome. Before they can make a decision, the door bursts open, and Kit tears past them with at least three PPOs on his tail, and the girls watch, their mouths hanging open and the camera fumbling as they try to capture his getaway.

They only manage to catch the very end of it, as he ignores the car waiting for him at the curb and takes the corner at a sprint instead. Frowning, I replay the video. There's no sign of blood anywhere, and the other bystanders don't seem alarmed or startled by anything beyond Kit's sudden appearance. So why is he—

The answer hits me like a punch to the gut, and for a split second, I can't breathe.

He knows I went after him. Or that I did something reckless, at the very least, and by now he knows I'm missing. And he is terrified.

"That was the last anyone's seen of him in public," says Guy as he returns his mobile to his pocket. "He was never the target, Evangeline."

Because I am. I have been from the start, and suddenly I understand why Singh has kept me under lock and key, hidden from our predators while Kit's been free to roam. He knew. Somehow, he understands Guy better than any of us.

"Why am I here?" I say, returning the peas to my jaw. It's growing more and more painful to speak, and I need the swelling to go down.

"Funny," says Guy, and he gestures for me to sit. "I'd like to ask you the very same question. Why *are* you here? In Oxford, with Lord Clarence?"

I ease down into the leather chair. The laptop is still open, the desktop still bright, and there are plenty of folders and files on display—bait, no doubt. But I refocus on Guy and reach for a strange little puzzle box near the laptop instead, fiddling one-handed with its sliding pieces.

"I don't know if you read the news," I say, moving my jaw

as little as possible, "but *Lord Clarence* and I've been dating for a while. Sometimes we visit each other. Wild concept, I know."

Guy's mouth twitches. "According to the media, you're supposed to be in America right now, with your head buried in the sand."

"I'd be pretty bad at hiding if everyone knew where I was," I say, toying with the box. The pieces don't fit together the way I expect them to, and I turn it over in my hand, trying again from a different angle.

Guy stares at me as if he can see right through my caginess, but I ignore him, focusing on the puzzle. The more I try to open it, the less it all makes sense, and I sigh, setting it back on the desk.

"What's your name?" I blurt. "Your real name. None of this 'Guy Fawkes' shit."

He tilts his head. "Out of all the questions you could ask me, that's what you want to know?"

"I'm just getting started."

He considers me for a moment longer, his arms crossed loosely over his chest. "John."

I snort. "I know John Johnson is an alias for Guy Fawkes. Try again."

"I didn't say John Johnson," he says. "Just John. Why do you prefer Evan to Evangeline?"

This takes me a moment to process—not the question itself, but the implication behind it. No one outside of my immediate circle calls me Evan in the UK. The media refers to me by plenty of nicknames—some more creative than others—but *Evan* has never been one of them. "Because *Evangeline* sounds pretentious. Did Kit tell you that?" I say, even though I know he didn't. Kit, more than anyone else, is extremely careful with how he refers to me in public, even to his supposed friends.

"Let's just say you and I have a mutual acquaintance," says Guy, and my breath catches in my lungs.

Ben.

"Do we?" I say with careful neutrality. "I didn't realize we ran in the same circles."

A faint smile crosses his lips, and as he drums his fingers against his elbow, I notice a gold signet ring on his pinky—the kind of ring that only nobility and their spawn seem to wear in the UK. The kind of ring Kit wears. The kind of ring my father and uncle wear. And definitely not a piece of jewelry a violent terrorist would wear simply out of habit.

I must stare a split second too long, because he slips his fingers behind his arm, hiding the ring from view. "I've always wondered how you and Lord Clarence ended up together. The king's daughter with a vocal republican. I certainly didn't have you pegged as an antimonarchist."

"You must *really* not pay attention to the news, then," I say with as much amusement as I can muster. "According to the media, I'm practically the face of the ABR."

Now that I've broached the topic, his expression returns to neutral, and he studies me with an intensity that makes me want to look away. "And are you?" he says, quieter now. "The face of the ABR?"

"Have you seen me on any posters lately?" I toy with the hem of Kit's cardigan, and when a loose thread starts to unravel, I idly wrap the yarn around my finger. "I don't like the monarchy. I think it's outdated, classist, obscene, and offers nothing of real value to anyone—either the people forced to live it or the people consuming it like it's reality TV. It's tradition for tradition's sake, and with the funds it takes to keep it going, we could probably solve homelessness and food poverty in a matter of months."

This seems to pique his interest, and he moves to the desk, perching on the edge and picking up the handheld puzzle I've left unfinished. "And yet you're the daughter of a king."

"And yet," I echo. "But while I don't care about crowns and thrones, I do care about my family. And there's nothing in this world that could tempt me to try to blow them up. Especially when I was in the building, too."

"A solid argument." His smirk of a smile is back, and with two hands, he works the puzzle box like he's familiar with every millimeter of its metal frame. "I can see why Lord Clarence likes you. He's very much of the same mindset, and I daresay you make a good pair."

I raise my eyebrows as the yarn continues to unravel. The hem hasn't changed, though, and I realize it's a patch of some sort. "I had no idea he didn't like the monarchy until a few weeks ago, so I really hope that has nothing to do with why he's dating me."

Guy chuckles, and it makes the hair on the back of my neck stand up. "If you're free to attend Oxford next year," he says, "I would be quite interested in having you join Fox Rex. We've never had royalty among us before. Lord Clarence is about as close as we've ever gotten."

My heart starts to beat a little faster. "I'm not royalty."

"And with any luck, no one in this country will be soon enough." He sets the puzzle down, and it's open now, its complicated pieces twisted to reveal an empty center. "Though I certainly hope no one else has to die in the meantime."

I can't tell if this is a threat or not. "How did you do that?" I say, eyeing the box.

"Patience." He nods to the puzzle. "Every time it closes, it's a little different. You can never open it the same way twice. That's what I like about it."

I start to unravel the yarn around my finger in order to pick up the box, but I feel something underneath the patch in the cardigan—something small, circular, and metallic, almost like a five-pence coin.

Almost, but not quite.

My pulse is pounding in my ears now. I recognize the rough texture of its edge, and without taking my eyes off the puzzle, I slip it into one of the deep pockets of Kit's cardigan before reaching for the box. Though I pretend to examine its pieces, all I can think about is the round object, and I set the box back down before my hands start to tremble.

"I've never been very good at puzzles," I say.

"Now that, I suspect, is a lie," says Guy, and he starts to reassemble it. "Would you be interested, then? In Fox Rex?"

A droplet of water drips from the bag of peas, perfectly in tandem with a bead of sweat that runs down my spine. "It depends," I say. "If Dylan is your best and brightest . . ."

"I assure you, he is not," he says, and he slides off the desk and makes his way over to the bookshelf behind me. I turn in the leather chair, watching him as his fingers glide over the various spines of historic warfare. Of the moments in history that changed the world. "We have many esteemed former members to count among our ranks, including several members of Parliament, courtiers and noblemen, lawyers, doctors, even an astronaut."

His fingers pause on the leather-bound book with no title, and I hold my breath. He tugs lightly on the top, sliding it out an inch or two from its snug spot on the shelf, but then seems to think better of it and returns it to its original position. I exhale silently, cursing whatever modicum of good sense he's decided to indulge.

"I'm not sure a royal bastard and accused terrorist would do much to enhance your ranks," I say. "But I suppose I can talk to Kit and give it some thought." I pause a moment, deciding on whether to chance it, but my mouth gets the better of me before I can think it all the way through. "I can't be the only rebellious royal who's ever held a grudge against the rest of the family."

He slips back around to the front of the desk, and I track him in my seat, adjusting the peas against my aching jaw. "Entire wars have been fought because some cousin or nephew or second son felt slighted," he agrees. "None of them have been part of Fox Rex, though. But wouldn't it be nice to have a patron like that? Imagine what our little club could accomplish."

His words turn the air to ice. "Shame there isn't one hanging around in the wings right now," I manage bitingly. "That would help recruitment more than I ever could."

The instant the words leave my lips, I know I've said the wrong thing. But instead of seizing my mistake by the throat, he simply regards me as his shoulders relax, and he perches on the desk once more. Something about his face softens, even as the glint in his eyes sharpens, but when he speaks, he sounds almost gentle.

"So that's what you want," he murmurs. "Proof."

It takes me a moment to backtrack and follow his train of thought, but once I do, I touch my lip self-consciously. "Proof of what?"

"We both know the answer to that." He takes a sip from his mug. "Lord Christopher Abbott-Montgomery, Earl of Clarence and nephew of the Queen, is the only member we have who is connected to the royal family. I hope to change that next year, with your arrival, but for now, I fear he is the closest our ranks come to being royal."

He doesn't say Ben's name, but his denial is proof enough that Ben really is part of this somehow, and Guy is protecting him. Why? Because Ben is funding their attacks? Because he's giving the ABR inside information about the family? My stomach turns at the thought, but I keep the disgust off my face. None of this is new information. Only confirmation, or at least as close as I'm going to get tonight.

"Maybe next year, then," I say, letting the edge return to my voice. "So long as you stop kidnapping me and threatening to kill my boyfriend."

"Kidnap?" says Guy, his eyes widening with innocent surprise. "I was under the impression you came willingly. My sincerest apologies, Evan. And again, I assure you, we have nothing but the deepest respect for Lord Clarence. He is an asset to our organization, and we protect our own."

His voice dips slightly as he says this last part, and I can't stop the shudder that runs through me. "I don't doubt it."

He smiles, as if we've come to an agreement after hours of negotiations, and he offers me his hand. "Now that we understand each other, I'm afraid I must be going. It was a pleasure, Miss Bright—truly. And I look forward to meeting again next year."

"Can't wait," I say, not bothering to hide my lack of enthusiasm. "Does this mean you aren't going to kill me?"

"Kill you?" He tilts his head again. "We at Fox Rex are revolutionaries, not murderers." He picks up the puzzle box, which is once again sealed. "Here—as a reminder of what's to come."

I take the box, confused, but he's still smiling as if nothing about this is out of the ordinary. "Am I supposed to open it?" I say, and he shrugs.

"That is entirely up to you." He nods toward me, the malevolent glint in his gold-rimmed eyes returning. "Do try to stay out of harm's way, Miss Bright. I would hate for anything to happen to you before we meet again."

He walks to the door, which opens on its own, making it clear that our conversation wasn't private. As soon as he's gone, I pretend to inspect the box again and place it in my pocket for safekeeping, only to palm the tiny tracking device that someone sewed into the hem of Kit's cardigan—a tracking device no one would be looking for, not when it's supposed to be his. I could activate the panic button, though if I really am about to get out of here unharmed, then the last thing I want is to end the mission early.

But while I still don't have the proof I need that Ben is involved,

I have enough hints and circumstantial evidence to know that with enough pressure, with enough *time,* Guy—John—will let something slip that he didn't mean to. That's all I need—more time. More time to talk to him. More time to earn his trust, as much as it can be earned.

My gaze drifts toward the leather-bound book, and as I wait for Dylan to fetch me, I pretend to browse the shelves again and slip the silver disc in the crevice between two misshapen spines.

CHAPTER EIGHT

Kit

Where is she?

Dylan, where the hell is she?

You have thirty seconds to tell me exactly what you've done with her, or I swear on all that is holy that you will spend the rest of your pitiful life regretting this.

WHERE IS SHE?

—Text messages sent by Christopher Abbott-Montgomery, Earl of Clarence, 1 February 2024, 6:07 p.m.

WHEN DYLAN FINALLY FETCHES ME from the study, he's sporting a fresh and quickly swelling black eye. He says nothing as he puts the bag back over my head, and only then do I allow myself an excruciating grin. I will never be Guy's ally, but I won't say no to his attempts to sucker me in.

The black van drops me off, still blindfolded, a quarter of a mile from my flat building. My hands are duct-taped together this time, but thanks to Ingrid, the PPO who sacrificed her life to save mine in the bombing, I know how to break that bond, and within minutes, I'm walking through the freezing cold toward the entrance of our building, trying to keep my teeth from chattering and causing even more pain in my jaw.

"Evangeline!"

My name explodes into a chorus as more than a dozen agents and personal protection officers swarm me, some pouring out from the lobby while others appear in the shadows around me, shielding my body with theirs. I'm so overwhelmed that I forget they have a real reason to be scared shitless, and when I stumble over my numb feet, a protection officer scoops me up and carries me into the lobby.

He and half a dozen other men with guns immediately cram themselves into a waiting lift, and before I know it, the doors are opening on our floor, which is also crawling with uniforms. Not just MI5 agents and PPOs, but police, too. Someone shouts, or maybe they've already radioed ahead, and as the overzealous officer finally lets me down, Singh appears amidst the chaos.

"Evangeline," he says, and I detect a distinct note of relief in his voice. "We have a doctor waiting. We've already alerted the local hospital, and we have a helicopter on standby to take you to London—"

"I'm fine," I say, my jaw agonizingly stiff from the cold. "Where's Kit?"

Singh blinks as he tries to usher me toward the nearest open door. "Lord Clarence is secure. You need to—"

"Where is he?" I dig my heels in, and to his credit, Singh pauses. "I'll talk to you and a doctor and everyone else after, but I need to see him. *Now.*"

Without further argument, Singh leads me through the chaos toward the flat Kit and I share. Yellow tape blocks off the entrance, but we both duck beneath it, and Singh guides me around the broken glass to the closed bedroom door. He knocks lightly, but before he can speak, I slip past him and push the door open, not wanting to keep Kit in agonizing suspense any longer.

But as soon as I do, something clinks against the door, and I pause, confused. A chunk of blue spherical glass catches on the edge, and as I try to figure out what it is, a familiar scent hits me, strong and almost overpowering.

Kit's bottle of cologne is shattered.

It's not the only thing that's in pieces. Picture frames and his alarm clock lie broken on the carpet, and even his laptop is cracked beneath a sizable dent in the wall. The things that don't easily break—pillows, books, even articles of clothing—he's torn apart, and my heart drops to my knees. Nearly all of his things are destroyed, but mine remain untouched.

"Kit?" I say softly, glancing around the dim room, lit only by the light filtering in from the main living area. I don't see him, and briefly I wonder if he's in the bathroom until a strange wheezing reaches my ears. Frowning, I venture inside, tiptoeing around the broken glass.

Huddled on the floor beside the bed, with his back against the mattress and his knees hugged to his chest, is Kit. His entire body trembles with silent sobs, and a dark trickle of blood runs down his forearm, pooling in the crook of his elbow. I inhale a silent breath of surprise and kneel slowly beside him, joining him on the carpet.

"Hi," I whisper. The light in the doorway shifts, and I realize Singh's brought backup in case—what, in case Kit tries to attack me? But I know what a breakdown looks like. I can feel the terror and anxiety pulsing through him, and it takes everything I have not to gather him in my arms and snap at the agents to get the hell away from both of us.

Several seconds tick by, but finally Kit raises his head enough to look at me. His eyes are rimmed with red, and there's a shallow cut on his chin that makes me want to cry. "Ev?" he whispers, as if he doesn't really believe it's me.

"I'm here," I murmur. "What do you need?"

He stares at me, his eyes pools of black, until he reaches for me with aching slowness. Like he thinks I'll vanish if he moves too quickly, and he gently cups my jaw and brushes his thumb against my swollen lower lip.

"Dylan?" he says jaggedly, and I nod, leaning into his warm palm.

"Don't worry. He paid for it." I touch his bleeding arm and try to find the source. "Are you hurt? What happened?"

He glances down, as if only just noticing the blood. "I thought . . . when they told me you'd been taken, I thought . . ."

He can't finish the sentence, but he doesn't need to. "I'm okay. I promise I'm okay," I say. "Dylan texted me. He told me . . . He made me think you were in danger if I didn't do exactly what he said, and—"

"You let him kidnap you?" Confusion and hurt flicker across Kit's face, and I shake my head. But after a moment, I reconsider and nod.

"I didn't know that's what was going to happen, but . . . he sent me a picture of you in the pub, and it looked like it was from some kind of rifle scope. I didn't think I had a choice," I whisper. "I'm sorry. I'm so bloody sorry. I panicked, and—and I didn't have time to *think*."

He's still now, so completely unmoving that I'm not sure he's even breathing. But though guilt washes over me like liquid concrete, sticking to every part of me and solidifying into stone, I know I didn't have much choice in the moment. I'd done the only thing I could do then, and now all I can do is murmur my apologies over and over until Kit finally slumps into my arms, his damp face buried in the crook of my neck.

After what feels like hours of simply holding each other, he sniffles into my collarbone, taking slow and steady breaths. "I've been having panic attacks since Liam died," he admits, his words tickling my skin. "They started at his funeral, the first time . . . the first time someone called me Lord Clarence. That was the moment I realized he was really gone, and I . . ."

My heart cracks open as he swallows hard, and I thread my fingers through his hair at the nape of his neck. I've never questioned why he hates his title, assuming it has to do with the pretentiousness of the whole aristocracy. But this . . .

"I spent that first year after his death numbing the panic and grief with drink and—partying, and all those pictures you saw from Ben's posts," he mumbles. "I was in therapy, too, for a while, but I dropped it when it didn't seem to help. It was a shit time. A really shit time. Things Ben or Maisie said would set me off without them realizing, and I couldn't look my mother in the eye or even speak to my father, not when he was so insistent on bringing up the responsibilities that should've been my brother's. It was too much. It's still too much sometimes. But then you came to England, and . . . the worst of it quieted. It became manageable."

Kit's arms are still tight around me, but he pulls me into his lap, and I rest my head on his shoulder, silent and listening.

"The panic attacks became easier to control," he continues softly. "At least for a while. But after Sandringham . . . they've been more frequent again, and I didn't want to tell you because I didn't want you to feel like they were your fault. They're not. Something inside me is broken, and I don't know how to fix it."

"You're not broken," I say, pulling away enough to peer at him. "You're not. You've been through a lot, and your brain is finding ways to cope, that's all." I hesitate. And I *am* making it worse, but I can't say that aloud. "I'm here, okay? Always. To talk, to—to distract you, if I can. Or if not, to just listen. Whatever you need. Whatever you want, all right? I love you."

The urge to say more nearly overwhelms me, but I bite my tongue as he nods, and that's enough for now. We fall back into silence as Kit leans against the edge of the mattress, me in his lap and our limbs tangled together. From the living room, I can hear the murmur of voices and the sound of glass being swept up, but no one disturbs us. Even Singh has left us alone for the time being.

"What happened?" he manages after what must be several minutes, his voice so low it's more of a rumble than a whisper. "With . . . Dylan."

I glance at the doorway once more to make sure we're still

alone. “It wasn’t just Dylan,” I admit softly. “He brought me to Guy Fawkes.”

Kit’s eyes widen, and in a hurried whisper, I tell him everything that happened, from the moment I realized he was missing to when I stepped back into our bedroom and found Kit like this. I don’t leave anything out, but I do save the best for last.

“And I think—I *think* I found the list,” I whisper, nearly breathless now. “I didn’t get a real look at it, but when Guy was talking about Fox Rex alumni, he started to pull this book out, and it didn’t have a title on the spine. And it wasn’t dusty like the others, so I think he handles it frequently. I noticed it before he got in the room, but I didn’t have a chance to check—”

“So you don’t know for sure?” says Kit. I shake my head.

“There were cameras on me the whole time, I’m sure of it. If I’d looked, it would’ve given the whole thing away. But I’m almost positive. And I left a tracker there,” I add. Instantly Kit’s eyes are on me again, wide and unwavering. “I found it in the hem of your cardigan, right here.” I guide his fingers to the unraveled thread that still hangs from his sweater. “I didn’t know it was there, but—”

“You didn’t activate it?” says Kit, his voice catching with disbelief. “You had a tracker and—”

“We don’t know it’s the list, not for sure,” I say. “And besides, we don’t have any proof tying Ben to Fox Rex or the ABR. But if I can get another face-to-face with Guy, and if I can make him believe I’m on his side—that we’re both on his side, and that we have no idea Fox Rex is connected to the ABR—then maybe we stand a chance at getting him to slip up.”

Despite the heaviness of the night, I feel like something fizzy is bubbling up inside me. For once in all of this chaos, I'm useful, and if Kit knows what's going on from the start, he won't have to panic. Even better if he's actually with me.

But I don't expect the way his expression grows guarded, and my buoyancy fades. "What?" I say, but Kit blinks, as if I've pulled him out of a trance, and he brushes a lock of hair from my forehead.

"Nothing," he says. "Have you told Singh any of this yet?"

I shake my head. "I promised I would after I saw you."

"The sooner, the better, I think," says Kit. "Once he knows you left a tracker, he'll want to activate it and—"

"I don't want to tell him about the tracker."

Silence fills the space between us, as hard and heavy as steel. "You don't?" says Kit, clearly struggling to understand. "But the list—"

"We don't know it's the list," I repeat. "And if MI5 goes in before we confirm it, we could be throwing away the whole mission for nothing. It's not worth it. Not when we still need proof that Ben's involved, too."

The muscle in his jaw twitches. "And if they try to take you again? Or me?"

My mouth goes dry, and I don't have an answer for that. The terror of losing him that ripped through me earlier—it still resonates now, carved into me like a scar from a lightning strike. And I'm not sure I can handle another round, either.

But I also can't handle another attack on my family, and while I'll do anything to protect Kit and make sure he never hurts like this another day in his life, I'll also do anything to guarantee that Ben never raises a finger against my parents and sister again. Or funds anyone who tries it in his name.

Kit seems to take my silence for what it is—confusion and overwhelm—and he pulls me gently to him once more. "We both need sleep," he says. "I'll clean up, and—"

"I'll help," I say. "We'll replace everything tomorrow, okay? Maybe take a shopping trip to London in disguise or something. Make it like none of this ever happened."

But it did happen, and as we both get unsteadily to our feet, the tension in the air makes it impossible to forget.

When we leave the bedroom to hunt for a vacuum, Singh and a medical team swiftly corner us, and Kit and I spend the rest of the evening being stitched up and interrogated within an inch of our lives. Again and again, Singh has me repeat everything I can remember about my encounters with Dylan and Guy Fawkes, and each time I skip over the part about the possible list and the tracker I left in Guy's office, I can feel Kit's eyes on me, but I do nothing to give the game away. Not until we have evidence tying Ben to the ABR, too.

This can't be for nothing. I refuse. I *refuse.*

Hours later, Kit and I finally collapse into bed, and we fall asleep tangled together, neither willing to let the other go. When I wake up in the morning, weak gray light streams through the open blinds, and it takes me a moment to remember what happened the night before. When I do, my eyes fly open as I grope around the empty bed, my heart already in my throat.

Kit. Where's Kit?

I stumble barefoot into the living room, vaguely aware that

someone must have vacuumed the glass shards out of the carpet the night before. The curtains are open, letting the cloudy dawn through, and to my relief, Kit stands at the stove, pushing something around a pan.

"Are you okay?" I blurt. He looks up and nods, and I immediately notice the dark circles under his eyes. "Did you sleep at all?"

"Some," he admits as I cross the dining area toward him, and he scrapes the contents of the pan onto two plates. "I made scrambled eggs and toast. I wasn't sure if you'd be hungry, but you didn't eat dinner last night, and—"

"Thank you," I say, wrapping my arms around his waist from behind and pressing my cheek to the fresh T-shirt that clings to his back. "I'm starving."

The air that felt so charged between us the night before has settled now, or at least I think it has. But when he turns to kiss me good morning, there's something strange about the look in his eyes—distant, maybe, or avoidant. Almost like he's ashamed.

I don't press, not when the wounds we opened last night are still so tender. And once breakfast is ready, we bring it to the dining table and sit down together like we always do. Like this is just another normal day in Oxford, and we're a normal couple whose entire world didn't almost end last night.

"So. Shopping day?" I say, flashing him a devil-may-care smile. "I was hoping to get an upgraded laptop anyway. My CPU can't handle some of the programs Singh is throwing my way, and—"

Kit clears his throat, and my smile fades. He still won't look at me. "Evan. Ev," he says, toying with his mug of tea. "I need to talk to you about something."

I spread butter across my toast as nonchalantly as possible. "Only if you want to," I say. "Whatever you're comfortable with. I mean it."

"I know. And I appreciate that," he says gruffly. "But . . . it's not about that. It's about—"

Our front door flies open with a *bang,* and the newly repaired frame almost cracks in half for the second time in less than a day. Kit jumps to his feet, placing himself squarely between me and the doorway, where I catch a glimpse of Singh and—

Victor Stephens, the head of palace security, along with half a dozen PPOs.

"Pardon our interruption, my lord," says Stephens with a bow of his head, and Kit's muscles clench even tighter than before. "Miss Bright, I'm under orders to take you into my custody immediately."

"What? Why?" I say, craning my neck to peer around Kit. "Is this about last night? Because I'm fine—"

"It's not about last night," says Singh, and his lips are pursed with what looks almost like . . . an apology? Sympathy?

No. It looks like grief.

"I'm to accompany you both to Balmoral Castle immediately," says Stephens. "It's His Majesty."

CHAPTER NINE

"Henrietta, what is your take on the sudden uptick of activity around Balmoral, where the royal family has been sequestered for the past month?"

"It's impossible to say for certain, especially with the palace refusing to comment. But we can confirm that at least two helicopters have landed on the grounds in the past hour, and local law enforcement has been called on to close the roads near the royal family's private Scottish retreat."

"Could this mean the palace is planning an announcement soon? One that might attract an . . . unusual amount of press interest?"

"Possibly. Likely, even."

"And the rumours regarding His Majesty's declining health?"

"I couldn't possibly speculate—"

"Of course not. But it wouldn't be such a leap, would it? After a month of no updates and the secrecy surrounding his medical status, there are certainly signs that a big announcement is coming, are there not?"

"One might suspect such a thing. Whether it has to do with His Majesty . . . to even speculate, given all the royal family has endured lately, would be utterly uncouth."

"But surely if there is an announcement coming, the public has the right to know?"

"And they will, when the palace has deemed it time. For now, we wish His Majesty and the royal family good health and continue to support his recovery."

—ITV News's interview with royal expert Henrietta Smythe, 2 February 2024

THE HELICOPTER FLIGHT FROM OXFORD to Balmoral is nearly three hours long.

I spend every second of it with my hand wrapped tightly in Kit's, and though our headphones allow us to speak, neither of us says much as we watch the United Kingdom pass by beneath us. I can't stop thinking about the last time I saw my father—nearly a month ago in a hospital in London, with machines keeping him alive as my mother sat over him, pouring every drop of herself into willing him to stay with her.

Did something happen? Tibby said he was getting better, but she also said she never actually saw him. Was Jenkins telling her the truth? I wouldn't put it past him to lie to her—to anyone other than family—if it meant keeping my father's health a secret from the vulturous media.

And if the worst happened . . . if he's really gone . . .

As the helicopter lands in the middle of a Scottish meadow near the gray stone castle of Balmoral, I already see media crews gathering at a blockade at least a mile away. Have they been there the entire time the royal family has been sequestered here? Or is something really happening? I don't have my phone anymore, but Kit seems to read my mind, and the moment we touch down, he's on his mobile, checking the BBC site for updates.

Nothing but speculation so far. Even that hurts, to see the vampires circling, ready to feed on whatever horrific news is about to change my family forever. I hug Kit's arm, taking a deep, shaky breath, and together we hurry across the frozen ground to the nearest entrance of the fairy-tale castle that my grandmother, Constance the Queen Mother, calls home.

Tibby is there to greet us, looking harried despite her dark tweed dress and artfully choppy bob. "I don't have any information," she says before I can even ask. "Jenkins won't allow anyone into the wing until you've arrived."

"What does that mean?" I say, my voice breaking with anxiety. "Are there doctors with him? Is anyone trying to—to—"

I don't know what I'm asking, but it doesn't matter. Tibby repeats herself, gentler this time, and she leads us into the castle at a quick pace I have no trouble keeping up with. I've never been to Balmoral before, but I barely notice the endless maze of rooms we pass, a blur of deep blues and greens and the occasional maroon. Dark oil paintings line the walls, and I'm already too horrified to feel anything at the sight of the astounding number of mounted deer heads watching us as we dart down the empty corridors.

He can't be gone. He can't be. Jenkins would have told me if there'd been any signs of decline. He would have made sure I was here, that I had a chance to say goodbye—

I stop short as we turn down yet another lengthy hallway. This one isn't empty like the others, though. Twenty feet away, standing in front of a full-length mirror as he adjusts his black suit, is my cousin, nineteen-year-old Prince Benedict of York.

Ben.

He doesn't look away from the mirror immediately. Instead, he finishes tying his solid black tie, and only then does Ben turn his sharp gaze toward us. Toward me.

"Ah, Kit," he says, though his eyes are locked on mine. "I was wondering if you were on your way. Maisie's been asking for you."

"I'll stop in to see her once we've settled," says Kit in the most neutral tone I've ever heard in my life. I don't know how he's managing—if I try to speak right now, it'll come out as a squeak or a scream, nothing in between, especially now that we're face to face with the reason my father is in this state to begin with. It's only Kit's grip on my elbow that stops me from lunging forward and clawing Ben's eyes out. That and the anxiety coiled so tightly within me that I can barely breathe.

"I'll let her know to expect you," says Ben, his stare still on me. "If you didn't bring a black suit, I have an extra."

Confused, I glance at Kit. There's no way the pair of them can comfortably share clothes, considering Ben is several inches shorter than Kit and built like a reed. But when what Ben is implying hits me, the air leaves my lungs, and it's all I can do to take one shallow breath after the other.

Kit tilts his head slightly, the barest of acknowledgments at Ben's verbal knife, and he wraps his arm around my waist. "If you'll excuse us," he says, and he continues forward, half carrying me with him.

Ben whistles to himself as we go, and Tibby hurries to open a hidden panel in the hallway. "This way will be quicker, I think," she mutters, glaring behind us. Neither Kit nor I question her as we head inside, and as soon as the thick door slides home, leaving us in a well-tended passageway that's probably about as secret as Alexander's middle names, I bury my face in my hands.

"Is he—the black suit—is that because—" I blubber, and Kit pulls me to his chest, where I promptly get his coat wet.

Tibby sniffs. "Benedict knows even less than I do," she says. "Why you'd believe a word that comes out of his mouth—"

"Tibby's right," says Kit, rubbing circles into my back. "He's just trying to get under your skin."

"Trying?" says Tibby with a scoff. "He gets off on seeing you like this, Evangeline. The only way we're going to find out what's happening with His Majesty is to go see for ourselves, so if you're quite done . . ."

Clearing my throat, I pull away enough to wipe my face with my sleeves. "Okay. I'm sorry. Can we—"

But she's already walking down the passage, her heels clicking with each step. I bury myself under Kit's arm as we follow, and when Tibby pops open another panel on the other side of the long passage, it's into an antechamber with an antique gold bench, four matching chairs, and no fewer than half a dozen PPOs guarding a pair of double doors.

"Miss Bright," says the nearest one, clearly startled by our appearance. "Er—Lord Clarence, Lady Tabitha. I apologize, but Jenkins was very clear that only Miss Bright be allowed—"

"I'll wait out here," says Tibby. My grip tightens on Kit's hand, and my pounding heart strains against my ribs, trying to break through.

"It's okay," says Kit, gently trying to undo my grip. "I'll be right out here, too."

But as one of the PPOs unlocks the double doors with an

electronic key card, I can't make myself move. Whatever lies beyond that threshold will define the rest of my life, and I can't face it. Not without him. If Alexander really is gone . . .

"Evan?"

Jenkins appears in the gap between the doors now, his expression grave. The purple circles beneath his eyes say more about the weeks I've been gone than words ever could, and his salt-and-pepper beard isn't as neatly trimmed as it usually is, though no one could possibly call it scruffy. Those small details are what make something crack inside me, and it takes everything I have to stop myself from surging forward into his arms. For years, Jenkins was my only constant—the only familiar person in my life, who picked me up from boarding school every time I was expelled and dropped me off at my new one, offering me a small sense of stability in between. He was the only person who ever seemed to care about me, but after I chose to go to Oxford and work with MI5 against his wishes, something in the bond between us broke. Forever, maybe, but while I desperately hope not, now is not the time to test that.

"Jenkins?" My voice is shaky, and I take a tentative step forward. "Is he—is my dad . . . ?"

He glances at the PPOs gathered in the antechamber and gestures for me to follow him inside. When I take a step forward, however, Kit doesn't, and considering I'm still holding on to him for dear life, that leaves me stuck.

"Lord Clarence may join us," says Jenkins, and I have no idea how to interpret that. Does he think I'll need the comfort? Or does Jenkins consider Kit family, since he is technically my father's nephew?

I don't think about it too hard. Instead, as soon as Kit is moving, I pull him forward, joining Jenkins inside an emerald sitting room. The only evidence of use is an untouched lunch tray sitting on a table near the window, and my pulse is pounding so loudly in my ears now that I can barely hear Jenkins as he speaks.

"What on earth happened to you?" he says, brushing his fingertips against my jaw. I blink like he's spoken a foreign language, and only then do I remember the swollen purple-and-blue bruise from the night before. The pain is still there, throbbing in time to my heartbeat, but my adrenaline and fear have spent the past several hours drowning it out.

"It's nothing," I say, flinching away as he touches an especially sensitive spot. "I'll explain later. My dad—what's going on? Victor Stephens, he said . . . it didn't sound good, and Ben's wearing black, and—"

"Evie?"

The sound of my name is faint and slurred, but I would've heard it clear as a bell even if the room were full of people. Immediately I snap my head around to a single door that stands half-open, and before Jenkins can explain, I've darted around a sofa and an ottoman, still dragging Kit along behind me as I step into the doorway.

On the other side is a bedroom, illuminated by weak daylight spilling through the gauzy white curtains. A hospital bed has replaced what was undoubtedly an antique monstrosity, and my mother sits on an uncomfortable-looking settee among any number of beeping machines. Her curly hair is a mess, and there's a small mountain of easels and sketchbooks in a nearby corner, but she's not the one who said my name.

Instead, my father, Alexander II, King of England and the Commonwealth, lies propped up in bed, his legs still wrapped in bandages and his arms sporting more tubes and monitors than I can count.

But his blue eyes are open, and he's smiling directly at me.

CHAPTER TEN

She's here.

You said you wanted to know when she arrived.

What, no reply?

Is there anything in particular you'd like for me to weasel out of her?

John?

—Text messages sent from a prepaid mobile,
2 February 2024, 11:27 a.m.

ALEXANDER IS ALIVE, BUT HE'S frail.

It's the kind of frail that nothing in life can really prepare you for—the kind where, as I wrap my arms around him, sobbing so hard I can barely breathe, the only conscious thought to pass through my mind is that hugging him too tightly might end up killing him after all.

I hear his words in my ear, a murmur of something comforting, but I can't make them out. He doesn't sound like himself. His mouth isn't working right, maybe because of the coma or the head injury or a combination of both, but I don't care. Hearing his voice again is more than I thought I'd ever have.

My mother joins us, sitting on the opposite side of my father's bed and hugging us both with such warm gentleness that it only makes me cry harder. Until this moment, I had no idea how scared I really was. How badly I needed Alexander to wake up. And now that he has, now that he and my mom are here, I let out every terrible emotion I've been holding in this past month, allowing the pieces of myself held together by vengeance and spite to crumble.

I don't know how long the three of us stay like that, but eventually one of my father's monitors begins to beep, and a nurse I didn't notice before steps up, waiting for us to detangle ourselves before she takes his vitals. From that short burst of activity—from nothing more than hugging me and my mom—Alexander is clearly out of breath, and anxiety twists inside me once more. Alive. Awake. But still at the edge of danger.

"Where . . ." he manages to slur, but he trails off, his lips still parted like the rest of his question is right on the tip of his tongue.

"Jenkins told us what you've been up to," says my mother instead, taking my father's hand. "But he didn't mention you'd taken up boxing."

I can see the worry in her eyes, even though she keeps her tone light for Alexander, and I gingerly touch the same spot Jenkins honed in on earlier. "You should see the other guy," I joke, but neither of them laugh. I feel Kit's presence behind me, and when I glance at him, he doesn't meet my gaze.

"You were one of the first things His Majesty asked about upon waking," says Jenkins stiffly from his spot on the other side of the bed. "I told him everything."

"Everything?" I say, eyebrow raised. Jenkins raises one right back.

"Everything. Including MI5's involvement."

Alexander clears his throat, though it does little to help his speech. "MI5 . . ."

"They have plenty to answer for," agrees my mom, her thumb stroking the back of his hand. "In the meantime, I'd like to hear the full story from Evie and Kit."

I glance at Kit again, and this time he's watching me expectantly. But when I open my mouth, I have no idea where to start.

"After the bombing," I say slowly, thinking over each word as I speak, "the Army of the British Republic—the antimonarchist terrorist group that took responsibility—claimed I was involved in the planning."

Lines appear in Alexander's forehead, and I know immediately from his confusion that no one has mentioned this part to him. "You . . . ?"

"I wasn't," I say hastily. "But—a lot of things happened really quickly that made it look like I had it out for the family. There was even a picture where Kit and I—we were photographed with one of the terrorists who was arrested at the site of the bombing."

"It was a setup, Your Majesty," says Jenkins, and I can already hear the regret in his voice at asking me to explain. With a single look, he silences me, and I gladly shut my mouth and lean into Kit as both he and Jenkins take the reins instead.

Together they paint a picture at a much more digestible pace, explaining as they go about Fox Rex and how both Kit and his older brother, Liam, were roped into joining. They break the news gently about the connection between a supposedly harmless but banned Oxford society and the Army of the British Republic, and Kit explains in detail how I ended up as the poster child for the most infamous domestic terrorist group the UK has seen this century, making sure to highlight the fact that I am not in any way, shape, or form an actual terrorist.

They leave out the parts about the Windsor Castle fire, I notice, and Maisie's brush with death at my supposed hands. Ben isn't mentioned at all, which rankles me, but I can tell by the way my father's gaze slips in and out of focus that he's already struggling to process everything. There's a good chance this won't be the only time he'll have to hear all of this information, and for now, I bite my tongue and let the cracks remain.

At last, after Jenkins has touched on the hospital threat that saw my critically injured father and the entire royal family evacuated to Balmoral, we reach the moment Agent Suraj Singh of MI5 asked Kit and me to help infiltrate Fox Rex and find the list of former members—and potential current ABR terrorists.

"And . . . you . . . said . . . yes," says my father in a whisper so hoarse that it crackles, but this time, I understand every word.

I nod without shame. "I had to. *We* had to. It's the only way to find the list—"

"It's not the only way," says Jenkins coolly. But when I look at him, his mouth is pinched, and his gaze is cast to the carpet.

"Kit and I have an in," I insist. "I've already spoken to Guy Fawkes—"

"You *met* him?" says my mother, horrified, and her hand flies to her throat. "Evie—"

"It's a good thing," I insist. "He trusts me, I think. And if we can just have a little more time—another two or three weeks to get closer to him—then I think I'll be able to convince him that I'm a bigger asset than Ben."

"Ben?" My father's complexion goes ashen, and I realize my mistake the instant my despicable cousin's name leaves his mouth. "He . . . still . . . ?"

I gulp. "He's behind it all. I'm sorry, Dad, I really am. I know you don't believe me, but we're so close to getting proof—*so* close, and if I can just get Guy to trust me—"

"I—believe . . ." My father shakes his head minutely, and his face crumples, as if this small action alone has caused him a world of pain. "No," he manages after a beat. "Evie . . . no."

I blink. "But Ben—"

"He said no, Evie," says my mother, sandwiching my father's hand between hers. "And I say no, too."

I look back and forth between them, stunned. "But—you don't understand. I'm close—I'm *so* close, and if Guy thinks he can trust me—if I can give him something Ben can't—"

Jenkins clears his throat. "It is, in any regard, a moot point. According to Victor Stephens, MI5 has spent the past eight hours coordinating with local law enforcement across the United Kingdom to make a series of simultaneous arrests targeting those they believe to be involved with both Fox Rex and the Army of the British Republic. It seems they intend to carry out those arrests today."

An icicle of dread pierces my chest. "*What?* But—why now? Why aren't they waiting for the real list?"

Jenkins glances behind me. No, not behind me—just above me to where Kit stands, his grip on my waist weakening with every passing heartbeat. "It is my understanding," says Jenkins slowly, "that they did in fact have this supposed list of former Fox Rex members in their possession."

My confusion burns away into agonizing clarity, and I crane my neck to look at Kit, who yet again won't meet my eye.

"I had to," he says simply. "It was too big of a risk to leave it."

Maybe this is true. Maybe, if circumstances were different, I'd even agree with him. But as it is, all I can feel is the boiling fury of betrayal and the pain of having the trust we've so carefully stitched together ripped out without a single care for what's left behind.

"You should've told me," I say, with steadiness I don't feel. Kit doesn't argue, and instead he lets go of my waist and takes half a step back, leaving the cold to sneak in where his warmth was seconds ago.

Alexander has questions—some of them articulate, others that no one, not even my mom, can fully make sense of. But after only ten minutes of this, the last of his energy wanes, and the nurse shoos all of us out, with the exception of my mother. I kiss his forehead as he falls asleep, his entire body seeming to sag with the weight of all we've put on his shoulders.

Kit and I leave the room side by side, though we're not touching. Jenkins remains behind in the sitting room, and while Tibby is waiting for us in the antechamber, she says nothing as we take a different exit, through a wing of the castle that looks like it hasn't been properly lived in for decades.

"I won't ask how he is," says Tibby at last, "but let it be known that you're both scaring me right now, and that's not an easy thing to do."

I exhale. "Alexander's awake," I say apologetically. "And speaking, sort of."

Her eyes shut in relief for two quick strides. "Good. State funerals are depressing affairs." But when she glances at Kit and me, I can still feel the question in her gaze. Why don't we look happy?

As Tibby leads us through the corridors, I replay Kit's confession in my mind again and again, and fury and frustration glow within me like hot coals, growing more unbearable with each footstep. And by the time we reach our guest room, I want to swear. I want to *scream.* But as I pull open the door to the living area, ready to ask for a moment alone with Kit, I come face to face with a tall, willowy girl with red-blond hair who looks every bit as furious as I am.

My half sister and heir to the throne, Maisie.

She's dressed in muddy riding gear, and her freckled face is pink from the cold. Still, not a single hair is out of place in her French braid, and her makeup looks pristine as she clutches her phone, her mouth set in a thin line.

"Maisie," I say, my spine stiffening. "We just saw Alexander. I thought—"

"What, that he was dead?" she says casually. "Maybe if you were both around more, you wouldn't be so shocked."

I stare at her, stunned, and her blue eyes flicker over me briefly before she focuses on something over my shoulder.

"I thought you, at least, would've known better," she says, contempt dripping from her voice, and I can practically hear Kit grimace.

"Mais, I'm sorry we couldn't tell you—"

"Oh, of course not," she says airily. "I'm only the heir to the throne. It's none of *my* business if my cousin and meddlesome half sister run off and chase terrorists for fun while the rest of us are stuck in Scotland. The entire world knows now, by the way. Or they will soon enough."

Before I can put any of the dozen questions suddenly crowding my mind into words, Maisie taps her phone and shoves it in my face, and the polished, steady voice of an anchorwoman plays on full volume.

". . . breaking news this hour as MI5 has announced the arrest of the terrorist known as Guy Fawkes, the supposed head of the Army of the British Republic."

The clip that follows shows Guy being hauled out the front door of a house in what must be Oxford, his forgettable face neutral and his gold-ringed eyes fixed straight ahead. And while I only catch a glimpse of the arresting officer, I immediately recognize Singh's profile.

"This is your doing, I suppose?" says Maisie, and I take her phone from her, my hands shaking.

Holy shit.

"Yes," admits Kit behind me, while Tibby leans in to catch a glimpse of the broadcast. "And we will explain everything as soon as we're settled in—"

"Please," says Maisie with a sneer, and she snatches her phone from my hands, leaving me staring blankly at the wall instead.

"I have better things to do than listen to your half-baked excuses."

With that, she shoulders her way past me and back into the hallway, and I listen to the echo of her boots against the wood of the corridor, my mind a dizzying hurricane.

It's over. Guy's been arrested. The Army of the British Republic has collapsed. Fox Rex is finished.

It's over, and Ben is still free.

"Ev?" says Kit, at my elbow now. I don't—can't—look at him.

"Tibby," I say, stepping into the Scottish country-chic room and shoving my shaking hands into my pockets. "We need a minute. Please."

"Very well," she says, and she eyes Kit up and down. "I suppose you remember where your room is."

He nods curtly, and I don't bother asking why he has a separate one. Right now I'm almost glad he does.

As soon as Tibby is gone and the door is closed, Kit leans against the back of the tartan love seat, his shoulders sagging. "I can't apologize," he says quietly. "I don't know if that's what you're waiting for, but it had to be done."

I cross my arms to hide my trembling hands as I pace in front of the enormous four-poster bed. "You should have told me," I repeat, and this time, he nods.

"I should have. I am sorry for that."

"Everything we worked for, every risk we took—it was all for nothing now."

Kit frowns. "They have them, Ev. They have Guy, and they'll have the rest of the ABR soon enough, if they don't already—"

"They don't have Ben," I snap, and silence falls between us, heavy and unmoving. Kit is frozen in place, his hand angled toward me like he wants to reach out, but there's too much space.

"Ev . . . we were never going to get Ben," he says carefully, like he's walking through land mines, and I want to smash something to pieces. "Guy only wanted you—*us*—to think we could. He was toying with us the entire time, and there was nothing we could do but play our ace—"

"Our ace was *Ben,*" I say, tears burning my eyes. "It was the fact that we know he's part of this, and if we can just get them to *admit it*—"

"If Ben is truly involved—"

"If?"

"—then he's the real prize, Ev. He grew up in the royal family. He knows more about how the entire institution functions than you and I ever will, and he knows Alexander and Maisie better on a personal level than nearly anyone in the world. Guy Fawkes would never turn him in to the authorities and risk all Ben knows about him, too, in order to hook you. Especially when the public already associates you with the ABR."

I stare at him, my mouth hanging open as I let my arms drop. "But—"

"Evan." He finally breaks the invisible wall between us, taking both of my hands in his and holding them so firmly that he feels like an anchor in a thrashing sea. "I love you. You've done more in twenty-four hours than the entirety of MI5 has managed in months simply by being your courageous, stubborn, utterly reckless self, and I *love* you for it. But I have stood by and almost lost you more times than I care to count, and all I want is for this to be over." He squeezes my hands, ducking down so his dark eyes bore directly into mine. "I am begging you, Ev. Let MI5 do their job now. If there's any chance of finding a connection between the ABR and Ben, they'll manage. And in the meantime, please, *please* let this nightmare be over for us."

I take a shuddering breath, and then another as he continues to hold my stare, his fingers lacing between mine. The worst part is, I know that if he'd simply told me he was going to Singh, this would all be okay. That the trust ripped out at the seams between us would still be there, and that we could find a way to mend the rest of the damage. But that gaping wound is bleeding freely now, and as I watch him, I have no idea how he can't feel it.

"You should've told me," I say one more time, my voice small and pitiful. And as I untangle my hands from his and head toward the door, the hope on his face drains away, and I know he can feel the wound now, even if he may not realize how deep it is yet.

CHAPTER ELEVEN

Now that members of the Army of the British Republic are being rounded up by the ever-vigilant MI5, almost a month after the bombing that killed eight innocent people and almost ended the reign of our beloved King Alexander, will Evangeline Bright and Lord Christopher Abbott-Montgomery finally be held accountable for their roles in the attack?

If the mountain of evidence that has surfaced over the past three weeks isn't enough to convince our counterterrorism experts that this dastardly duo must finally be taken seriously, we at the *Regal Record* have unearthed pictures of Evangeline deep in conversation with the accused leader of the ABR, known only as Guy Fawkes. The pair are photographed in a private setting, reportedly discussing yet another attack on the royal family, this time at Balmoral—the alleged cause of all the fuss in Aberdeenshire this morning. Click below to view our exclusive gallery.

At what point do the people of the United Kingdom stop allowing royals and the rest of the aristocracy to slip their gilded handcuffs and start demanding real justice?

—*The Regal Record*, 2 February 2024, 1:14 p.m.

SOMETHING IS LICKING MY TOES.

I jolt awake, disoriented and confused, and jerk my leg away from the warm tongue. I'm sprawled out on a couch in a drawing room deep within Balmoral, and as my heart races, a small black-and-white spaniel pops up from the other side of the sofa, cocking its head as its pink tongue hangs out of its mouth.

"Shit," I say in an exhale. I know Constance breeds dogs, but I always assumed she skins them alive to make fur coats or something. Not lets them roam around like pets. "What are you . . . Stop that!"

"Ah, you're finally awake."

Tibby appears in the doorway, silhouetted by warm light from the hallway, and I scowl. "How did you find me?"

"Do you really think you don't have your own personal protection officers here?" she says. "I see you've made a friend."

I sit up and run my fingers through my messy hair, then do the same begrudgingly for the puppy. "Does Constance know she's missing a dog?"

"Probably," says Tibby. "Was your bed not to your liking?"

"Didn't get the chance to try it out. Kit and I had a fight."

"How unfortunate." She doesn't sound the least bit surprised. "When you make up, please keep in mind that the Queen Mother prefers that all unwed couples sleep separately."

"Not going to be a problem," I mutter, and pain stabs me unexpectedly. Maybe I'm overreacting—Kit was right, after all. I was being reckless, leaving the list there with only a tracker to lead us back. But that doesn't change the fact that he still went behind my back and broke my trust without even trying to talk to me first. If I can't trust him . . .

But does he even trust me anymore, either?

"What time is it?" I say, mentally sidestepping those quicksand thoughts. The heavy curtains are closed, and it's impossible to tell if it's still light out.

"Nearly five o'clock," she says, checking her phone. "Which is why I'm here. You've been summoned to a meeting of the Privy Council."

"The—what?" I say, confused. "Aren't they all in London?"

Tibby doesn't answer as she digs through her handbag, and a moment later, she produces a hairbrush and a stick of gum. "If you wouldn't mind. We're already late."

I could refuse to go—I really am exhausted—but given all that's already happened today with MI5 and the ABR, my curiosity gets the better of me. And after popping the gum in my mouth and running the brush through my hair, I follow Tibby out the door, the puppy trotting happily at my heels.

Minutes later, we reach a sitting room with a table that seats twenty and a cabinet displaying hunting trophies that are undoubtedly older than some American states. Maisie, along with my stepmother, Queen Helene, and my grandmother, the Queen Mother Constance, are seated on one side of the table, and my uncle Nicholas, the Duke of York, stands behind them as they all face an enormous monitor.

". . . can't ignore the public outcry," insists a red-faced man named Doyle, the royal press secretary, amidst more than two dozen somber individuals all appearing on-screen. "Something must be done now that the relevant arrests have been made—"

"I agree," says Ben, catching my attention like a white-hot hook. He's mostly concealed on the other side of Nicholas, but I can tell he's still wearing that damn black suit. "With photographic evidence out there to prove their involvement, it's only a matter of time before the public will lose all trust in the monarchy if we don't launch an official investigation. It doesn't matter who they are or who they're related to—"

Someone clears their throat behind me, and only then do I realize Kit has followed us into the room. He stands an unnerving distance away from me, his hands shoved into the pockets of a cardigan and his back ramrod straight.

"I take it you're talking about the pictures published by the *Regal Record* this afternoon," he says stiffly, and I look between him and Ben, confused.

"What pictures?" I say, and Ben steps fully into view, looking every bit as polished as he always does.

"The pictures that show you cozying up to the suspect known as Guy Fawkes," he says, and my stomach drops. The only time I've been anywhere near Guy is last night, and there's only one way Ben managed to get his hands on that camera feed. It's proof—not anything I can use as evidence, maybe, but it's still *proof.*

"It's 2024," I point out. "Pictures can be easily faked."

Ben smirks. "Is that really the defense you plan on using? The leader of the ABR has already publicly called you out for participating in the bombing and getting him access to our family—"

"If I may interrupt," says a familiar London accent, and though he doesn't speak loudly, Singh has the kind of authoritative voice that not even Ben can ignore. Which is probably a good thing, considering I'm only now catching on to something I should've realized the moment I discovered Ben and the ABR were working together.

He plans to pin everything he's done on me.

My insides are in knots as Ben gestures for Singh to go ahead, and the MI5 agent who has potentially ruined my life clears his throat. "Your Majesties. Your Royal Highnesses. Today's arrests are the direct results of the hard work and courageous action from members of MI5 and local authorities, but also—especially so—from Miss Bright and Lord Clarence."

Even though the ambient noise was already quiet, the silence becomes oppressive now, like a weighted blanket that's smothered all the air out of the room. "Pardon?" says Constance, as if she hasn't quite heard him correctly.

"Miss Evangeline Bright and Lord Clarence, ma'am," repeats Singh, "were instrumental to our mission in finding individual members of the ABR and tracking them down for questioning and arrest. The pair have spent the past several weeks working undercover in Oxford at our direction and under our protection, and though we cannot yet share all the details of their mission with you, I can tell you, without a doubt, that if it hadn't been for their willingness to come face to face with the terrorist known as Guy Fawkes—whom they both knew to be behind the bombing—we would be no closer to arrest than we were the day of the attack. They are heroes, ma'am, and I—MI5—this country owes them a deep debt of gratitude."

All eyes turn toward us now, and my face heats. Even the puppy at my feet licks my ankle, and I bend down to scoop her into the crook of my arm, if only to buy a moment of relief from those stares. And Ben's menacing glare.

"Kit? Is that true?" says Helene, baffled.

"Not necessarily the hero part, but the rest of it," he admits reluctantly, stepping up beside me. "Since I was already . . . associated with Fox Rex, Agent Singh asked for our help in finding a rumored list of ABR members. We agreed, and Evangeline has been with me in Oxford since I left London. We've been using our connections to infiltrate Guy Fawkes's inner circle. Seems she did a better job of it than me," he adds with a glance my way, and I look at the puppy again, scratching her soft black fur.

Ben leans down to whisper something in Maisie's ear, and they both glance at me before exchanging another whisper. I try to ignore it, but the assignment I gave Maisie before I left for Oxford slithers through me, leaving a trail of nausea behind.

Keep him close. Let him think he's won. Let him think you hate me.

Nicholas's jaw twitches. "You had no right to ask that of them," he says to Singh, who nods in agreement.

"I wouldn't have done so unless it was of the utmost urgency, Your Royal Highness. By agreeing, they saved our investigation months, possibly years, and my agents ensured they were protected at all times."

"Ah, yes, because nothing says *protected* like a purple jaw and a swollen lip," says Nicholas, his scowl deepening.

On the giant screen, Doyle clears his throat. "So . . . you're telling us that they aren't terrorists. That they are, in fact, the reason the arrests happened in the first place?"

"Indeed," says Singh, and Doyle rubs his face with his meaty hands, clearly forgetting his audience.

Ben shifts his stance, his foot tapping erratically on the polished floor. "I for one am pleased that justice is served," he says in what has to be the bullshit statement of the century. "But pictures are pictures, and the public will always assume there was a palace cover-up to protect them."

"You're right, Your Royal Highness," says Singh in a deceptively light voice. "The chances of the public accepting that Miss Bright and Lord Clarence are completely innocent of all charges leveled against them are nonexistent."

"It's a disaster," bemoans Doyle. "Unsalvageable. The king's daughter and the queen's nephew, caught up with terrorists—even if they're innocent, His Royal Highness is right. There's simply no way we can coax the public into believing them—"

"On the contrary," says Singh. "I believe that if we go public with the story—the *full* story, mind you, or as much as we can declassify in a timely manner—then we'll have a real opportunity to win over the British people. There's little more that buys loyalty and compassion than allowing someone in on a secret, and what bigger secret is there right now than what Miss Bright and Lord Clarence have gone through, all in the name of protecting their family and country?"

One, two, three seconds of silence, and then chaos erupts.

"You want to go *public*?" explodes Nicholas.

"Have you any idea how vulnerable that would make Kit? And Evangeline?" says Helene, and I'm impressed she remembers to include me, even as an afterthought.

"Tell the people the truth?" gasps Constance, like this is the most absurd thing she's ever heard.

"Do you have any idea how many ways this could backfire—" begins Doyle, but they're all drowned out by Ben's guffaws.

"You want to turn them into heroes?" he says over the shouting coming from the crackling speakers. "Evangeline can't even be trusted with a solo appearance, and Kit—" His entire body shakes with laughter now. "We all know you'd rather be holed up in a cave somewhere than have a camera pointed in your face."

The shouts die down as everyone yet again turns toward Kit and me, because Ben might be the biggest arsehole in Britain, but he's hit the nail on the head. Kit and I are exactly the wrong people for this. If it had been Maisie in Oxford instead of me, she could polish this shitstorm of a situation into a diamond that would redefine history. A new age of Great Britain would rise up in her making, and the monarchy's future would be secured for at least another five generations.

But my biggest contribution to this country has been my ability to sell salacious tabloids. Even on days when the public likes me, I'm only useful as a laughingstock or some long-running gag. Calling me a hero, or claiming I'm some superspy who helped take down one of the biggest domestic threats to British soil since the real Guy Fawkes himself—it's a joke. And everyone here knows it.

But because it's Ben who pointed it out, and because it's his laughter that echoes around the room as the rest of the volume dies down, I look at Kit. He's looking at me, too, and though there's still an enormous distance between us, a space I'm not sure we'll ever be able to fully cross again, I shift the puppy into my other arm and touch his hand.

"If there's a way to make it work," I say, "then I'd rather have the truth out there than let everyone think we're traitors."

Kit swallows, his Adam's apple bobbing. "I agree," he says quietly.

Doyle frowns. "It would take more than just a statement from the palace. The public would expect interviews, appearances, perhaps even a book or . . . or a ceremony of some sort."

I blanch at the idea of a ceremony, or anything celebrating weeks of me sitting around and one night of sheer recklessness. But I can't admit how little I really did, or how much I don't deserve the credit. Not in front of Ben. "We'll do what we have to do," I say after the slightest of nods from Kit. "Just . . . release a statement, and we'll go from there."

Ben scoffs again. "Ridiculous," he mutters. "No one will buy it."

"Maybe not," says Singh. "But let's give it a try, shall we?"

CHAPTER TWELVE

"I would like to personally thank Lord Christopher Abbott-Montgomery, Earl of Clarence, and Miss Evangeline Bright, daughter of His Majesty, for their vital aid in the fight against the Army of the British Republic. Without their courage and daring, yesterday's arrests of more than three dozen suspected members of the ABR would not have been possible, and we owe them an enormous debt of gratitude for placing both their lives and reputations at great risk to help us find those responsible for the terrorist attack on our nation and our king."

—Transcript of the prime minister's speech addressing the arrests of the suspected ABR terrorists, 3 February 2024

KIT SLEEPS IN HIS OWN room that night, an arrangement I'm trying to pretend was my idea, and I only have my toe-licker for company as I turn restlessly over and over again, struggling to convince myself that the world as I know it hasn't ended.

I don't have a clue what will happen now that we've given

Singh and Doyle the green light to go public with what we were really doing in Oxford. The least-terrifying scenario I can come up with is that no one really cares—that the public is so busy with their own lives that they simply accept MI5's word for it, agree that Kit and I aren't terrorists, and move on to the next great scandal.

The worst scenarios, however, are too numerous to list. Pitchforks. Protests. Prison. My head on a stake. Kit's head on a stake. Just because the palace declares us innocent doesn't make us so in the eyes of the public, after all, and what proof do we really have except our word? And while Kit's may still be worth something, mine has long expired.

Tibby drops the bomb on me at breakfast. "The prime minister gave a speech twenty minutes ago, thanking both you and Kit," she says as I feed bits of egg to the puppy. "It's already making headlines around the world."

"Great," I mutter as the puppy rolls on the carpet, begging for belly rubs. I reluctantly give in, but only because it means I have an excuse to avoid my plate. "Do you think anyone will actually believe him?"

"Does it matter? It's the truth. The opinions of others are like . . . like farts," she says, and I do a double take. "They're occasionally smelly enough to notice, but they always disappear into the ether eventually."

I grope around for my phone, only to remember that I no longer have one. "I'm going to need you to repeat that as soon as I have another mobile," I say. "Because *that* is going to be my ringtone for the rest of my life."

"Don't be ridiculous," she says, though I swear she cracks a smirk. "Now come. You're nearly late for a meeting with the crisis management team we've looped in from London."

This is the first I'm hearing about it, but I'm so exhausted and anxious to see Kit that I don't argue. Every part of me misses him, and even with the toe-licker curled up beside me all night, it still felt wrong to be without him in a way I can't put into words.

The puppy follows us through the maze of corridors until we reach a sunny dayroom, complete with a lit fireplace and blue-velvet sofas, with no plaid or dead carcasses in sight. Kit sits at a table facing another oversized monitor, and the natural light emphasizes the deep shadows beneath his eyes. He clearly didn't get much sleep, either.

"Hi," I say hesitantly, not sure where to sit. He rises and pulls out the chair beside him, and my heart stutters before my brain sternly reminds it that this is who Kit is—polite and chivalrous to a fault. He'd do the same for a stranger, and reading any kind of intention into this is just one more way for me to silently torture myself.

"Good morning," he says as I join him, and though there's an awkward pause, he kisses my cheek before I take a seat. Apparently the torture's going to happen whether I like it or not. "I see your new friend is back."

It takes me a beat to realize he means the puppy, who is now happily chewing on the heel of my slipper. "I don't think Constance has noticed she's missing yet."

"She must've seen you two together yesterday," says Kit,

reaching down to scratch the puppy behind the ears. "Maybe she knows you'll take good care of her."

Doubtful, but I keep my thoughts to myself. Instead, even though Tibby is standing near the door, tapping furiously into her mobile, I say, "I missed you last night."

Kit's hand stills. "I missed you, too," he says, quieter now as he leans in toward me. "Constance is . . . very particular when it comes to sharing rooms, and I thought you wanted time to yourself, after . . ."

"I thought I did, too," I admit. "But I want to talk and—and figure this out. I just . . . I need to *understand* why you didn't tell—"

"Good morning!"

A chipper voice with a posh accent breaks through our conversation, and Kit and I both jerk upright like we've been caught making out. On the screen is a stunningly beautiful twentysomething woman with glossy chestnut hair, piercing hazel eyes, and a smattering of freckles so perfectly placed on her heart-shaped face that they look like a work of art, and suddenly I wish I'd bothered to put on some mascara. But there's something about her that's familiar, too, and I frown, trying to place her.

"Astrid?" says Kit, his mouth dropping open. "Is that really you?"

The woman—Astrid—beams. "Who else?" she says, making a "ta-da" motion with her hands. "I was hoping no one would tell you. I wanted it to be a surprise."

Kit laughs—a lighthearted chuckle I haven't heard from him

in weeks. "It's you, then? The fixer from London? I should've bloody known."

"When you need the best, you hire the best," says Astrid, and she winks. "Oh—how terribly rude of me. Evangeline, my name is Astrid Clark, and I'm an old friend of Kit and Liam's. I'm also a partner in the crisis management firm Tucker and Clark—"

"The youngest person to ever make partner in the firm," says Kit pointedly, and she fans her face like she's blushing.

"Stop. Stop! We both know it's all nepotism."

"I don't see Connor there with you," he says. "And isn't he five years older?"

"Seven," she corrects with an impish grin, and part of me withers and dies. "All right, enough with the flattery. We have magic to work and a disturbingly limited amount of time to make it happen. I'm looping in the palace PR team now."

As she clicks a few buttons, I glance at Kit. The way he's gone from somber and careful with me to this gregarious social butterfly with Astrid makes a strange, jagged sensation slice through me, and I can't help but wonder which version of him is the truth.

Our eyes meet, and he laces our fingers together, stroking the back of my hand with his thumb. He thinks I'm jealous. Maybe I am, but when I search the hollowness in my chest for any burning insecurity or animosity toward this gorgeous, accomplished friend of the person I love, all I feel is a cold and abiding sadness for what now stands between me and Kit. And every part of me that has, again and again, lost friends and family and all the places and things I ever dared to love is screaming at me about another loss to come—this one so deep that I can't even begin to fathom it.

I miss most of the introductions from Doyle's staff, too focused on Kit's warm hand against mine. It's the anchor I need in the spiraling sea of anxiety and grief that threatens to consume me, even though he's still here and with me and mine. But I can feel the strings between us being cut one by one, and all I desperately want is for him and I to be okay again.

At first, everyone feigns politeness as they debate the best way to handle the now-public knowledge that Kit and I were involved in the investigation into the ABR, but the meeting eventually devolves into a battle between Astrid and Doyle, who seems determined to keep things as traditional and *downplayed* as possible.

"That's not going to work," says Astrid flatly after Doyle interrupts her with yet another *slight modification* to her surprisingly tactful and considered suggestions. "The whole point is to make bloody certain the entire world knows what happened in Oxford, and a subtle course will only put us right back where we started. If whoever's in charge has problems with our approach, then we'll reevaluate, but for now, we *will* be answering calls from every reputable news agency and chat show in the country. We *will* be speaking to both current and former royal correspondents about book deals. We *will* be entertaining pitches from every major producer and studio that is interested in a *favorable* adaptation of their harrowing—"

"A movie?" I blurt. "You want to do a *movie*?"

"Yes," says Astrid calmly as Doyle opens and shuts his mouth like an outraged fish. "Nothing influences public opinion like a good film, Miss Bright, and that's what we'll be aiming for—something of quality. Not a cheesy made-for-TV movie with a shoestring budget, but something with a celebrated director and known cast, released in theaters worldwide—perhaps even worthy of the BAFTAs or the Oscars."

My eyes widen, and I look at Kit, who appears every bit as shell-shocked as I feel. A movie. Someone else playing me. Someone else playing *Kit.*

"If we can get the palace's permission to use royal locations," continues Astrid, typing furiously now, "and if we can find an appropriate screenwriter to work in tandem with the author of our choosing, then perhaps we can have the film fast-tracked and released at the same time as the book later this year—"

"Astrid," says Kit quietly, and it takes her a moment to look up. "I think that's enough for today."

"What?" she says, confused, and she glances between what must be his face and mine on her screen. "Oh. Look at the time—my apologies, Kit. Er, Lord Christopher. I suppose you have a flight to catch, don't you? I'll drop by Oxford over the weekend and go over more details with you. And, Doyle, you can brief Miss Bright. Or I'm happy to do so if you can't be trusted."

Doyle is so red now that he looks like he might explode, and while normally I'd be delighted, my head is spinning, and I'm slow to absorb exactly what she's saying.

"Flight?" I manage, glancing at Kit once more, before Astrid continues as if I haven't spoken.

"I'm arranging a live interview with the BBC for next week—

we'll of course prep you thoroughly, but Kit—Lord Christopher—I wanted to make sure you'll be available."

Kit nods, not looking at me. "I'll make it work."

"Lovely," she says. "Miss Bright, Lord Christopher, I'll speak with you soon. Doyle, I look forward to continuing this delightful verbal brawl over email."

As soon as we've all disconnected, I turn to Kit, my mind still racing. Movie. Live interview. *Flight.* "What was she talking about?"

Even though he didn't bring anything with him to the table, he glances around our shared space, as if searching for his things. "I, er—I've decided to head back to Oxford," he says. "I've already missed too much of this term, and I'd rather not have to repeat it."

A block of ice forms in the pit of my stomach. "I don't understand," I say, but he rises to his feet, his hand leaving mine, and panic surges through me. "Kit—I'm not—whatever this is really about, can we please talk—"

"I was going to tell you." He finally meets my gaze again, his brown eyes full of something I'm too afraid to name. "Yesterday morning, right before Stephens interrupted us, I was about to tell you that I texted Singh. I couldn't sleep, and all I could think about was losing our one chance to finish this, and what might happen if they came after you again—what almost *did* happen, and—" He rakes his hair back in a defeated gesture. "I'm sorry I didn't tell you before I did it, but I couldn't make myself wait another moment, not with your life on the line. I'm done, Ev. I'm sorry I'm not strong enough to stay, then or now, but even being here . . . seeing you so upset, knowing it's my bloody fault that

Ben is still free to do what he pleases . . ." He rubs his face. "I'm sorry. I need—a break. Space. Please."

I stare at him, rooted to my seat. "A break?"

"Just for a little while. To get my head on straight. To—I don't know. Recalibrate. To stop feeling like this. Like everything is a threat, even—"

He shuts his mouth before he can finish that sentence, but a sickening feeling washes over me, and I know exactly what he was going to say.

Even you.

There's a knife in my chest now, buried so deep that I'm amazed my heart is still beating. This is what the end looks like. No shouting matches, no blowouts, no long-drawn-out feuds. Just two days of torture, and then this. A break. Space. A girl who makes him laugh that isn't me, and heartache that will never go away. I know he truly intends for it to be a break, but I also know what it really means when people say they'll keep in touch.

"Okay," I say, so softly I can barely hear myself speak. I stand to join him, but there's a chasm between us now that only grows wider with each passing moment. "When . . . ?"

"Term ends on the ninth of March," he says, and my insides twist. That's more than a month from now.

"Can I visit?" I say, but as soon as the words leave my mouth, I know his answer. Kit reaches for my hand, squeezing it with shattering gentleness.

"Let's play it by ear. I'm not in a good place right now, and I don't want to . . . say anything or . . . do anything that might . . ."

He trails off, and I don't know what he thinks he could possibly say or do around me that he might regret. But then the sight of our bedroom in Oxford flashes through my mind, with all of his things smashed to pieces, even though mine remained untouched.

He heads toward the door, and it's only then that I notice his suitcase tucked into a corner. The sight of it rings like a bell in my head, making this all too real, and my heart pounds.

"Wait," I gasp, hurrying after him. Kit obediently turns back, and suddenly I see his weariness. I see the fear etched into every faint line and furrow of his skin. And in his soft sigh, I hear the terrible truth—that I'm the one causing so much of this agony.

Tears prickle in my eyes. If I don't say something right now, I know—I *know* I will lose him, as sure as I know that the sky is blue and the English drink way too much tea. So I open my mouth and let the words tumble out.

"I'm sorry," I croak. "For everything. For getting into that van. For falling for some ridiculous setup. For not telling Singh about the tracker the moment I got back to the flat. For wanting to stay longer and put you—put both of us in even more danger—"

"There's no need to apologize." Kit cups the uninjured side of my jaw, his thumb stroking my cheek, and the way he stares into my eyes is devastating. "You want to stop Ben from hurting the people you love, and there's nothing wrong with that. I just . . ." He takes a deep breath. "I don't know how much more of this I can take. I love you, Ev. I always will, more than my own life. But it isn't supposed to hurt like this."

I always will. Like this really is the end.

Another invisible string connecting us severs, and my stomach lurches, threatening to bring up my breakfast. "Okay," I manage again, but this time it comes out small and broken. "I'm sorry."

"Don't be—" he begins, but I cut him off, because it's either that or burst into tears, and suddenly I can't stand the idea of him seeing me cry.

"Text me when you get there," I say shakily. "Or—Tibby. Text Tibby. My phone . . ." I trail off. Another reminder of why this is happening. "I'll see you in March."

"Evan . . ." Kit moves toward me, trying to close the distance, but I step back. I don't want to hurt him more than I already have, but if I don't find the connection between Ben and the ABR, then my bloodthirsty prince of a cousin will never stop coming after me. After my parents. After Kit and everyone I love. And Ben will get away with murder—literally.

But now I know it will also cost me the best thing in my life, and those two facts can't fit together in my mind, like two puzzle pieces that are both the wrong shape and size.

Tears leak from the corners of my eyes despite my resistance, and I brush them away. Kit reaches for me again, but his hand stops half an inch from my face. Close enough to feel his warmth, but not his touch.

"Just give me time," he says softly. "That's all I ask."

"Okay," I repeat. He frowns, and I know it's not what he was hoping to hear, but it's all I can say.

"I love you," he says again, all sincerity and faith, and this, at least, gets a tiny, trembling smile out of me. It's true, but now I know it isn't enough.

"I love you, too. More than my own life," I say, echoing his earlier words. It's also true, and it was always enough, or at least I thought it was. But now I know it's the fatal flaw between us.

He hesitates, and before either of us steps away, he leans down and brushes his lips against my cheek in another chaste kiss. That's all it is, but it devastates me to my core. Because now I know it really means goodbye.

He doesn't say it, though. Instead, he picks up his suitcase and gives me one last, long look before stepping out the door. And though every cell in my body screams at me to follow, I stay glued to the rug with the puppy at my heel as he leaves, taking any chance I have at real happiness with him.

CHAPTER THIRTEEN

EVANGELINE AND LORD CLARENCE OFFICIALLY CLEARED BY MI5—'GOVERNMENT ASSETS, NOT SUSPECTS'

—*The Daily Sun*, 3 February 2024

EVANGELINE BRIGHT AND LORD CHRISTOPHER ABBOTT-MONTGOMERY 'INSTRUMENTAL' IN HELPING BRING DOWN ABR

—BBC News, 4 February 2024

LORD CLARENCE BACK IN OXFORD, ATTENDING LECTURES DESPITE HERO STATUS—WHERE IS EVANGELINE?

—*The Daily Sun*, 5 February 2024

AMERICAN PRINCESS—NOW ROYAL SPY?

—CNN, 6 February 2024

EVANGELINE AND LORD CLARENCE RISKED ALL TO PROTECT FAMILY AND COUNTRY, CLAIMS PALACE INSIDER

—BBC News, 7 February 2024

SOURCE: EVANGELINE KIDNAPPED DURING MISSION, THREATENED BY HEAD OF ABR—STILL WANTED TO CONTINUE DESPITE ROYAL WISHES

—*The Daily Sun*, 8 February 2024

TIMELINE OF THE OXFORD OPERATION: WHAT WE KNOW SO FAR

—*London Independent Standard*, 9 February 2024

PRESIDENT PARK COMMENDS EVANGELINE BRIGHT FOR BRAVERY, ISSUES OPEN INVITATION TO WHITE HOUSE

—CNN, 10 February 2024

LIVE INTERVIEW WITH EVANGELINE AND LORD CLARENCE SET FOR TOMORROW NIGHT—'ALL WILL BE REVEALED'

—BBC News, 11 February 2024

THE WEEK THAT FOLLOWS IS torture.

Tibby tries to cheer me up by showing me headlines from around the world—headlines that endlessly praise me and Kit for bravery they don't even have context for—but all that does is remind me of everything I didn't do to protect Kit, and every mistake I made in my relentless pursuit of trying to take Ben down.

I don't so much as try to come to terms with that guilt and grief as I do wallow in it, and between VidChat prep meetings with Doyle and Astrid, I haunt my guest room like an agoraphobic ghost, accompanied by the loyal spaniel puppy and occasionally an annoyed Tibby. The only time I leave is when I visit my parents, spending as much time with them each day as I can before it's obvious that Alexander is pushing himself to stay awake for me.

The one silver lining in all of this is that he's recovering faster than any of his doctors expected. His memory is improving and his words are mostly intelligible now, barely a week after regaining consciousness, and he only slurs when he's tired—usually the first sign that I need to find a reason to leave. His left leg, which was shattered in the bombing and isn't healing properly, is now the biggest problem his medical team is facing, and I try to pretend I haven't heard the whispers of what they might need to do if things don't change. But it's written in the way my mother's smile grows tighter each time I visit, and despite the surgeries he's already endured, despite the odds he's already defied, I know Alexander is nowhere near out of the woods yet.

On the third day of this, Tibby hands me a new phone without comment, and it takes me all of two minutes to realize that the ringtone is, in fact, her reluctantly repeating *fart* a dozen times in her uppity accent. It's the only thing that makes me grin in this strange, endless week, and I do my best not to think of how miserable I must look if she's willing to do that for me.

I don't text Kit. I want to, desperately, but I'm determined to give him the space he needs. And selfishly, I know that if I try to reach out and he doesn't reply, my heart will permanently shatter, and I'm already in too much pain to put myself through that.

But when my text notification goes off hours later, I nearly drop my phone as I scramble to unlock it. Did Tibby tell him she replaced it? Or maybe he's been texting, and I forgot to check—

It's not him, though. Instead, it's from a number I've never messaged before, even though it's saved in my contacts.

Lady Primrose Chesterfield-Bishop.

Rosie

i've been following the news . . . did you take him down, too??? xx

I stare at my screen as the puppy snores softly beside me on my bed. Rosie, my half sister's former best friend, is the reason we know Ben is guilty. She's the one who revealed back in January that Ben runs the *Regal Record,* the royal gossip site focused on destroying me and Kit. She even confessed that he'd been blackmailing her into slipping him pieces of gossip and writing articles for him—a practice she swears she's since stopped—and she's the reason we know exactly why he's doing it in the first place.

But Rosie and I aren't exactly friendly, and I can't remember a time we've ever talked, just the two of us. Which makes her text all the more baffling. But the more I study it, the more I realize that even though she's undoubtedly seen the endless headlines, the *him* she's referring to isn't Guy Fawkes.

Evan

Just the ones you've heard about. I'm sorry.

Rosie

damn. is there any chance . . . ? xx

Evan

I don't know. It's a long story.

Rosie

i can ring if you'd like xx

I have a pretty solid idea of what Maisie would say if she ever discovered I'd spoken to Rosie behind her back, especially about Ben, and it isn't good.

Evan

Can't. Puppy is sleeping.

Rosie

you have a puppy??? xx

It's almost funny how easily this distracts her, and I take a picture of the puppy and send it to her. Seconds later, Rosie replies with a string of heart and rainbow emojis.

Rosie

what's the name??? xx

Evan

She doesn't have one yet.

Rosie

you have to give her one!! xx

Evan

Can't. She's Constance's.

Rosie

i won't tell if you won't xx what are her parents called??

Evan

Not sure. All of Constance's dogs are named after shades of blue. Zaffre, Indigo, Cobalt, Sapphire.

Rosie

jade??? lapis??? azure??? omg TIFFANY!! xxx

I wrinkle my nose. The thought of using Constance's naming convention makes my skin crawl, even more than naming the puppy does. I don't want to create a bond that will inevitably break when it's time to leave Balmoral, just like every other relationship in my life, and I know for damn sure I can't take another loss right now. But I'm also positive Rosie won't let up until I give her a name, and Tiffany is not it.

Fine. Constance likes the color blue, and I like nothing more than to annoy her.

Evan

Poppy.

Rosie

a flower name! love it!!! xxx welcome to the family, poppy bright!!

I don't know why this makes me tear up, but it does, and all I want is to tell Kit about it. About Rosie texting, about the puppy's name, about how much I miss him—every bit of it. Instead,

I set my phone down, ready to call it a night, but only a minute later, it buzzes again.

Rosie

thank you, by the way . . . i know i'm probably the last person you want to hear this from, but thank you for trying. even if ben gets away again, what you and kit did was really, really brave, and i'm so proud of you. i hope one day we can be friends (and snickers and poppy, too!!) xxxxx

I sniff and wipe my eyes with my shirt. There are a dozen things I could say in return—that I didn't do it for her. That I would love for her dog, Snickers, and Poppy to be friends, even though I'm not sure she and I ever could be. That Maisie won't forgive her no matter how close she is with me. That I'm sorry we didn't take Ben down, too.

Instead, I press the text long enough to heart it, and leave it at that. It's the only thing that doesn't feel like a betrayal of Maisie, Kit, or myself.

SOMEHOW, I SURVIVE until we're only twenty-four hours away from the live interview.

Doyle and his team spend the entire day going over the preselected questions with me, making sure I have my answers down and know exactly what information is still classified. No mention of Ben, but I'm encouraged to talk about my experience with Guy Fawkes, whose real full name I still don't know. Dylan is, to my deep dismay, still on the loose, and any details about his identity are strictly off-limits, although I'm welcome to refer to him as a *violent fanatic of the ABR* when it comes to my supposed kidnapping—which I'm also encouraged to play up, especially with my bruised jaw and healing lip still obvious.

Thanks to the endless reminders and dire warnings from a visibly sweating Doyle, I'm late seeing my parents that evening, and instead of taking the long way through the castle to their wing, I cut through the more populated corridors. My footsteps are silent as I move through the hallway, but when I turn a corner, I hear a sharp gasp.

"Stop!" shrieks Maisie from the other side of a heavy wooden door. It's cracked open, and I rush over, ready to put an end to whatever's going on when—

Maisie starts to laugh. Confused and alarmed, I peer through the doorway. She's sprawled out on the scarlet sofa, trying to squirm away as someone with slicked-back blond hair mercilessly tickles her sides.

Ben.

"Admit it," he says. "I won that race."

"Never!" she declares, laughing so hard now that it sounds like she might be crying. "You were—a nose behind—and—you—*know it!*"

"Do I?" says Ben, and I can see his wide grin from my vantage point. "Because I also recall *you* and Isla taking off half a beat early, which would mean Rory and I more than made up the distance—"

"Are you—calling me—a cheater?" says Maisie, trying to sound serious as she smacks his hands away. "Because I—would—*never*—"

At that exact moment, she glances straight at the door—and at me. Her laughter dies in her throat, and even Ben's tickles don't draw them out of her. Instead, her eyes go from the color of the summer sky to icy pale, and I step out of view, exhaling softly.

"What?" says Ben, and I can sense his gaze through the thick wood.

"Nothing," says Maisie. "Just one of the maids. Is it dinner-time yet? I'm starving."

"Ought to be," says Ben. "Do you want to—"

"Will you check? I'll only be a moment."

He huffs. "While I'm at it, would you like me to fetch you some tea and biscuits? Coffee, perhaps, or should I draw you a hot bath?"

I hear a soft thump that sounds a lot like a pillow. "Don't be an arse. I'll be in the dining room in a minute."

"Whatever you say, Your Royal Highness." Ben's footsteps echo through the room, but just as I'm about to duck behind a sweeping velvet curtain that's probably as dusty as Constance's opinions on social etiquette, I realize he's heading the other way. There must be another exit, and thankfully Ben chose the one that doesn't lead directly to me.

What little luck I have runs out, however, when Maisie clears her throat. "Are you going to show yourself, or should I expect all my conversations to now be fodder for eavesdropping?"

Gritting my teeth, I step into the room and close the door behind me. "I wasn't eavesdropping. I heard you screaming."

"*I* wasn't screaming," she says. "Maybe *you've* never had family to horse around with, but I—"

She stops herself before she can finish that thought, and I do my best to let her blistering comment roll off me, even though it hit home.

"I wasn't screaming," she repeats herself stiffly. "I'm fine. But thank you for your concern."

"Sure," I say, the word clipped, and I nod toward the other door I can now see. "Has he let anything slip? Anything useful?"

Maisie narrows her eyes. "If he had, I would've been open and honest with you, unlike *some* members of this family."

I wince. "I'm sorry—I really am. If I could have looped you in—"

"And who, exactly, was stopping you? MI5? Because the last time I checked, the crown ranks somewhere above Agent Singh. I can keep secrets—"

"This secret could've gotten me and Kit killed," I say. "This has nothing to do with your pride, Maisie. We didn't tell *anyone* because we couldn't risk them letting something slip. Not just you, all right? Not even my mom knew. And you were spending so much time with Ben—"

"I've been spending time with Ben because *you* told me to," she hisses. "You told me to keep him close and convince him that he's back in my good graces, and that's exactly what I've done. Now you're punishing me for playing my part?"

"I—of course not. I wanted to tell you. If there was any way I thought you could've helped—"

"You never gave me a chance, did you? You've no idea what I could've accomplished."

"I—" I bite my lip. "You're right. I'm sorry, and I'm asking for your help now. We didn't find anything on Ben in Oxford, which means unless Guy Fawkes is willing to talk, we have no way of proving Ben's involvement. Which means—"

"I know what it means. I'm not an idiot," she says hotly, but her gaze is unfocused now, and there's a faint line between her eyebrows. "And you expect me to do what, exactly? Confront him about it? Invade his privacy like you do?"

I frown. "I don't know. Maybe not that, but—anything that might give us a lead."

"And what if there is none? You've been convinced he's guilty for so long that you're not even willing to consider the likelihood that he isn't. You tracked down the ABR *and* its leader, yet you still didn't find anything to tie Ben to the attacks. Isn't it time to explore the possibility that you're simply biased, and that he isn't the person you think he is?"

I stare at her, stunned. "Did you lose a brain hemisphere somewhere in the Highlands? Of *course* he's part of this. There's a good chance it was all his idea in the first place. Rosie—"

"Do *not* talk to me about that traitorous snake," she snarls. "Do you have any idea what it's like, being surrounded by people you love who constantly lie to your face? All I want is one person I can trust, Evan. One single bloody person who won't try to use me or betray me for their own gain."

"And you think *Ben* is that person?"

Her silence is all the answer I need.

I shake my head, speechless. Maisie was with me and Kit when we confronted Rosie. She heard the whole story—she knows Ben runs the *Regal Record* and has been behind every bit of slander from the start. She knows that Ben was blackmailing Rosie. That the entire reason he's been doing this is because Maisie, who likes boys about as much as most people like root canals, will probably never have an eligible heir of her own.

She knows. She *knows.* So why is she doing this?

"If you really need help," says Maisie at last, "you could ask your new friends at MI5. I'm sure they'd be thrilled for another chance to kiss your arse."

"They've already tried," I mutter. "Please, Maisie. You know him better than anyone—"

"Kit knows him, too," she says. "Oh, wait. You also bungled that up, didn't you?"

"Don't," I manage, though it comes out as more of a wheeze.

"Oh? Is it not true? Because from what I've heard, you somehow took the one good thing you both had and threw it away with such finesse that even I'm impressed. The way you broke his heart—"

"You have no right—"

"I have *every* right. Kit is like a brother to me, and I've loved him long before you were in the picture. From the sounds of it, I'll love him long after you're gone, too. He told me what happened in Oxford, you know—how you recklessly risked your life and nearly destroyed him in the process."

"I didn't—" I begin, but the protest dies on my lips. Because I did. "That's not—"

"That's not what happened?" she says, eyebrow raised. "You've no idea what he's been through, losing Liam, and yet you insist on making him relive that trauma again and again. Not only that, but you actively put his life in danger. You asked him to possibly *die* for you, Evan. How am I supposed to forgive that? How is *anyone* supposed to forgive that?"

"I didn't ask him to—I didn't want any of that!" I burst. "I tried to keep him safe—"

"But how could he have possibly been safe when he was with you?"

I hear it now—the real hatred in her voice—and it slices through me like a white-hot knife. Maisie squares her shoulders, and with one final sneer, she storms across the room and through the other exit, leaving me wrecked in her wake.

CHAPTER FOURTEEN

The mysterious June 2022 death of William Abbott-Montgomery has finally been revealed as a suicide.

—Excerpt from *The Regal Record*, 12 February 2024

WHEN TIBBY KNOCKS ON MY door early the next morning, I'm wide awake, still reeling from my fight with Maisie.

Though I managed to sleep a little the night before, it was restless at best, with dreams that haunted me even after I woke up in a cold sweat. Now I stare at a crack in the curtains, watching the pitch-black sky slowly lighten to gray as Maisie's words repeat in my mind again and again.

You asked him to possibly die for you, Evan. How is anyone *supposed to forgive that?*

Tibby steps inside, and instantly I know something's wrong. She typically wakes me like a tornado, taking pleasure in ruining my morning before it's even begun, and her making an effort to be discreet is never a good sign.

"What is it?" I say, sitting up. She must hear the urgency in my voice, or maybe the exhausted defeat, because she doesn't try to take the sting out of what comes next.

"The *Regal Record* posted an article overnight, announcing

Liam's death as a suicide," she says, and all the warmth leeches from my body in a single exhale. "They're trying to discredit Kit and cast uncertainty around everything he says during the interview tonight—"

"Has anyone talked to him?" I say, throwing the covers off despite the chill. "I need to call—"

"Maisie has already spoken to him," she says, and I bite the inside of my cheek. Tibby has no idea Ben runs the *Regal Record,* but Maisie does. Is this enough for her to realize that Ben will never spare either of them as long as she—we—stand in his way?

Somehow I doubt it. "What did Kit say?" I say, pulling open the doors to my armoire.

"I've no clue. Maisie's at breakfast now. I'm sure she's eager to discuss the matter before you leave for London."

Maisie likely wants nothing to do with me, but I'm not about to miss my chance to demand answers from her. I rush through the morning essentials, and once I'm dressed and reasonably presentable, I head toward the dining room at a pace that has Tibby struggling to keep up. As we go, she fills me in on our packed schedule before the interview tonight, but I'm barely listening as I cut every corner close, nearly mowing down at least three footmen and a maid.

"How is he?" I say as I burst through the double doors of the dining room. Helene, Nicholas, and Constance all look up in alarm, but Maisie, who sits several seats away from them, barely gives me a passing glance as she types into her phone.

"Evangeline," says Nicholas, the only friendly face among the four of them. "What an unexpected surprise. Please, help yourself to the buffet—"

"Thanks, but I'm not hungry," I say, my stare locked on Maisie. "You spoke to Kit, didn't you?"

Maisie's thumbs move at the speed of light. "Of course I did. I rang him first thing."

"What did he say? Is he all right? Has he talked to his parents or—"

"Is this about that dreadful article on that blog?" says Helene. "I thought Doyle was taking care of that."

"We've always been unable to get posts taken down off that site," says Nicholas with a grimace. "Really, poor Edgar and Amira. And Kit, too, of course. Some things are meant to remain private, and how those vultures got that information to begin with . . ."

He trails off and takes a bite of his eggs, and I glare at Maisie, who knows damn well how the *Regal Record* came across that little tidbit.

"Is this that . . . royal what's-it rag?" says Constance, giving the puppy at my heels a disapproving look, and I grit my teeth. Why does Nicholas seem to be the only one who cares?

"Yes, Grandmama," says Maisie sweetly. "It's that terrible online journal that writes all sorts of nasty things about—"

"*What* is the meaning of this?"

A red-faced Prince Benedict of York storms into the dining room, followed closely by a scowling protection officer. Poppy cowers behind me, and I ball my hands into fists as all of my impotence shifts to anger. There is nothing I want more than to break his nose right now, and it's only because of his unexpected fury that I hesitate.

"The meaning of what, darling?" says Helene as she butters a scone.

"I'm to have a minder wherever I go now," announces Ben indignantly. "Even during private interactions with family members. And I've been banned from all official meetings of the Counsellors of State."

Helene raises an eyebrow, but while Nicholas also looks mildly surprised, it's Constance who sits up straighter, clearly affronted. "Who is responsible for this?"

"Isn't it obvious?" says Ben, shooting me a death glare. "There's only one person here who hates me. Did you take advantage of Uncle Alexander's addled state and convince him I'm the bogeyman?"

My jaw tightens painfully, and all my rage finally breaks free. "If I wanted you banned from Balmoral, I wouldn't have to lie."

"Enough," says Constance, and her cup of tea hits the saucer with a clatter. "I'll speak to Stephens and get this sorted. Clearly there's been a misunderstanding."

"At the very least," says Ben bitterly. "I've never done anything to warrant such treatment."

I snort so loudly that I startle myself, and all eyes turn to me. "Did you have something you wanted to say, Evangeline?" says Helene coolly.

I glare at Ben. "Anything I have to say, I'll say it during the interview tonight. I think that's fair, don't you, Ben? No fun handing out spoilers."

His soulless eyes narrow. "If I were you, I'd make sure to brush up on defamation laws in this country before saying anything too outrageous. Especially since you seem to be lacking any real evidence to back up your lies."

"Am I?" I say. "I guess we'll just have to see, won't we?"

I step forward, intending on leaving it at that and hurrying back to my phone to text Kit, but Ben's arm snaps out in front of me, his palm hitting the threshold as he blocks my way.

"Your interview with Kit is at the Maychester Hotel, isn't it?" says Ben, his voice carrying beyond me. "I certainly hope for your sake that MI5 managed to round up every member of the ABR. Otherwise I shudder to think of what might happen tonight. It's likely to make what happened to Uncle Alexander look like child's play—"

Before I know what's happening, I shove Ben up against the threshold, my elbow digging into his throat. His pulse flutters against my skin, but he doesn't even try to fight me off, and the entire room—even his minder—is completely still.

"Don't you dare say my father's name," I growl, bared teeth and all. "After what you did, you have *no* right—"

"If you're implying that I had anything to do with what happened to Uncle Alexander, then you're utterly mad," says Ben with a sneer. "I've done nothing but support his recovery—"

"You haven't been allowed anywhere near him." I press my trembling elbow harder into his throat, and he makes a choking sound. "Just in case you try to finish the job."

"I didn't—do—*anything,*" insists Ben. In a burst of ferocity, or maybe panic, he finally shoves me away, and I stumble back toward the table. "I would never—"

"Of course not," I snarl as something wild overtakes me.

"You never do your dirty work yourself, do you? That's what the ABR was for."

He slams his fist into the wall, leaving blood smears behind. "I *refuse* to stand here and listen to this character assassination," he howls, straightening to his full height. "Father. Grandmama. Aunt Helene. Maisie. If you're all willing to entertain this madness, then by all means. But I will not waste my time defending myself against these ridiculous claims."

Ben stalks away, and satisfaction rushes through me as he vanishes from sight. Good. Let him disappear. With any luck, after the interview tonight, the only time I'll ever have to see him again will be in a courtroom when I give testimony against him.

But once he's gone, the silence in the dining room is resounding. "Well," says Maisie at last, and she rises, taking her phone and another piece of toast with her. "Now you've done it, Evangeline."

She, too, strides out of the room, and something cracks inside me—my heart, maybe, or any sense of hope I still had that my sister hasn't been fooled by a murderer. Fighting back tears, I lean against the dented wall and rub my eyes, wishing more than ever that Kit was still here.

"That," says Constance in a deadly voice, "was the most inappropriate display of—of sheer *lunacy* I have ever witnessed. I am *appalled* by both your actions and your words, Evangeline, and I will not suffer having the likes of you in my presence—"

"She's telling the truth, Mother," says Nicholas with a long-suffering sigh. "Ben is a devious little shit, and frankly he's lucky she didn't try to break his nose. He certainly deserves that and more."

"Nicholas!" exclaims Constance. "Benedict is your *son*—"

"He knew about the bombing," I say as Nicholas takes another bite of egg. "I don't know if he's been funding the ABR or feeding them information or both, but he knew exactly what was going to happen that day."

"Don't you dare speak of my grandson in such a way," says Constance. "He is a prince—"

"He's a terrorist."

"He has no reason to harm a fly," she retorts. "He lives a life of luxury—"

"As third in line to the throne," I say. "And until I arrived, he was practically guaranteed to get the crown someday. But Ben knew Alexander was still in love with my mom, and he also realized that if my parents ever get married and I decide to have kids, they'll be next in line, not him. Seemed highly unlikely a year ago, but when I suddenly showed up, he panicked."

Constance stares at me like I'm speaking in ancient verse, and before I can stop myself, the entire story spills out of me in a painful rush. I tell her every terrible thing that Ben has done since I arrived in England. How he helped Jasper drug me and then tried to pin Jasper's death on me. How he told Dylan exactly where Kit and I would be the morning we were shot at Sandringham. How Ben bugged my rooms and made me think I was having auditory hallucinations.

I tell her how he was behind the fire at Windsor Castle, and how he specifically targeted my mother in order to burn her alive. Without naming our source, I tell her how Maisie, Kit, and I managed to confirm both Ben's motives and his methods through someone he was blackmailing, and how we're sure there are other victims. I tell her about his connections to the ABR and Guy Fawkes, and how even MI5 is investigating him. I show her pictures, video, the threatening texts he's sent, evidence I've collected—I give her everything I have in under ten whirlwind minutes, barely stopping for breath.

"And the *Regal Record,*" I say at last, lightheaded and knowing I'm treading on dangerous ground, but I have to make her understand. I have to make all of them understand. "We know that's Ben, too, from the same source he's blackmailing."

"That's him?" says Nicholas, his frown twisting with disgust. "He wrote the article about Liam?"

I nod. "Tibby thinks the *Regal Record*—Ben—is trying to discredit Kit before the interview and make sure no one trusts him."

Helene shakes her head slowly in disbelief. "And he used Liam's death, of all things, to do it. As if Edgar's family hasn't been through enough."

Constance, who's been completely silent this entire time, walks wordlessly toward the door. "Constance?" I say, but she turns down the hallway without explanation. I follow as the puppy trots at my heels, her tail wagging. "Constance, you can't tell anyone else—it's still an open investigation—"

I fall silent as we pass a footman, but Constance quickens her strides. I can't let her walk away with all the information I've given her, not when I have no idea what she plans to do with it, and so I stay with her, my heart thudding against my ribs.

At last we emerge into a familiar wing of the castle—the guest apartments. Ben's personal minder stands guard in front of a nearby door, and he steps aside as Constance reaches for the knob and throws it open, revealing a dimly lit guest suite.

"Grandmama?" says Ben from behind an antique writing desk, and he slams his laptop shut, jumping to his feet. "What are you—"

"From this moment on," she says, her voice full of steel, "you are no longer welcome on my property, or on any royal property where I have a say in the matter."

Ben blinks, and we both look at her at the same time. *"What?"* he gasps, echoing my shock.

"No true prince would ever behave in such a manner as you have," she continues, "and no grandson of mine would ever threaten our family."

His eyes flicker toward me. "Whatever Evangeline's told you, it isn't true—"

"I am not interested in your attempts to further manipulate me. I have been kept in the dark for far too long, but that ends today. Should you ever show your face in my presence again, I swear I *will* see you punished to the fullest extent of the law for all you've done to my son."

Ben's jaw tightens, and he grips the edge of his desk like it's the only thing keeping him from exploding. "You're choosing a mongrel over me? I'm your grandson. I've done nothing but put this family first again and again—"

"Lie to me one more time, and I will also have Alexander cut your allowance to nothing," she says coldly. And with a single glance back at me, she adds, "At least this mongrel has integrity and courage. Unless one is careful, even the purest of lineages can be bred into monstrosities. The only kind thing to do then is to drown the pups before they spoil the bloodline any further."

Before I can process just how nasty this insult is, Ben spits at her feet—only to be strong-armed to the other side of the room by his minder.

"You'll regret this!" he shouts as Constance turns on her heel and strides back down the hallway. "That bitch will burn the entire monarchy to the ground—she'll destroy everything—*everything*—"

I follow her, numb with disbelief, and only when the echoes of Ben's tirade finally fade does Constance stop in front of a window, her eyes shining with tears. I want to cry, too, but for an entirely different reason, and I scoop Poppy up and bury my nose in her fur.

Nicholas believes me. Helene believes me. Somehow, impossibly, Constance believes me, too. Maisie doesn't, but does it really matter when Ben isn't allowed on royal property anymore? Alexander and my mother will finally be safe, or as safe as they'll ever be. It isn't over—it'll never be over, not while Ben is alive and still has a chance at the crown—but for now I can finally breathe.

"She likes you," says Constance, her voice tight with emotion. I pull my face from the puppy's fur and frown.

"I guess so," I say. "I'm sorry. I keep trying to shoo her away, but she won't leave. She's a good girl, though."

Constance nods brusquely, once again staring out the window. "She's the wrong color for breeding. It happens sometimes, despite how careful we are. Her lineage is strong, but she's no good to us here. You can have her, if you'd like."

I stare at her, the silence between us crackling like static.

Constance is offering me a puppy.

I've never had a pet before, but I know a peace offering when I see it. Not just a peace offering, but an apology—one that, to Constance, must be the equivalent of eighteen years of remorse. And so, even though I don't have the faintest clue how to care for a puppy that can't be more than a few months old, I nod.

"Thank you," I say, and I hug Poppy a little closer as she licks my cheek. "I'll take excellent care of her, I promise."

"Obviously," says Constance, and she turns away to dab her eyes. "I'll make sure the staff at each royal residence knows how to meet her daily requirements. Her diet is tailored to her breed, and she'll need extensive training—"

"You're giving Evan a *dog*?" Maisie appears from a nearby room, her cheeks pink and her blue eyes wide. "I've been begging you for a puppy for *years*—"

"The dog chose her," says Constance. "There's nothing I can do. Besides, when you ask for a puppy, it's always the pick of the litter. This one's barely more than a mutt. Now," she adds, taking a shaky breath and focusing her full attention on Maisie. "I expect you knew as well, did you? About what your weasel of a cousin was up to all this time."

"Of course," she says, undeterred by the change in subject. "Who do you think told the PPOs to put someone on him?"

I blink. "That was you?"

She rolls her eyes. "*You* certainly don't have the power. As soon as I saw the article about Kit and Liam, I made the call."

Constance straightens, and somehow the shine of tears in her eyes has disappeared. "We won't have to worry about Benedict's antics any longer. I've made it clear he isn't welcome here—at Balmoral or on any other royal property."

"Good," says Maisie, raising her chin. "It's about time Mummy and Uncle Nicholas looped you in. I've been pressing them to for ages—"

"Wait," I say, my mind still reeling. "Maisie—the things you said about Ben yesterday—defending him and—"

"Really, Evangeline," she says with a mixture of haughtiness and hostility. "For an internationally renowned spy who's single-handedly taken down the biggest domestic terrorism threat in the United Kingdom, you're awful at recognizing the signs of when someone is listening at the door."

Ben. Of course he came back to eavesdrop. "So everything you said—you didn't mean it?" I say, confused as I yet again mentally run through our argument the night before. About Ben, about Kit, about all of it.

"Oh, I certainly meant some of it," says Maisie with a single raised eyebrow. "Grandmama, why don't I escort you back to the dining room? Mummy and Uncle Nicholas are waiting, and I'm sure you have questions."

"Several," she says, taking Maisie's offered arm and glancing at me once more. "Do try not to disgrace the family during your interview tonight, Evangeline. We'll all be watching."

CHAPTER FIFTEEN

Evan

Are you okay? Tibby told me about the article. I'm so sorry.

And I'm sorry for texting, too. I wasn't sure if you wanted to talk to me or not, and Maisie said she already spoke to you, but . . . I'm always here for you. And we don't have to talk about it if you don't want to, I promise. I just wanted to make sure you know you're not alone.

I love you. I'll see you tonight.

—Text messages from Evangeline Bright to Christopher Abbott-Montgomery, Earl of Clarence, sent February 12, 2024, 7:48 a.m.

I TEXT KIT THREE TIMES before I hop in the shower, and by the time I step out of the hot water ten minutes later, I'm already reaching for my phone to see if he's replied. He hasn't—he hasn't even read the messages—and throwing all caution to the wind, I call him.

It immediately goes to voice mail.

I wait five agonizingly long minutes before trying again. Once more, the phone doesn't even ring, and all I get is a robotic voice instructing me to leave a message.

By the time my teeth are brushed, my hair is dry, and I'm dressed in cozy travel clothes that cost more than my entire childhood wardrobe, I've called him twelve times more, each with the same result.

"Did Kit change his number?" I say as I step into my bedroom, where Tibby is playing tug with the puppy and a cashmere sock.

"Is he not answering?" says Tibby without glancing up.

"And he's not reading my texts."

"His mobile's probably off," she says. "Now that the rest of the world is waking up and news of Ben's article is spreading."

She says this in a tone that makes it clear she overheard everything in the dining room, including the revelation about Ben and the *Regal Record,* and I grimace. "I'm sorry I didn't tell you. I should have, but—"

"No, you shouldn't have," says Tibby with a scowl. "There was no pressing need for me to know, as annoyed as I am with you for it. You *can* trust me, though, for the record. Should anything like this come up in the future."

"I trust you more than I trust almost anyone else," I point out. "It was just . . ."

I trail off, not knowing how to put it into words, but Tibby nods anyway. "Yes, it was. Now, if you don't mind waiting until the plane to put your makeup on, His Majesty has requested to see you before we leave."

"He has?" I say, surprised. He was so out of it yesterday that I wasn't even sure he remembered the interview was happening, let alone knew what day it was.

We waste no time making our way to Alexander's private wing, and the protection officers let me and the puppy in without a word while Tibby waits in the antechamber. I knock on the bedroom door, not wanting to burst in and startle Alexander—or worse, accidentally catch a glimpse of a sponge bath or a catheter change—and a moment later, Jenkins opens the door.

"Oh, lovely," he says. "His Majesty was afraid you wouldn't make it before your flight."

"Pretty sure the pilot isn't going to leave without us," I say, and while normally I'd offer Jenkins a hug, his posture is as stiff and formal as it has been since I arrived at Balmoral. I hate the distance between us, but nothing except time and a substantial amount of groveling on my part is going to bridge it, so for now I pretend nothing is wrong and turn to face my parents.

Except it's only Alexander today, sitting up in bed and slowly feeding himself from a breakfast tray. A nurse watches over him, ready to help if need be, but he's doing a damn good job on his own, all things considered.

"Where's Mom?" I say as I perch on the couch she usually occupies. Poppy curls up at my feet, happy to play with a discarded rag my mom uses for watercolors.

"I asked to speak to you alone," says Alexander, his voice stronger than it was the day before, and he sets down his fork.

"Why?" I say, suspicious. There aren't many things my parents keep from one another.

Alexander hesitates, then reaches for something on the corner of the tray. It's a small black box, unmistakable in purpose, and as soon as I see it, I feel like I've been punched in the gut.

No. *No.*

"You said—on Christmas, you said you'd never force my mom into a role she didn't want," I manage, "and we both know she doesn't want to be queen."

"This is what we both want, Evie," says my father gently, and he sounds so much like himself again that the tears springing to my eyes aren't only out of frustration and fear. "She and I've been talking about it for a very long time, what we would do if we had the chance, and titles, roles . . . none of that matters. But being her husband . . . having her as my wife . . . that would mean more to me than . . ." He shakes his head slowly, seemingly at a loss for words.

"But—she would hate royal life," I say, my stomach in knots. "And forcing her to live it—"

"I would never, just like I would never hurt her again. Our marriage would be between us. The kingdom and Commonwealth would have no place in it."

"Tell that to the millions of people who have *very* strong opinions about our family," I mutter. "It'll make her a target. The media will never leave her alone—"

"Is that a reason to never give her the happily-ever-after I promised her decades ago?" says my father, and I swallow hard. "I will protect her. She will never have to take part in any ceremony she doesn't wish to attend. She won't even have to take the title of queen, if she'd rather not. All I want is to love her with everything I have—"

"You don't have to marry her to do that," I protest, but he keeps going.

"—and I am done living by everyone else's rules. My life does not belong to the people of this country, or to the government. It is mine, to live and do with what I like, and this is what I want, Evie. This is what she and I both—"

He stops suddenly and clumsily wipes his wet eyes, and guilt stabs me deep in the chest. I know how much they love each other. I've seen it countless times, and I've heard it in every story they've told me about their life together, both before and after I was born.

But I've spent my entire life trying to protect my mom from people who would make her feel less than for her mental illness, or worse, try to rip her to shreds for the things she's done that she couldn't always help—things that weren't her choice—and the thought of putting her in the line of fire like this, all for a ring . . .

"You and Helene are still married, though," I say in a small voice. "Separated, sure, but—"

"I've instructed my lawyers to begin divorce proceedings, with Helene's blessing," says Alexander. "Considering she and I are both eager to move on with our current relationships, I'm hopeful it will be as quick and problem-free as possible."

I can't imagine Helene making anything *problem-free,* but I don't say that. Instead, I shift from the couch to the edge of his hospital bed, where I clasp his hand between mine.

"Dad," I say quietly, one of the few times I've called him that. "Is there any other way?"

He looks me straight in the eye, his gaze more focused than it has been since he's woken up from his coma. "Would you be satisfied," he says, barely louder than a whisper, "if no one took the love of your life seriously? If you'd been through so much together, fought for every small step you've taken side by side, and yet everyone treated you as a laughingstock because of . . . of circumstances and mistakes? If it were Kit, would you be satisfied with this?"

My heart skips a beat at the mention of Kit. I haven't told my parents about our so-called break—that would make it feel real in a way I couldn't take. But I understand what Alexander means. And if our positions were reversed, I'd be willing to fight anyone and everyone who turned the love between Kit and me into a punch line.

"No," I admit. "Do you really need their approval, though? Or—validation?"

"Of course not. But I do need yours."

I press my lips together and stare at that damn box. "If you and my mom get married, then I'll be legitimized, and everything Ben is afraid of will happen. Which means he'll only come after us harder. We've already almost lost you once, and my mom . . ." I trail off. I'm not sure if he knows about the fire at Windsor. "I don't—I *can't* lose either of you. Okay? I can't."

"You won't," he says, and he squeezes my hand with surprising strength. "And I won't lose either of you. I know I made you this promise once before, but I swear on all I am, Evie, that I *will* protect you and your mother. I *will* protect our family. After all we've been through . . . after what happened in January . . . I have a second chance. *We* have a second chance, and all I want to do with it is to spend the rest of my life with her. This is how it should've been from the start."

I think about my own future laid out before me. It glows with possibility and potential, but the moment I picture experiencing it without Kit, the shimmer of promise disappears entirely. With him, it's a real future, but without him, it's nothing—just a map of maybes. And that's what my parents have been living all this time without each other, scraping together moments when they can, navigating the kind of shit that no two people should ever have to go through together or alone, yet somehow managing to do both at the same time.

I ache at the thought of facing that empty future without Kit, and I ache for my parents and all they've lost already. I can't do that to them again. No matter how afraid I am, no matter how much more danger we'll be in, they deserve that glow of potential. They deserve all the happiness in the damn world.

"Okay," I finally say, and my father studies me, his eyes wide.

"Truly?" he says, as if he doesn't quite believe it. "You'll give us your blessing?"

I nod, not sure I can say it twice. "On one condition."

"Anything," he says, and even though he really shouldn't be saying things like that, I'm past taking advantage of it. For the moment, at least.

I glance at the corner of the room, where Jenkins sits at a small table near the window, reading through documents. "Jenkins has to forgive me," I say. "*Really* forgive me, not just say so."

He raises an eyebrow, and I know he's listening to every word. Alexander chuckles weakly. "I'll see what I can do," he says, also peering at Jenkins. "Though it may be best to give him some time."

"As long as it's before the wedding," I say. "Otherwise, you'll just have to cancel the whole thing."

This, at least, gets the tiniest of smiles out of Jenkins, and that's enough for now.

"Can I see the ring?" I say, and Alexander nods. When he reaches for it, however, his hand begins to shake, so I pick up the box and open it.

Inside is a beautiful emerald-cut diamond with a cluster of three smaller stones artfully arranged on either side—mint green, rose pink, and lilac, the shades my mom favors for her abstract paintings. The design is unconventional, and definitely not something I'd ever see on Helene's or Constance's fingers, but it suits her perfectly.

"She'll love it," I say, shutting the case and setting it back on the tray. "When are you giving it to her?"

"As soon as I'm well enough to get on one knee," he says. "Or . . . I suppose if that isn't happening anytime soon, then until I can't stand waiting any longer."

Thirty-six minutes later, as Tibby and I sit in the back of a town car on our way to the nearest private airport, my mom sends me a text from Alexander's mobile:

Mom

I said yes!

And the image attached shows the ring on her finger, looking every bit as beautiful as I knew it would.

CHAPTER SIXTEEN

I've been booted from base camp.

You've been what?

She convinced them I was a threat,
and I'm now persona non grata.

Inconvenient.

But not incapacitating.
Are you settled?

Yes. Scoping out the crowd before noon.

They'll be looking for you.

I'm not an idiot.

No, you're not, unlike John. Text me the
details when you have them. If there's
an opportunity, we need to take it.

Security will be a madhouse.

You nearly got her once.
I believe in you.

Inspiring.

—Text messages between two prepaid mobiles,
12 February 2024, 9:47 a.m.

AS OUR PLANE FLIES OVER the Scottish countryside, dreary and gray in the morning mist that's slowly burning away, I curl up in my seat and stare at my three unread texts to Kit. Would I be violating his request for space if I sent another? Probably, but it's taking every last thread of self-control I possess to resist, and I distract myself by running my fingers through Poppy's soft fur as she snores in the armchair next to mine. She's wearing a pink collar now with a gold name tag, a surprise gift from Rosie, and I click out of Kit's text to send a thank-you note to her instead. That takes all of thirty seconds, and then I'm staring at my unread and unanswered texts to Kit again, my mood as dismal as ever.

Is he with Astrid right now, prepping for the interview? I can picture the easy back-and-forth between them, the familiarity that feels more like casual friendship. Is she taking advantage of our so-called break? Is he? She's exactly his type, based on all the—

Wait.

Wait.

Holy shit.

I pick up my phone again, my thumbs flying, and within moments, I'm scrolling through one of the *Regal Record*'s photo galleries, which is full of pictures from Kit's club outings before we met. And, more significantly, the girls he's gone home with. While I hate myself already, the depressed part of me needs an answer, even though the rest of me knows it won't help a damn thing. I click through the gallery, picture after picture of stunning beauties he's slept with, until—

—a picture I've seen before, dated back to early autumn 2022, right after Kit moved to Windsor. She's ducked behind Kit as they leave whatever club they met in, but I can see part of her nose, cheekbone, and one of her stunning hazel eyes, as well as her mane of chestnut hair flowing out behind her. It's longer in the picture, nearly to her tailbone, but it's still every bit as glossy as it was during our VidChat a week ago.

Astrid Clark.

I throw my phone back on the table like it's bitten me, my eyes wide and my heart pounding. It's one thing to know that these girls exist, or even to meet one, but to see her flirting with him—to see him flirting back right in front of me—

"I see you're lurking in places you shouldn't be."

Tibby sits down in the armchair across from me and sets two fresh coffees onto the table. She sighs in agitation, which isn't surprising, considering she's spent the flight so far bickering with Doyle's assistant, but all I can do is stare at her, my mind racing, unable to put anything into words for a good ten seconds. Tibby, of course, stares right back.

"Did you know?" I manage, trying to rein in the chaos of emotions storming inside me. "That—that our crisis management handler is Kit's ex?"

"I knew they were close," says Tibby. "Which I thought they'd made clear during your meeting."

"Yes, but—I thought they were friends," I say, my voice strangled. "Why did no one mention this?"

"Likely because it isn't relevant, since Kit is with you," she says. But my traitorous eyes choose this moment to tear up, and I can barely make out her blurry form leaning toward me across the table. "Evangeline. Evan. Tell me what's going on."

I open my mouth, then shut it. How the hell am I supposed to explain? "Kit's—mad that I risked my life in Oxford," I mumble. "And he has every right to be. But he wanted a . . . a break. To think about our relationship."

It's more complicated than that, of course, but I can't bring myself to go into detail, and Tibby doesn't push. If anything, she seems to read between the lines, and she taps her perfectly manicured nails on the table. "I see," she muses. "A valid reason to need to step away, but I expect it's done you no good."

I shake my head and sniff wetly. "It's not about me. I just want him to be okay."

"Of course it's about you," she says. "You're part of this relationship, too, and it's shit that you're *both* going through this. And the more you repress your own feelings, the less likely you two are to ever work through it properly. Is that what you want?"

I imagine the moment I'll see him today—a moment only hours away—and think about it being the last. Or at least the last moment where hope and love still burn between us. My eyes start to overflow, and I shake my head again, turning to stare out the window.

"I didn't think so," she says with surprising gentleness. "Now, how are you really doing?"

She must know—she's been with me every single day, after all, but I take a deep breath and tell her anyway. "I miss him. None of this feels *real* without him, and I keep thinking of him and—and Astrid, and—she made him laugh when he was miserable, and—" I gulp and wipe my eyes with my palms so hard that I see stars.

"And you think someone he *might* have shagged once over a year ago could hold a candle to everything you've been through together?" says Tibby. I shrug.

"She doesn't come with the baggage I do. She doesn't give

him panic attacks or—or make him worry, or scare him half to death."

Tibby considers me for a long moment, as if something has just occurred to her. "Did you read the article from this morning?"

"The one on the *Regal Record*? Of course not," I say, making a face and wiping my wet eyes with my sleeve. "Kit told me what happened months ago. I don't need Ben's salacious take on it."

"Fair," says Tibby slowly, "but in this case, I think you might want to read it anyway. There may be . . . details in it that Kit might not have mentioned. For good reason."

I stare at her, my mouth already open to object, but something overtakes me instead. She wouldn't suggest it if it weren't important. I warily pick up my phone once more, scowling at the picture of Kit and Astrid, and navigate back to the *Regal Record*'s homepage. The article about Liam is at the top, and while I intend to skim it, halfway through the second paragraph, my body goes cold like I've plunged into the depths of the freezing ocean.

> ***The mysterious June 2022 death of William Abbott-Montgomery has finally been revealed as a suicide.***
>
> ***The body of the 21-year-old son of the Duke of Dorset was found with a self-inflicted gunshot wound in the family home in Somerset by his younger brother, Christopher Abbott-Montgomery. According to royal insiders, while William—known as Liam to friends and family—left no note, a difficult breakup is thought to be the catalyst.***
>
> ***The Duke, with help from his sister, Queen Helene, and brother-in-law, King Alexander, was quick to smother all mentions of William's death in the media, let alone any leaks about the manner of his demise, leaving those who knew Abbott-Montgomery to assume an accident or brief illness. Even Christopher, only eighteen at the time of the tragedy, was sworn to secrecy, and he has done a masterful job of keeping his family's skeletons hidden ever since.***

If the current Lord Clarence is willing to keep something as important as his brother's death by suicide a secret from friends and family, then what's stopping him from lying to the public about his experience with MI5? And after Queen Helene's confession of a sham marriage and adultery earlier this year, can we really trust a word coming from the mouth of any Abbott-Montgomery?

Kit found his brother's body. I don't know why I assumed Liam died far away from Kit, or that the manner of his death hadn't involved blood and gore and horrific violence—maybe because of how close the Abbott-Montgomerys are to the royal family, and the idea of anything messier than a bottle of pills is unthinkable in those circles. But a bullet wound. A devastating scene that Kit must still see in his more difficult moments—maybe every time he closes his eyes.

"He never told me," I whisper as I skim the rest of the article, which is of course nothing more than Ben bad-mouthing Kit after he's just flung him into a fiery pit of despair. It's a damn good thing we're thousands of feet in the air right now, because if I were still at Balmoral, I would hunt the sick asshole down and ensure his family line ended with him.

"Of course he didn't," says Tibby. "What do you expect? 'Oh, I suppose I'm not too keen on marinara sauce because I found my brother's body after he shot himself in the head. Pass the salt, would you, darling?' "

My stomach turns at the mental image that flashes through my mind. "Obviously not, but—we've talked about all kinds of hard things. I just thought . . . I don't know. I thought he would tell me something like that."

"That's what I'm trying to get through to you," says Tibby. "You're convinced that *you're* the one causing his panic attacks and anxiety, but I think that while what you've been through together certainly hasn't been helping, the intensity of his reactions goes far deeper than you. He lost his brother less than two years ago under horrifically traumatic circumstances, ones his family has refused to acknowledge. He certainly didn't cope well before your arrival, and he's been so busy supporting you since that, quite frankly, it rather seems like he's been suppressing his own trauma in favor of helping you through yours."

I pull my legs to my chest, so cold now that I'm trembling, but I hardly feel it. All I can think about is the sight of Kit huddled against our bed in the dark, tormented and bloody and broken. I didn't understand his pain at the time, or why it hit him so hard—because we'd gone through it before, because of the circumstances behind the kidnapping, because he was the one who was supposed to be putting himself in danger, not me.

But now I know. It was me—it was always me—but it will always *be* me, too. I can't take away his pain. I can't heal his trauma. There's nothing I can do to erase the horror of the terrible things he's been through, or the scars left behind that will always be part of him. I can't fix this with words. I can't fix this with actions. I can't fix this with promises. I can't fix this at all.

I rest my forehead against the window, not caring that Tibby can definitely see me crying now. I thought part of it would be up to me, that I would have some control over what happens next, even if I have to beg and plead and promise Kit that I'll never put myself in danger again. But I can't fight these demons for him, and he's already walked away and given up on us.

There's nothing I can do anymore.

"I realize you're both in a difficult place in your lives," says

Tibby, "but for what it's worth, Kit loves you, and sometimes a break really *is* just a break—"

"Tibby," I say shakily. "I don't want to talk about it anymore. Please."

She sighs, as if I'm yet another hindrance to an annoying problem she's been trying to solve for ages. "Very well. Get it all out now. There will be no crying during the interview, at least not about him. No longing gazes, no letting the public know you two are on the rocks—"

"Tibby, *please.*" My voice cracks, and I finally look at her again. "Just leave me alone."

She purses her lips. "It's my job not to, and I have no intention of starting now. But I will drop the subject, if you insist—"

Someone clears their throat, and Tibby and I both look up at the lanky figure of Doyle's assistant, who's gone pale and is clutching the back of the seat across the aisle.

"Sorry, sorry, very sorry," he says, his words stumbling all over themselves. Tibby mutters something under her breath.

"Are you here for a reason, Miller?" she says, and he hesitates.

"Astrid, er—Miss Clark's just messaged," he says. "Apparently Lord Clarence is, er . . ." He clears his throat. "Well, he's missing."

CHAPTER SEVENTEEN

ROYAL FANS GATHER OUTSIDE HOTEL TO GREET EVANGELINE AND LORD CLARENCE

Royal watchers and fans of Evangeline Bright, daughter of His Majesty and Laura Bright, and Christopher Abbott-Montgomery, Earl of Clarence, battled the February chill to spend all day lined up in front of the Maychester Hotel in Mayfair, eager to show their support for the royal couple-turned-spies.

Though the pair were seemingly universally reviled for their apparent roles in the bombing of the Modern Music Museum in London on the 12th of January, MI5 has released several statements over the past week making widely known the couple's heroic—and historic—efforts to help corner the leaders of the terrorist organization the Army of the British Republic. Though neither Bright nor Clarence have spoken publicly about the monthlong operation that centered on the city of Oxford, where Clarence attends university, that is expected to change tonight as the pair are interviewed live on air by Henrietta Smythe, former member of the Royal Rota and author of *Royal Rebel,* the unofficial biography of Bright released in December.

"I can't believe they managed to keep it from us this whole time," says Fiona Quint, a fourteen-year-old fan from Watford. "Can you imagine how dangerous it must have all been? And we even heard Evangeline was kidnapped!"

Rumours of a royal abduction have been all but confirmed by MI5, though details remain scarce, as has any information regarding Bright and Clarence's exact roles in the investigation.

Clarence was photographed daily attending his lectures, but Bright was never spotted by the general public, a feat considering she is now one of the most recognizable celebrities in the world.

Tune in to BBC One at 7 p.m. for the full live interview.

—*The Daily Sun*, 12 February 2024

AT 6:30 P.M., THIRTY MINUTES BEFORE the live interview is set to begin, there's still no sign of Kit.

How Astrid lost him, I have no idea—nor, apparently, does anyone else on his security team, which has been scrambling since the moment they discovered his flat in Oxford empty that morning.

I call him again and again, hoping for a miracle each time I press his number, but it never rings. Instead, I get his voice mail for almost exactly an hour after we land until the message changes, declaring his inbox full.

"Are you prepared to do this yourself, Evangeline?" says Astrid, who's been pacing a path into the carpet of our suite at the Maychester Hotel. Even her growing apprehension doesn't detract from how dazzling she looks in person, her posture perfect and her skin glowing, but when I look at her, all I can see is Kit's touch. "If we cancel now, the entire campaign will be called into question—"

"I strongly disagree," cuts in Tibby, who sits cool and collected on a love seat as she plays with my puppy. Despite how often Astrid has addressed me directly today, Tibby has answered for me every single time. "Given the spread of the *Regal Record*'s tasteless article over social media and in the more unsavory corners of the internet today, I'm certain the general public would understand if we rescheduled."

"No," says Astrid, "they would not. They'll spin conspiracy theories out of it, and this supposedly isolated incident will be enough to pull more than the usual crackpots into it. Kit *must* be here, and if he isn't—if he's really going to let us down like this—then Evangeline needs to be prepared to go on by herself."

"She won't be by herself," says Tibby, still supremely unbothered. "She'll have Agent Singh with her."

"Unless she's been in a secret relationship with Singh for almost a year, then that's hardly anything to work with," says Astrid, and I turn away from the pair of them and pretend to study my reflection in the mirror.

Louis Jenkins, the official royal stylist, has done a magnificent job making me look like a polished version of *me* for once, with a soft leather jacket, fitted black jeans, and Dr. Martens that lace up nearly to my knees. But all I care about is the empty chair and vanity next to me, and the cluster of stylists still waiting in case, by some miracle, Kit does show.

If he was going to make it, though, he would have called, or found some way to get in touch—if not with me, then with Astrid. Worrying everyone down to the last minute isn't his style, and my stomach is in knots so tight that it takes me a moment to realize that everyone is now staring at me.

"What?" I say, nonplussed.

"Are you willing to do this alone?" repeats Astrid, her frustration clear. "Because it's fairly obvious by now that Kit has no intention of being here, and—"

"On the contrary," says a heart-achingly familiar voice, and we all turn simultaneously.

Standing in the hallway, flushed and looking like he's run a half-marathon, is Kit.

He's here. He's real, or at least I think he is—he must be, judging by the way Astrid rushes forward and throws her arms around him, and he greets her with a kiss on the cheek.

I turn away, a lump the size of Big Ben in my throat. He may be here, but he's not mine anymore. That much is also obvious.

"Where have you *been*?" demands Astrid, and I hear the rustle of Kit's coat and scarf. "We've been trying to reach you all bloody day."

"I had to turn my mobile off. Someone leaked my number to the press," he says. "I went to Somerset to talk to my parents and—figure out how to handle this, I suppose. Or, rather, to tell them I'm going to address it openly tonight. I have a short list of questions I'll allow, if Smythe wants to go there and there's time. I won't let anyone use Liam against us."

"Lovely," says Astrid with a hint of bitterness. "So good of you to loop me in."

"Are you saying you wouldn't have been the tiniest bit tempted to tell one of your more upstanding contacts where I was, or what I'm planning to do?" he says, and I stare at my nails, freshly painted a sparkly silver.

"I—of course not," she protests. "But I would've wanted to come with you."

This crushes something inside me—maybe what's left of my heart—and I stand before I know what I'm doing. "Loo," I mumble, not looking at anyone, and I hurry to the nearest door, ducking inside and closing it behind me with a soft click.

Only then do I realize it isn't a bathroom, but a dimly lit bedroom, complete with ornate gold furnishings and crisp taupe sheets that look brand-new. With an inward sigh, I perch on the edge of the bed, wishing I could burrow under the covers and forget everything for a little while. That would be infinitely easier than facing the nightmare outside that door.

But in the silence of the bedroom, noise from the main room filters through, and I can hear both Astrid and one of the stylists calling Kit's name.

"We don't have time for that," insists Astrid. "We barely have time to run a bloody comb through your—"

"I don't care." Kit's voice is surprisingly close to the door, and I sit up straighter, my heart thudding. "Five minutes."

"We don't *have* five minutes," says Astrid. "Kit, it's a live interview—"

The door opens, flooding the room with light, and Kit steps inside, his silhouette appearing only briefly before he shuts and locks the door behind him. Astrid immediately tries the handle, and as soon as she realizes she can't get in, she begins to knock.

"Kit—*Kit!*"

He ignores her and steps toward me slowly, as if I'm an injured animal he's trying not to startle. "I'm sorry," says Kit softly. "I shouldn't have left."

I pull a pillow to my chest, confused. He doesn't owe me an apology. He doesn't owe me anything at all. "You needed space. You needed a break—"

"I shouldn't have left." He emphasizes each word as he steps forward again, as slowly as before.

"You were upset—I hurt you—"

"I—shouldn't—have—left." Two more steps, and now he's so close that I can touch him. He can touch me. But neither of us does. Instead, he kneels, resting his hand on the edge of the bed. "I've spent every moment since regretting it, but I was too afraid of myself to return. I attended my lectures because I had to, but when I wasn't, I was working through everything I've been avoiding for the past year and a half. Since Liam died."

I swallow, my mouth suddenly dry. "I'm so sorry," I say, my voice crackling. "I had no idea—"

"Because I never told you," he says. "I never let you see that darkest part of me. If I had, you would've understood what I've been trying to fight, what made everything that happened with the ABR and Fox Rex that much worse for me. But you couldn't, because I never gave you that chance. It wasn't on you, Ev. It was never on you."

Something hot and wet slides down my cheek, but before I can wipe it away, Kit's hand is there, barely brushing my skin. I squeeze my eyes shut and lean into his touch, hating myself for it. Hating myself for needing him so badly when I've already put him through hell.

"Kit?" Astrid knocks again, harder this time. "You two better not be shagging in there. We need to move, *now.*"

Yet again, he ignores her, his soft touch all I can feel. "Tibby just mentioned that you found a picture of me and Astrid from . . . from before," he says, and I freeze. "I never told you about her, did I?"

I can't believe he wants me to speak right now, but I manage it, barely. "No. I don't—"

"She'd been dating Liam for two years when he died," he says before I can finish telling him I don't want to know, and the words disappear from my tongue. "She's always blamed herself, even though it wasn't her fault. It wasn't anyone's fault. We used to spend time together right after it happened—sort of a grieving party of two situation, since we couldn't really talk to anyone else about it, and sometimes she came out with me. But we were just friends, Ev. We still are, and that's all we've ever been."

Something in my brain clicks, and I remember the line from Ben's horrific article. *A difficult breakup is thought to be the catalyst.*

The terrible swirl of despair and hopelessness I've felt about Astrid vanishes all at once, and I open my eyes. She isn't a replacement. She isn't even a predated artifact. She's a friend—a gorgeous friend, but one his brother was with for too long for that to ever be Kit's thing. I take a deep breath and let it out slowly as Astrid knocks again, but it's easy to ignore, even though a large part of me now feels bad for how much stress we must be causing her.

Friends. They're just friends.

"I'm sorry," I whisper at last, fighting another wave of tears. "For hurting you. For—for making it worse even if I didn't know the whole story. I shouldn't have been so damn reckless—"

"You wouldn't be you if you weren't so damn reckless," he says with a faint smile. "It's part of what I love about you. And I won't pretend that everything's better, that a week of intense therapy is enough to fix that part of me. I've got a long way to go, and this won't be my only mistake. But the difference between us, Ev, is that you didn't know. *I'm* the one who knew that you've never trusted anyone to be in your life long enough to properly love you, and I'm the one who knew how badly walking away would hurt you. Yet I did it anyway, and I am so bloody sorry."

He cups my face now, inching closer as his thumb brushes my cheek and his dark eyes lock on mine. "I'm permanent," he promises, his voice barely a whisper, but there's an unyielding strength to it that makes everything he says unshakable. "I was from the moment we first spoke. I simply didn't want to scare you away. But now I'm afraid I've done it anyway, so—there it is. I'm yours, endlessly and for eternity. Always on the good days, but especially the bad. Whether you'll still have me or not—and I wouldn't blame you for not trusting me to stay, not after this—I'll be here for you regardless. I had a glimpse of what my life would be like without you, and it's no life at all, Ev. Certainly no life I'm interested in, and I refuse to live it."

He takes my hand gently, threading his fingers through mine, never with enough strength to prevent me from pulling away if I need to. Or want to. But I don't.

"In whatever capacity you'll have me, I am here," he whispers, his gaze pleading now. "I will always be here. I am yours. I am *yours.*"

I'm trembling again, and I don't know why, but it's uncontrollable, and I feel like all the blood has been drained from my body. This is what I've wanted since the moment he walked away in Balmoral—everything so exactly right that part of me wonders if I'm still on the plane, and this is a dream. A cruel, tragic dream I never want to wake up from. Everything in me screams to kiss him, to let this end and to let things go back to the way they were before, but they'll never be like that again. Not completely, no matter how hard Kit and I try to pretend. Pain lives between us now, shading every moment, unavoidable and no longer something we can ignore. And if I say okay, if I kiss him and throw my arms around him and move on like everything is fine, then that pain will continue to fester within us until something unfixable breaks.

I can't hurt him like that. I love him too much to put him through that kind of agony ever again, and he clearly loves me too much to let that pain get in the way of us being together. Which means there's only one thing I can do.

"I need to tell you something," I say, my voice thick with tears. Astrid is going to kill me for undoubtedly ruining my makeup with minutes to go before the interview, but I can't find it in me to care. "Two things, actually."

"Anything," he says. "Whatever it is, it doesn't matter—"

"My mom and dad are getting married," I whisper, because it does matter. It's everything I've been worried about since I found out that their supposed one-night stand was actually a once-in-a-lifetime love. "As soon as his divorce goes through. Which means . . ."

I trail off. I can see it in the way Kit's gaze grows distant for a moment that he knows exactly what it all means.

"Okay," he finally says, squeezing my hand again. "We'll just have to figure it out then, yeah? I know we haven't really discussed it, but—I'd like a family someday, if you would, too. Not immediately, of course, but I don't care who our potential children grow up to be. And if it means getting to spend my life with you—"

"That's not—" I can barely force out the words. "That's not what I'm afraid of, Kit. I don't know if I want kids, but if I decide I do, you're the only person I'd want to have them with." I exhale sharply. "I told Constance everything. About Ben, I mean, and all he's done. Everything from—from Jasper and the video to the shooting and the ABR and the bombing and the *Regal Record,* and the article he wrote about . . ." I shake my head. "Nicholas and Helene backed me up, and she kicked Ben out of Balmoral. And banned him from every royal property in the UK."

Kit gapes at me. "Constance? Really?"

"Really. She even gave me Poppy—the puppy—as an apology," I say. His stare is too intense now, too hopeful, and I fix mine on our joined hands instead. "There's a chance we might never have to worry about Ben again, with the ABR gone and Dylan in the wind. But . . ."

"But," says Kit slowly, "there's a bigger chance he'll never stop, and that we—and later our potential children—will be his main targets."

I nod, still not looking at him, but when I open my mouth to speak again, he stands long enough to sit on the bed and wrap his arms around my shoulders.

"Then we'll keep fighting until we know it's over," he says into my hair. "I won't let him hurt you again, or our family, real or hypothetical. Whatever it takes, we'll do it."

But I can hear the strain in his voice, and I know what this promise is costing him. The panic attacks, the pain, the memories, the knowledge of what he could lose at any moment—all because of my recklessness. All because bringing Ben to justice is more important to me than making sure the person I love most is happy and healthy and whole.

I can't put Kit through that anymore. Not if I want to live with myself, and not if I want to be the partner he needs and deserves.

"No, Kit. It's over," I whisper, and the words cut through me like a scythe. But I will never let anything short of fate get between Kit and me again, and Prince Benedict of York is *not* fate. "You were right. It's time for me to start trusting our security and MI5 to do their jobs, and that means letting them handle Ben. All I want now is to forget he ever existed and live the rest of my life with you."

Kit goes still beside me, so still that for a moment, I think he's even stopped breathing. "You're sure?" he whispers into my hair, and I nod.

"Positive."

He shifts beside me and brushes his lips against mine in the sweetest, softest kiss he's ever given me. "Okay," he says. "I love you, Evangeline. More than my own life."

The way he says it feels ominous, and I kiss him back, wrapping my arms around him until I'm not sure I can let go. "I love you, too. Always on the good days," I whisper, echoing his earlier words, "but especially the bad."

At last there's no ignoring Astrid's incessant knocks, and we reluctantly part. But before Kit unlocks the door, he offers me his hand, and I take it. Things between us won't always be perfect. This is just the first step in a healing process that might very well take years. But as long as I'm with Kit, life will always be better. And I never want to be without him again.

CHAPTER EIGHTEEN

HENRIETTA SMYTHE: Were you frightened? It was all a rather dreadful ordeal, from the picture Agent Singh has painted.

EVANGELINE BRIGHT: I wasn't scared for myself. I was scared for Kit. He was the one going to his classes—lectures—every day, facing the paparazzi and people who hated us.

SMYTHE: Because they thought you were terrorists.

BRIGHT: Because they thought we were responsible for killing eight people.

SMYTHE: It's amazing so many believed it, considering you two were in the Modern Music Museum at the time of the bombing. You could have both been killed.

LORD CLARENCE: Evangeline almost was. Her personal protection officer, Ingrid Straw, was one of the eight people killed, and she gave her life to protect her. If she hadn't pushed Evangeline out of the way . . .

[pause]

BRIGHT: I owe my life to Ingrid, and I will never, ever forget the sacrifices she made. And we will never forget the courage and determination of everyone involved in hunting down the ABR and finally allowing the families of those who died in the bombing to seek justice for their loved ones.

SURAJ SINGH: That's what we at MI5 signed up for—to protect this country and her citizens from people like John Phillip Michaels, formerly known as Guy Fawkes, the head of the Army of the British Republic. But Evangeline and Lord Clarence didn't have to do this.

BRIGHT: Yes, we did.

SINGH: No, you didn't. You were comfortable and well protected right where you were, and no one in their right mind should've ever asked you to get involved in something so dangerous.

CLARENCE: Except for you.

SINGH: Yes, well, no one's ever accused me of being in my right mind. But it did make sense—Lord Clarence already had a connection with a supposedly defunct Oxford club we believed to be loosely associated with the ABR, and with John Phillip Michaels already making the outrageous claim that Evangeline was involved, we decided to call his bluff.

SMYTHE: Some have called the move reckless.

BRIGHT: We were aware of the risks. But we were also very aware of the fact that by using our connections, we could potentially save Agent Singh's team months or possibly years by putting ourselves in an uncomfortable position.

SMYTHE: So you're saying you were willing to put your own lives in jeopardy if it meant bringing the ABR to justice sooner, and potentially stopping countless others from also losing their lives and loved ones?

[pause]

CLARENCE: Yes.

BRIGHT: It was never about being . . . brave or anything like that. It was about . . . it was about my dad, too. And finding the people who tried to kill him.

SMYTHE: So it was also personal.

BRIGHT: I—we were just trying to protect our family. We knew the ABR wouldn't stop coming after us until my sister and Kit's aunt and—everyone we loved were dead. And we couldn't let that happen if there was even a single thing we could do to try to stop it.

CLARENCE: Evangeline doesn't like to think of it as brave, but when she asked me if I'd go with her to Oxford—if I would help her and MI5 in the investigation, because by then, I could tell she'd already decided, whether I went with her or not—it was the most courageous and selfless thing I'd ever seen. We didn't know then what would happen next—we didn't know what the consequences would be. If the ABR would find us first, or if we'd even succeed in infiltrating the club that fed into the ABR. But Evangeline didn't care about any of that. Nothing in the world could have convinced her that it was too dangerous, or that it wasn't her place to try. Evangeline was determined to do everything she could, no matter what the country thought of her—of us. By then, I already knew I loved her, but that was the moment I really, truly fell in love with her. I don't know how anyone could've witnessed that kind of selfless and stubborn determination and not done so.

SMYTHE: Did you have any hesitations yourself, Lord Clarence? Considering what we unfortunately now know about what happened to your brother, William, and the toll that must have taken on both you and your family.

[pause]

CLARENCE: Of course I had hesitations, and every moment Evangeline and I were there together, I was terrified—truly terrified—that something would happen to her, and I would never see her again. But if Liam taught me anything in life, it's to take each moment as it comes and keep moving forward to the best of my ability and morality. And I also couldn't step aside and do nothing when it was fully in my capacity to help. Liam is the reason I had those connections to the Oxford club in the first place, the ones that eventually led to the ABR, and in a way—a big way—Liam is the reason we were able to find these terrorists before they claimed another life. He is as much a part of this as Evangeline and me, and I will always be grateful to him for being the best brother and guide in life that I could have ever asked for, even in death.

SMYTHE: I was very sorry to hear of your loss, and even sorrier now to know the cause and circumstances behind it.

CLARENCE: Thank you.

SMYTHE: May I ask what this club is that you keep alluding to?

SINGH: I fear that's still classified, as the investigation is still in the beginning stages.

SMYTHE: Of course. Would it be too much, then, to ask after His Majesty's status?

[pause]

BRIGHT: I don't think he'd mind too much if I mentioned that this morning, he promised to watch this interview live with the rest of the nation.

SMYTHE: He's conscious, then? And well?

BRIGHT: He's on the mend and furious that Kit and I put ourselves in danger. But he gets it, I think. Or at least I hope.

SMYTHE: I imagine he's very, very proud of you.

BRIGHT: I hope so, but . . . I'm just glad the ABR can never hurt him or the rest of my family again.

SMYTHE: And how are you two? You've been dating since July, is that correct? That's an awfully short period of time to suddenly be thrown together in what is essentially the death-defying thriller of the year. How has your relationship held up?

[pause]

CLARENCE: As they say, the strongest steel is forged in the hottest fire, and Evangeline and I have never been closer.

BRIGHT: He's a good one. I think I'll keep him for a while.

CLARENCE: Just a while?

BRIGHT: Maybe forever.

—Excerpt from the BBC One interview of Evangeline Bright, Christopher Abbott-Montgomery, Earl of Clarence, and Agent Suraj Singh, by Henrietta Smythe, 12 February 2024

THERE'S A MOMENT AFTER THE interview is over, when Henrietta Smythe has shaken our hands and everyone is standing around congratulating themselves on a job well done, when Kit guides me to a corner of the hotel suite and wraps his arms around me like he alone can protect me from every miserable minute of what we've just had to do.

"Are you okay?" he says softly, his lips brushing the shell of my ear. I shake my head against his dark button-down shirt, sliding my arms beneath his suit jacket and hugging him in return, ignoring the mic pack still hooked to his belt.

"Not really," I say just as quietly. "Are you?"

"Not yet, but I will be," he admits, his voice thick and on the verge of breaking. He was cool and composed throughout the interview, which picked apart every salacious detail of the past two months that Henrietta Smythe could get her hands on, from the bullet wound that we shared at Sandringham to what our living arrangements in Oxford were like to what really happened when I was kidnapped by Guy Fawkes himself—or, as I now know, John Phillip Michaels, the son of one Baron Michaels, which is so ironic that I almost choked when Singh told us right before the interview began.

But now Kit is beginning to show the cracks, and I hug him tighter, determined to hold him together as best I can.

"I'm just glad it's finally over," I whisper. The walls I've struggled to build over the past month begin to crumble, too, and I sniff into his chest, a wet sound that should embarrass me, but Kit buries his nose in my hair, and I don't care about anything but him. "I love you."

"I love you, too," he murmurs. "Whatever happens now . . . it was worth it. *You're* worth it."

"So are you," I manage shakily. "Thank you. For being you. For being here. For loving me. For all of it."

I can feel his faint smile against my scalp, and he kisses the top of my head. "Loving you will always be my greatest privilege and greatest pleasure, Ev. Never doubt that for a moment."

Neither of us realizes that the cameras are still rolling. And the next day, when our interview is being replayed and dissected endlessly on social media, and by gossip sites and news channels that were cursing our names only a week ago, that's the clip they show the most.

That's the clip that changes everything.

SEVEN MONTHS LATER

CHAPTER NINETEEN

Rebel, Princess, Terrorist, Spy—and Instant Bestseller

If Henrietta Smythe's first foray into Evangeline Bright's life, *Royal Rebel,* released in December 2023, was a sympathetic look into the curious and sometimes pitiful life of the illegitimate American daughter of His Majesty, King Alexander II, then consider this to be a tour de force of an apology for ever casting Miss Bright as a victim.

Instead, in *Rebel, Princess, Terrorist, Spy,* Smythe shows the now 19-year-old Bright for what she truly is: a survivor hell-bent on protecting her family and loved ones no matter the risk involved. Despite the Hollywood-esque plot based on the real-life spy mission to find and capture John Phillip Michaels and the rest of the Army of the British Republic, the narration takes care to highlight both Bright and her partner in supposed crime, 20-year-old boyfriend Christopher Abbott-Montgomery, Earl of Clarence, as human beings rather than polishing them with a superhero sheen. They are flawed. They make mistakes. They even argue in the narrative, which, according to Smythe, contains "no fabrications, inferences, or filling in of blanks." Every word in the book is true, including a read-it-to-believe-it account of Bright being kidnapped by Michaels, the head of the ABR, though the narration is straightforward with the fact that some details are still classified. An updated edition will be released after all legal matters surrounding the arrests have concluded, according to the publisher and a spokesperson for MI5. Both Bright and Clarence are expected to be called as witnesses during Michaels's upcoming trial.

The highly anticipated film adaptation is also set to premiere this week, with members of the royal family—including the subjects themselves—in attendance. Though typically adaptations take years to develop, produce, and edit, Smythe worked side

by side with a team of screenwriters to ensure the film could be rushed into production this spring. Thanks to the generosity of both the royal family and Oxford University for allowing most of the real-life locations to be used during production, the book and the film are set to be released within days of each other. A savvy move from Buckingham Palace, considering the popularity the young couple are currently enjoying.

Written after a series of in-depth private interviews with both Bright and Clarence, *Rebel, Princess, Terrorist, Spy* is a captivating, edge-of-your-seat thriller, made all the more so for knowing it is, according to the author and subjects themselves, entirely true.

★★★★★ 5/5 Stars

—Book review from *The Daily Sun*, 8 September 2024

THE MONTHS THAT FOLLOW THE live interview are a blur.

Our schedule of appearances is endless as Kit and I are ushered all across the UK, then continental Europe, Australia, and a dozen American cities. Charities, talk shows, podcasts, magazine spreads—if there's a way for Astrid and Doyle to exploit the public's newfound love for us, they take it, and despite our faces being everywhere, no one seems to grow tired of us.

I tell myself that it has to end eventually, but Astrid is a genius at stringing the public along. Anytime their interest in us even remotely wanes, she releases a juicy tidbit, about the movie or book or our relationship. She's especially fond of engagement rumors and behind-the-scenes photos of Kit and me looking ridiculously in love, which I never see her take. And, of course, Astrid never asks before she posts. My life no longer belongs to me, but while I know that this is supposed to be a good thing—that we *want* the public to adore us and root for us—I can't help but wish, more often than I should, that Kit and I were back in our flat in Oxford, alone in our bedroom, wrapped together and just—*being.*

My sister is, of course, furious. At first, I think she's still mad at me for not telling her what we were doing in Oxford, but once she starts to shun Kit, too, I realize she's jealous. I don't blame her. She was born for this kind of attention—a spotlight that never turns off, where our every move is analyzed, and we have whole fandoms dedicated to us now. Maisie does, too, and has since the day she was born, but to no one's surprise, she's terrible at sharing even a fraction of the limelight.

It only gets worse when, in April, Tibby announces that Kit and I are outpolling Maisie in whatever unhinged popularity contest the palace PR department has created to no doubt rein in the egos of the royal family.

"Why would anyone even *ask* the public to rank us?" I say from a fitting platform, while Louis Jenkins hems a gown I'm supposed to wear for an upcoming gala. "Has this been going on the whole time I've been here?"

"It's been going on for decades," says Tibby, tapping her tablet. "And no one told you because you were at the bottom of the approval polls for months, and you tend to get a bit testy whenever someone points out that you could be doing more to appease the public."

"I don't care what anyone thinks of me," I protest, shifting in my sky-high heels, which were not designed to bear weight this long.

"If that were true," says Louis cheerfully, "then you wouldn't be racing about trying to make the world love you."

I scowl. "I'm trying to make sure they know we're not terrorists. There's a difference."

"If you say so, darling," says Louis, and he winks at me before shifting his attention back to my dress.

"I wouldn't feel too guilty about it," says Tibby as she scratches Poppy behind the ear. "Maisie's still coming in fourth, well ahead of the Queen, Prince Nicholas, and the traitor. Neck and neck with the Queen Mother, though, which is rather a surprise."

I do the math. "Wait—who's third? Alexander?"

Tibby raises her eyebrows. "His Majesty is first. Naturally."

"Naturally," I echo, but the relief that floods me is like cool water on a July day. The people still love him, even though they haven't seen my father in months. Some corners of the internet keep trying to spin conspiracy theories, claiming that he died in the blast, but while the uncertain timeline of his recovery is stressing out Jenkins, Doyle, and pretty much everyone else involved with the constitutional monarchy, no one is pushing him. Especially when he still has to relearn how to walk.

What no one says out loud is that Kit and I aren't just doing PR for ourselves—we're a distraction, too, buying Alexander time and keeping the heat off him. And it's working. Everywhere Kit and I go, we're greeted by an ever-growing legion of fans who call themselves *Pearls*—apparently a combination of *princess* and *earl,* never mind that I'm not a princess and *earl* is a courtesy title. It's sweet at first, taking selfies with them and hearing their stories, listening as they tell me how they believed in Kit and me all along, even though it's probably bullshit. But as the numbers grow, the more extreme some get—especially with Kit. They grab at him, hold up signs proposing marriage, and one even tries to cut a lock of his hair. I have a few die-hard fans, too, but the most they really do is break down into tears and hug me too tight and refuse to let go when it's time for me to move on.

At last, after an incident that ends with three fans trampled and scratch marks down Kit's arm, our security insists that our walkabouts and direct interaction with the crowd end. I'm relieved, and not only because the crowds unnerve me now. No one says his name, but I've never forgotten that Dylan is still out there somewhere, and as long as he's free, Kit and I will never be completely safe.

We never talk about Ben, either, even when we're alone at night, my head against Kit's chest as I listen to his heartbeat. Sometimes I do a quick online search to see if Ben has popped up anywhere, but he's a ghost. Maybe that's part of why Kit and I are so happy, or at least why we're able to find so much comfort in each other. It isn't perfect—Kit's continued with his therapist multiple times a week, and I started speaking to my own shortly after our live interview. But we listen to each other now. We communicate. We do our best to be there for each other and to heal as well as we can, and even when we accidentally touch scar tissue or a wound that's still open, we find a way through it. Because a life without Kit isn't one I'm interested in living, either, and nothing—especially not my stupid pride—is worth losing him again.

In July, shortly after Maisie and I turn nineteen and celebrate our shared birthday apart, the fire damage that Ben caused is finally repaired. Alexander is moved from Balmoral, where he's spent the spring and summer slowly getting better under the watchful eyes of my mother and Constance, back to Windsor Castle. Though both Kit and I are offered our usual separate rooms, we decide to move into a larger suite together. And only once we arrive home, exhausted after a whirlwind trip to Canada, do we discover they're Helene's old lodgings.

"This is weird, right?" I say as we explore the renovated apartment for the first time. Instead of red and gold furnishings, like my old rooms, everything is in lifeless white and silver. My mother's artwork hangs on the walls, though, replacing whichever long-dead royals have been on display for possibly centuries, giving the room a much-needed splash of color.

"Very," admits Kit, peering out the window. "We really ought to check with housekeeping to make sure they've changed the sheets."

"And sanitized the sofa," I say. Kit chuckles.

"Maybe we should track down a can of disinfectant spray, just in case," he says, wrapping his arms around me from behind.

"It definitely can't hurt." I lean my head against his shoulder, casting my gaze around the new apartment. *Our* new apartment. "Thank you. For all of this."

I don't just mean moving in with me. I mean everything we've been through together over the past year, and as Kit's grip tightens around my waist, he seems to understand. "Always on the good days, but especially the bad," he whispers, his warm breath tickling my ear. "Let's grab some provisions from the kitchens and see how long we can hide out here without anyone else finding us, yeah?"

"I'd give Tibby an hour at most," I say morosely. It never takes her long to track me down. "But it's possible she doesn't have a key yet."

"I'm willing to take that chance," says Kit, nuzzling my ear. And even though we're only in Windsor for forty-eight hours before heading back on the road, they're the happiest days we have all summer.

Before long, it's nearly autumn, weeks before my first term at Oxford University begins, and the movie premiere and book launch are finally here. It's what all this touring has been leading up to—to make sure that when the public watches two actors playing us on-screen, that they're already familiar with who Kit and I really are. That when they read the book, they picture us, not strangers they've never given a shit about.

The point of the tour was to make them love us. The point was to make damn sure that when they see what we went through—or at least the dramatized, declassified version—that their hearts *ache* with how close Kit and I supposedly came to death. We need to be real to them so this book and this movie are real, too. So when the credits roll, or they reach the last page, their tears or smiles of triumph are for friends. That they feel like they could call us up and invite us over for tea, if they wanted.

Or at least that's been Astrid's plan all along. I'm not convinced it worked, and as the sun slowly rises on the day of the premiere, I lie awake in bed, staring at the ceiling and trying not to picture an entire theater of people dead silent after the movie ends tonight.

I don't want to go. I don't want to watch two shiny starlets pretend to be me and Kit and act out every awful thing we went through together, taking razor blades to scars I might not even know are there. But tonight I have to sit through all of it, wearing a ball gown meant for a princess and pretending none of it bothers me. Because while the public may think we belong to them now, while they may try to cut Kit's hair and hold on to me so hard that I can't breathe, at least they don't think we're terrorists anymore.

Kit groans in bed beside me, his arm tightening around my waist as he stretches his legs. "All right?" he whispers.

"No," I admit softly, turning to bury my face in his shoulder. "Do we really have to go?"

" 'Fraid so. It'd be taken the wrong way if we didn't."

"Yeah, but—" I shake my head. It's too late to chicken out. Months and months too late. "How are we supposed to take any of it seriously when we know what really happened? When we *lived* it?"

"Who says we have to take it seriously?" he says. "We can make a game of it. Start with a bucket of popcorn, and eat a kernel whenever something's off."

"There's not enough popcorn in the world for that," I grumble, and he chuckles.

"We'll find a way to make it bearable, I promise."

I want to believe him, but I can't imagine ever being okay with sitting in a theater full of people all watching the movie unfold, believing every word, every movement, every action happened, like it's a documentary instead of a piece of propaganda. Because that's what it really is. Make them love us, make them pity us, and maybe they'll forget they ever thought we were murderers.

"Wait until you see my dress," I mutter. "I think they stole it from a costume shop. Some ostentatious number with so much fabric that I look like an unmade bed—"

"It's not that bad, Evangeline," says Tibby, striding through the door without knocking. I sit up straight, and the covers fall down, exposing the oversized T-shirt I'm wearing, but Kit is shirtless.

"Tibby!" I cry. "You need to *knock.*"

"Why?" she says as she draws the curtains open, and the pink sunrise spills inside. "I heard you speaking. You were awake."

"We could've been—" I shake my head as Kit sits up, too, running his fingers through his messy hair. "Kit isn't wearing a shirt!"

"*You* are," she says pointedly. "Are you wearing pants, Kit?"

He checks under the covers, even though we both know he is. "Seem to be," he says mildly.

"Then I hardly see the problem," she says. "Now, do you want the good news?"

I narrow my eyes as Kit climbs out of bed, his pajama bottoms long and perfectly acceptable as he grabs his robe. It may only be September, but it's still freezing in the castle. "What good news?" I say suspiciously. "Your definition of 'good,' or mine?"

"You'll like it, trust me. I had nothing to do with it," says Tibby as she steps into the small room that acts as a closet. "Astrid says there's no reason for the pair of you to stay for the film."

"Really?" I climb onto my knees as the heaviness in my chest vanishes. "Do you actually mean that, or is this a trick to make sure we're smiling on the red carpet?"

"Why on earth would you have to watch?" says Tibby, her voice distant as she riffles through my clothes. "Astrid has already written your comments for you, and there's no need for either of you to ad-lib. Besides," she adds, "I know you both far too well to let you run loose with something as dangerous as an actual opinion."

I look at Kit, and he looks at me, and we share a grin so wide that my face actually hurts. "Thank you, Tibby," I call, and I mean it. "Even if you didn't have anything to do with it."

"I'll happily take the credit for this if you don't blame me for what else I have to tell you," she says, walking out with a soft gray sweater and a pair of black trousers.

"What?" I say, my amusement instantly fading, and she hesitates long enough that a pit forms in my stomach.

"Singh rang me first thing this morning, before I'd even had my coffee." Which is clearly a cardinal sin, according to the look on her face. "Apparently John Phillip Michaels wants to speak to you, Evangeline."

"No," says Kit instantly. "Absolutely not."

"John who?" I say before it clicks. "Wait—*Guy Fawkes?* He wants to talk to me?"

Tibby nods. "As soon as possible, which he seems to think translates into today, of all days. He claims it's important, and he's apparently gone on a hunger strike until—"

Before she can finish, my phone on the nightstand vibrates. Frowning, I glance at the caller ID. Lady Primrose Chesterfield-Bishop, who hasn't written a word to me since accepting my thanks for Poppy's collar seven months ago. And, as far as I know, is still at the top of Maisie's shit list.

I look at Kit, who can't see my screen from his angle. "Rosie," I say, and his eyebrows shoot up. "Why would she be calling me?"

"At this time of morning, no less," he says, his shoulders still tight from the mention of John Phillip Michaels. "Only one way to find out."

I suck in a breath and reach for the ringing phone, the cloud of dread hanging over this day only growing. "Rosie?" I say, switching the call to speaker. "Is everything okay?"

"He did it," sobs Rosie, her voice thick and almost unintelligible. "He finally posted the pictures. I thought—it's been so long, and I thought maybe he wasn't going to, or maybe—maybe he thought I could still be useful to him, but—a boy I dated this summer texted me a screenshot from this awful website. It's me. They even have my face in some of them, and the freckles on my—"

"The photos Ben was blackmailing you with?" I say, struggling to keep up. But there's only one person "he" could be. "Today? Just now?"

Rosie cries even harder. "I haven't spoken to him since January! I swear, Evan, I've stayed out of his way completely. I don't answer unknown numbers or emails, and I've got my security locked down—"

"I believe you," I say hastily. On the other side of the bed, Kit's arms are crossed tightly over his chest, and his jaw is clenched like he's ready to punch something. He and I both. "Can you text me the site? Maybe we can find the originals."

"That's—that's not all," says Rosie, and she pauses to blow her nose. "I—I took Snickers for—for a jog in the park just now, and—and someone was following me, I'm sure of it. I had to—to stop and catch a cab, I was so scared."

I freeze, and once again, I lock eyes with Kit. Neither of us says a word, but I can tell he's thinking exactly the same thing.

Dylan.

I shift my gaze to Tibby and mouth, *Stephens?* She shakes her head, and I know why. Rosie isn't royal, and Victor Stephens won't lift a pinky to help her, even if it is Dylan. "Did you see their face?" I say urgently. "Was it paparazzi, maybe? Did you notice anything at all?"

"Nothing," says Rosie miserably. "Just shadows and a silhouette, but I swear someone was there, Evan."

"I believe you," I repeat, and she lets out another soft sob. "Listen—I'm going to send someone to talk to you, all right? It might be police, or it might be MI5. And I'm going to see if there's anything palace security can do for you." Tibby's opinion be damned. "Just do me a favor and don't open the door to anyone without a badge. And if you see anything else suspicious, call 9-1—I mean 9-9-9, okay?"

"Okay," says Rosie with a miserable little sniff. "I'm sorry. About everything."

"I know you are," I say with all the gentleness I can muster. "Don't take any chances. I'll be in touch, all right?"

It takes another minute or so of reassurance for her to hang up, and once she does, I glare at Tibby. "Whatever you have to tell Stephens, get him to send someone over there. And let Singh know that Dylan might be stalking Rosie."

Tibby sighs. "You can't just wave your hand and make things so, Evan, especially on a day like today—"

"Singh will want to talk to her anyway," says Kit. "And if

Stephens isn't willing to send someone, then I'll hire security for her."

"Just make it happen, Tibby. Please," I say. And with my phone still clutched in my hand, I hurry out of the bedroom, through the sitting room and library Kit and I now share, and out into the main corridor, which is bustling despite the early hour. I have to duck around two housekeepers and a footman before I finally reach the door I'm interested in, but when I see who's standing in front of it, I skid to a halt in my bare feet.

A Secret Service agent.

"She didn't," I mutter, and flashing the muscled man a tight smile, I knock hard on my sister's door. Sure enough, it opens seconds later, but it isn't Maisie who greets me.

Instead, it's a tall, handsome teenage boy with black hair and a jaw that could cut diamond, and as soon as he sees me, he breaks out into a massive smile.

Thaddeus Park, President Park's son.

CHAPTER TWENTY

I'm here! FRONT ROW at the red carpet!!!!! by the entrance wearing a pink ROYAL REBEL shirt and holding a yellow sign! If I get a selfie I will DIE!!! #brightgomeryforever

—Twitter user @dutchessdame172, 10 September 2024, 7:05 a.m., London, UK

"EVANGELINE!"

Thaddeus's voice booms through the corridor, twice as loud as anyone else in the castle would dare to be this early in the morning, and he wraps his arms around me in a bear hug like we're old friends. In reality, we've only met once—at a state dinner last December, though I know he's been in contact with Maisie frequently. Obviously, since he's come all this way to see her. And, I suspect, thinks she might be interested in dating him.

For once, I have nothing to do with that, considering Maisie was the one who managed to ruin her three-year relationship with one Lady Georgiana Greyville—Gia, the third in the trio that was once her, Maisie, and Rosie. Given Maisie's sour mood ever since, I think it's safe to say she isn't over the breakup yet.

But Thaddeus either doesn't know her well enough to recognize the signs, or Maisie's putting on the performance of a lifetime around him, because his thousand-watt grin could light up all of London.

"Thaddeus?" I say, stunned. "What are you doing here?" I look back and forth between him and Maisie, who's standing on a platform while a woman with white hair hems her pale blue gown—presumably for the premiere tonight. My sister must have heard me come in, but she's staring resolutely in the mirror, as if nothing exists outside of her own reflection.

"Nothing could stop me from missing the premiere," he says. "Unfortunately I had a charity appearance in Seattle yesterday, so I had to take a red-eye, but that's what caffeine is for, right?"

"And naps," says Kit, who steps into the doorway and offers his hand. "Never too old for a good one. We haven't had the pleasure. I'm Kit."

"Ah, the boyfriend," says Thaddeus, and he shoots me a conspiratorial wink as he shakes Kit's hand. "The pleasure's all mine. We're going to be friends, you and I."

"Seems like we already are," says Kit easily. "Maisie invited you, then?"

"Yes, I invited him," snaps my sister, and she holds out her arms for the seamstress to make adjustments to her bodice. Her collarbone is poking out more than usual, and I notice that padding has been added to her corseted top—something she normally doesn't need. "I figured there's no better time to introduce the world to my boyfriend."

If I were drinking something, it'd be all over Maisie's dress now, despite the fact that she's several yards away. "Your *what*?"

"Oh, have you made it official, then?" says Kit, as if this is something he's been looking forward to. "Brilliant. Gia will be thrilled. She's coming tonight, too, did you hear?"

This last line is directed toward me, which is a good thing, considering Maisie is slowly turning a shade of red I've never seen before. "She is?" I say, barely managing to swallow my surprise and play along. "I can't wait to see her. Tibby mentioned she's seeing someone now, too?"

"Mm, one of the actresses in the film," says Kit. "Odd—isn't it the one who plays you, Mais?"

If ever there was a moment that my sister's head might actually explode, this is it. "Lovely," she mutters through a jaw so tight that I can barely understand her. "I'm sure they're very happy together."

"No doubt," agrees Kit, and he loops his arm around my waist. "By the way, we wanted to let you know that Rosie's pictures are out."

This sudden shift in topic seems to take some of the fury out of Maisie's sails, and her eyes narrow in the mirror. "The pictures . . . ?"

"You know the ones," he says calmly, handling her with deftness I will never manage. "Just thought you ought to know."

Maisie's throat constricts. "Seems like the chickens have finally come home to roost, then," she says at last. "I hope she enjoys reaping what she's sown."

This is such an oddly cold thing to say, even for Maisie, that all I can do is stare at her. Thaddeus also frowns, clearly confused. "Pictures?" he says. "Chickens? I'm lost."

"Don't worry about it," says Kit, clapping him on the shoulder. "We'll see you tonight, yeah? I'll be the version of me not on the big screen."

Thaddeus grins again. "I'll keep that in mind."

With the same ease with which he dealt with Maisie, Kit guides me back out the way we came, and only once the door is closed do I manage to find the right words.

"She doesn't care," I burst. "She just—doesn't *care.*"

"To be fair, they have an entire lifetime of history between them, and Maisie values loyalty above all else," says Kit. "Something she now thinks Rosie has none of. Give her time. She'll come around and contact her eventually, but not if we push."

This is so monumentally unfair that I don't know what to say, but in reality, what did I expect? I'm not sure *I* forgive Rosie yet, or that I ever fully will, especially when she was partially responsible for the fire at Windsor that could have—*should* have—killed my mother, and almost took Maisie's life instead. I can't blame Maisie for refusing to look past it, especially when she'll always bear the physical scars. But the coldness with which she dismissed it all rankles me, and while these two things—all the reasons Rosie doesn't deserve our sympathy, and all the reasons we should give it to her anyway—can both be true, I don't know how to reconcile them with each other. Or the fact that Maisie's dragging Thaddeus into this mess, too.

"Why do you think Ben posted them today?" I say quietly

once we're far enough away from Maisie's apartment to guarantee some modicum of privacy.

Kit frowns. "The pictures? I don't know. Because of the premiere, I suppose."

"He doesn't do anything at random, and he wouldn't wait this long just to waste the timing," I say. "It *has* to be because of the premiere. But Rosie isn't invited. She and Maisie aren't even speaking."

"Ben doesn't know that," says Kit. "Or at least we don't think he does. He could be trying to make Maisie look bad, especially if he expects her to be photographed with Rosie."

"Maybe," I mumble, but it doesn't feel strong enough. "Maybe he's trying to prove he still has power over us. But that's a really big hand to play for no good reason, especially when he doesn't have anything else."

"His carefully laid plans have blown up in his face again and again, and he's probably getting desperate," says Kit as he opens our door, which is much closer to Maisie's and my parents' apartments than my old suite. "He may be trying to force himself into the narrative and scare us."

Before I can respond, Tibby looks up from her spot at our dining table, where someone's laid out three breakfast trays. "There you are," she says, clearly miffed. "Do you think, today of all days, that you might do me a favor and not run off?"

"Sorry," I say, even though I'm not. "I had to tell Maisie about the pictures."

Tibby sighs, but at least she doesn't admonish me further. Instead, she gestures for Kit and me to sit down in front of our plates, making it clear breakfast is not optional this morning.

"Have you decided what you'd like to do about John Phillip Michaels?"

Right. Because the Rosie and Maisie drama isn't enough of a side quest for today. "Did he say why he wanted to talk to me?"

Tibby shakes her head. "Only that it was important."

"Everything's important when you're stuck in prison," says Kit testily, and he pours us both cups of tea, adding the perfect amount of milk to mine.

"You don't owe it to him. You don't owe him anything at all," adds Tibby. "His trial is soon—he may just be trying to delay, or to get some press coverage to spout whatever shite he thinks might get him off."

"Probably. But what if there really is something important?" I counter.

"And he's just remembered, despite having had half a year to do nothing but think?" Tibby gives me a look. "Even if he *did* have important information he's been holding back, that doesn't mean you have to respond to him with any urgency. He's responsible for the deaths of at least eight people. He doesn't get to make demands on his victims."

I start to reach for my cup, but stop short at that. Is that how Tibby sees me? Sees Kit? As his victims?

"It could be a trap," says Kit. "Or some sort of mind game."

Tibby snorts. "I certainly wouldn't put it past him."

Neither would I, but it still doesn't feel right. And as I mull it over, something sparks in my mind. "What if *he's* the desperate one?" I say suddenly. "What if . . ."

My gaze darts to Kit's, and my heart begins to pound. He

holds my stare for a long moment, his lips pursing. "You think he'll give up Ben," he says, and it isn't a question.

"Maybe," I say, itching to stand up and pace. I'm onto something. I have to be. "He knows that's why I was in Oxford, and he must know I won't help him otherwise. If there's even a chance he'll offer evidence . . ." I swallow hard. "Kit. This could be it."

"I know," he says softly. And I can tell from the way he averts his eyes that he also knows nothing in the world will stop me from making that trip if there's even the remotest possibility we're right.

"Then you can talk to him all you want," says Tibby, "*tomorrow.* Today's all booked up, and if you try to play that royal renegade game with me, I *will* have a PPO sit on you until it's time for the premiere. You *cannot* miss it, Evangeline. There is simply too much to do before then to fit in a trip to the bloody nick—"

"Okay, all right, fine," I say, picking up my fork and stabbing a hardboiled egg. "Tomorrow, then. It'll give me a day to figure out what to say to him."

"I'll make the arrangements," says Tibby, mollified. "Kit? Shall I include you in these plans?"

He's quiet at first, and I look at him again as he shifts uncomfortably beside me, his gaze locked on the rim of his cup. "Yes," he says at last. "I'll go. I have a few things I'd like to say to him, too."

"About Liam?" I say, and Kit nods, but he still doesn't look at me. Just like we don't talk about Ben, we don't talk about John Phillip Michaels, either.

But maybe this is our chance for closure. We didn't get it in

Oxford, but maybe confronting John will offer us that sense of finality. Of a job well done, or at least of a job *done.* It'll show us that this wasn't all for nothing, and that has to be worth the anticipation of facing him one last time before we do our best to forget he ever existed. Even if we risk causing yet another wound between us, one that might never heal completely.

CHAPTER TWENTY-ONE

"I'm Samuel Frick, and this is Ashleigh Wallace, and we are here on the red carpet in London for the premiere of *Rebel, Princess, Terrorist, Spy,* one of the most anticipated movies of the year—"

"One of the most anticipated movies of our lifetime! Look at this crowd! Thousands have gathered here in Leicester Square, where the stars of the big screen are joined by real-life royalty from around the world!"

"And speaking of real-life royalty, it looks like the British royal contingent are arriving now. Ashleigh, who are you most excited to meet tonight?"

"Evangeline, of course! Her and Lord Clarence—can you think of a more stunning couple?"

"None come to mind. Considering they're one of the most photographed couples in the world, it's no wonder they're so fierce about protecting their—"

"Oh my god! Is that Princess Mary? And—*First Son Thaddeus Park?* Did you know they were dating?"

"No clue, Ashleigh. But they're gorgeous together, aren't they? Her Royal Highness's couture gown is simply breathtaking—"

"Did he just kiss her hand? *Did he just kiss her hand?*"

"We'll find out all the details as soon as they make their way to us. Oh, those *heels*! We'll also ask who she's wearing, and if she considered a tiara for the evening, though she seems to have opted for a lovely diamond comb instead—"

"The other car! Is that Queen Helene? Or—well, former Queen, though I'm not sure we know what her title is now that the royal divorce has been finalized. But that's definitely the Duke of York, gorgeous as ever. It's lovely to see them looking so happy together. And—who's that with them?"

"That would be Laura Bright, mother of Evangeline and His Majesty's former mis . . . companion. She certainly looks stunning in that flowing watercolor gown, doesn't she? Though we've never seen her at a public event before, tonight we may finally get the chance to ask her the important questions, like who she's wearing and what impact her internationally renowned artwork has on her fashion choices—"

"Sam. *Sam!* Do you see what I see?"

"Er, what is that, Ashleigh?"

"The ring! Do you see the ring on her finger?"

"I—is it the one on her left hand?"

"*Yes!* She isn't wearing anything else, not even earrings. Is it—can you see it?"

"I can. And . . . well, perhaps there isn't anything *former* about her relationship with His Majesty after all."

"Is it possible? Only weeks after his divorce to the former Queen has been finalized, is the King engaged to Laura Bright?"

—*Entertainment Now Live Red Carpet* event,
10 September 2024

THE CAR KIT AND I take to the premiere is the last one to arrive.

I hear the crowd half a mile before I see them, though there's no missing the fireworks that seem to light up Central London. The movie studio and palace have gone all out for this spectacle, and that's exactly what it is—something meant to be gawked at. Even I have trouble tearing my eyes away as we pull to a stop at the head of the red carpet.

"Ready for this?" says Kit, his fingers laced in mine. He looks incredibly handsome in a navy tuxedo, his dark wavy hair artfully disheveled, like there's a *reason* the crowd had to wait for us, and in the low light, I want to make that fantasy the truth.

"No," I say, but I gather my clutch and kiss him anyway. That's the exact moment the door opens, revealing us to the fans, and their screams triple in volume, a relentless onslaught of auditory waves that nearly bowl me over.

I break away from Kit with a sheepish smile, because I really didn't plan that. He touches the corner of my mouth, as if fixing a smear of lipstick I know hasn't budged, before climbing out first. The screams rise to a frenzy, and every camera is pointed toward us as he offers me his hand. Wordlessly I take it, exiting the town car in what feels like slow motion—until everything speeds back up again, slamming us into the reality our PR team has created.

"Evangeline! *Evangeline!*" The shouts are all around us, and while Kit is as much a part of this as I am, it's my name that rises to the top. I don't know how he must feel about it, but he squeezes my hand and raises it to his lips, kissing my knuckles as he meets my eye. Whatever he's thinking, the fact that I'm the one they're cheering for doesn't seem to bother him at all.

Countless flashes go off, and I'm momentarily blinded as someone ushers us up the carpet toward the gauntlet of photographers, fans, and reporters. My dress, which is a figure-hugging, floor-length scarlet gown with an ostentatious glittering train that Tibby is in charge of wrangling, is arguably a showstopper, but it's also a giant pain in the arse. Even now, I'm still struggling to keep my balance underneath the heavy layers of fabric, but Kit never lets go of my hand, and I grip his like it's the only thing stopping me from falling flat on my face. Which it probably is.

"Where are the others?" I say into his ear, and he glances around, using his height to his advantage. Finally he nods toward the photographers, and as a few people ahead of us step aside, I spot the last person in the world I expect to see.

"Mom?" I call, even though there's no way she can hear me over the din. Instantly my palm is sweaty in Kit's. "What is she doing here? Is Alexander here, too?"

Kit shakes his head, still scanning the area. "Maisie and Thaddeus are doing interviews right now. Your mum is with Aunt Helene and Nicholas, but she isn't posing for pictures."

I suck in a deep breath. She wasn't supposed to come. She never said a word about this—never gave any indication that she was planning on leaving Alexander's side, and every single one of his advisers, Jenkins included, made it damn clear that *he* couldn't let his first appearance after the bombing be a movie premiere, no matter how important it is for the royal family's image.

Why is she here? I glance around, plastering a smile on my face as I wave to the crowd, though I'm really searching for—what? John Phillip Michaels in a teal scarf? A bouquet of blood-red gerbera daisies with my name on it? That's over now, I tell myself, even though it doesn't feel like it'll ever be. Half the police force in London are here, including snipers on the roofs nearby, and after everything that's happened, if even the slightest hint of a threat appears, I know our army of PPOs won't take any chances.

But Ben and Dylan are still on the loose, and on a night like tonight, anything feels possible. Especially the worst-case scenario.

"Please tell me you don't plan on standing here all night," hisses a voice in my ear. Tibby appears beside me, stunning in the plain black dress she's chosen to wear, and she gestures toward the photo call area. "Smile and wave to your fans, take a few pictures, and then we'll head to the interviews. Do you remember your answers?"

"Of course," I say through a tight smile, my lips barely moving. "My mom is here."

"Is she?" Tibby sounds surprised, but when I glance at her, her expression is as impassive as always. "She obviously wants to support you. Don't let her down."

Leave it to Tibby to take my panic and use it against me, and I dig my heels in as Kit steps toward the photographers. "No, wait," I say. "Fans first."

After the assaults we've both endured at the hands of some of our more enthusiastic new friends, I don't blame him for looking less than thrilled about putting ourselves in that direct line of fire again. But the crowd barriers are packed with security, and we have to squeeze between police officers to shake hands, take selfies, and hug those who've stood outside all day to meet us. Some people greet us like old friends. Some squeal too loudly for us to understand what they're saying. One middle-aged woman in a pink shirt even bursts into sobs after babbling her undying love to both of us and asking Kit to sign her marriage proposal written on a neon yellow poster—which he does, with good humor, letting her know this unfortunately doesn't make things legal in the eyes of British law.

By the time we make our way down the line, neither of us has lost any hair, gained any new tears in our clothes, or accumulated any fresh mental scars, and Tibby is practically beside herself.

"We have seven minutes. *Seven minutes,* Evangeline, before we have to be inside," she hisses. "Did you have to greet everyone?"

"Yes," I say, waving at the cheering crowd once more before heading to the photo call area. "They've been waiting here all day."

Tibby grumbles, but seems to mellow out once Kit and I are posing for the cameras, turning this way and that as the photographers shout our names. By now I should be used to it, but it never stops feeling like they're trying to steal a piece of our souls as they take picture after picture, as if there can never be enough. I hate it, but I don't stop smiling, even when two freakishly familiar people join us.

"Oh my gosh, it's really you!" cries an American girl three inches taller than me, her dark hair tumbling down her back in perfect waves. She catches me in a hug, and it takes me a beat to realize this is Riley Monroe, the actress who plays me in the film.

"And it's you!" I say, trying to match her excitement as I hug her back, ignoring the flashing cameras. Astrid's firm insisted on keeping Kit and I separate from the actors playing us—Riley and an eerily handsome man named Greyson Thatcher—on the promo circuit, and I have no doubt that both Riley and Greyson have been carefully coached to time our first meeting in front of these cameras.

"It's lovely to meet you," says Greyson in a posh accent very much like Kit's, and he leans in to kiss my cheeks. He doesn't look enough like Kit for me to stare, but Riley is a taller, perfected version of me, as if someone photoshopped an exceptionally good picture of me within an inch of its life, and I can see the surprise on the real Kit's face as he, too, greets Riley.

"Thinking of trading up?" I tease in his ear once the four of us start posing together for even more pictures. Kit grins down at me.

"No such thing when it comes to you," he murmurs, giving me a quick kiss on the lips, causing another wave of screams from the fans and a blinding explosion of light from the photographers.

At last, after the four of us spend several minutes posing in every possible combination, a red-cheeked Tibby ushers us along toward the interviews.

"Time blindness is not an attractive trait," she mutters so only Kit and I can hear her.

"Pretty sure that's why I have you," I say, scanning the clusters of people still hanging around. While Helene and Nicholas speak with a reporter I recognize from ITV, my mother is nowhere in sight.

Hoping that she went inside the theater, I hug Kit's arm while Riley and Greyson break off to do their own interviews, and Tibby guides us toward a pretty blond woman and a man in a cerulean suit that matches his short mohawk.

"Evangeline! Lord Clarence!" the woman squeals, and I force a warm smile. "What a wild event! First off, let us congratulate you on the film—"

"And, of course, the real-life events that led to it," says the man, his tone much more even. "Now that you've had time to settle back into royal life, how are you feeling?"

"Stunned," I say, looking around, as if I can't quite believe we're here. Which I can't, but I'm playing it up for the camera, exactly as Astrid instructed. "This is incredible. Neither of us ever expected anything like this—how could we?"

"It's rather surreal," agrees Kit, his arm slipping around my waist. "All we wanted was to protect the family and the people of the United Kingdom to the best of our limited abilities, and seeing what it's turned into . . ."

He shakes his head, but this is a sentiment we've repeated again and again throughout the year, never once making the mistake of seeming like we think we deserve it. Because we don't. It's all manufactured anyway, for the greater good of the monarchy, a fact that's never too far from the forefront of my mind.

They have a few more bland questions—have we seen the film already, what do we expect, how involved were we in the making of it, and what do we think of the crowds here tonight—and I sense Tibby stepping forward to end the interview when the blond blurts out one more question.

"We hear congratulations are in order, Evangeline—an engagement between your mother and His Majesty! You must be so excited! Has a date for the wedding been set?"

I freeze, my eyes on Kit. How do they know? It couldn't have been a press release—Doyle would never do anything to steal headlines from the premiere tonight. Did my mother say anything? No—she wouldn't announce it without Alexander's approval. And without warning me first.

"I . . ." I search frantically for something to say. Do I deny it? But what happens when they *do* announce the engagement? Do I confirm? How do these two random American reporters even *know*?

"His Majesty is focused on his recovery," says Kit smoothly, and his hand splays comfortingly on the small of my back. "We are very proud of the strides he has made, and we know he is eager to resume his full duties as soon as he is able."

This is such a sidestep that even I can't blame the reporters for their crestfallen faces. But it's the woman who rallies quicker, and as Kit starts to lead me away, she shoves a microphone within millimeters of my mouth.

"What about you two? When should we expect a big announcement of your own?" she says, clearly desperate to get something usable out of us. But while the most I can manage is a tight smile, Kit chuckles.

"When we have something to announce, we'll be sure to do so," he promises, and before either of them can press, he hurries me away, Tibby following at a quick pace.

"I've changed my mind," she says in a clipped voice. "No more interviews. How on earth did they find out about—"

"They didn't know," says Kit through a wide smile, waving to another cluster of fans in the stands. "They were fishing."

"But how—"

"My mom's probably wearing her ring," I realize, holding my hand up to cover my mouth so no one can read my lips. "She almost never takes it off."

Tibby groans and proceeds to curse whichever stylist let my mother leave Windsor wearing it, while I silently curse whoever let my mother leave Windsor at all. The only silver lining to the American reporters' curveball is that Tibby lets Riley and Greyson deal with the rest of the interviewers, while she leads us quickly through the doors of the theater with plenty of time to spare.

As soon as we duck inside the cool, dark building, a coil in the pit of my stomach unclenches, and the urge to take off my heels is almost overwhelming. Before I can weigh the pros and cons—mostly of what Tibby would do to me if I tried—I spot a familiar head of auburn hair in the glitzy lobby, which is slowly emptying as everyone filters into the theater for the premiere.

"Mom!"

She turns around in time for me to catch her in a tight hug, and she wraps her arms around me in return, stronger than ever before. "Evie! Look at you—you're stunning," she says into my hair. "I'm so proud of you, sweetheart. All of this . . . it's because of you and Kit, every bit of it."

I don't have the heart to remind her that it's all PR. "Thanks," I say, and I mean it. "I can't believe you're here. I thought you were staying home with Alexander."

"We both always planned on surprising you tonight," she admits, finally letting me go. She touches my hair, which is in a half-up, half-down do with strategically placed diamonds that are meant to look like a diadem. "But your father is having a bad pain day, and he didn't want to distract you."

"Really?" I say. "Jenkins had nothing to do with it?"

"Jenkins makes an excellent mother hen, but we all know who rules the roost," says my mom, amused. "Alex insisted I go without him, and so here I am."

As she touches my cheek, I notice the engagement ring she is most definitely wearing, and I sigh inwardly. At least we have our answer there. "Thank you," I say again, catching her in another hug, even more grateful now for all the security stationed around the theater. "I'm really glad you made it."

"We both are," says Kit, and my mother opens her arm and pulls him into the embrace, too. It's a sweet moment, warm and almost like we're in our own little bubble—until I hear several clicks of a camera phone. I instantly stiffen.

"Just thought you'd want a photo," says Thaddeus Park, who stands ten feet away, drink in one hand and phone in the other. Maisie lingers nearby, but her back is turned to us, and I spot Gia in a slinky silver dress on the other side of the sparsely populated lobby, laughing beside a tall redhead who has the bone structure of a supermodel.

"Send it to me," requests Kit, which is much more polite than anything I can think of to say.

"Sure thing," says Thaddeus, completely oblivious to the tension he's caused. "Here, let me pull them up. I took a couple."

While he shows Kit and my curious mother the results, I join my sister instead, not trusting myself to keep my cool. At first I say nothing, and I'm not even sure Maisie's noticed me as she stares blatantly at Gia and the actress.

"You're certainly enjoying the spotlight tonight, aren't you?" she says at last, breaking the silence between us.

"Mm, every bit of it," I say, sarcasm dripping from my words. "Does Thaddeus know it's all for the cameras?"

Maisie tilts her head. "Who says it is?"

"The way you've been staring at Gia is a pretty good hint," I say. "Or are you staring at the other girl? Are you upset that she doesn't look like you?"

"What are you talking about? She's stunning. Of course she looks like me."

"That's not what I—" I begin, but Maisie huffs and stalks over to Thaddeus before I can get in another word.

"Come on," she says nastily, grabbing his elbow as he's in the process of typing out Kit's number. "Let's get seats before we're stuck next to them all night."

As Maisie and a baffled Thaddeus head off, I rejoin Kit and my mother, who wraps her arm around my bare shoulders. "Are you going in, too?" she says.

"I—we're not sure yet," I say, glancing at Kit. Now that my mom is here, maybe we should join her, but I still loathe the idea of sitting through two hours of our fictionalized trauma. "Do you have a place to sit?"

She nods. "Helene and Nicholas are saving me a seat. I didn't think you two would want to stick around and watch."

I'm unnerved that she knows me so well, considering we barely saw each other while I was growing up. But I'm even more unsettled by the idea of my mom being buddy-buddy with my former stepmother. Helene, at least, seems to have cooled it with the menacing threats now that she knows it was Ben, not me, who was responsible for the fire at Windsor. But I still don't trust her.

"You're sure?" I say, and my mom nods.

"I'll let you know how it is," she promises. "You two stay out here and protect your peace."

She hugs us both once more before following Maisie and Thaddeus, who end up directly behind Gia and her date in the line to get into the theater. Kit and I wait as the final warning announcement is given and Riley and Greyson are ushered inside, and finally, once we hear the rumblings from the theater begin, we seek out a small table near the corner of the bar, and a server gets us two nonalcoholic drinks and a basket of every snack they're offering.

"Ah, the royal treatment," I say, popping a salted peanut into my mouth. "How do you think the movie starts?"

Kit pauses, cocking his head. "From the sounds of it, with the morning of the bombing."

I stop cold, second peanut frozen between my forefinger and thumb. "You can hear it?" I say after a beat, and sure enough, a bass-filled tremor shudders from the closed theater.

"Enough of it," he says grimly, and suddenly I am very, very glad we chose to stay out here. But my mom . . . Maisie, Helene, Nicholas, even Tibby . . .

"Shit," I say, barely stopping myself before I rub my eyes and ruin the hour of work that went into the makeup I'm wearing. "I can't believe no one warned them."

"Probably wanted their genuine reactions," mutters Kit. "Nothing better for PR than a crying princess. Likely have a bloody camera shoved in all their faces."

The server drops off our drinks, and I silently wish I'd ordered something with a kick to it as I down my ginger ale. But when I go for another snack—something that looks vaguely cheesy—Kit takes my hand.

"Can we talk about that interview?" he says, and I frown.

"Which part of it?" I say. "Because I think you're right. They didn't know for sure. They saw my mom's ring and were fishing—"

"Not that part of it," he says, and he takes a deep breath. "The last part. When they asked about us."

I blink. "Wait—about us getting engaged, you mean?"

He nods. "I realize this isn't the most romantic setting—quite possibly it would win an award for the least, given the circumstances—but I've been thinking about it a lot lately. Not in any imminent way," he adds hastily at what must be the look on my face. "But it's certainly been on my mind. Is there . . . Do you . . ." He hesitates. "Is that something you've been thinking of, too?"

My brain sputters, and it takes me a full five seconds to comprehend that he's asking if I've been thinking about marrying him. "I mean—not *actively,*" I admit, which I immediately realize is the wrong thing to say. "I just—of course I want to marry you. That's completely the plan. One day, when we've both graduated and have jobs and—you know. All that stuff. If you want to, I mean." I swallow. "Do you?"

"Yes," says Kit, and there's no hesitation in his voice. His fingers curl around mine. "I'd marry you in a heartbeat. But I know you have reservations, and there is never any pressure. Or rush."

Reservations. He makes it sound like I'm not sure, and something about that sits wrong with me. "I—I'd marry you in a heartbeat, too," I say, even though I know I don't sound nearly as convincing. "Really, I would. It's not about us. You're the best thing in my life, and as far as I'm concerned, we're a done deal, as long as that's what you want, too. I just . . ." I shake my head. "I'm nineteen. You're twenty. I haven't even started university, and we've had one hell of a year, and supposedly our brains aren't even fully developed yet, and I just want to be—*settled,* you know? Or at least have some idea of what the rest of our lives together will look like before—before—"

"I know," he reassures me, folding my hand between his. "Astrid brought it up to me, that's all. Multiple times," he adds wryly.

"Astrid?" I wrinkle my nose. "Why does that have anything to do with . . . Oh."

They want an engagement to top off the tour and premiere. Like icing on a cake with a diamond-shaped cherry on top. My skin starts to crawl, and I shift in my seat uncomfortably.

"That's what I *don't* want," I say firmly. "For this—for any of it to be a damn show. The world already thinks that we belong to them, that—that what's between us is somehow their business, too. But no one gets to decide when we get engaged, or when we get married, or when we have kids, if we even have kids at all—no one except us, okay? I don't care if it takes us twenty years to get there—"

"Twenty years?" says Kit, amused, and his eyebrow quirks.

"—I will not have *any* part of the real thing be dictated by Astrid, or Doyle, or *anyone,*" I say with every ounce of conviction I feel. "I mean it. If one of us proposes, I want it to be because we really mean it—"

"I'll be the one proposing, thank you," says Kit, squeezing my hand.

"I can propose if I want to," I insist.

"Centuries of the famed Abbott-Montgomery chivalry will force me to say no and break your heart," he says, a playful hint in his tone, "only to turn around and propose right back, you know. The dynamic will be terrible. It's best just to let me do it."

I roll my eyes. "Fine. You can do it. But I mean it. If it happens—"

"When."

"—*when* it happens, the only factors are you and me, okay? Nothing else. *No one* else. No pressure, no rush, like you said."

"I promise," he says, bringing my hand to his lips and pressing them against my knuckles once more. "Just you and me. Nothing and no one else matters."

Exhaling, I let my shoulders slump a bit, right as the theater door opens. Someone slipping out after the intensity of the bombing scene, no doubt, but I can't see who it is from our corner. "Thank you," I say. "And when you do . . . not to ruin the suspense, but I'll say yes." It's not even a question in my mind. "I just don't see the harm in waiting until we're older when we know it's forever anyway."

Kit chuckles. "By that logic, there's no harm in not waiting, either. But I understand. We've given them plenty to talk about for now. This is just for us, on our own time, when we're both—"

"*There* you are."

Tibby's voice cuts through the quiet bar, and we both turn in our seats. She hurries toward us as she furiously types something into her phone, the *click-click-click* of her heels signaling her urgency.

"What's happening?" I say. "Is everyone okay? Did the movie really open with the bombing? Is my mom—"

"It began with news clips from that day, and real footage of you both and His Majesty," says Tibby with a dismissive wave. "Surprisingly tasteful, all things considered, but still not something I wanted to relive. Have you checked your mobile?"

"What?" I glance at my clutch, which sits abandoned between a basket of peanuts and the cheesy things. "No. What's going on?"

"You have a text from Singh," she mutters. "And possibly a dozen missed calls, unless he went directly to harassing me."

I pull my phone out of my clutch, and sure enough, I have seven unread texts and four missed calls. "What happened?" I say, dread creeping in, and Kit's hand slides over my knee.

"It's John Phillip Michaels," says Tibby, and my insides turn to ice. "He's dead."

CHAPTER TWENTY-TWO

John Phillip Michaels, leader of the ABR and the alleged architect behind the bombing of the Modern Music Museum that killed eight and critically injured His Majesty, has died by apparent suicide in his cell whilst awaiting trial on charges of treason, terrorism, and murder in the first degree.

He was 25.

—Breaking news alert from the BBC, 8:24 p.m., 10 September 2024

JOHN PHILLIP MICHAELS—GUY FAWKES—is dead.

I should feel relieved, and part of me is. The man in the teal scarf, who stalked me for weeks and actively tried to kill not only me, but also my father and Kit, is gone. I never have to worry about turning around and coming face to face with those chilling gold-rimmed eyes again.

But none of it makes sense, and as I stare at Singh's text messages, the room starts to spin.

Singh

Need to talk ASAP.

Singh

Damn, premiere's tonight. Calling now.

Singh

Good time for you to choose to pick up, Bright.

Singh

Bloody hell, you're live on TV. Trying again in a minute.

Singh

Evangeline. This is important. Partying can wait.

Singh

Michaels is dead. Apparent suicide. Bloody guards let him keep his belt. Can't say much more. Looking through footage now. Will update in a minute.

Singh

Footage missing. Might be nothing, but I've alerted your security. Calling Tibby now.

"Singh says there's footage from the prison missing," I say, my mouth painfully dry. This can't be happening. "Why would there be footage missing?"

"He could've bribed the guards so there was no recording of his death," says Kit. He's pale, even in the dim light, and his grip on my knee tightens.

"Or someone else could've bribed them so they don't know what really happened," says Tibby, and it's the first time I've heard her sound genuinely frightened. "It's unlikely, but not impossible, especially with someone as high-profile as Michaels. And it seems like that's what Singh is thinking, too."

"You mean . . ." My pulse races. "Someone could've done this to him?"

"Or paid a guard to do it for them," says Tibby, glancing at me. "We don't happen to know anyone who likes to have other people do their dirty work, do we?"

My jaw tightens. "Is there any chance John really did . . . ?" I can't finish that sentence, not in front of Kit. But I don't have to, because I'm already answering my own question. "No. He *wanted* to go to trial and make sure everyone knew what he'd done and why he'd done it. There's no way he would've deprived the entire world from hearing his—his *manifesto* on why the monarchy deserves to be destroyed."

"Someone could have threatened him," says Kit quietly. "Or his family."

"He doesn't have any siblings, and I'm willing to bet he loathes Baron Michaels," says Tibby, looking around the otherwise empty lobby. "Well, they're not pulling people out of the theater, so that has to be a good sign. They don't think whatever's happened is a security risk."

"Do you think anyone in there knows?" I say. "Should we at least tell my mom and—"

My phone vibrates in my hand, and I fumble it in surprise, nearly sending it straight to the ground. I catch it before it can skydive off the table, only to see a video call request on the screen.

Rosie.

"Evan?" Her image is blurry when I accept the call, but it quickly clears, revealing her puffy, tearstained face. "Did you hear?"

"I heard," I say grimly. "Are you okay? Did something else happen today?"

She shakes her head, her lips pressed together so tightly that the skin around her mouth is blanched. "Do—do they think it was Ben?" she whispers, and I can barely hear her despite the quiet of the bar.

"I . . ." I look between Tibby and Kit, but neither of them has any answers. "I don't know. It's impossible to say this early on. It could've just been . . . you know. His choice."

Rosie inhales a sharp gulp of air, and a sob escapes her. I mentally kick myself for not checking in with her earlier. After her phone call this morning, I should have at least followed up after lunch.

"Are you okay, Rosie? Did anything else happen?" I repeat.

"N-no," she sobs. "But—but I'm scared, Evan. What if—what if it was Ben? What if I'm next?"

My heart sinks. "He won't come after you, Rosie. Not for writing a few posts." But even as I say it, I know that's not all she did. She helped with the fire, too, which almost killed Maisie and should've killed my mom. She fed him information that helped him with who knows how many of his schemes—maybe ones we don't even know about—and he has every reason in the world to come after her. She can testify against him, and with all she knows and all she's done for him, she can easily be the linchpin to expose him and put him away for treason.

Shit.

"The man in the park stalking me," she says shakily. "What if it was Ben? Or—or Dylan? It could've been, couldn't it?"

"Maybe," I say, trying to sound unconvinced. "Did security stop by?"

Rosie nods. "There's someone outside my door right now, but—I'm too afraid to leave. And what if Ben gets to me anyway? If he got to John Phillip Michaels in a prison cell, then killing me won't be any—any trouble at all—"

That's all she manages before breaking down into even more tears, and I grimace, glancing up at Kit and Tibby. "Hey, Rosie?" I say. "I'm going to come see you, okay? Right now. Just to make sure you're okay."

"But—but the premiere," she sobs.

"I'm not watching the movie anyway," I say. "I'll be right there, okay? Let your guard know."

She nods shakily, and while she's wiping the snot from her face, I hang up. "You don't have to come," I say to Kit. He hasn't spoken to her since we used Rosie's crush on him to trick her into confessing, and it's been an awkward night as it is.

"You know I am," he says. "We'll take extra security with us, just in case. Rosie's not wrong, you know."

"I know," I say miserably. "That's what I'm afraid of."

Tibby scoffs. "Are you mad? I don't care how distraught she is. This can wait until morning. You *must* be there after the credits, and there's barely an hour and a half left—"

"Then I guess we have an hour and twenty-nine minutes to make it back," I say. "Rosie doesn't live far, right?"

"No more than fifteen minutes away," says Kit, and he stands, offering me his hand. "Tibby?"

She grinds her teeth, her nails digging into her designer bag. "Fine," she says crisply. "But if you're not there when the lights go on, then I will make bloody sure everyone involved knows exactly whose idea this was."

"Naturally," I say, and I take Kit's hand and hop off the stool, unable to fully shake the echo of Rosie's cries. "Let's hope this place has a back exit."

We arrive in front of Rosie's townhouse less than twenty minutes later, and sure enough, there's a mustached officer standing guard outside her gate. He greets the three of us with a nod, and as Tibby tries to wrangle my train and make sure I don't catch it on anything, Kit and I hurry up the walkway arm in arm.

My hand trembles as I knock on her door, and I'm not sure what I'm more afraid of—that Ben really may be responsible for John Phillip Michaels's death and coming after Rosie, too, or what her reaction might be upon seeing me and Kit again. Either way, I don't have much time to think about it when the door flies open, and a tearstained Rosie stands on the other side, her mouth hanging open in shock.

"K-Kit?" she manages. "I didn't know you were coming, too."

"I'm sorry," I say. "We both wanted to make sure you were all right. Is that okay?"

Rosie takes a moment to consider it, but at last she nods, a tiny gesture that isn't at all convincing. Still, she steps aside to give us room to enter the foyer, and as we do so, an adorable white dog much smaller than Poppy trots into the room.

"Oh, hi," I say, bending down as much as I can in this scarlet atrocity of a dress. "You must be Snickers."

His little tail wags as I scratch him behind the ears, and Rosie walks listlessly into the white marble kitchen. It's sizable for London, and it's more of an aesthetic than a functional space, which isn't surprising when it comes to Rosie and her obsession with social media.

"He doesn't usually like strangers," she says, perching on a white leather barstool beside a massive bouquet of pink and red roses. She reaches into an unwrapped magenta gift box on the counter, pulling out a chocolate. "But I suppose you're not really a stranger. I've told him all about you."

"You have?" I say, and as I join her, Snickers disappears into another room, his tail still wagging. "He's really sweet. How old is he?"

"Seventeen months." She nibbles on the chocolate, staring at the intricate design. "The guard outside said you hired his firm, Kit?"

Kit nods, and he heads toward the electric kettle to boil some water, presumably for tea. "We were hoping for palace security to step in, but with the event tonight, there was no one to spare," he says, and I can sense the guilt rolling off him. "We didn't want to leave you vulnerable, even for a day."

She sniffs and looks him in the eye at last. "Thank you. It means a lot to me and Snickers. And thank you for coming by. You really didn't have to."

"I think we did." I study Rosie. She's in sweats—the worn kind most people never leave the house in, not the designer type, and her curly blond hair is lank and a little greasy at the roots. She looks terrible, and suddenly I'm glad we're here. Not that we can really do much other than sit with her, but at least it's something.

"The flowers are really pretty, too," says Rosie, and one of her dimples appears as she offers me a tiny smile. "Maybe a little overboard, but I really appreciate them. They're beautiful."

"Flowers?" I say, confused, but she's already rearranging the giant vase of roses. "Oh—those?"

"Of course," she says, her smile growing, and she looks behind me, to where Tibby is lingering by the door, no doubt watching the time like a hawk. "Tibby, did you send them and put Evan's name on them?"

"Send what?" says Tibby, sounding distracted. "The flowers? Er—no, I'm afraid not. Perhaps Fitz did?"

Rosie's expression falls. "No, Maisie hasn't spoken to me since . . . well, you know." Her throat constricts, and I frown.

"She hasn't reached out to you since January?"

"Of course not," says Rosie with a sigh that speaks volumes. "It's all right. I didn't expect her to, not after . . ."

I press my lips together. I'm not sure I can fault Maisie for that one, not after Rosie's involvement with the fire and blatant betrayal. But considering how close the two were for nearly all their lives, part of me—the part of me that thinks I know my sister better than I clearly do—expected Maisie to at least reach out to . . . I don't know. Yell at Rosie. Or find some sense of closure. But then again, maybe that was Gia's influence on her. Maybe Gia was the glue holding the three of them together, and with her gone, there's no hope for reconciliation between Maisie and Rosie, either.

The thought is devastating, and I'm trying not to picture the way Maisie was watching Gia from across the lobby less than an hour ago when suddenly I see it. Tucked among the roses, nestled in a clump of crimson and blending in so well that at first I think it's an illusion. But it isn't.

A single blood-red gerbera daisy.

"Rosie," I say, a fireball of panic forming in my chest. "How do you know these came from me?"

"The note, silly," she says, and she hands me a plain but heavy card that rests beside the vase.

Dearest Rosie,
I'm sorry you couldn't be at the premiere tonight. Thinking of you and the part you played in our journey.
Love,
Evangeline

The handwriting looks nothing like mine, and I sure as hell wouldn't use "dearest" as an opening. Or sign it with "love" when Rosie and I barely know each other. My heart is pounding, and I set the card down, careful not to touch more of it than I already have.

"We need to get out of here," I say, searching the kitchen as if Ben is lurking in the shadows, ready to strike. *"Now."*

"You're scaring me," says Rosie, her eyes wide as she pinches another bonbon between her fingers. "What's going on? Evan—"

"Ev?" Kit is by my side now, and my pulse is so fast that I'm dizzy. "What—"

But then he lets out a curse so unlike him that I know he sees it, too. That damn flower. That message, specifically for me. How did he know I'd be here? How did he know I would come?

He didn't. It was a gamble, and now I have to get Rosie out of here before she and I both lose.

"No time to explain," I say as Tibby pokes her head in, and I take Rosie's elbow. "Come on. Tibby—tell them we're coming out, and we need a security team here as soon as possible. It's urgent."

To her credit, she doesn't question me, and Kit takes Rosie's other arm as we head toward the door, leaving the bouquet behind. Is there a bomb inside? Is someone—Dylan, undoubtedly—already in Rosie's townhouse, waiting to kill us? My mind whirls with possibilities, each worse than the last, but just as we're about to step out into the night air, Rosie stops.

"Snickers!" she cries, and she deftly slips out of our grips and bolts back inside. Kit and I exchange a horrified look, and he darts after her before I can even think to kick off my heels.

"Rosie, no!" I cry. "We'll come back for him!" But even as I say it, I know I'd do exactly the same thing for Poppy. And so, as Tibby rushes back toward the door with our PPOs following her, I hurry after Kit and Rosie, cursing every inch of this dress train and how much it slows me down.

I hear footsteps overhead, and Kit's voice calling for her, too. But his pleas quickly turn to yet another curse, and he bellows, louder than I've ever heard him before, *"Evan! Tibby!"*

With my heart in my throat, I rush upstairs, and something in the back of my dress rips as I turn down the hallway, but I don't care. Kit is kneeling in a doorway that leads into a pink-and-white bedroom, and I see Rosie's feet twitching before the rest of her comes into view, sprawled out on the carpet.

She's seizing.

"Rosie—Rosie, you're all right," says Kit as he hovers over her, clearly unsure what to do. Foam forms at the corners of her mouth, tinged pink at first before turning undeniably red, and my stomach turns.

"What happened? Did she fall?" I say, kneeling on her other side. Kit shakes his head.

"I found her like this. She's never had seizures before."

"We need to turn her so she doesn't choke," I say as heavy footsteps thud up the staircase. "If she bit her tongue—"

But just as Kit and I start to ease her onto her side, the seizing stops. For one horrible moment, her green eyes open to meet mine, and I can see the fear and pain in hers before they roll into the back of her head. A torrent of blood spills from her mouth, and she stiffens once more as every muscle in her body seems to tense, before—

It's over.

"Rosie?" I say as two PPOs rush into the room, and I touch her warm cheek. "Rosie. *Rosie.*"

The larger of the two shoulders me aside, and he presses his fingers to her neck. "I can't feel a pulse," he announces to the other, and my insides turn to molten lead.

"What?" I say. "No, that's not right—she's okay, she just had a seizure—"

But they're doing CPR now, the chest compressions hard and fast and deeper than I've ever seen on any show or movie. I can hear her ribs snapping as Rosie lies there motionless, showing no sign of pain. No sign of life. No sign of anything at all.

"What happened?" says the second PPO, and I shake my head, baffled and unable to speak. This doesn't make any sense. None of it makes any sense.

"Evan, Kit," says Tibby from the doorway, and it's an unspoken order, not a request. But I can't move. I can't tear my eyes away from Rosie, who two minutes ago was talking and breathing and—and *living*, but is now nothing more than an inanimate body, her sweatshirt soaked in her own blood. Vaguely I hear a whimpering sound behind Tibby, and when I finally look at her, I see Snickers in the hallway, cowering at the commotion.

Snickers. He's okay. I'm okay, and Kit's okay, but Rosie—

"Ev." Kit's beside me now, helping me to my feet. I'm trembling so hard that I can barely stand, but he gathers me in his arms, carrying me the same way he did after Jasper attacked me. I can feel him step over Rosie's legs, and my stomach lurches violently.

"It was just a seizure," I say as he sets me back on my feet on the other side of the doorway. Tibby immediately wraps her arm around me as well, but I slip out of her grip and kneel down to scoop up the quaking dog. As I do, I chance one last glance back into the bedroom, where the PPOs are still performing CPR on Rosie's lifeless body. She's so impossibly pale now that she blends in with her white rug, and I bury my face in Snickers's fur.

This can't be real. She was *fine* minutes ago. We were going to leave. We were bringing her to safety. How is she—how is she like that, and Kit and I are okay? *How?* We're the real targets, not her. Why is she the one on the floor, not us?

But as the three of us head down the steps and through the kitchen in one awkward huddle, I spot the single daisy among roses once more, and my blurry vision drifts to the box of chocolates on the marble counter. They're expensive, handpicked ones, not the cellophane-wrapped packages that come premade. They're the kind Rosie, an aristocrat, would be used to getting. The kind she wouldn't question.

The kind that could easily be tampered with.

Before I can put my suspicions into words, Tibby ushers Kit and me through the front door and into the night air, where flashing lights reflect on the neat row of expensive townhouses, and the wail of sirens fails to muffle the words echoing through my head.

Rosie is dead.

Rosie is dead.

Rosie is *dead.*

And Ben's the one who killed her.

CHAPTER TWENTY-THREE

"Henrietta, are you surprised that His Majesty is rushing into a second marriage so soon after finalizing his divorce with Her Majesty Queen Helene?"

"Well, it has only been weeks, but after all we've learned about their marriage in the past sixteen months, it's fair to say that they've been married in name only for years—possibly for the majority of their union. Her Majesty has already publicly moved on with the Duke of York, which is as scandalous a match as there is, in my opinion, and with all His Majesty has been through since the bombing, surely we as a country can allow him this happiness in marrying the woman he has apparently loved since he was a teenager."

"So you see this as a happy ending to a decades-long love story?"

"I do. Not to speak ill of our queen or of the marriage that produced our beloved Princess Mary, but while they may be royalty, we must remember that Their Majesties are also human. And it has been clear from the moment we found out about Evangeline that His Majesty has been leading a life outside the public eye, one he cherishes a great deal. We simply did not know how much until now."

"Do we have any details of the wedding yet?"

"Buckingham Palace has released a statement saying that a small civil ceremony will take place in the 'near future,' and there is no word yet as to which titles, if any, Ms. Bright will take."

"Considering what the country thought of Laura Bright little more than a year ago, what should we expect the public reaction to be?"

"It's hard to say. The stigma against mental illness will never go away completely, especially coupled with the heinous act Ms. Bright committed when she wasn't in her right mind—"

"Trying to drown four-year-old Evangeline in a bathtub."

"Yes, if you'd like to be crass about it. But as we know, she received years of in-patient treatment and is still under the care of doctors to this day, and she was not charged with a crime. Paranoid schizophrenia is a complex mental illness with many facets—"

"And is it not controversial, having a queen with such a . . . complicated history?"

"Of course it is, and to imply otherwise is naive at best. But I would certainly not wish to be judged by the entire world for the single worst moment of my life, and yet Laura Bright is risking exactly that by marrying the man she has loved for decades, despite knowing it will put her in an unfriendly spotlight for the rest of recorded history. That alone tells me all I need to know about how much they love each other, and I for one hope they are able to finally have their happy ending. Or happy beginning, as it is."

"But what about the legal implications of such a marriage?"

"I don't see the problem. Henry VIII saw to it nearly five hundred years ago that our kings and queens could divorce, if they so choose, and Ms. Bright has never married. Or, as far as we know, had a relationship with anyone other than His Majesty."

"Yes, but this is more a question of succession—a game of heirs and thrones, if you will. With Princess Mary and Evangeline born on the same day, would a union between His Majesty and Laura Bright not throw the current line of succession into question?"

"Ah, I see. After His Majesty and Ms. Bright marry, yes, Evangeline would legally be legitimized. But the line of succession excludes someone in Evangeline's position from being placed in line without an act of Parliament, something that, as much as we all love Evangeline, I highly doubt would be passed anytime soon, barring another royal crisis."

"I see. So regardless of which girl was born first, the line of succession will not change?"

"I . . . well, now that you've brought it up, I must admit this isn't something I'd given much thought. But should Evangeline have any legitimate children, those children *would* be automatically placed in the line of succession, as would any legitimate child born of royal blood."

"And if Evangeline is older than Princess Mary?"

"Well. That would certainly make things interesting, wouldn't it?"

—ITV News's interview with Henrietta Smythe,
10 September 2024

BY THE TIME OUR RANGE Rover pulls up the gravel drive and stops at the entrance to Windsor Castle, it's nearly four in the morning, and my parents are waiting for us beneath the awning, their faces knit with unspeakable worry.

"Evie," says my mother, sweeping me into her arms the moment I plant my feet on the drive. "Are you all right?"

I shake my head and cling to her, unstable as I am after hours of questioning and interviews from both Scotland Yard and MI5. Though Kit, Tibby, and I were only inside Rosie's townhouse for eight minutes, I've gone over every single detail so many times that those eight minutes are seared into my memory now, and everything else—even the cool predawn breeze—feels unreal. Like I'll be stuck in the last moments of Rosie's life for the rest of mine, no matter where I am.

"It's been a long night," says Kit tiredly as he climbs out after me, refusing to leave my side. There were nearly two horrible hours when we were separated at the start of questioning, when I did nothing but request a lawyer and stare at the wall as tears streamed down my face, and I silently prayed to whatever deity I could think of that somehow, someway, Rosie would survive. But something Kit or Tibby said, either to the police or the familiar MI5 agents who soon joined the investigation, must have cleared us of suspicion, because we were reunited in time for Singh to arrive and inform us that Rosie was really, truly gone.

"The police treated you fairly?" says the low, rumbling voice of my father, and Kit nods.

"There was some trouble at the start," he admits. "Whoever did it sent a . . . er, bouquet and some chocolates we suspect were laced with poison, and they did so under Evan's name."

My mom hugs me tighter before letting me go. "We heard," she says, giving me a once-over. I'm still in the awful scarlet gown, though the oversized train is now wrapped around my bare shoulders like a shawl. "Singh said he sorted it out, though?"

"He did," says Tibby, joining us from the front of the Range Rover. "They're gathering footage from Rosie's security system to find out more about the delivery, since she didn't leave the house after her morning walk. But that's all he was able to pass on to us before they let us go."

Alexander curses quietly. "The palace lawyers are on it," he promises. "And the police have agreed to a media blackout regarding your involvement. We'll sort this all out before the press can hurl any fresh allegations."

I don't care about any of that. I should, probably, but somehow getting accused of terrorism and trying to murder my own father has numbed me to any other accusations, especially when they're so blatantly false. "Rosie's dead," I say—the first time I've spoken the words out loud. "Ben was behind it. I *know* he was. The bouquet—there was a gerbera daisy, exactly like the ones he sent me—and Guy Fawkes—John Phillip Michaels—he's dead, too. It's not a coincidence. It can't be. He's tying up loose ends, and Rosie's one of them."

My mother and father exchange a look. "We spoke to Singh as soon as they released you," says Alexander. "And he agrees that that's the most likely scenario. We all do, Evie. The problem is—"

"Evidence," I say with a heavy sigh, as if the word is escaping me like air from a deflating balloon. "But how are we supposed to find any if he keeps using other people and covering his tracks? He killed *Rosie.* He can't just get away with—"

A pair of headlights flashes at the gate, and we all look as another Range Rover approaches. Confused, I glance at Kit, but horror slowly dawns on his face, and it takes me a moment to catch up.

There's only one member of the family with the nerve to come home at four o'clock in the morning. And if she's been partying since the premiere . . .

"You didn't have to wait up," says Maisie as she opens her own door. Her heels hang from the tips of her fingers, and her hair is slightly mussed as she steps onto the gravel drive barefoot. "Kit, Evan—where on earth have you two been? The entire audience was buzzing about where you'd run off to after the premiere, and do you know who they asked? *Me.* Again and again, like I'm your bloody minder."

Maisie doesn't know. Wherever she's been, no one has bothered to text her. No one's told her that her lifelong best friend died tonight.

"Maisie . . ." says Alexander when it becomes apparent no one else is going to speak.

"Daddy, I'm an adult," she says as she picks her way across the gravel to the smooth stone walkway. "I can stay out as late as I want."

"It's not that," says Kit, his voice thick. This must be enough of a hint to catch Maisie's attention, because she immediately looks at him, her brow furrowed.

"Then what is it?" she says. "Is it Thaddeus? Because he's back at his hotel, and we didn't do anything. We just went to a few after-parties and a club or two, nothing outrageous. Nothing for the press to get their knickers in a—"

"It's Rosie," I say with as much gentleness as I can muster, because it shouldn't be Kit. It shouldn't be Alexander. The news won't be any easier to hear from them, and they're both already on shaky ground with her. But my so-called relationship with my sister is completely torched. "She—she's gone."

Maisie stares at me for a terrible moment that seems to twist in on itself like a fun house mirror, the world between us distorting until nothing makes sense anymore. "Rosie?" she says at last, the ghost of a scoff in her voice. "What are you talking about? She hasn't gone anywhere. You were yelling at me this morning about—about—"

"I'm sorry, Mais," says Kit quietly, and he reaches out to touch her, only for her to rip her arm away. "We think Ben poisoned her. There's an investigation, and—"

"What are you saying?" says Maisie shakily, and she drops her heels on the ground. "Rosie isn't gone. She's not—bloody hell, Kit, *what are you saying?*"

Kit's throat constricts, and one look tells me he's struggling to hold himself together. "Rosie—" he tries, but his voice breaks, and even in the low light, I can see the tears shining in his puffy eyes.

"Rosie is dead," I manage thickly, because there's no other way to say it now. "She called me at the premiere when she heard about Michaels's death. She was afraid Ben was coming after her, and so Kit, Tibby, and I headed over to her place to—to see her. But it was too late. There was a bouquet—roses and a daisy, just like the ones Ben sends me—and a half-eaten box of chocolates. As soon as we saw the flowers, we tried to get her out of there, but . . . the chocolates must have been poisoned, because she seized, and . . . everyone did everything they could. They worked on her for—for a really long time. But . . ." Now my voice catches, and I take a deep breath. "I'm so sorry, Maisie. She didn't make it."

My sister stares at me like I'm something so nightmarishly

surreal that she can't comprehend what she's looking at, and I know that feeling. I felt it the day I discovered why my mother lost custody of me, and I felt it when I saw Ingrid's unrecognizable body next to mine in the bombing. I felt it tonight, too, seeing Rosie lying there with her eyes open, staring at nothing with pink foam at the corners of her mouth, and—

I squeeze my eyes shut and push the mental image away, even though I know it won't go far. And that's when I feel the sharp sting against my cheek.

A slap. Maisie slapped me.

"You're lying," she snarls, but she's trembling now as she bends over to pick up her shoes. "You're all lying. Whatever this is—it isn't funny. It isn't *funny.*"

She turns to Alexander, who leans heavily on his cane, but when he grimaces and says nothing, I can see both the hope and fury die in her eyes.

"Daddy," she says, and there's a note of pleading in her voice. "It's not true. Rosie would never—she can't—"

Maisie cuts herself off like she's choking on the words, her shoulders shaking with grief as reality sets in. Kit reaches for her once more, but she jerks away yet again.

"Don't *touch* me," she gasps, doubling over as if someone's punched her in the gut. "Don't—bloody—"

And then she's running across the sharp gravel, to the immaculately kept grass and into the dark garden beyond. Kit makes a move to go after her, but Alexander shakes his head.

"Let her go," he says to Kit, even as he gestures for one of her PPOs lingering nearby to follow. "She'll come to us when she's ready."

But as I watch her silhouette disappear into the unsettling shadows of Windsor Castle, I can't imagine a time Maisie will ever be ready to accept that Rosie is gone. And I'm sure—as sure as I am that tonight will live in my memory for the rest of my life—that Maisie will never, ever forgive me for this.

CHAPTER TWENTY-FOUR

Did the royal family arrange John Phillip Michaels's death to cover up the truth about Evangeline Bright and Lord Clarence's involvement in the ABR? Or is it a coincidence that the 25-year-old terrorist leader, who up until his death continued to insist that Evangeline played a key role in the January bombing of the Modern Music Museum, was found dead in his prison cell mere weeks before his trial was set to begin?

Who was powerful enough to have him killed? Who had the means, the motive, and the opportunity to do so? Only one family checks all those boxes, and it certainly wouldn't be the first time they've gone to great lengths to cover up a royal secret—such as just how long the former Queen Helene and the Duke of York have been involved.

Click on the gallery below to go back in time on the journey of their forbidden love affair, from their hot and heavy touches at the premiere of *Princess, Rebel, Terrorist, Spy* last night to their adoring and intimate looks at Princess Mary's christening in 2005.

That's right, dear readers. *2005.*

—*The Regal Record*, 11 September 2024

IN THE THREE DAYS BETWEEN the night of the premiere and the afternoon of Rosie's funeral, not a single media outlet mentions her death.

It should be everywhere—one of Princess Mary's best friends dying from poisoned chocolates while Kit and I watched, helpless to do a damn thing. I brace myself for the media onslaught the next day, and then the day after that, but it's like it never even happened. In the papers and online, at least.

Maisie doesn't leave her apartment for those entire three days. Kit and I don't venture out from ours much, either, but we at least pretend to be human in the face of our—mostly Kit's—grief. I'm still reeling from watching Rosie die and all the guilt that comes with knowing she thought those damn chocolates were from me, but he's the one who really knew her. They'd been friends for years, and it wasn't exactly a secret that she wanted to be more. She was infatuated with him, and the crushing regret of having used that against her back in January must cause him no end of shame.

Singh stops by twice—once the day after to clarify a few points in our statements, and once the morning of the funeral. As he settles into a seat at our dining table, Kit pulls me into our bedroom, everything about him riddled with anxiety.

"Ev," he says quietly, as broken as I've ever seen him. "I know we're part of this investigation, and there's nothing we can do to excuse ourselves from it. But . . ." His brow knits, and I reach up to smooth it over, as if it's that easy.

"But it's a lot," I whisper, and his Adam's apple bobs.

"I can feel the seams in me coming undone, and all I can think about is—is what would've happened if Rosie had offered you the chocolates, too. Or if it had been something sprayed on the flowers, or . . . or . . ." He shakes his head, and I can see a slight tremor as he moves. "I don't want to fall apart again, Ev, and it's taking everything I have to hold myself together."

I clasp his hands between mine, alarmed by how cold his are. "Oxford won't happen again," I say, keeping my voice low. "I promise. Have you spoken to your therapist since . . . ?"

"No," he admits. "I should. I keep meaning to."

"Then how about this," I say. "You stay here and call your therapist. Make an appointment for this morning or later today, after the funeral. And once that's done, take a long, hot shower or—or bath, or whatever you think will relax you, okay? I'll see what Singh wants."

I raise his hands to my cheek, letting my warmth chase away the chill in his skin. Kit takes a few deep breaths, then nods. "Okay. You'll tell me what he says?"

"Every word," I promise. "Thank you for trusting me."

"Always." He slips his hands from mine only to hug me, holding me for a few beats longer than usual. I can feel his heart racing against my chest, the *thud-thud-thud* a reminder that this hasn't fixed everything—maybe it hasn't fixed anything at all—but at least we're trying together this time. That's the step we've been missing.

Once Kit has excused himself to make the call, I head back out into our shared sitting room to face Singh, two fresh breakfast trays, and the mountain of questions between us.

"We have no evidence that Prince Benedict or Dylan Baxter were involved," says Singh, heading me off before I can speak. "Scotland Yard tracked down the delivery boy who dropped off the flowers and chocolates, and he's clean."

"He is?" I say, confused. "You're sure it was the chocolates? Could it have been something else?"

Singh pours himself a cup of tea and dunks a cookie—biscuit—in the hot liquid. "It'll be a while before toxicology can confirm, but they're as sure as they can be that it was the chocolates. Good call on that," he adds, as if that's something I should be proud of. All I feel is slightly sick.

"Do you know where the packages came from?" I press. "Are there any more leads? There have to be, right? They didn't just—*appear.*"

"We're working on it," he promises. "It's early days yet. Very early days. These things take time."

The urge to scream rises up within me, primal and so overwhelming that I almost can't tamp it down. "It was Ben. It *had* to be Ben. There's no one else who would come after Rosie—"

"She had some online stalkers we're looking into," he says. "A few exes that weren't the kindest. We're considering every avenue, Evan, and that includes ones that don't fit your narrative."

"I don't care if they fit my *narrative* or not. I just want whoever did this to be found."

Singh watches me. "Well, the card points to you. That certainly says something."

I freeze, my hand halfway to my own cup of tea. "Am I a suspect again?" I say, my heart pounding. "Because Kit and Tibby were there, and—"

"No, no, nothing like that," says Singh with surprising reassurance. "I simply mean that whoever it was certainly wanted to pin it on you, didn't they?"

I exhale, relieved, even though proving my innocence no

longer feels like the priority. Maybe because I've had to do it again and again, and I'm sick of it. "Which would point right back to Ben," I say.

"Yes. Or someone else who has a grudge against you," he adds. "Like Michaels."

"Who's dead," I say flatly, pushing aside my own regret for not visiting him the day of the premiere. Nothing could have convinced Tibby to make room in our packed schedule for a trip to a penitentiary, and there's no faulting myself for that one. It was inevitable. "Any leads there?"

Singh raises an eyebrow. "You're full of questions today, aren't you?"

"Isn't that why you're here?" I say, picking up a piece of toast and nibbling on the corner. "Otherwise this could've easily been a text. You want to brainstorm with someone who's even more paranoid than you are."

" 'Paranoid' isn't the word I'd use," he says, digging into a bowl of fresh fruit. "At least not to describe myself. Any thoughts?"

I think for a moment as I slowly chew, my unharnessed thoughts flitting from one dead end to the next. I know it's Ben. I know it as well as I know my own damn name. But without proof—without a sufficient trail of evidence—my certainty is worthless.

"I don't have all the pieces," I say at last. "I don't think any of us do. But people like Maisie and Kit . . . they know Ben better than I ever will. And if we want to start somewhere, we need to start by talking to them. That's the only way we're going to outsmart him."

"By surrounding him like a pack of wolves and picking him apart until he has no choice but to give up?" says Singh, and I nod, hating myself for even thinking of dragging Kit into this.

"More or less. How did Michaels die without anyone seeing him hang himself?"

"Apparently the CCTV system in the prison was having technical difficulties."

Now it's my turn to raise my eyebrow. "Right. And you're checking into the people who could've made that happen?"

"Naturally. You wouldn't happen to know anything about Michaels that could be useful, would you? He *was* asking for you."

I hesitate, then shake my head. "I told you everything," I say, and it's the truth. Or at least I think it is, but as soon as I've said it, the so-called chat with him in his study replays in my mind, beat by beat if not word for word. And then, in a flash of memory, I glance at the Victorian writing desk nearby, which neither Kit nor I actually use, considering we're more adept at email than we are handwritten letters.

There, sitting innocuously between a gold container of several fancy fountain pens and a picture of Kit and me taken over the summer, sits the puzzle box Guy Fawkes gave me.

I still haven't cracked it. Maybe I should have tried harder, but after he was arrested, it didn't seem to matter anymore. Still, I know that if I mention it now, Singh will take it and I'll never see it again, and something in me bristles at that—at the idea that I'm not good enough to solve it on my own. Which is ridiculous, because this is literally a case of life and death, but it really *can't* matter, can it? Now that the case is solved and Michaels is dead. It's just a toy he gave me to drive me bonkers, and to distract me from the real game at hand.

But that game is over now, and all I have left is an unsolved puzzle. I open my mouth to mention it, but before I say a word, something stops me. My pride, or maybe whatever strange bond was forged between me and John Phillip Michaels in that study. This is personal, between him and me, and I can't stand the thought of anyone else trying to open it.

"I'll tell you what," says Singh, breaking the heavy silence between us. "I'll gather together what I can and meet you back here after the funeral. Bring the people you trust."

"Not many of those," I say without thinking, and Singh offers me a grimace of a smile.

"That's how you know you're doing your job right," he says. "I'm sorry about your friend, Evangeline. I'll see you afterward."

He stays only long enough to finish his fruit and tea, and I see him to the door. As soon as I close it behind him, I wipe the sad smile from my face—my default these past few days—and turn toward the desk.

In three quick strides, I take the puzzle box and turn it over in my hand, and once again I start to twist its pieces, trying to find a solution that seems like it can't possibly exist.

AT A QUARTER to noon, Kit and I make our way hand in hand to the drawing room closest to the private family entrance. He's barely said a word all morning, and I don't press, only telling him what he needs to know about my meeting with Singh—and that there will be another one after the funeral, if he decides to attend. He said nothing to that, either, but at least it wasn't a straight-up refusal.

I curl up beside Kit on the uncomfortably ornate sofa, tracing patterns over his palm with my fingertips and resting my head on his shoulder as we wait for the others. I made sure to tuck a pack of tissues beside Guy's puzzle in my shoulder bag—which is the exact shade of black as my knee-length dress and jacket—and I'm trying not to be obvious about watching Kit for any signs of his flat expression slipping when the others finally start to trickle in.

A subdued Helene and Nicholas are first, stopping by from their apartment in Kensington Palace so they can accompany Maisie. Helene's eyes are red, and though Nicholas looks unaffected, he's as attentive to her as I am to Kit. It's only then that I remember Rosie's mother is one of Helene's best friends, and the guilt in my gut twists even tighter, making me wish I hadn't eaten breakfast.

"I can't believe Alexander isn't coming," says Helene, dabbing her eyes with a black silk handkerchief. "Of all the things to miss . . ."

"You know he can't, my darling," says Nicholas, pulling her close. "His presence will draw attention away from Rosie and the Chesterfield-Bishops, and the pressure of his attendance is the last thing they need today. He called Lucy and Stuart earlier this morning to offer his condolences, and Jenkins has already sent flowers and a sizable donation to the charity they chose to honor Rosie's memory. Sometimes that's all that can be done."

This sounds reasonable to me and what little etiquette I've

absorbed, but Helene still buries her face in Nicholas's shoulder, her own shaking with silent sobs.

To my surprise, Thaddeus Park is next. Kit rises to greet him, and I follow his lead, allowing Thaddeus to hug me like we've both lost a family member instead of someone he never met.

"Good of you to stay for this," says Kit, his voice rough as Thaddeus sits down in an armchair near us.

"I want to make sure Maisie is okay," he says, and he clears his throat, glancing around—and snapping his gaze right back to us as soon as he spots the crying Helene. "Speaking of, where is she? Isn't it nearly time to go?"

Kit checks his phone. *11:56.* "It is," he admits, though he looks miserable at the idea of facing Maisie for the first time since the hours after Rosie's death. I'm not looking forward to it, either.

But if I can spare him this much, then I will. "I'll go get her," I say, standing and smoothing out my dress. "I'm sure she's on her way."

I'm sure of no such thing, but before either Kit or Thaddeus can protest—or worse, insist on coming with me—I kick off my heels and hurry out of the drawing room, making my way up the corridor that wraps around almost the entirety of the U-shaped castle. The royal apartments aren't far, and as soon as I reach Maisie's door, I knock, not at all surprised that she hasn't even left her rooms yet.

"Maisie?" I say. No answer. "Maisie, it's me. We're all waiting for you in the drawing room. Are you okay?"

More silence. I press my ear to the door, and through it I

can hear the ticking of the grandfather clock that sits in Maisie's living room. Between soft clicks, however, there's something else—something soft and muffled, but it's there, even if I can't tell what it is.

Knowing I'll probably be paying for this invasion of privacy for a very long time, I pull the lockpicks I always carry out of my bag and get to work on her door. I've had enough practice now, especially on the old hardware in Windsor, that I have the door unlocked in under fifteen seconds, and I nudge it open slowly, grateful the staff keeps the hinges well oiled.

Someone is definitely crying inside. Slipping my picks back into my bag, I tiptoe across the soft cream rug and peek around the corner into Maisie's large sitting room. Part of me expects a mess like the last tantrum she threw, with broken treasures everywhere, but the room is pristine, as if housekeeping has just been through.

"Maisie?" I say softly. As soon as I speak, the crying stops, but at least now I can tell where it was coming from.

I peer around a massive bouquet of white roses, to the space between a cream sofa and a tall window. Maisie sits huddled beneath the narrow ledge in a sky-blue nightgown, her hair a mess and her face bare of any makeup, and an open photo album is in her lap.

The pictures already tucked into the pages are of three little girls—unmistakably Maisie, Gia, and Rosie, laughing and playing and completely oblivious to the painful future that lay ahead of them. And in a neat stack at Maisie's side are more photos, these much more recent.

"Maisie," I whisper, my heart breaking for her. "I'm so sorry."

"I don't understand how she can just be . . . gone," she says without looking up. Her voice is hoarse, as if she's spent all night crying. Or screaming. Or both. "We used to talk about what we would do when we were grown-ups. About what it would be like when I was queen and they were my ladies-in-waiting. It was always 'when,' not 'if.' Of course it was never 'if.' Who thinks like that?"

I have, I realize, ever since I lost my grandma and my childhood in one fell swoop. I was way too young to have to question the stability of my universe, but when's the right time? When you're nineteen, like Maisie is now? When you're in your twenties, like my parents were when my mom got sick? "I'm sorry, Maisie."

She finally looks at me, her eyes so red and puffy that her irises look oddly lavender in the light. "You could have saved her. You were *right there,* and you did nothing."

A knot the size of a walnut forms in my throat, and for a moment, I can't breathe. "There was nothing we could do. We tried to get her out of there, but it was too late—"

"There's *always* something you can do," says Maisie, and though she sounds every bit as exhausted and deflated as she looks, there's an edge to her voice as dangerous as a chainsaw. "You could've warned her. You could've told her not to touch anything until you got there. You—you could've saved her, and you didn't, and *you* are the reason she's dead."

She exhales, her entire body seeming to expel whatever demons have been haunting her these past three days, and with a shuddering gasp, she buries her face in her hands and starts to cry. I crouch down beside her and gently slip the album from her lap, ignoring the cut of her words—her very true words—as I do my best to stop her from crying on the photographs.

"If you—if you hadn't come here—if you'd just—stayed in the States, where you belong," bawls Maisie, the tears falling harder and faster with every word, "then she'd—still be alive. She'd—she'd be okay, and Ben—"

Her whole body is racked with sobs now, and knowing it might cost me my hand, I finally muster the courage to reach out and touch her shoulder. "You're right," I say, my eyes welling up, but I blink hard, forcing those tears back down. "If I hadn't ended up here, Ben would've never . . . done what he did. And Rosie would likely still be alive."

The fact that I'm agreeing with her is apparently so startling that Maisie seems to barely notice that I'm touching her. Instead, she pulls her hands from her face to stare at me again, this time like I'm some kind of venomous snake. "You shouldn't be here. No one wanted you here. *I* didn't want you here. And now—now—"

"Maisie?"

A familiar voice, high and cautious, sounds from the doorway, and I can practically see Maisie's heart stop. Slowly she pulls herself to her feet, and judging by the painful way she moves, she's been sitting beneath that windowsill for hours.

"Gia?"

Kit and Gia stand in the doorway, both looking like they're not sure they're allowed inside. But that doubt is quickly banished—for Gia, at least—as Maisie stumbles forward, her nightgown tangling around her legs as she closes the distance between them and throws her arms around her.

I expect Gia to hesitate, or maybe not to hug her back at all. But instead she's there in an instant, supporting Maisie as she collapses in her arms, and the pair of them sink to the carpet together, clinging to each other like there's nothing as solid and grounded as they are. Kit gingerly sidesteps them and makes his way toward me, and I loop my arm around his waist, hugging him closely.

"She got here quickly," I say, low enough so only he can hear.

"I invited her yesterday to ride with us to the funeral," he says, his voice still heavy with sorrow. "I thought perhaps there was still one wrong we might be able to right in all of this."

At first I'm not sure, but as I watch the pair of them hold each other, Gia running her fingers through Maisie's tangled hair and Maisie sobbing into Gia's neck, I can see shades of the same relief and desperation I felt the moment I saw Kit in that greenroom so many months ago. Maisie may be temperamental and deep in the throes of grief, but she is Gia's as much as I am Kit's, and I pull him a little closer.

"We need to put an end to this," he says softly, burying his nose in my hair, and I nod just enough to show my agreement.

"It was Ben tying up loose ends," I whisper. "It had to be. I refuse to believe it's a coincidence that Rosie and Michaels died on the same day."

"As do I," he murmurs, but there's a note of wariness in his voice, and I find his hand, lacing my fingers through his.

"You're sure about this?" I say quietly. "About—going after

Ben?" After everything Kit went through while we were at Oxford, after everything that nearly broke us apart, I can't stand the thought of putting him through that again, even if it means leaving Ben to Singh. But he nods and brings my hand to his mouth, pressing his warm lips to my skin and holding it there for a beat longer than he ever has before.

"If he did this to Rosie, we're next." He pauses, and I meet his dark eyes. "What time is that meeting with Singh?"

CHAPTER TWENTY-FIVE

REMEMBERED: LADY PRIMROSE CHESTERFIELD-BISHOP, 18

Lady Primrose Chesterfield-Bishop, born 7 October 2005, died at age 18 on 10 September 2024 of unknown causes.

The adored only child of Lord Stuart and Lady Lucile Chesterfield-Bishop, Rosie, as she was known to friends, family, and her half-million social media followers, was a close friend of Princess Mary and beloved by the entire royal family. She is survived by her parents, her grandfather, Alastair Chesterfield-Bishop, the Earl of Brodrick, aunts Lady Susanne Nellsworth and Lady Julianne Humphrey, and her faithful companion, rescue dog Snickers.

The private funeral takes place today, and family has asked that in lieu of flowers, donations be made to Canine Chums Charity of Surrey.

—*The Daily Sun*, 13 September 2024

ROSIE'S FUNERAL IS HELD AT the church where she was christened, just outside of London. It's a beautiful building with stained glass windows and enough seating for hundreds, but every guest has already been ushered inside by the time our fleet of Range Rovers arrives.

There's a small but determined group of paparazzi in a roped-off section near the entrance to the church, and none of us—not even Thaddeus—glances their way as we all head inside. It's too much to hope for that they might be respectful, and instead they call out as we pass.

"Mary! Is it true? Were you fighting when she died?"

"Do you know what happened, Mary?"

"Helene, how do you feel knowing it could've been your daughter?"

"Christopher, is it true you two dated? Did it end badly?"

"Mary, will you miss your former best friend? Or are you glad she's gone?"

It's heinous, and I nearly break just to tell them to eat shit. But my arm is linked with Kit's, and I can feel the tension in his grip as we approach the entrance. If I break, so will he, and considering the way color floods his cheeks, he might have more than just a few choice words for them.

We all hold it together until the church doors close behind us, and only then do I hear my sister release a soft sob. Gia is beside her in an instant and holding her close, and the pair stand wrapped together as Maisie cries into her shoulder.

"They're waiting for us," says Helene after nearly a full minute, and she dabs her eyes with her handkerchief. "We shouldn't hold them up longer than we already have."

Gia helps Maisie fix her smeared mascara before we venture into the main body of the church, where a man and a woman stand at the foot of the aisle, waiting for us. They're both dressed in black, and while the tall man is older and washed out, with only a few wisps of hair left, the much younger woman resembles Rosie so closely that there's no mistaking them for anything other than mother and daughter.

“Your Majesty.” The woman curtsies to Helene, who quickly reaches out to take her elbows and guide her to rise.

“Not today, Lucy,” she says before embracing her. “I am so, so very sorry for your loss.”

“Th-thank . . .” Lucy’s voice hitches, and her eyes flutter shut as she clearly tries to compose herself. I turn away, hugging Kit’s arm and glancing around the crowded church instead. Every single pew is full, except for the first row, and my stomach drops. I don’t know what I expected—to hide in the back, maybe, and pay my respects from a distance—but sitting front row at Rosie’s funeral knowing I’m the reason she’s dead is a form of karmic punishment I wasn’t prepared for.

I force down the nausea, however, as we all offer our condolences to Lord and Lady Chesterfield-Bishop one by one. They greet me and Kit as warmly as they do Maisie and Helene, and I’m instantly aware that no one’s told them we were there that night, or about the series of events that led up to Rosie’s death. But we know—we all know—and even Kit seems to want to keep his distance as we follow everyone up to the front pew, within feet of the white casket that’s covered in pink roses. He trails Thaddeus to the very end of the row, next to a woman who’s holding Snickers in her lap.

“Hey, boy,” I say softly, scratching him behind his ear. He wags his tail morosely and, without hesitation, climbs into my lap instead. The woman looks vaguely relieved.

“You’ve got him, then?” she whispers, and I nod. “Good. Lady Lucy wanted to take him, but he gave her a sneezing fit, so I volunteered to come along and watch him. But I really don’t like dogs.”

"We've got him," confirms Kit in a low rumble as the priest—preacher?—bishop?—climbs to the pulpit at the front.

The funeral is long but beautiful, with her mother giving a tear-filled eulogy and several of Rosie's relatives and friends coming up to speak. Gia goes to the pulpit as well, regaling the audience with a few sweet stories from when the three of them were children, and later, as teens, that show how close they were. But it's when Maisie stands, her hands shaking and her face so pale I think she might faint, that a heavy hush falls over the crowd.

"Rosie . . ." Maisie clears her throat, but it does little to dislodge the sorrow from her voice. "Rosie was my best friend. Will always be my best friend. Her presence was a shining star, the kind that brought light to all who knew her, and we were incredibly lucky to have her for as long as we did. We just didn't know to cherish it at the time."

From my lap, Snickers barks, and Maisie's gaze snaps to me, her eyes welling with tears. "She deserved better," she says, seemingly barely able to get enough air into her lungs to speak. "From me, from the world—from . . . from everything life threw at us. She brought so much happiness to everyone who knew her, and yet all she wanted was to be loved in return. How hard is that?" Her voice cracks, and she hastily wipes her cheek. "How hard is it to love someone who's nothing but sunshine? It shouldn't be. Yet so many of you took her for granted. *I* took her for granted. I thought she would always be here, like the sunshine she was. But now it's midnight, and it feels like the sun might never rise again."

Snickers wiggles in my lap, and before I can stop him, he hops onto the ground and scurries up the steps to the dais. Maisie bends down and scoops him up, and she buries her damp face in his fur, seemingly unaware—or not caring—that she's crying in front of hundreds now.

"But—even on the darkest of days," she continues, her words trembling, "we remember the sun's warmth, and how it made us feel. We remember those happiest of times, and we look forward to the moment we meet again. And we will," she adds brokenly. "Rosie is as much a part of me as everyone I've ever loved and ever will love, and I will carry her with me—we will all carry her with us as a little bit of sunshine to remind us that night will not always be so dark, and that the morning will come again, in this life or the next. That's the gift Rosie gave us—to never fear what comes next. To live like the sun is shining on us, because she is, and she always will be."

When she steps down, Gia envelops her in her arms once more, with Snickers sandwiched between them. Their embrace lingers until the priest—preacher—officiate returns, and only then does Gia take Maisie's free hand and lead her back to the pew.

I know I shouldn't, but I can't help but glance at Thaddeus, who seems completely unperturbed by this public display of something more than friendship. After a split second, his gaze meets mine, and he offers me a lazy half smile.

"It's cool," he whispers, leaning in so only I can hear him. "I know she was never really into me. But we both got what we wanted, so no complaints."

I frown. "What did you . . . ?" I say so quietly that I practically mouth it.

Thaddeus's smile grows. "No matter what happens, I'll always get to say I dated the future Queen of England."

Despite the grief that weighs heavily over the room, I almost—*almost* laugh. I bite my cheek instead, and though Kit's fingers are already laced in mine, he shifts closer and presses a kiss to my hair, letting me know he also heard.

A Spice Girls song plays as the coffin is carried out by the pallbearers, two of whom are Kit and Nicholas, and it seems like an absurdly fitting way for Rosie to say her final goodbyes. But all I focus on is the way Maisie and Gia are locked together, seemingly caring for Snickers, but the touches between them, the way they look at each other, the words they whisper—it gives me hope that maybe, despite everything they've both been through, they really will have each other now. And maybe my sister will finally find some peace.

LATER THAT AFTERNOON, once we've all returned to Windsor, a subdued Jenkins leads us to the conference room on one of the upper floors, where Alexander and Singh are waiting. Half a dozen files are placed neatly around the table, and Kit, Maisie, Gia, and I all take our seats, each in front of a red folder. No one touches theirs.

"The Director General of MI5 has granted me permission to share these with you today," says Singh as I fiddle with Guy's puzzle. "*With* the understanding that the contents of these files are classified, and nothing here leaves this room. Is that clear?"

Maisie, who is still holding Snickers in her lap, bristles at being spoken to like she wasn't born with a silver spoon up her arse, but the rest of us—even my father, who sits at the head of the table—nod.

"I'll be sure to ring Belinda and thank her," he says as he picks up the first file and flicks through it. I tuck the puzzle into my pocket and do the same, laying the contents out on the table. They're documents pertaining to Rosie's death, including pictures of her townhouse, with police tape and evidence numbers everywhere. I quickly cover up the ones of her bloodstained bedroom carpet.

"What's the point of these?" says Gia, also flinching away from the first file and digging into the next. I discard it as well, picking another from the bottom of the pile instead. This one includes an incident report from the shooting at Sandringham, as well as stills from security footage and, most intriguingly, a roundup of Ben's whereabouts that day—and the twenty-four hours beforehand.

"Evangeline?" prompts Singh, and I clear my throat, setting the second file aside and opening a third. The Windsor fire.

"These are the incidents we think are connected to Ben, aren't they?" I say, and Singh nods.

"Heavily redacted in some cases, and I've spared you details you don't need to bother with. But yes," he adds. "These are all separate incidents that we believe Prince Benedict may have had a hand in."

Gia's eyes widen. "Including—wait, including Rosie's death?"

Maisie slips her hand into Gia's as I explain what happened that night, and why Kit and I are both convinced Ben had something to do with it. "But we don't have proof," I say, gesturing to the files. "That's the problem with all of this. We have enough theories to put Ben away for about a hundred lifetimes, and enough tenuous connections to not look completely delusional, but—"

"But there is no solid evidence connecting him to any of these crimes," says Singh. "And though Evangeline has been targeted several times by His Royal Highness, she does not know him well enough to guess the hows and whys of these crimes, including the connections he may have had to pull them off without dirtying his own hands."

"And that's why we're here?" says Maisie, still scratching Snickers. "To pool our knowledge?"

"Yes," I say, glancing sidelong at Kit. I expect him to look stricken, but while there's a furrow in his brow, he looks every bit as determined as I feel. "We can't trust anyone else. We know Ben is working with Dylan Baxter, and he was working with John Phillip Michaels—"

"The terrorist?" says Gia, her voice rising as she looks again to Maisie, who grimaces. "Wait, really?"

"Really," she mutters. "And we know Ben's responsible for setting the fire at Windsor, too. Or that he at least blackmailed Rosie and someone else into doing it for him."

Gia's mouth drops open, and the string of curses that escapes her is so delightfully vile that my respect for her triples.

"That would be this file," says Singh, opening the one on the Windsor fire. "And a solid place to start, considering we still haven't figured out who the other accomplice was. I've compiled a list of all staff members on duty during that time period, though of course you would all be the ones to ask for details."

I scan my copy of the names, but while I recognize some

of them, most are a mystery to me. "Were any of them cross-matched to the list of Fox Rex members we got from Oxford?" I say, and Singh shakes his head.

"An excellent theory, but no. No member of the palace staff was found on Michaels's list."

"Damn," I mutter. So much for making this easy.

"That doesn't mean His Royal Highness didn't have something on a member of staff he was able to use against them, however," adds Singh. "So please consider the possibilities carefully."

I scan it again. I recognize my housekeepers, a few of the footmen I joke around with when they're not being sticks in the mud, and of course the PPOs who follow us around constantly. But my depth of knowledge about what goes on in the castle when the royal family isn't around is shallower than a puddle on a sunny day, and I'm useless.

"Does anything stand out to you?" I say to Maisie, and though she still doesn't seem pleased that I have the audacity to speak to her, she does at least shuffle through her papers until she finds the document.

"The number of staff was limited then, because of the bombing," she says, dropping a kiss onto Snickers's head without her gaze wavering. "And it would've been someone who had access to the royal apartments, which also reduces the possibilities. There's Jenkins, of course—"

"He was at the hospital with Alexander," I say, shooting my father a look, as if he could possibly corroborate this.

"Naturally," says Alexander. "And I trust Jenkins with my life."

"Then there's Fitz," says Gia, glancing over Maisie's shoulder. "I always thought he was a weasel."

"Tibby thinks he's incompetent," I offer. "But I'm also pretty sure she thinks everyone is incompetent."

Maisie sniffs. "I like that he's incompetent. It gives me a reason to have a go at him. What?" she adds when I blink at her. "Mummy says I have to find a discreet way to express my less . . . gracious sentiments, and therapy is far too much of a risk. Could you imagine the stories they could sell if I actually told a therapist the truth?"

I roll my eyes. "We can put Fitz down as a 'maybe.' It's not Tibby."

"Oh?" says Maisie, eyebrow raised. "And how can you be so sure?"

"Because if she wanted to kill me, she could've done it about a hundred times by now. *And* made it look like Kit was responsible."

Kit sits up straighter. "Right. Remind me never to get on Tibby's bad side," he mumbles, raking his fingers through his hair. "I don't recognize many names on the list, but whoever it is, what we do know is that, between Rosie and Michaels, Ben is tying up loose ends. Whoever aided him with the fire will be targeted, and soon."

"Unless . . ." Maisie pauses, and both she and Snickers tilt their heads at exactly the same angle at exactly the same time. "Unless they already have been."

"What do you mean?" says Singh, immediately opening his laptop.

"My housekeeper's assistant," she says. "I think her name was . . . Molly? Polly? Dolly? No—here it is, Holly McIntyre. She was there that week, possibly even that day. I remember because she helped me clean up a broken vase. But I didn't see her after we got back from Balmoral, and my housekeeper told me it was because Dolly—Holly was in a car accident. Her brakes were tampered with by an ex, supposedly, and she had a spinal injury, so she couldn't work anymore. I had Fitz send flowers, of course, but I didn't think anything of it at the time. Except that men are terrible and don't deserve women, naturally."

Singh types a quick note into his computer. "I'll look into it immediately. There may be CCTV footage of the accident, or even the tampering, if they weren't careful."

"What about footage from the morning Rosie died?" I blurt, and everyone turns to look at me—even Singh, fingers still poised above the keyboard. "She went for a jog around the park with Snickers, and she thought she was being followed. I know the CCTV footage from that night was a bust, but maybe—"

"I'll make it a priority," says Singh. "I believe someone from my team spoke to her after the incident, but concluded there wasn't a threat at the time."

"We called in an independent security team to help," says Kit, and he pulls out his mobile. "I've got the number here. They ought to be able to give you further details."

"And Victor Stephens spoke to her, too," I say, gripping the document so hard I wrinkle the page. "He might know something."

"On it," promises Singh, and he looks around the room again. "This should be enough to keep me busy for now. Look through these files as soon as you can, and if anything comes up—I mean anything at all—contact me directly, day or night."

"Thank you, Agent Singh," says Alexander. He rises slowly,

and they exchange a firm handshake. "The moment you have any news, please let Jenkins know. While the last thing we want is to implicate a member of our own family—"

"The last thing we want," corrects Maisie, "is for a member of this family to try to kill the rest of us."

Alexander's grim smile falters. "I will not allow it to happen again. Is that understood?" he says to Singh. "No matter what it takes, I will protect my family at all costs."

"Understood," says Singh, and he offers me a small nod before gathering his laptop and hurrying out the door, leaving us to pore over the files in search of a spark that might, for once, start a fire we control.

CHAPTER TWENTY-SIX

SINGH: I apologise, I know it's early, but I just got off the phone with your father, and I wanted you to know that you were right. The individual following Rosie in Hyde Park was Dylan Baxter.

EVANGELINE: What? How did you—

SINGH: His face was hidden, but we traced him back to a flatshare in Hackney and raided it a few hours ago. It was definitely Baxter, and we found receipts and other significant evidence that we believe will tie him to Rosie's death once toxicology comes back.

EVANGELINE: But you didn't find him.

SINGH: No. We didn't find him.

—Phone call between Agent Suraj Singh and
Evangeline Bright, 6:18 a.m., 14 September 2024

KIT AND I ARE ALREADY awake, showered, and dressed when Tibby arrives at seven o'clock that morning, yet she doesn't seem at all surprised to see us sitting at the dining table, both of us in foul moods.

"I take it Singh told you," she says, and I nod once as I stab at a piece of pear with my fork.

"He apparently hasn't been back there since the night he

murdered Rosie," I mutter as the pear slips away, nearly sliding right off my plate. "He could be anywhere by now."

"Out of the country if he's smart," says Kit grimly. "Which unfortunately he is."

"They should have his picture everywhere," I say, furiously chasing the piece of fruit around the plate. It manages to slip away each time, and I curse. Loudly.

Tibby pointedly picks up my knife and spears the pear for me, then hands me the utensil without a word. "It seems your father has thoughts on this development as well, as His Majesty has called a mandatory family meeting later this morning. I've already adjusted your schedule. In the meantime," she adds, "are you planning on eating your breakfast or torturing it? Because if you're feeling particularly violent, I can arrange for the PPOs to help you work out some of that aggression."

I nibble the piece of pear Tibby subdued for me. Kit and I haven't worked with a PPO on self-defense since Ingrid died in the bombing, and while there's a fair chance Tibby might be kidding, that's actually not a bad idea. "I could get sweaty," I say, glancing down at my T-shirt and leggings. "Do you think they'd teach me how to punch without breaking my hand?"

Tibby snorts. "If you can manage to reach their chins with your tiny Tyrannosaurus rex arms, I'm sure they'd be delighted. Kit?"

"Always happy to watch Evan try to hit things," he says, sipping his coffee. "Any idea what this meeting is about?"

"Haven't a clue," says Tibby, already tapping her phone screen. "But whatever it is, I'm certain you two won't be the only ones with a temper."

* * *

A PAIR OF PPOs spend the next three hours walking Kit and me through some practical self-defense moves, mine in particular tailored to my height. It's exhausting, sweaty work, exactly like I'd hoped, and by the time Tibby calls an end to our impromptu seminar, my limbs are wet noodles and I desperately need a nap. But we have just enough time to shower and change again before Tibby escorts us to the white drawing room, and I pause in the doorway, frowning when I see who's gathered near the roaring fireplace.

Alexander and my mother, of course, along with Maisie, Helene, and Nicholas. But Venetia, Duchess of York, is also there, standing opposite Alexander, her head held high and her expression set like she's expecting a fight. Has someone told her what her son has been up to? Has Ben himself already poisoned the well and made sure that his mother believes his lies?

Holding Kit's hand, I move gingerly to an empty sofa near the edge of the gathering, not sure what to expect. My father is standing despite the clear effort it takes, his hands shaking slightly as he leans on his cane. But while his body may be weak, the look on his face is anything but.

"Does Benedict no longer consider himself part of this family?" he says to Venetia, and she crosses her arms, her posture stiff.

"I told him to stay away. With all the false accusations against him, I don't trust any of you to treat him like your blood," she says, and it's the most serious—and venomous—I've ever heard her sound. Ben has definitely been lying to her.

"False accusations?" counters Alexander. "Such as?"

Silence settles over the group, and Venetia shifts her stance awkwardly. "Accusations about—well, I certainly won't give you any ideas," she blusters. "But I do know you haven't treated my Ben fairly since the incident with Evangeline, even though he's bent over backward to apologize and ask for forgiveness, and I refuse to stand by and let this family continue to bully him for what was, admittedly, a lack of good grace, but is hardly treason."

"Funny you should say that," says Alexander as I bite the inside of my cheek to stop myself from objecting to Ben's audacity. "I take it you heard about the fire at Windsor that nearly killed my daughter."

Venetia's reproachful gaze shifts to Maisie for a split second. "I sent a bouquet and a get-well-soon note, of course. And I am very glad that you've recovered so well, my darling."

Maisie tilts her head in the slightest of acknowledgments, and it's only then that I notice how tense she is. Not just stiff, like Venetia, but almost like every muscle in her body is tight enough to snap at the slightest touch.

"What would you say," says Alexander, "if I told you that we have considerable evidence that Benedict was the one to arrange the fire?"

Venetia scoffs. There isn't even a moment, a beat when she considers it or processes the possibility—she simply rejects it. "I would say you were unconscious and have no way of knowing what happened, but even if you weren't, Your Majesty, my son was with me in Italy the entire time. There's no way he could have set the fire."

"I didn't say he set it," says Alexander. "I said that he arranged for it to be done."

She raises her chin another inch. "Ridiculous. He would never—"

"The evidence says otherwise."

"What evidence?" she snaps. "Footage? A recorded conversation?"

"Testimony from the two people he blackmailed to do it for him," says Alexander, and rather than the stunned silence I expect, Venetia starts to laugh.

"You have the word of two people, both of whom you could've easily paid off or influenced in any number of ways," she says, shaking her head. "That isn't evidence, Your Majesty. That's just another way to accuse my son of things he would never do."

Alexander takes a steadying breath, and though I can see his legs shake, he doesn't move to sit down. "Your son is likely connected to the ABR," he says bluntly, "and MI5 is investigating him for potential involvement in the deaths of John Phillip Michaels and Primrose Chesterfield-Bishop, both of whom he had regular contact with."

"I see," says Venetia, her perfectly lined eyes narrowing. "So now you're accusing my son of breaking into a prison and making a terrorist hang himself, are you? And that girl—he's told me about her, that they remained good friends after their breakup. Why would he have any reason to hurt her?"

"He released graphic photographs of her on the internet the day she was murdered," says Alexander plainly. "Photos he took. Photos he was in."

"If he was in them, then why would he release them? Wouldn't the connection be obvious?" she snaps back. "Give my Ben some credit, at the very least. And Nicky—" She looks at her ex-husband, who sits beside Helene with his hands clasped between his knees and his gaze fixed on the fire. "Are you going to say nothing to defend your own son?"

"I've seen the evidence, Vee," says Nicholas wearily. "I tried to deny it, too, but there's nothing we can do for him now except try to stop him from ruining the rest of his life."

"We are also certain that he gave the shooter insider information on our security at Sandringham the morning Evangeline and Kit were shot," continues Alexander. "He knew where they would be—"

"How?" cries Venetia. "How could he have known any of that? I *refuse* to believe that my son, my twenty-year-old son, who is the funniest, sweetest, most giving person I've ever known, could be capable of *any* of these terrible things, let alone all of them."

"We don't always know a person—" begins Helene, but Venetia turns to her so quickly that she nearly trips over her own stiletto heels.

"No, we don't," she says nastily. "Especially our best friends. I know what this is really about. The same sordid secret you've always kept hidden, isn't it? Does Ben know? Is that why you've done this to him? To discredit him? To make sure he can never tell, even though he already knows what's at stake?"

I blink and glance at Kit, but he looks as confused as I am. Helene shakes her head.

"Venetia, this has nothing to do with—"

"Because I've kept your secret for you," she snarls. "For years, I haven't said a word to anyone, or even so much as hinted. I could've made millions off of it, you know. I could've gone down in history. But I've honored my side of the bargain, and this is the thanks I get?"

Nicholas rises to his feet. "Vee, Helene is telling the truth. This has nothing to do with that and everything to do with more than a year of mounting evidence—"

"Evidence *you* can't show me!" Venetia stomps her heel into the patterned rug, and Maisie flinches, curling into herself. "Everyone in this room knows Nicholas should be the rightful heir to the throne, and that my son should be next. But you insist on this—this *farce,* this *insult* to every monarch that's come before you—"

Maisie flies to her feet, and before anyone can try to stop her, she sprints out of the room, two red splotches on her cheeks and her blue eyes overflowing with tears. I give Kit another look, beyond confused now. But his focus darts between Venetia, Alexander, and Helene and Nicholas, and I can practically see him working out some kind of puzzle in his head.

"Enough," says Alexander in a quiet, deadly voice. "How I choose to conduct my family's business is none of yours."

"Of course it is, when it's my family, too," insists Venetia, her volume only rising. "I've given up *everything*—"

"And been highly compensated for it," says Alexander in that same lethal tone. "Is that what this is about? Money?"

Venetia grits her teeth. "This is about *honesty* and *integrity,* and the lies you've built your entire reign upon. If you continue to target my son, then let me make myself perfectly clear—your secrets will no longer be safe with me. I don't care what it costs me," she adds with the kind of defiant bravado that makes it clear she definitely does. "Maybe it's finally time that everyone knows what this family has really been up to."

With that, she pivots toward the door opposite the one Maisie fled through and walks away, her head held comically high and her back painfully arched. We all watch her go in silence, and it's only once a footman closes the door behind her that Helene breaks.

"Alexander . . ." Her voice is thick with unshed tears, and she and Nicholas are both on their feet now.

"I'll take care of it," he says heavily, finally sinking down onto the nearest ottoman with my mother's gentle help. His entire body is trembling, and I stand, like there's something I can do about it. Like there's something I can do about any of this when I have no clue what's going on.

Except as Helene and Nicholas hurry to follow Maisie, I glance at Kit once more, and the look he's giving me—the wide-eyed, shell-shocked expression of someone whose entire world has just been rocked—makes me pause, and Venetia's words finally brand my brain like hot steel.

Everyone in this room knows Nicholas should be the rightful heir to the throne, and that my son should be next.

But that would mean skipping over Maisie, which doesn't make sense. Does Venetia think that Alexander should've never been king? Because he went to the United States to live with my mother when they were younger? Because he wasn't there the day his father died? Because he intended on abdicating and changed his mind? Or—

Her threats to tell the world. The way Maisie flinched and curled up into herself, like Venetia was about to beat the royal titles right out of her. The tension in my sister's body, as if she knew what this was all about from the very start.

Because she *did* know. She knew the moment Venetia showed up without Ben—she had to.

Which means this has everything to do with Maisie. And if Venetia's implying that Maisie isn't the rightful heir, and Maisie can't even bring herself to deny it . . .

In one roaring instant, everything snaps into place. The pieces of a puzzle so inconceivable that I've never even considered it before. A possibility so absurd that only Ben would think to test those boundaries and see if they break. But unlike our accusations against him, all the evidence is there, circumstantial and otherwise.

Maisie isn't Alexander's biological daughter. She's Nicholas's.

Holy shit.

Holy *shit.*

Holy shit.

It's my turn to gape at my father, and to my surprise, he's staring at me in return. "Is Venetia right?" I say, my mouth dry and my tongue oddly clumsy. "Is Maisie really . . . ?"

"Maisie is of royal blood," says Alexander firmly. "Just as you are."

"But I'm not the next Queen of England," I say. "I mean, don't get me wrong, I really don't care about legitimacy or succession or any of that, but—" But Maisie does. And royal blood doesn't matter when it's from the wrong person. "Does she know?"

"Yes," he says, and he takes my mom's hand, folding it in his. "It was a condition of the agreement Helene, Nicholas, your mother, and I made at the start."

"That you would—you would raise his kid?" I say, and the room starts to spin. I sit down again next to Kit, who still looks as wild-eyed as I feel. "Wait—is that why you didn't divorce Helene? Is that why you didn't abdicate and stay with my mom and—and is that why you weren't there for me?"

The questions land with a resounding thud, as if I've dropped a boulder in the gilded splendor of the white drawing room, and suddenly everything is quiet. Even the crackling of the fire seems to be muted, and my father's grip on my mom's hand tightens. "I—"

"It was a choice we all made," says my mother as Alexander swallows hard and stares at his feet. "And no one is pretending it was easy, Evie."

"Seems pretty easy to me," I say, my insides churning like someone's poured lava down my throat. "Alexander could've left and had us. You two could've been together, he could've been my dad—my *real* dad—but instead he chose to stay in a job he hated and raise his brother's daughter with a woman he didn't even love, all because—what, because that's what he was supposed to do? Because he didn't want to embarrass himself or admit that his wife cheated on him?"

"Because I didn't want to ruin Maisie's life before it had begun," says Alexander, and my vision distorts from a potent mixture of hurt and fury.

"What about *my* life?" I say, my voice ragged. "What about Maisie, sure, but what about *me*? Did you even remotely consider what my life would be like without you? Or has Maisie always been more important, just because she's Maisie?"

Alexander shakes his head, his face splotched with red. "You—

at the time, you had your mother and grandmother. And if Helene, Nicholas, and I had gone public with the truth about Maisie, or even part of the truth . . . Helene wasn't willing to hide the pregnancy, not when she knew I would never put her through the humiliation of admitting that the baby wasn't mine. We simply had no real choice."

"Of course you had a choice," I snap, and a surge of grief and spite I don't expect rise within me, nearly choking off my words. "You had a choice, and you chose Maisie and Helene and—*this.* And you left me and my mom alone."

"Evie—" says my mother, reaching for me, but I pull away before she can even get close.

"Don't," I say, hot tears running down my face. "You let him go. You *let him go,* even though it meant I wouldn't have a dad, and we would be alone. And when everything fell apart—when—when you got sick—"

My throat closes, and I can't finish, but I don't need to. We all know what happened next. When my mom got sick and lost custody of me, I had no one but my grandma. And when my grandma died, I had no one at all. The entire time, I could've had someone—I could've had a father, a *family,* and my mom wouldn't have felt like she had to send me away to boarding school. I would've had something solid, something real, something *permanent* instead of a desperate yearning I kept locked away and refused to acknowledge out of the fear that it would only make the pain worse.

I could've felt loved. I could've felt *safe,* and like I really belonged somewhere, to someone. But instead I spent my entire childhood and teenage years in a constant state of uncertainty and fear of ever getting too close to anyone, knowing damn well that if I did, they would disappear soon enough.

People aren't permanent. Or they weren't, before Kit. Before London. Before my father. But even he didn't want to be my dad, despite the fact that all he had in England was a family that wasn't his and a life he didn't want. It doesn't matter that he loves my mom more than anything. He didn't love *me* enough. He didn't want *me* enough. And somehow, knowing that he could've been there—that it was his choice all along, and he'd chosen to stay in England—it hurts so much more than when I thought I was nothing to him at all.

"I didn't let him go," says my mom, stepping toward me slowly, her hand hovering halfway between us, like she knows I'll bolt if she tries to touch me. "We stayed together for as long as we could, sweetheart. And if I hadn't gotten sick—"

"But you did," I say brokenly, forcing the words past the knot in my throat, and I refocus on Alexander. "And *you* still weren't there."

"Because Betty, your grandmother—" he begins, but I've already heard his excuses.

"I don't care. I would've done *anything* to be there for either of you no matter what my grandma said. You made that choice. Before, I could understand, since you had Maisie here and couldn't exactly walk away. But now . . ." I shake my head. He still couldn't have walked away, not when the entire world thought Maisie was his. But he could've done *something* instead of ignoring me all those years, and I wipe my cheeks, furious and spiraling as everything I thought was solid turns to smoke, giving me nothing to hold on to anymore.

"Ev . . ." Kit brushes his fingers against my elbow in a gentle question. I don't pull away, even though my skin crawls at the thought of being touched right now. But it's Kit. Even if I can count on no one else, at least I can count on him.

"Can we go?" I say, my eyes welling up again, and the look he gives me is so full of pity that I want the earth to swallow me whole.

"Of course," he says, and he wraps an arm around my shoulders and leads me toward the door. My mom and Alexander say nothing, and I'm grateful. This isn't something a few apologies and excuses will fix. The foundation of my entire life has shattered, and I have no idea how to put the pieces back together—or if I'll ever be able to trust either of them again.

CHAPTER TWENTY-SEVEN

Over the past twenty-four hours, we've received an uptick in anonymous tips in regards to a particularly juicy—and flat-out treasonous—rumour that's been making the royal rounds for nearly two decades. And while we always make sure to vet our sources before sharing anything substantial, there's simply too much smoke to ignore.

Before we announce anything that might be considered treason ourselves, we ask you to examine a few facts we know are true, straight from the royal family themselves:

The former Queen Helene and the Duke of York have admitted to having had an affair for nearly a year now, likely longer. Photographic evidence of how close they've been over the years is below, but of course we cannot claim to know what goes on behind palace doors.

We know that His Majesty was having an affair with Laura Bright in 2004, when Evangeline was conceived. At the same time, Princess Mary was also conceived, and the pair were born on the same day: 1 July 2005.

Her former Majesty also admitted that His Majesty was, at the time the dual pregnancies were discovered, planning on leaving her and abdicating the throne to his younger brother, which indicates that a significant breakdown of their marriage had already occurred, and it's unlikely they were still . . . maritally engaged.

One must wonder, then, if there might be any truth to the vicious whispers between courtiers and throughout the aristocracy that perhaps Princess Mary is not His Majesty's daughter after all. We have even received a copy of a supposed DNA test that claims to prove this, which is included in the gallery below, though we ask our readers to keep in mind that the source is, as of yet, unverified.

Still, could it be true? Could our sweet princess be—gulp—*illegitimate?*

—*The Regal Record*, 16 September 2024

I KEEP TO MYSELF FOR the next two days, refusing to leave our bedroom, let alone the apartment.

Kit chases everyone away—including my parents, who visit every few hours in an attempt to convince me to talk to them. Tibby is banished to the sitting room, where she mostly works on our upcoming appearance schedule and digitally organizes my wardrobe, according to Kit. And I huddle under a quilt in bed with Poppy, my eyes locked on my laptop as I read every single article I can find about Maisie's life.

I read every birth announcement, every milestone, every birthday post, every article about her achievements—her first days of homeschooling, her awards for horse-related things I don't understand, her first public appearances, Christmas cards, every time she's ever been present on the balcony for Trooping the Colour and other important events. Each time she's been a tiny bridesmaid at a wedding for one of her million godparents. Snapshots shared from Balmoral and Sandringham and other family holidays. Paparazzi photos of her when she's older, the walk to church Christmas morning, boating adventures that seem to universally make her look like a windswept model. I dig so deeply through multiple search engines that eventually I only find duplicates, and then I start using keywords on different social media sites to see if I can find more.

I read about every moment of my sister's life that only happened because Alexander chose her instead. Every glimpse of the comfort and emotional safety she had that I didn't. It isn't just jealousy that eats away at me—it's longing and self-pity and a deep, primal need to be loved that has never fully been sated.

But I don't hate her for it. I don't even stop thinking of her as my sister, because she is. The choices our parents made aren't her fault, and I can't bring myself to hold them against her, even though I know she's held plenty of things against me.

"I don't know how to go out there and face them," I admit to Kit two days after the family meeting that sent shock waves through both our lives. "How am I supposed to ever believe a word Alexander says now? How am I supposed to even look him in the eye?"

We're sitting up in bed with our empty breakfast trays at our feet, a paperback in his hands while I'm a hundred posts into a blog devoted exclusively to Maisie's fashion choices over the years. He slips a bookmark between the pages and turns toward me, giving me his full attention in a way I'm not sure I deserve after two full days of wallowing.

"Alexander knows he needs to earn back your trust," he says, tucking a wayward lock of hair behind my ear. "And I'm certain he's willing. Just because things aren't okay right away doesn't mean they won't be in time."

"Easy for you to say," I grumble. "You don't have to deal with them anymore if you don't want to."

"With any luck, I'll be *dealing* with your parents for a very long time," he says with a faint smile. "Eventually it might help to speak with them. Not right away, but . . . when you're ready."

"I don't know if I'll ever be ready to talk about why he didn't love me or want me enough to be my real dad," I mutter, leaning into Kit. "Even if he really did let my grandma bully him into staying away from me after my mom got sick, that hurts, too, you know? You think your parents will do anything to keep you safe and be with you—"

"And if those two things are incompatible?" says Kit gently. I frown.

"What do you mean?"

"If keeping you safe and being with you were two parts of a Venn diagram that couldn't touch."

I sigh. This is exactly the argument Alexander made to me during our first heart-to-heart—that being there for me the way I needed him to be would've put me in danger, simply by exposing my existence to the press. "But it happened anyway. Everyone still knows who I am."

"Now that you're an adult, yes," agrees Kit. "Imagine this level of fame and interest when you were four years old, while your mother was severely ill and going through the legal process. Imagine the amount of worldwide attention that would have attracted, and how that would have changed everything for you."

If Alexander or even my mother had asked me to think this scenario through, I would've refused out of sheer spite. But because it's Kit, I let myself sink into the daydream that, moment by moment, looks more and more like a nightmare instead.

Paparazzi shouting at four-year-old me. Hunting us down at my grandma's condo. Surrounding my mother's house, even though it was undoubtedly empty for the years she was going through inpatient treatment. Harassing her doctors, the nurses, the staff—anything to find out a morsel of information. Blackmailing them. Paying them off for clues. Not allowing my mom the opportunity to heal in peace and privacy. Not giving Alexander the chance to visit her every weekend, like he did the whole time.

It would have changed everything. I would've been a completely different person—maybe still hidden away at boarding schools to protect my privacy, but that would've only lasted for so long. And it wouldn't have just been my bad behavior that forced me to switch schools so often. I would've been hunted, even though I was still a kid. I would've been known as the King's bastard daughter my entire life, and by now, at the age of nineteen, I would've never given him a chance to explain himself. Ever.

"Things would've been worse," I finally admit. "A lot worse."

Kit nods. "I think so, too."

"But . . ." I rub my face, pressing my palms into my eyes. "All he had to do was choose me and my mom instead of Maisie and Helene. Nicholas could've married Helene, and Maisie could've been born legitimate, and no one could've stopped them. And everything would've been the same."

Kit studies me for a long moment. "Is that what you really think?"

"Yes," I say, determined now, but after another beat, I huff. "Okay, it would've been a rough few months, maybe a year—"

"Even the most loyal of royalists would've lost their bloody minds at the thought of Alexander abdicating, divorcing his pregnant wife, and his brother stepping in to take his place," says

Kit. "They would've had to go public with the affair in order to legitimize Maisie, and that alone would've done more damage to the monarchy than—well, anything any monarch has ever done, I suppose. Kings have been beheaded for less."

"It's not the seventeenth century anymore."

"No, it isn't," he agrees. "And we know now what some people are willing to do in order to see the monarchy abolished. Nicholas, Helene, and Maisie—that mess would've been more than enough for people like Dylan and John Phillip Michaels to get the following they needed to see their so-called revolution through."

I'm quiet for a long moment, my fingers dancing silently over the smooth keys of my laptop. "So you're saying that Alexander sacrificed his relationship with me in order to save the monarchy," I say finally. "Because that isn't helping."

Kit shrugs. "I'm saying we won't know until you're ready to talk to them. But there's a pretty good chance there was much more at stake than either of us realizes."

I grit my teeth and ease my laptop closed. He's not wrong, and while I'm not mad at him for it, I'm mad at the situation for being nuanced. I want to be angry. I *am* angry, and no matter how many facets there are, I have every right to be. But I also love Alexander more than I ever thought I could, and I love my mother with blind faith. If she thought it was a good idea, or at least the only workable option, then there's a possibility—a small possibility, but one that still exists—that she was right.

"I'll consider talking to them," I finally mumble, sinking down onto the pillows and giving a sleeping Poppy a scratch behind her ear. It's late morning now, but I haven't even showered yet, let alone changed out of my pajamas. There's no point, not when I have no intention of leaving the bedroom today.

Kit kisses my cheek. "Thank you," he says. "Only when you're ready, though, all right? There's no pressure—"

A muted knock sounds from the other room, and he and I both pause. "I thought Tibby was meeting with Louis until lunch," I say.

"And your father has his doctor appointment right around now, too," he says, glancing at his watch. "Maybe it's tea."

Either way, I'm not interested, and as he rolls out of bed and heads into the other room to answer the door, I cocoon myself and Poppy in the quilt again, closing my eyes and trying to picture what my life would've been like if Alexander had been there for all of it. I think I would've been happy. I would've known I was loved. But what would the rest of it have looked like? Would we have had any privacy at all? Or would the paparazzi have followed Alexander to Virginia, always fascinated with the King who gave up his crown for love?

". . . want to speak with her," says a haughty, all-too-familiar voice from the sitting room, and I sit up again, the blanket falling to my shoulders.

"She's not up for visitors right now, Mais," says Kit, sounding exasperated. "It's not my decision—"

"If *I'm* ready to talk, then she certainly ought to be," says Maisie, and I can practically see her tossing her strawberry-blond hair over her shoulder. No wonder she's so damn beautiful, with both Helene's and Nicholas's genes working together. Not that

Alexander is a troll, but between the brothers, Nicholas definitely won the genetic lottery.

I roll out of bed without thinking and, with the quilt still wrapped around my shoulders, I plod to the door and open it, revealing my sister and Kit standing nose-to-nose in the sitting room. She's dressed in a pale blue jumper and gray trousers, and her makeup is impeccable despite the obvious emotional blow she's been dealt.

"It's okay," I say to Kit. "We can talk, Maisie. If you really want to."

"Of course I want to," she says, giving Kit a victorious look. "I brought tea, too. A special brew from India. It's supposed to help with nerves."

I raise an eyebrow as a footman enters with a tray and a teapot, and he sets both down on the dining table. As soon as he leaves, Maisie gives Kit another pointed look, and he clears his throat.

"I suppose I ought to . . . make sure the rest of the castle is still standing," he says, and he gives me a quick kiss before ducking into the main corridor. Maisie closes and locks the door behind him, and I sink into a chair at the dining table.

"Special tea?" I say, eyeing the pot. "Please don't tell me you've picked up a drug habit in the past few days. It would explain why you're so—*calm* about all this, but still—"

"And give the press the opportunity to make a terrible 'Her Royal Highness' pun? Never," she says with a scoff, as if I've mortally offended her. She takes a seat near me and pours the tea for both of us, and it smells like cinnamon, cloves, and something nutty. "We need to talk."

"Obviously," I say, wrapping my hand around my cup and blowing on the hot liquid. "Has Alexander tried to speak to you?"

"Yes," she says. "And he told me that you . . . know now. About everything."

She says this in a flatly neutral tone, and I study her, looking for cracks in her imperious facade. "Yeah, it was sort of obvious once I had a minute to think," I admit. "Kit knows, too."

"I'm surprised he didn't figure it out years ago," she says, like we're discussing nothing more scandalous than the weather. "Daddy trusts you, of course, but I'm here to make a deal."

"A deal? What kind of deal?"

She eyes me over the table, her nails tapping against the polished wood. "That's up to you, I suppose. What do you want for your silence?"

My stomach turns, and I pull the quilt tighter around me, flashing back to the moment I realized she was the one who had pushed Jasper Cunningham to his death. She'd tried to buy my silence then, too, but that was before we knew each other. Before we trusted each other.

"Maisie, I'm not going to—listen, I know you're in a shitty position, but that's because of Venetia and Ben, not me—"

"It's only a matter of time," she says with a shrug that's painfully impersonal. "So let's head that off at the pass, shall we? Or is that what you want? An unnamed favor in the future? Because I suppose I could agree to that. Either way, I'd rather not have you or anyone else holding this over my head for the rest of my life, so if you wouldn't mind doing me the courtesy of naming your price—"

"Maisie. *Maisie.*" I have to say her name twice to get her to stop speaking. "I'm not going to blackmail you. I don't care who your mother slept with, all right? Whatever happened back then is none of my business, and I won't say a word to anyone. You're still my sister, and I'd never do that to you."

She stares at me. "But we're not sisters," she says, and it's not a protest. Just a fact. "We're cousins. Alexander and Nicholas are brothers—"

"I don't care. Alexander raised you as his daughter, and that makes you my sister, okay? That's it. End of story. Unless you don't think of me as yours."

"Of course I think of you as my—" She stops herself suddenly, and to my surprise, her blue eyes fill with unshed tears. "Evan. Evangeline. Maybe you don't realize the seriousness of the situation at hand—"

"I get what this means for you and the country." But I've been so buried in my own misery that I really *haven't* thought much about how heart-wrenching this must be for her, and how traumatic it must be having to live with this, especially considering her role as the future queen. "How long have you known?"

Maisie dabs her overflowing eyes with a cloth napkin. "Since I was eight. Mummy, Daddy, and Uncle Nicholas sat me down one day and told me that, while Daddy was of course my father and always would be, Nicholas was my biological . . ." She shakes her head again, as if she can't even bring herself to say it. "I didn't understand at first. I was so young that I didn't even know how babies were made. I just . . . thought it meant I had done something wrong, I suppose."

I take a deep breath and release it slowly. Eight years old. "That's really damn young to have your entire world blown to pieces," I say, and she laughs humorlessly.

"Yes, well. You were four." She looks at me, and for a moment, there's warmth between us for the first time since January.

"How did Ben . . ." I hesitate. "How did he find out?"

She swallows and reaches for her tea, then pulls her hand back into her lap to fiddle with the cuff of her sweater. "I don't know. Daddy thought I'd told him when we were kids. We were like brother and sister then. We *were* . . ." She pauses, grimacing. "But I never said a word. I somehow understood how important it was to keep our secret, even from Benny, and the shame I felt . . . well, we didn't have that kind of relationship, did we? Even then, I knew something was off. He didn't make me feel safe, and I would've never trusted him with anything that made me so vulnerable."

"So . . . Venetia?" I guess, and she nods, dabbing her eyes again.

"It's likely. Unless he overheard something. Mummy and Nicholas aren't always discreet, after all. And the DNA test the *Regal Record* posted—"

"The what?" I say, stunned, and half my body twists toward the bedroom Kit and I share, as if I can reach my laptop from here. "A DNA test?"

Maisie nods, and she gives up on dabbing now, wiping angrily at the tears dripping down her cheeks. "I found it last year, when we were searching Ben's room for the laptop. It was in the—"

"The manila envelope," I interrupt, my eyes widening. I can picture it in my head—the large yellow envelope concealed beneath the decades-old adult magazines that Ben had hidden inside his wardrobe. I hadn't thought much about it at the time, but clearly I should've been paying attention.

"The manila envelope," she echoes quietly in confirmation. "That's when I realized he knew. It was a copy, not the original, and it's old—from around the time we were born. It must have been . . . to confirm that I was . . ."

Again she doesn't finish, and I exhale. Of course Ben would've dug something like that up. "Alexander knows all of this now, too?"

She nods, her leaking eyes still on the untouched tea. "I knew Ben would use it against me somehow, but I never thought he'd go this far. It's sadistic. It's *cruel.*"

"It's disgusting." And exactly the kind of thing I wouldn't put past Ben. "The *Regal Record* is just a gossip site, Mais. No one knows Ben runs it except for us. The palace can deny and discredit the accusations, and the entire country loves you—no one's going to give it a second thought."

"Of course they will," she says, her nose growing stuffy as the tears flow freely down her face now. "They were ready to believe the worst in you."

"But I didn't grow up in front of them," I argue. "No matter what supposed evidence the *Regal Record* posts, it will *never* add up to the word of the royal family, okay? Alexander loves you. He won't let Ben win this one."

The words cut me to ribbons, but while they've been my own personal hell these past two days, Maisie gives me a look so blatantly hopeful that it's instantly worth the agony. "Do you really think so?" she says, her voice catching. "Because all I can think about is—is that it's out there now. Eventually everyone will know, and—and they'll hate me."

"It won't come to that," I say, because it's the only thing that sounds like the truth anymore. "Alexander chose you, and he'll do anything to make sure that doesn't happen."

She gives me an odd look. "What do you mean, he chose me?"

I shake my head, trying to stave off the return of my pity party of one. "It doesn't matter. I just mean—he chose to be your father, and he'll do anything to keep you safe. All of this—everything our parents went through, it was all because of how much they love you. Don't you see that? Alexander kept his crown to protect you. Helene and Nicholas stayed apart so you could be raised as the legitimate heir to the throne."

"And you didn't have Alexander because he was too busy being my father to have time to be yours," she finishes, her tone slightly strained now.

"That's not what I—that's not the point," I say as firmly as I can. "The point is, you are so damn loved, Maisie, and the entire family—the entire *palace,* and most of the country is going to fight for you. No one's going to let Ben win over some easily forged piece of paper. You have everyone you need on your side, including me, okay?"

Maisie lets out another soft scoff. "You can't help. No one can undo this, and when everything grows to a fever pitch and they demand another DNA test—"

"Then that's what we'll give them," I say, because she's wrong. There is a way I can help. "I'll give them my blood, and we'll pretend it's yours. As long as they don't test it against Helene's, it'll show that you're Alexander's biological daughter."

Maisie stares at me as if she hasn't heard me right, and I settle back in my chair, cradling my still-hot teacup to my chest.

"You'd do that for me?" she says, stunned. "Even though I've been awful to you?"

"Only some of the time," I say with a shrug. "The rest of the time, you're not so bad. And either way, you're still my sister."

A fresh sob escapes Maisie, and she buries her face in her hands. "But—Ben will figure it out—he'll know what we did—"

"So what? Let him shout about it from the rooftops. Maybe a few people will have their conspiracy theories, but you're the one who told me that there are corners of the internet that claim you were switched at birth." I raise my teacup near my lips. "There are always going to be rumors, but we can do our best to make this one look ridicu—"

"Stop!"

Maisie's hand flies out, slapping the teacup out of mine before I can register what's happening. Hot liquid flies everywhere, but thankfully it's been long enough that when some of it lands on my neck, it doesn't scald my skin.

"*Maisie!* What the hell—" I begin, but she's already grabbing the partially sodden napkin she's been using as a tissue and wipes away the spill on my neck.

"Did it get anywhere else?" she says urgently, and I stare at her, bewildered.

"I don't think so. What's going on?" I say, following her lead and mopping up the remaining droplets with a fresh napkin, then arranging the quilt on the floor to absorb the rest of the spill.

Only then, my heart still pounding, do I take a good look

at Maisie. Her face is bloodless, and her hands are trembling so badly that she isn't even trying to hide it. A sick shade of green tinges her skin, and I scoot back in my seat, trying to avoid the potential splash zone.

"I'm sorry," she gasps, as if she can't get enough air into her lungs. "Evan, I'm so bloody sorry. Ben—he said if I didn't—he gave me twenty-four hours, and—if I didn't, he would tell everyone, and—and I didn't know—I can't sleep—I didn't think there was another way—and I thought—I thought you wouldn't try it, because of what—of what Jasper did, and I thought I'd tell him I tried, and maybe that would buy me some time, but—"

Maisie breaks down into full-body sobs, her shoulders shaking and her skin now blotchy and red. I can't understand half of what she's trying to tell me, but as soon as she mentions Jasper, I look at the shattered teacup on the ground, and shock and horror creep over me like ice-cold vines.

The tea. There's something in the damn tea, and whatever it is, Ben gave it to her. To give to me. And she did it. Or at least she tried. And I almost drank it.

I almost *drank it.*

"You're telling me," I say slowly, fighting to keep my voice steady, "that Ben sent you tea, and he gave you twenty-four hours to give it to me. And if you didn't, he would . . . what, post the DNA test?"

"I don't know," cries Maisie. "I don't *know,* but he said—he said it would be worse, and—I didn't think you'd trust me, not after Jasper. I'm sorry, Evan. I'm so bloody *sorry.* I didn't think there was any other way. But then—if you're serious about another blood test . . . if you'd really do that for me . . ."

I stare at her, and her image seems to distort in front of me, like there's a haze between us that's twisting her features into something monstrous. "You just tried to kill me," I say, eerily calm now that I'm sure.

"No, Evan—please, I didn't think you'd drink it—I just wanted to tell Ben I'd tried, and—and maybe—"

"He'd give you more time. To what?" I say, tilting my head. Her face turns into a Picasso in front of me, and I'm vaguely aware that the room around me is spinning. Not because of any poison, but because of the battering ram of emotions violently breaking down my defenses. Because my sister, one of the few people in the world I really, truly trust, just tried—and almost succeeded—in doing what Ben's failed to achieve for the past year, all because I love her enough to let my guard down around her.

"To—to—I don't know," she answers at last, snot and tears clinging to her upper lip. "To come up with a solution, maybe. I don't *know.*"

She breaks down into another wave of sobs, and that's all I need to hear. Numb to everything but the ache in my chest, I stand and walk out of the sitting room and into the castle beyond, and even when she cries my name, her voice shattered and full of the same agony I feel at this rupture between us, I refuse to look back.

CHAPTER TWENTY-EIGHT

"We have the pleasure of being joined today by His Royal Highness Prince Benedict via VidChat as we discuss the stunning attack in Kenya, where four poachers were killed earlier this week by the herd of elephants they were tracking. Your Royal Highness, you've recently spent quite a bit of time on the reserves in Kenya, haven't you?"

"I have. It's been a pleasure to see so many of these intelligent, compassionate creatures in their natural environment, and it's no surprise to me that they banded together to protect their own."

"A video of the attack has gone viral, and while we must caution viewers about its graphic nature, I'd also like to point out the herd's choice of approach. I don't know what else to call it other than 'strategy.' It's remarkable, isn't it?"

"It really is. It's a teachable moment as well, I feel, about underestimating those around us, animal or human."

"That's a fascinating insight, Your Royal Highness. Do you have plans to return to Kenya anytime soon?"

"Sadly, no, not with term starting next month."

"Ah, yes, that's right—you, Princess Mary, and Evangeline Bright are all set to go to university in the coming weeks. We've heard rumours that the royal wedding might even take place before then. Can you give us a hint, perhaps?"

"I'm afraid my uncle would throttle me if I gave too much away, but I will say that I'm likely to need a new tux before a new textbook."

"Good man, good man. No doubt you're excited to welcome Evangeline into the family, especially after all the last year and a half has brought."

"We're thrilled. She's like a sister to me, and we're quite eager to have another our age in the family."

"And can you share whether there's any truth to the rumours about her being legitimized and her heirs potentially placed in the line of succession ahead of you?"

"There's . . . plenty I could say about that, but I will admit that as of right now, there *is* a crisis in the palace over the line of succession. But Evangeline isn't the main topic of conversation there."

"That's not quite what we expected to hear. Are there any details you're able to share at this time?"

"I . . . well, I suppose it's already out there, which is part of the problem. It's *the* problem, really, considering it's never been a secret in the family. They won't like me talking about it, and I fear there may be some form of retribution for this, but with it already made public, it'd be best announced by someone who loves her deeply, and for whom it changes nothing."

"Does this have something to do with Evangeline?"

"No, though of course I love her, too. We're a very close family, which is what makes this so difficult for everyone involved. It's Mary."

"Princess Mary? Is she ill?"

"No, no, nothing like that! She's in perfect health. But I'm afraid our parents have been lying to the public—out of love and necessity, you see—all her life."

"Lies? What sort of lies?"

"Well, my aunt has all but come out and admitted it, though she was . . . flexible with the timeline. It's no secret now that she and my father, the Duke of York, have had an affair, though they claim it only began in the past year. I'm afraid that's the start of the lie—a lie that has been necessary to protect Mary from the wrath of the public and the family from utter humiliation. As I said, it's no secret between us, but for obvious reasons, it was necessary from the beginning to make sure that no one else knew how long their affair has really been going on."

"Oh. *Oh.*"

"Precisely. I fear Mary is not my cousin but in fact my half sister, and a product of the decades-long affair between my father and Hele—"

[cuts to commercial]

—ITV News's interview with His Royal Highness Prince Benedict of York, 17 September 2024

BEN'S INTERVIEW AIRS LIVE THE next morning, and it's instantly banned from all British media. Not that anyone legitimate would touch it, considering his treasonous claims, but whatever special relationship the palace has with the BBC and other proper news channels works, and it only airs on television once.

Unfortunately, digital recording and the internet exist, and it's gone viral within fifteen minutes.

On any other day, I would've been in Maisie's room, listening to her tantrum or her sobs, handing her tissues and doing everything I could to comfort her. But today, less than twenty-four hours after she tried to poison me with Ben's tea, I can't bring myself to do anything other than recognize the dull thud of finality in the pit of my stomach.

This is it. Whatever comes next, this is the turning point where nothing will ever be the same. And short of me dying like the good little corpse I'm not, there's nothing any of us could've done to stop it.

"Tibby says that Alexander's been in a crisis meeting with Astrid, Doyle, and his other advisers all morning," says Kit as he brings our lunch trays to bed, where I'm yet again huddled with Poppy, watching with little interest as various social media feeds light up on my laptop. "But she expects he'll call a family meeting as soon as they're done. Bloody hell—they've forgotten our tea *again*."

"I'll start the kettle," I say quickly before he can try to call the kitchen. As soon as I returned to our suite yesterday, I asked Tibby for a minifridge full of water bottles and an electric kettle, along with a selection of tea packets and mugs, and while these are the only luxury items I've ever asked for, she still eyed me like I'd lost my mind. But the thought of ever drinking tea from one of the royal services again—or watching Kit do so—makes me sick to my stomach, and I hop off the bed and hurry to boil some water.

Even though my back is turned, I can feel Kit watching me, and I know what's coming next. He didn't ask about the new additions the evening before, when tea wasn't included with our dinner trays, or this morning, when I was already in the process of making it for him as Tibby burst into our room with breakfast. But that ticking clock was always going to be a short one, and once I've poured two mugs of boiling water and dropped packets of Earl Grey inside, I know my time is up.

"Is there any particular reason we have our own kettle now?" says Kit, and there's no accusation or wryness in his voice—only patience and curiosity.

I press my lips together, still facing the tea instead of him. I didn't tell him what Maisie tried to do, even though the smart thing would be to warn him. Just because she failed once, after all, doesn't mean she won't try again.

But Kit loves her like a sister. He grew up with her, and he's already lost his brother and Ben. I can't—I *won't* do anything to put a wedge between him and Maisie, even when it means dealing with the aftermath of this on my own.

"I'm feeling a little more . . . anxious than usual lately, with the wedding so close," I say. "And it's kind of nice, isn't it? Making our own tea instead of relying on someone to bring it to us. Like how it was in the flat."

I hear the rustle of blankets, and then Kit's warm arms envelop me from behind, his cheek resting against my head. "It is nice," he agrees, his voice low in my ear. "As long as that's all it is."

I nod, my mouth dry. I hate myself for lying to him. "We know Ben likes to drug drinks."

"And chocolates," he says grimly. "I suppose we could live off Pizza Express until we go back to Oxford, if you'd prefer."

"Tempting," I say with a small smile. "But after what happened to Rosie, Alexander's being a lot more careful with the food and kitchen staff. And I can't go completely off the deep end."

"No, no, can't have that," he agrees, his arms tightening around me. "C'mon. Let's get a bit of food in you before Alexander calls that meeting. I've a feeling it'll be a long one. Do you think Maisie and Gia would like to join us for lunch?"

"No," I blurt a little too quickly, and he pauses, peering down at me. "I mean—Maisie's obviously going through a lot right now, and I doubt seeing me will help." In our own twisted version of "The Prince and the Pauper," I'm weeks away from being legitimized, while Maisie is facing down the barrel of public bastardom. "Besides, the meeting is going to be a mess. I wouldn't mind a few minutes of peace and quiet first."

Even though I can still feel Kit's burning questions, he doesn't press, and we head back to the bed with our mugs of tea. The story of Ben's interview has reached American news sites now, and my compassion for my sister and all she's going through fights a violent war with the very real fact that I should be dead by now, if she'd had her way.

Tibby knocks on our door soon after, and the three of us head up to the conference room, which I expect to be packed with advisers and assistants. Instead, as Kit opens the door for Tibby and me, I'm struck by how empty the room is. Maybe the others have already left, but the only people who remain are Alexander, Doyle, Astrid, and Jenkins, each of whom look like they've spent all morning banging their heads against a wall.

"Ah, Evie, Kit, you made it," says Alexander, and when he tries to smile, it looks like a grimace of pain. I haven't seen him since the confrontation with Venetia in the white drawing room, and I can't bring myself to offer him a greeting other than the smallest of nods. He returns it, his face falling, and I can't help but wonder what he would think about Maisie's stunt with the tea. Would he try to make excuses for her? Or would he take my side, for once?

I sit at the far end of the table that's meant for two dozen, and Kit joins me as I pull the damn wooden puzzle from my pocket, more as something to fidget with rather than in any hopes of finally solving it. I've spent hours messing with it since Rosie's death, but there's something about the wooden shape that doesn't make sense to me. Something that was maybe obvious to John Phillip Michaels, but that kind of spatial intelligence isn't my forte.

"What's that?" says Kit quietly as the rest of the family trickles into the room. Helene, Nicholas, my mother, and finally Maisie, whose hair is unwashed and whose face is tinged with gray. I can't look at her, and so I show Kit the puzzle box instead, holding it in my palm.

"Just one of those brainteaser things," I mumble, already feeling guilty for not telling him it's the same puzzle John Phillip Michaels gave me back in February. But now is definitely not the time. "I can't figure it out."

"That's because this bit is twisted the wrong way," he says, his brow knit. He takes it from me, and his nimble fingers work some strange magic, flipping one of the wooden pieces, only to drop the puzzle in my hand once more. "Try that. It should work now."

I blink at him. "How did you see that?"

He shrugs. "The wood grain didn't match the rest. It must've been moved out of position."

Stunned, I focus on the puzzle again, and sure enough, the pieces turn easily now, just like they did under John Phillip Michaels's deft touch. Had he flipped it like that on purpose? Or had I accidentally jammed it in one of my early attempts to solve it?

"Thank you all for being here," says Alexander, even though

there are fewer than ten of us. Kit and I remain separated from the others, though I notice Jenkins has moved closer to us, bridging the gap. "I suppose everyone is aware of what this is about."

"That *wretch,*" spits Helene, her posture rigid and her eyes red. "This is treason, Alex—"

"I'm aware," he says miserably, and my mother sets a hand on his arm. "But I can't very well haul him in front of an executioner, can I?"

"There are other ways of achieving the same goal," mutters Helene, and the look Nicholas gives her sends a chill through me. Ben may be Royal Enemy Number One, but he's still Nicholas's kid. "He's put the entire monarchy at risk—"

"He also made it clear that he expects the crown to retaliate, ma'am," says Astrid from her spot across from Doyle. "And anyone who believes him will also deify him should the royal family try to seek vengeance for this."

"It isn't *vengeance,*" protests Helene. "It's all li—"

But she falters then, and heavy silence fills the room. It isn't all lies. Ben has the truth on his side, for once, and there's nothing anyone here can do about it.

"How did he even get his hands on that bloody test in the first place?" says Alexander, and this time his quiet rage is directed at his brother. Nicholas exhales sharply.

"I've no idea," he says raggedly. "I've kept it, of course, but it's locked in my personal safe—"

"And you're *certain* you never gave him the passcode?" says Helene, making it obvious they've had this conversation before. Nicholas nods.

"The only one who's ever laid eyes on it other than the three of us is Venetia," he admits. "But even then, she didn't have a copy. It was never in her possession."

"You showed *Venetia*?" Helene's face is cherry red now, and she clutches the front of her cardigan with a death grip that I'm sure she wishes was around Ben's neck. "How *could you—*"

"It was part of our settlement," mutters Nicholas. "I don't know *why* she wanted to see it, but she did. Closure, maybe. It doesn't matter. She knew that if she ever told a soul, her allowance would be cut off, and she'd be cast adrift from the family. There's no way she would've ever risked it."

"But Ben has nothing to lose," says Maisie, her voice rough. "He's playing his last hand, because there are no repercussions for him that aren't already coming."

"And because it's true," adds Kit, and heads swivel our way. I stare resolutely down at the puzzle box in my hands, refusing to meet anyone's eye. "It's ironic, in a way, after all the lies he's told to get himself here."

Alexander sighs heavily. "We have contacts all over the world searching for Ben, but there's been no reported sign of him, and the interview this morning was from an untraceable connection. Even if we do manage to ping his mobile or laptop, he's smart, and there's a high probability he's made his way to a country that doesn't have an extradition treaty with the UK."

"Can't be king if he can't return to Britain," mutters Maisie.

"Yes, but the monarch cannot be convicted of any crime," says Alexander.

"Brilliant," says Helene crisply. "Then you can be the one to swing the ax, and no one can punish you for it."

Nicholas rubs his eyes, while Alexander doesn't even acknowledge Helene with a glance. "What we need is a way to get him onto UK soil," says my father. "A lure of sorts."

"He doesn't do any of his dirty work," says Kit, and he sets a comforting hand on my knee beneath the table. "I suppose he used to have an army of people willing to jump when he called, but that's likely dwindled as of late."

"Dylan could still be working with him," I say, not meeting anyone's eyes. "But we don't have any way to get ahold of him."

"Then the message will have to be public, without being obvious," says Alexander, and he looks between us all. "Any ideas?"

"For now," says Astrid delicately, "I think our best bet is to mitigate the damage, rather than to try to hold the source accountable. As I mentioned, because of what he said during the interview, any maneuver the palace makes against him will only be seen as confirmation of the rumors, and an attempt to silence him. Whatever our next move is, we *must* be aware of how it will look to the public."

"We could always deny the accusation," says Doyle with less bluster than usual. Even he sounds drained. "Then again, by acknowledging the rumors at all, we validate the conspiracy."

I shake my head, my fingers turning pieces in on themselves in a pattern I'm only beginning to notice. "It doesn't matter what the palace does. Ben's third in line to the throne. By talking about it publicly—like he's some sort of expert and only wants what's best for Maisie—he's already confirmed everything. There's no putting this genie back in the bottle, and like everyone keeps saying, Ben has the truth on his side this time. He won't retract no matter what you threaten to do to him, not when he knows this is his last shot. Not when, between Helene admitting to the affair and the discrepancies with the timeline, the public is primed to believe him."

Yet again, silence falls over the conference room, and all I hear for a moment is the soft *click-clack* of the puzzle pieces sliding against one another. I'm making progress, and my fingers fly faster as my pulse begins to race.

"We could always put out our own DNA test," says Maisie in a small voice, and my head snaps up so fast that a muscle in my neck cramps. "To prove that I am . . ."

She trails off, and it takes ten full seconds for Nicholas to state the obvious. "But you're not," he says with gentleness I've never heard from him before. "And while I want nothing more than to claim you for all the world to know, it does put the monarchy in a pickle. Which is the *only* reason I didn't do so before you were born."

"I know," says Maisie quietly, offering him a sad smile. "You've already told me."

In that moment, despite all that's happened between us, I feel a deep stab of pity for Maisie. For Helene. For Nicholas, for Alexander, for my mother, for everyone who's had to put the monarchy before love again and again and again. It's bullshit, and they all deserved better. They all *deserve* better.

"We could still do a DNA test," presses Maisie, a note of desperation in her voice. "Claim that Daddy was worried, with all the rumors and Mummy admitting to an affair, so he privately asked for one, but the results were . . . well, as they should be."

I know exactly where she's going with this, of course, but no one else at the table seems to understand. "This is not American daytime television, darling," says Helene with a haughty sniff. "We do not *debase* ourselves in such ways."

"There would've been no need if . . ." begins Alexander, but he seems to think better of it and clears his throat. "While that's certainly one angle to consider, we cannot tamper with the results without risking creating even more of a problem for ourselves, should someone talk."

Though I can barely see Maisie at the edge of my vision, I sense her gaze flickering toward me. "What if it was Evangeline's blood instead? The results would be positive, wouldn't they? So no one would question them."

The room goes dead silent, and beside me, Kit stops breathing for a moment. Everyone is looking at me now, but I'm still staring at my puzzle, sliding pieces as fast as I can, as if that will somehow tune out what's happening around me.

"You'd be okay with that, right, Evan?" says Maisie, and her voice breaks slightly. "If it would—put an end to all this?"

My tongue feels like lead, and my mind is screaming at me to—I don't know. Walk away. Run, if I have to, from this circus sideshow. From being a pawn, from letting myself be used like this by someone who was willing to watch me die yesterday. Because that's the only reason she's being nice now, isn't she? Because she still needs me. She needs my blood to get out of this, and she knows the chances of me helping her have dropped dramatically in the past twenty-four hours.

"We can consider it an option," says Doyle gruffly after it becomes clear I'm not going to answer. Kit's hand tightens around my knee, and I can feel him staring, waiting for me to look at him, to communicate what I'm feeling to some degree. But I can't, not without giving it all away. So I don't. Not yet.

Astrid toys with the ends of her glossy hair. "As for other options, we'll of course argue that the original test was forged—"

"Naturally," agrees Doyle, scribbling something down.

"—but it's entirely possible that there's a record somewhere, and someone will talk," she finishes. "So that may backfire on us, too."

"So what *can* we do?" says Helene, her voice a bit higher now. "There must be something, even if it isn't a perfect fix."

"Telling the truth is out," says Astrid plainly. "Not if you want the line of succession to remain the same. It would also risk putting an end to the monarchy itself, with how it would shatter the trust between the palace and the public."

"Simply not an option," says Alexander firmly, while Helene shakes her head.

"Agreed," says Astrid. "Which would leave Maisie's idea of a DNA test using Evangeline's blood—"

"Not happening," says Kit, and the whole room once again turns to look at us. Even I glance up at him, surprised by the protectiveness in his voice. But his mouth is set, his brow is furrowed, and the hand on my knee is now tracing invisible patterns over my leggings, as if to assure me that he's on my side, regardless of what it costs us both.

I could kiss him right here, in front of the entire family. But I don't, only because I know it would embarrass him. Instead, I manage a tiny smile meant only for him, and in that exact instant, I feel something click in my hand.

The puzzle box.

It's open.

"Very well," says Astrid in a clipped tone, clearly not happy with Kit laying down the law. "Then that leaves us with one viable option: discrediting Prince Benedict."

"And how would we do that?" says Nicholas, sounding flustered. "He may be a lot of things, but he's still my son—"

"From what I've heard, he's done plenty of things to this family that would show malice on his part," says Astrid. "Things that wouldn't even require a felony conviction, should it come to that. The incident with Evangeline and the video, for instance, or the revenge photographs he released of the poor Chesterfield-Bishop girl. Yes, the public would certainly see it as retribution from the palace, but it would also tear his reputation to shreds."

"But would that move the needle when it comes to what the public believes regarding the princess?" says Doyle, dabbing his forehead with a handkerchief.

Astrid shrugs. "It sure as hell won't hurt. Pardon my French."

Alexander considers it. "It would also become glaringly obvious that we have lied to protect the children multiple times, and the monarchy *cannot* be caught in a lie."

"It doesn't come without its costs," agrees Astrid. "But by discrediting Ben . . ."

Their voices fade into the background as I stare at the tiny black chip that rests inside the hollow of the puzzle box, and even though I've seen dozens of them before, it still takes me nearly thirty seconds to fully believe what I'm looking at.

It's a SIM card.

John Phillip Michaels—Guy Fawkes—gave me a puzzle with a SIM card inside.

It could be a trap—some kind of virus to steal information from my mobile, but something screams in the back of my mind that that isn't right. There's a reason he wanted to talk to me the day he died, and this, I'm positive, was it. He wanted to make sure I still had the puzzle. He wanted to make sure I was still working on it, because this SIM card was meant for me. Not as a trap. But as a key.

My hands tremble as I pull my mobile from the pocket of my hoodie, and it takes me longer than it should to open the SIM compartment and exchange mine for the one in the box. My pulse is hammering, and I can feel Kit's eyes on me yet again as I restart my phone. While I wait for it to reboot, I take all of three breaths, and as soon as the main screen pops up—no password, no lock, nothing to keep me out—I start to explore.

Phone logs. Text messages. Images. Even voice recordings. My mind spins, and I finally look up at the rest of the table, vaguely shocked that they're still locked in the same conversation, as if the entire world hasn't just turned inside out and upside down.

"We need Venetia," says Nicholas. "If we try any of this without her support, she'll do everything she can to make our lives miserable. Believe me, I've been there. It isn't an enjoyable experience."

"Venetia won't budge," points out Alexander.

"And even if she did," says my mother, who's been quiet up until now, "what real difference would it make? She can't control Ben. No one can."

"We don't need to *control* him," says Helene through clenched teeth. "We need a way to remove him from the bloody—"

"I have an idea," I say shakily, and my voice comes out as a squeak. No one stops talking—over me, over each other, layer after layer as they fight about the best bad route to take.

And so I stand, clutching my phone like it's the key to eternal life, and I bang my free fist on the table so hard that my hand starts to throb. Instantly everyone turns my way again, and this time, that's exactly what I want.

"I have an idea."

CHAPTER TWENTY-NINE

"Here we are, Henrietta, yet again talking about the newest explosive story to come out of—well, Buckingham Palace this time, isn't it?"

"The palace has issued no official statement regarding Prince Benedict's interview this morning with ITV News, nor can we expect them to address it at all, considering the heinousness of His Royal Highness's claims."

"Does that mean you don't believe Prince Benedict when he claims that . . . well, I suppose we have to say it, though we ask you all to keep in mind that we are merely restating the prince's *alleged* accusations to pass along the information to you, our viewers, rather than to perpetuate any sordid tales that would not bear repeating, should they have come from any lesser source."

"A disclaimer if I've ever heard one."

"Yes, I'm sure the lawyers have been working on it all day. Here it is, then: In case you've missed it, the third in line to the throne, Prince Benedict of York, has come out with an extravagant claim that his cousin, Princess Mary, heir to the throne, is in fact his half sister through his father, the Duke of York. And considering that Queen Helene has already admitted to an affair with her former husband's brother . . ."

"It's like something out of a soap opera, isn't it?"

"Straight out of *EastEnders*, Henrietta."

"Yes, well, we must keep in mind that Prince Benedict himself was an infant when this affair supposedly occurred and is therefore making these claims from secondhand knowledge, if that, as there's simply no way he could remember any of these events himself. And while of course we must always consider the slight possibility that such a scandal is true, it's highly, *highly* unlikely, given this is a revered institution, not a Hollywood movie."

"But that doesn't change the fact that this revered institution is made up of flawed human beings who have already admitted to having a stormy and extremely complicated relationship among themselves during those years and beyond."

"Indeed. But to *fathom* the thought that they would allow something like this to happen, in a time of DNA testing and when Alexander himself already wished to abdicate . . . I have a hard time believing that he would abandon the love of his life, Laura Bright, who was already pregnant with his child, to remain married to a woman who was not only allegedly having an affair with his brother, but who also carried his brother's child and was trying to pass the baby off as the heir to the throne. It's absurd."

"And if they didn't know?"

"The date on the alleged DNA test posted online that claims to confirm Princess Mary is the Duke of York's child was supposedly taken while Her Majesty was in her first trimester, before the pregnancy was even announced to the public. So, should all this be true—which is *deeply* unlikely even under the most forgiving of circumstances—His Majesty would have, in fact, walked away from his own biological child with Laura Bright to remain King and pretend to be a father to his own brother's daughter. It's completely illogical, especially for someone who claimed he didn't want the crown. None of it adds up."

"Or perhaps His Majesty was part of a solution that protected his niece, brother, wife, and the royal institution itself from unnecessary humiliation."

"Throughout history, we've seen plenty of examples of what the monarchy is willing to do to protect its image, and had this truly been any sort of scandal in the making, this would have been properly taken care of long before it ever became a problem."

—ITV News's interview with Henrietta Smythe, 19 September 2024

IT TAKES ALEXANDER, SINGH, AND half the palace's lawyers two days to put the plan into place.

The whole production is actually impressive, considering every royal and legal precedent they're working around, but I stay out of it beyond my singular contribution at the meeting, content to hear general updates from Tibby and leave it at that.

Kit and I focus on expanding my—and eventually our—patronages instead, both of us determined to act like the monarchy isn't one wrong move from falling apart. Maisie tries to visit seven times in those two days, but I ignore her pleas, leaving Kit to turn her away. He does so again and again without asking why, but the question grows heavier between us until it threatens to break something, and I know we're on thin ice.

"Was the DNA test her idea?" asks Kit during lunch on the second day, minutes after he's turned her away again.

"Maisie's?" I say casually, stirring chunks of grilled cheese sandwich straight into my tomato soup.

"Yes, Maisie's," says Kit, ignoring his own bowl. "You don't want to give her your DNA, do you?"

I check the clock. *12:19.* Forty-one minutes to go. "It's a long story. I'll do it if it comes to it. If . . . if all this doesn't work."

"If it doesn't, then no one's going to force you," he says

protectively. "You're worth more to this family than backup DNA and an easy way out, Ev."

"Tell that to Maisie and Helene," I mumble. A DNA test that proves Ben wrong *is* an easy out, or at least an easy way to turn down the temperature on the roaring hell that has become Maisie's life. And it's only a matter of time before Maisie isn't the only one knocking on my door.

But I don't owe her a damn thing. I can give her my blood if I want to, if it comes to it, but the bond between us will never be the same. I'll never be able to trust her again, and I will always question her motives and whether she even wants to be family at all. That, more than the poison, more than Maisie bringing up the DNA test in the meeting, is what hurts the most.

"It'll work, right?" I say, even though Kit's already reassured me a dozen times.

"It'll work," he says, his voice low and certain. "It's about bloody time the palace lawyers earn their keep, and they won't let an opportunity like this slip through their fingers."

Except it's not up to them, and that's the most terrifying part of all. None of us can do a damn thing about this except wait, and I'm crawling out of my skin as the clock ticks closer and closer to one o'clock.

The door bursts open without warning, and Tibby hurries into our sitting room. "Evan, I hope you're wearing something appropri—" She stops mid-sentence and sighs, taking in my Reignwolf T-shirt and hot-pink leggings. "I suppose that'll have to do. Find a jumper and let's go."

"Go?" I say, my heart crashing into my ribs. "Where?"

"Buckingham Palace," she says, already rushing to the bedroom to pick out a sweater for me, her heels clicking against the floor faster than my pulse. "We've been summoned, and we're late."

OUT OF ALL the places I expected to go today—which was nowhere, admittedly—outside my father's Buckingham Palace office was the very last I would've guessed.

A pair of PPOs stand on either side of the doors, neither looking at me or Tibby as we approach at a swift pace. Between them stands Jenkins, his spine so straight and stiff that it looks painful, and that's how I know this is serious.

"Evan." Jenkins's strained expression softens slightly when he sees me, and for a moment, I almost forget about the tension between us that's lingered for the past eight months—tension I'd very much like to get rid of, even if Jenkins has made damn sure we're never alone long enough to talk it out. "You made it."

"Of course we made it," says Tibby, flustered. "You didn't give us much time."

"I gave you as much as I had to give," says Jenkins, and Tibby narrows her eyes. "They're inside, Evan, and they should be finishing up soon."

"Inside . . . ?" I glance at the crack between the office doors. "You want me to go in? Right now?"

"His Majesty requested you specifically," says Jenkins.

"Who else is in there?" I say, lowering my voice. Helene and Nicholas, surely. Maybe even Maisie.

"Just the three of them," he says. "His Majesty requested that everyone else, myself and the PPOs included, step out until the matter is settled."

My heart isn't hammering anymore. It's down in my stomach, sitting like a lump of ice, waiting for something to restart it. I shouldn't be here. I don't *want* to be here. But Jenkins knocks without asking for my opinion, and when I hear my father's faint call in return, he opens the door.

"Evangeline, sir," says Jenkins. And taking a gulp of stale palace air, I step inside the massive office that houses a single mahogany desk, where three people are gathered.

"There you are." My father sits with regal authority in his chair facing the door, and I can see his tight smile from forty feet away. "I'm glad you made it."

His guest—a blond woman I never wanted to see again—spins around in her seat, and instantly I'm nauseated. "You invited *her*?"

"Hello to you, too, Venetia," I mutter, taking a few ginger steps toward them. Singh, who stands at my father's side wearing a navy suit and a stone-cold expression, offers me the slightest of nods. I return the gesture as my stomach does cartwheels, threatening to expel the soup I never got to finish.

"I invited Evangeline here today in case you had any questions or . . . hesitations, shall we say?" says Alexander, refocusing on Venetia. What little warmth he greeted me with is gone, and he's every bit as cold as Singh.

Venetia shakes her head almost violently, and now that I'm closer, I can see how red and puffy her eyes are. Her mascara must be waterproof, though, because it's still holding on for dear life. "This is blackmail. Retribution for telling the truth. Everything here is circumstantial—"

"Some, yes," agrees Alexander. "But not all of it. And certainly not the worst of it."

I slowly move behind the desk, giving Venetia a wide berth as her lower lip starts to tremble. "My Ben never did any of this. He was with me the whole time—"

"We both know his physical location doesn't matter," says Alexander, giving her a heavy, unwavering look I never want to be on the receiving end of. "You've seen the evidence, Venetia, and you know the charges he's facing should you not be willing to cooperate. Whatever happens next is entirely up to you."

Her eyes fill with tears, and I linger in the corner as I try to get a good look at the document in front of Venetia. I already know what's in it, or at least the general idea, but morbid curiosity has always gotten the better of me.

"I knew," says Venetia at last, her voice venomous as she jabs a manicured nail at Alexander. "About the affair. I found out weeks before I gave birth to Ben. *Weeks.* Do you know what it's like to lie in hospital, all alone with your newborn son, knowing that your husband is celebrating by shagging your best friend?"

She plucks a tissue from a silver box at the corner of the desk, but instead of daintily sniffing, she blows her nose so loudly that it sounds like a foghorn.

"I kept your secrets all these years, Alex. I could've told the entire world and made tens of millions, but I didn't, because I still loved you all. And this is how you repay me?" She gestures with her damp tissue toward the document in front of her, like it's a plate of feces she's supposed to eat. Which, metaphorically, isn't all that far from the truth. "This is what decades of loyalty has earned me?"

"Ben did this to himself," says Alexander, with more sympathy than I expect. "I'm sorry you're caught in the middle of it, Venetia. But I am offering you a way to protect him one last time."

"Protect him?" Venetia laughs, sitting up straighter in her seat. "You call this *protecting* him? It'll take everything from him. *Everything.*"

"Not his life," says Alexander quietly. "And make no mistake, Venetia. That is what's on the line here."

He nudges the paper toward Venetia and offers her a fountain pen. Venetia's jaw works, and even from nearly ten feet away, I can hear her teeth grinding.

"I can't," she says at last, her gaze dropping to her lap. "My entire livelihood will disappear."

Alexander exhales, and I can't tell if it's full of relief or frustration. "You have my word that you will be taken care of for the rest of your life, in the manner to which you are currently accustomed. You are still family, Venetia, regardless of what this document says."

Venetia closes her eyes for a long moment, and when she opens them again, they're focused directly on me. "This is your fault," she whispers, but there's no fight behind it anymore. Just quiet resignation. "If you hadn't come here, none of this would've happened."

Her words are so eerily reminiscent of Maisie's that it takes me a moment to swallow the knot that forms in my throat. "No, it's not," I manage. "It's Ben's fault. He's the one who chose to do this, and he won't stop until one of us is dead."

"And I assure you," says Alexander, "that person will not be Evangeline."

The cords in Venetia's neck stand out, and at last she picks up the fountain pen and signs on the dotted line with an angry flourish.

"I love my son," she says, fury dripping from every word as she caps the pen and sets it down with inhuman control.

"And I love my daughters," says Alexander.

"Daughter. Singular," snaps Venetia as she stands. "You only have one, in case you've forgotten."

Alexander rises with her, though it takes him a moment as he struggles to fully support himself on his bad leg. "I've known I wasn't Maisie's biological father from the moment Helene told me she was pregnant. But Maisie has been mine from the day she was born, regardless of biology, and it has never changed how much I love her. It has never changed how much any of us have loved her."

Venetia tosses her blond waves over her shoulder and, without another word, turns to go. The three of us—Alexander, Singh, and I—watch her strut nearly the full length of the office before she stops in her tracks, turning toward us once more.

"Evangeline was born first, wasn't she?" she says. "What are you going to do about that, Alex? Lie to the public some more?"

"It's just a crown, Vee," says Alexander with a sigh. "And a heavy one at that. Let's all agree it's ruined enough lives for now and leave it there, shall we?"

A hint of something—victory, maybe, or rage-fueled madness—flashes in Venetia's eyes, and this time, when she starts toward the exit again, she doesn't stop.

We all watch her go, and as soon as the double doors close behind her, my shoulders slump, and Alexander sinks back into his seat.

"Well, that was easy," says Singh, plucking the paper from the desk and examining it. "Even signed and dated in the right place."

"Give it to Jenkins. He'll make sure it reaches the right hands," says Alexander, and he turns to me. "Evan, do you have a moment? It's important."

He knows I have a moment. He knows I have the whole damn day, and even if I didn't—even if I had to run out to some charity appearance or interview—he's the King. I can't exactly tell him I have something more important to do, as tempting as it is right now.

But at the same time, I know that if I did make up an excuse, he would let me go. It's my choice whether to stay, and part of me—a big part—is tired of being upset. I'm sick of feeling like a guillotine is hanging over me, ready to sever the bonds I've spent the past year and a half creating with people I now love. I'm ready for this hell to end, one way or the other, and so reluctantly, I nod.

Singh quickly collects the various folders and documents splayed out on Alexander's desk, snapping them all into a leather briefcase before hurrying out the door. Once he's gone, I perch in the second chair in front of my father's desk, the one that hasn't been warmed by Venetia for the past half hour.

"Why did you want me here for that?" I say once we're alone. "Sounds like you already had her cornered."

Alexander raises a single shoulder in a shrug. "I asked you here because nearly all of our evidence involved you, either directly or indirectly, and I wanted Venetia to look at you—really *look* at you—and make her choice."

"So you were manipulating her," I say. That makes much more sense than wanting me here for any other reason.

"I didn't want to give her an opportunity to forget all the harm her son has caused," corrects Alexander gently. "And, most important, I wanted you to see the result of everything you've had to endure at Ben's hands. While this was all Ben's choice from the beginning, you are the reason this . . . agreement happened."

In a perfect world, none of this would've happened at all. I hug my knees to my chest. "Why did you choose to stay with Maisie?"

I've asked the question before—sort of, in the white drawing room the day the whole Maisie mess exploded—but this time, I don't try to talk over him or ask a barrage of questions that I now know aren't so easy to answer. Alexander takes his time, seeming to sense that I'm willing to give it to him.

"Do you remember your first full day here?" he says at last. "The conversation we had just before the investiture ceremony?"

"Right after Constance called me a mangy stray at a dog show? Sure. Hard to forget."

He grimaces. "Do you remember how that conversation ended? When I told you that all I wanted was to shield you from the consequences of my greatest mistake, and you—"

"Didn't take it well? Yeah," I say, a sour taste filling my mouth. "Sort of hard to interpret that any other way than me being your greatest mistake."

"I was afraid that's what you took away from that," he says, rubbing his eyes wearily. "You were not my greatest mistake, Evie. You are and always have been my greatest joy."

I snort in disbelief, but he presses on, refusing to leave me with the wrong impression this time.

"My greatest mistake," he continues, "was choosing to remain with Helene and the crown over living the life I wanted with you and your mother, and leaving you to go through what you did alone. I didn't know what would happen then, but if I'd had any idea at all . . ." He sighs, and it's so deep that it sounds like he's expelling his soul. "I did choose you, Evie. I chose both of you. The intention was always a double life until Maisie was of age. That was my nonnegotiable part of our deal. The four of us even had plans to introduce you two as sisters—to spend holidays together when we could, to be as much of a family as possible. But . . ." He hesitates. "Venetia was right. You *were* born first. And Helene . . ."

He doesn't need to finish for me to understand. Helene felt threatened, given her own precarious situation with Maisie. Even though I wasn't legitimate, I was still Alexander's, and I was older. And therefore any invitation my mother and I may have had into Alexander's public family vanished.

"Can't really blame her, I guess," I mumble. I have zero interest in the crown now, but who knows what would've happened if I'd grown up knowing the whole story. I could've been more like Maisie. Or worse, like Ben. The thought alone is enough to make me sick to my stomach.

"I certainly can blame her, and I always will," says Alexander in such a haunted voice that the hair on my arms prickles. "She had me cornered, and she used her position to take you from me, despite our agreement. I couldn't walk away without destroying Maisie's life and quite possibly the entire monarchy, and while I would've been fine with the latter . . ."

"Maisie didn't do anything to deserve it," I finish for him, picking at a loose thread on my leggings.

"No, she did not. Nor did you, for that matter. And those of us who should've reaped what we'd sown paid our own prices, but never the ones we deserved."

I finally look at him again, taking in the dark circles under his eyes and the red lines that surround his blue irises. "Dunno," I say. "I think being married to Helene for twenty years was a pretty good place to start."

He chuckles faintly. "Suppose so. But the real punishment," he adds, serious once more, "was being separated from you. I cannot tell you how many times I wished I'd ignored Betty's request and remained in your life, or how often I almost brought you here to stay after her death. But I knew it was too late by then, and I feared that you would never forgive me for taking you from all you knew and loved, and . . ." He shakes his head, his eyes watery now. "We lost too many years, and I can never make those up to you. But I *can* make sure you know that I never, *ever* chose anyone—not even Maisie—over you. And I never will."

A tear slides down his face, and despite my deep-seated bitterness and hurt, I'm on my feet before I'm even consciously aware of it. One moment, I'm huddled in the chair, and the next, I'm at my father's side, sliding my arms around his shoulders and pressing my cheek to the top of his head.

"We lost too many years," I agree, my throat tightening. "But we have them now, right?"

"Right," he confirms, the word breaking under its own weight. "Thank you, Evie. For giving me a chance even when I didn't deserve one. I will never let you down again, I swear it."

I snort softly into his sandy hair. "You're my dad, not a saint. Arguments are okay. I just . . ." I swallow hard. "I just need to know you're on my side. That I'm not disposable to you, the way I am to everyone else in this family."

"You're not—" He pulls away, his eyes narrowed. "This has to do with Maisie, doesn't it?"

My heart sinks. "I'll do the DNA test if she wants, but no, it doesn't exactly feel great to be used like—"

"I don't mean that," he says. "She told me what happened between you two."

Now it's my turn to stare at him suspiciously, and I lean against the edge of his desk with faux nonchalance. "Which thing, specifically?"

He hesitates. "She told me about the tea Ben sent, and that she tried to get you to drink it."

Suddenly the office around us feels like the size of a coffin, and I stare at him, hardly daring to believe my own ears. There's no way Maisie would ever admit to that—*ever.* "What—" My voice squeaks, and I clear my throat. "What about it?" I say, because I'm absolutely sure that whatever Maisie told him, it wasn't the whole story.

"That Ben laced it with something deadly, and that he gave her twenty-four hours to make you drink it, or else he'd tell the world about her paternity," says Alexander calmly. "Considering the pickle we're all in now, and the fact that you're still breathing, I guessed the rest of the story correctly."

My jaw works, and for twenty full seconds, I can't think of a single thing to say. "She slapped it out of my hand," I finally manage. "She said she thought I wouldn't touch it, because of—what happened with Jasper, but—I trusted her. I *never* thought she'd . . ." I grip the edge of the desk. "Why did she tell you? Did she think I would?"

"I don't know," says Alexander. "But I'm glad she did, for multiple reasons. It was the incident that seemed to hit Venetia the hardest, for one, but I also wish you'd both come to me when it happened."

"I didn't want her to get in trouble," I say, even though it's much more complicated than that.

"Darling," he says, sandwiching my hand between his. "When someone tries to kill you, no matter who it is, I'd prefer you tell me immediately rather than keep it secret. It makes keeping you alive much easier."

"Even though it was Maisie?"

"Especially then. Considering she stopped you from drinking the concoction, and considering she came to me about it with the evidence we need to charge Ben with attempted murder, Singh is offering her full immunity."

"Of course he is," I mutter, even though the last thing Maisie needs—the last thing any member of this family needs, including me—is for this to turn into a legal shitshow.

"But," says Alexander slowly, "if you want to press charges, that is entirely your prerogative. And I will fully support you with the legal might of the palace behind you."

I stare at him like he's just promised to start a war against France for me. "You—you'd do that?"

He nods. "There are no circumstances under which what she did was either understandable or acceptable, and I will certainly not be making excuses for her. If she hadn't had a change of heart . . ." He trails off, clenching his jaw. "Regardless of your choice, she's lost as many privileges as I can feasibly take from her, and she *will* be apologizing and staying out of your way from here on out, unless you request otherwise. She broke your trust—our trust—and I do not care how frightened or desperate she was. There is no excuse for not coming to me. None."

Something inside me thaws a little at that, and my grip on the desk relaxes. "You'd really go through the scandal of having her arrested? For me? Even though I'm fine?"

"Yes," he says, looking me straight in the eye. "I mean it, Evie. You are every bit as important to me as she is, and you have never—*never* been extra or disposable, or even the slightest bit lesser in any way to me. You are my daughter, and I have loved you with everything I am from the moment I knew you existed. And I will do whatever it takes, for however long it takes, for the rest of our lives if need be, for you to believe me."

Pushing off the desk, I hug him again, speechless. He embraces me in return, tight and unyielding, even though I know he would let go in an instant if I asked. But no matter the distance or tension between us, there is one thing I believe now that I didn't when I arrived in England last year:

He's not just my father. He's my dad, in every way I've ever wanted. And while we may have endless obstacles in the road ahead of us, this is the first time they've felt smaller than the bond growing between us. We may not be totally okay today or tomorrow, and with Maisie, I might never be again. But at least now that hope feels permanent.

CHAPTER THIRTY

CHANGES COMING TO LINE OF SUCCESSION—WHO'S IN, WHO'S OUT?

With the Royal Wedding less than twenty-four hours away, palace courtiers have confirmed that a massive change is coming to the line of succession.

With the buzz around Princess Mary's alleged illegitimacy only growing over the past weeks, as the palace has steadfastly refused to comment on the rampant rumours that have plagued our beloved princess, many members of both the public and the media have speculated that it is Mary, current heir to the throne, who may be the one removed from the line of succession. As unlikely as that may seem to those outside the palace walls, one anonymous adviser close to His Majesty has confirmed those suspicions.

"His Majesty and the former Queen know they've been caught, and there's nothing they can do about it now. Better to take care of the problem as it is—with Princess Mary's permission, considering she doesn't want a reign that will only be questioned and ridiculed—than to let it fester and create distrust between the public and the monarchy."

Another source deeply entrenched in the royal family's day-to-day life agrees. "After being mocked for weeks, Mary is done. She's happy to shed the burden of the throne, and she sees this as a chance to live the rest of her life as her authentic self. The crown will pass to the Duke of York and his heirs, including Prince Benedict of York, likely much sooner rather than later, considering the whispers that His Majesty plans to abdicate once the next election cycle is finished. He's quite serious about living out the rest of his years with his new bride and daughter, and he wants nothing to get in the way of their peace and happiness together."

A royal announcement is reported to be coming soon after the wedding between His Majesty and Laura Bright tomorrow afternoon, the details of which have been kept private. Though the ceremony is expected to take place at St George's Chapel at Windsor Castle, an appearance on the balcony at Buckingham Palace is anticipated soon after the statement regarding the line of succession.

—*The Daily Sun*, 4 October 2024

IN THE WEEKS LEADING UP to my parents' wedding, I don't see any sign of Maisie.

As far as I know, she's still at Windsor, but at the same time, I'm not exactly keeping track of her. It's possible she's spending time at Kensington with Helene and Nicholas, or maybe at St. James's Palace, Constance's London home. Either way, I'm grateful I don't have to look her in the eye, considering I still don't know how to feel about what she did—both the whole attempted-poisoning thing and the turning-herself-in thing, possibly to give Alexander and Singh the evidence they need to convict Ben if it comes to it.

I keep busy most of the time anyway, between appearances with Kit, self-defense training with varying PPOs, and helping my mother with the few parts of the wedding she's been entrusted with. The menus are set; the location is set; even the flowers were chosen for her by a flock of royal wedding planners who barely listen to a word she says. But she gets a say in her hair, makeup, and dress, though she's restricted on which silhouettes she can wear. The flock *does* eventually decide she's allowed to wear certain shades of white, even though I obviously exist.

But since she's never been married, *and* since she and Alexander were engaged before he married Helene, it's all some giant religious technicality, and in the end, the Archbishop of Canterbury even agrees to officiate the ceremony. Which is, according to the media frenzy that follows this announcement, a deeply controversial decision.

"Alex just texted," says my mom, who hates using phones and only has my number and Alexander's in hers. "Victor Stephens says he's arrived."

"Really?" I say, twisting to look at her and earning myself a disapproving *tsk* from Louis, who kneels next to the fitting platform I'm standing on, his mouth full of pins as he alters the hem of my bridesmaid dress. "They'll have someone on him the whole time, right?"

"Naturally." She tucks her phone away in the pocket of her apron and picks up her paintbrush again, studying me. "Are you sure you're ready for this, Evie? I'm worried."

"Don't be, Mom," I say. "Really. I know exactly what I'm doing."

Except I don't, and *I* am definitely worried, even if I don't want her to be. I'm worried about everything—what could go wrong, what might go right, and what elements we need to pull this off with as few hitches as possible. I'm not sure I have them all, even though I've run through the scenario a zillion times in my head, out loud, and on paper, with as many different people as I can.

Something is missing, though, and I can't put my finger on it. And if I can't figure it out by tomorrow, I might be the reason Ben gets away with all of it.

"What about you?" I say, smoothing my hands down the front of the fitted bodice. My mother may be restricted to shades of ivory and pearl, but she insisted that Maisie and I choose splashes and combinations of our favorite bold jewel tones for our dresses. "Are *you* sure you're ready for this?"

She seems to realize that we're not talking about Ben anymore, and she smiles a bit dreamily as she focuses on her canvas. "Sweetheart, I've been ready since I was nineteen."

"I don't mean—" I begin, but Louis slides the final pin out of his mouth and motions for me to turn.

"Other side, my dear," he says, and I do so, watching my mom in the huge trifold mirror now. "Perfect. Hold still."

Once I'm sure I'm not standing wrong, I try again. "I don't mean marrying Alexander. Obviously you're happy about that, even though the ceremony's going to be about as stuffy as a turkey on Thanksgiving."

She laughs. "That's one way to put it. But I don't care about the details, Evie. Just the person waiting for me at the end of the aisle. I can take a little stuffiness if it means getting to spend the rest of my life with him."

I understand that sentiment more than I want to admit. "What about the paparazzi?" I say. "The endless commentary from all corners of the world? Everyone having an opinion about you, even though you've never met? The rumors, the gossip, the—the lack of privacy—*everything*—"

"Yes," says my mother emphatically, and she looks at me through the reflection, paintbrush hanging in midair. "Evie, I understand why you're nervous. I am, too, for plenty of reasons. But this isn't like it would've been when your father and I were young. It's different now. We'll be well protected, and while we won't be able to hide from the world completely, we're far more prepared for the difficult moments. For better and for worse, right?"

"Right," I say, and I press my lips together, trying not to frown and give myself away. But she's my mom, and even though we spent seven long years of my childhood apart, she still knows me better than anyone.

"What about you?" she says gently. "How are you feeling about this?"

"I . . ." I hesitate, and even though I don't mean to, I glance down at Louis. His dark eyes meet mine, and he clears his throat.

"I need to fetch a few things for your other dress," he says, and he stands, brushing his hands together. "I won't be a moment."

"Take your time," says my mother, and we both watch him go. As the door closes, her gaze returns to me, and I take a deep breath, horrified to feel my eyes prickle.

"I'm . . . I don't know how to feel," I admit softly. "Not that I don't want you to be happy. I do, more than anything. You and Alexander deserve to be together, and I never want to hold you back from that. But . . . after everything that's happened, with Ben and—and the ABR, I don't think I'll ever be able to stop worrying about you both."

"Oh, sweetheart." She sets her paintbrush down and pulls off her apron before closing the distance between us with a hug. "That's called love, darling. And anxiety, but a good therapist can help with that."

I hiccup. "Sometimes I wish it were just the two of us again,"

I mumble, hugging her fiercely, even though I know Louis will be aghast at any creases in the delicate fabric of my dress. "I wish we could go back in time and stop everything bad from happening, and it could just be the two of us. And Grandma, but I wouldn't want to live with her. I'd want to live with you. And be a family with *you*. I want those years back. I want it all back."

"Oh, Evie." She rocks me side to side, even though I'm almost a full foot taller than her on this platform. "It was never just the two of us. Alex was always there, even when you didn't know it, and my mom . . . she was always there, too, loving us both with everything she had. You and I were never an island, and I'm so sorry I ever made you feel like we were. I did so many things wrong—"

"No, you didn't," I say firmly, burying my face in her shoulder.

"Yes, I did," she counters gently. "But every parent does. We just don't always know it until much, much later. And the choices Alexander and I made . . . believe me when I say we would give anything to take those back and to give you the childhood you deserved."

I shake my head, realizing a beat too late that I'm getting snot on her shirt. "I didn't want any of that. I just wanted you."

"I'm sorry," she whispers, hugging me even tighter now. "I had a hard time coming back to myself for a while, no matter how badly I wanted to be there for you. But I'm here now, and I love you so very, very much, Evie. That will never change."

I think of her as an in-patient for years, with Alexander in the visitors' lounge waiting for her to let him back in. I think of all the horrors she must have held over herself, all the guilt she must've wallowed in, and all the fear she must've felt—must still feel even to this day—and I press my cheek to hers and finally let her go.

"Just promise me that you and Alexander won't be one of *those* couples," I say, wiping my nose with the back of my hand. "You know, the ones who forget everyone else once they're married and only ever want to spend time with each other."

I can tell from the look in her eyes that it takes her a beat to realize I'm joking, and when she does, her mouth widens into a smile, and she holds out her pinky to me. "Promise. Just as long as you promise me that you and Kit won't be one of *those* couples, either."

I hook her pinky with mine. "Promise. But that won't be for at least another decade. Some of us like to take our time, you know."

She raises an eyebrow. "Sure, kiddo. Does *he* know that?"

"Yes," I say. "I think so. Probably."

"Keep telling yourself that," she teases, tucking a lock of hair behind my ear. "Either way, you've certainly found yourself a good—"

There's a soft knock on the door, and my mom and I both look up in time to see Maisie poke her head inside. "Oh," she says, her face falling right as my stomach drops. "I didn't know . . . sorry. I'll come back later."

"No, no," insists my mother. "Come on in, Maisie. I was hoping you'd be early. I want to see you and Evie wearing your dresses together."

She was *hoping* Maisie would be early? I give my mother a betrayed look, but she ignores me as Maisie reluctantly slips inside. "Where's Louis?"

"He'll be back," says my mom. "You can change in the other room. Your dress is hanging next to mine."

Maisie nods, her eyes fixed on the rug as she scurries down the hall. As soon as the door clicks shut, I glare at my mom.

"You *invited* her here?" I hiss, keeping my voice down. "Why—"

"Because she's your sister, and she's already been through enough this past year," says my mom, giving me a look that deflates the worst of my aggravation. Or, quite possibly, panic. If Maisie was willing to go after me, there's no telling what she might do to my mom the day before the wedding, and the urge to drag Maisie out of the room and throw her back into the main corridor is unfathomably strong.

"*She's* been through enough?" I whisper, my voice squeaking. "No one's tried to kill *her* three, maybe four times!"

My mother clasps my hands, her skin cool and smooth. "Evie. We have two choices here. We can take what happened at face value and never forgive her—"

"Yes, because she *almost killed me,*" I hiss again. Why does no one seem to understand that part?

"Or," says my mom patiently, "we can look at it from her point of view."

I gape at my mom. "*Her* point of view? She's not the one who almost—"

"From what she told Alexander—and yes, I'm inclined to believe her, all things considered—she didn't think you would drink it," says my mom, brushing the backs of my hands with her thumbs in a calming rhythm. "She was trying to buy herself more time. A stupid move, yes. A dangerous move, absolutely. She should've gone to your father the moment she discovered Ben's note. But people aren't always rational, especially ones your age—"

I huff, but she ignores me.

"—and the three of you have had far too much weight on your shoulders, between you and Kit helping MI5 and Maisie having to carry the monarchy while Alexander was healing. We all make bad decisions sometimes. You can either hold it against her for the rest of your lives and make you both miserable, or you can try to find it in yourself to accept her apology and give her the chance to rebuild the trust between you."

I clench my teeth so hard that a jolt of pain cuts through my jaw, and for a moment, I think I've cracked a tooth. "How am I supposed to trust her now? She could've killed me. If she'd hesitated for even a second—"

"But she didn't," says my mother. "And believe me, I certainly won't be drinking anything she offers me for a great long while, either. But we're family now. And while you are under no obligation to put yourself in danger or in another uncomfortable situation, one lesson I hope you've taken from the way you've been treated by the public is that the truth isn't always obvious from the surface. And sometimes, all someone needs to be their best self is a chance to prove to you who they really are."

I stare at her. "You're turning the past year and a half into a life lesson? For *me*?"

"I'm pretty sure reality's already done that," she says with a faint smile. "But it doesn't hurt to be reminded every once in a while."

I mutter a few curses—which I would normally never dare to say in front of either of my parents—but at last I glance at the still-closed door and try to swallow my anger and sense of betrayal. Neither goes down easily, but at least they make it past the lump in my throat.

"Fine. I'll talk to her," I mutter. "*After* the wedding tomorrow. I can't handle another distraction. Everything's fragile enough as it is, and if one tiny thing goes wrong—"

"I think I might be able to help with that," says a small voice from the door, which is now cracked open. My first instinct is to lash out at the obvious fact that she was eavesdropping, but then again, how many times have I listened in on conversations in this place?

And so, with gritted teeth yet again, I spit out, "How?"

Maisie pushes the door wider until her gown shows—a gorgeous turquoise, emerald, and gold number, complementing the magenta, purple, and emerald dress I wear. "I know Ben better than anyone, remember?" she says. "If he doesn't talk tomorrow, it could all be for nothing. *I* know how to make him talk."

I eye her for a long moment. "You know what the plan is, then?" I say to Maisie, and she nods.

"Mostly. Daddy told me the broad strokes, and I heard Stephens talking to some of the PPOs about a few details. I've had nothing to do but think it over, and I have some ideas I would *love* to try."

"Do any of them involve poisoned tea?" I say before I can stop myself, and Maisie's expression once again collapses.

"I . . . Evan, I really am sorry," she says, her voice low and crackling with what I think might actually be sincerity. "I should've told you the moment he sent it. It should've never gone as far as it did, but I didn't know who I could trust. I didn't know who might be watching me and working for him, and I knew if he told the world, at least some of them would believe him, and—" She stops herself and buries her face in her hands for a beat, then pulls away, as if that alone has done enough to compose her. "It doesn't matter. I did a terrible thing, and I will do whatever I can, for however long it takes, to prove to you that that wasn't me. That I never intended . . ." She trails off and takes another deep breath, her blue eyes meeting mine. "*Whatever* it takes, Evan. Including helping you catch this arsehole. And after everything, if the public continues to believe him, then I won't fight it. We can just . . . let the crown go to your heirs instead. As long as it doesn't go to him, and as long as there's some way we can be sisters again . . . that's all I care about."

I don't believe her. Not fully, anyway, but the sincerity on her face, the pleading in her tone, and the blatant hope in her eyes—it's almost too much, and if I didn't know Maisie was a terrible actress, I wouldn't believe her at all. But she's awful. And there's no way she's pulling this out of her arse if she doesn't at least sort of mean it.

I take a deep breath and release it slowly, giving myself time to think. My mom's right—I don't need to make any decisions right now. I can let Maisie earn my trust back, if she even really wants to. But a painful, hollow pit inside me is screaming to let her back in, even if I can't fully trust her. That she's my sister, that anything she did under Ben's coercion can't count against her, and that if I can forgive Rosie, I can forgive Maisie.

And that hollow pit has a point.

Besides, the part of tomorrow that's missing—the thing that doesn't feel right, the cracks that Ben might very well find a way to slither through . . . as I stare at Maisie, as I stare at my sister, I'm positive she'll know how to fill them. And trap Ben for good.

I don't have to forgive her yet. But I still love her, and if I'm going to give her the chance to rebuild the trust between us, destroying a common enemy sounds like an excellent place to start.

"Okay," I say. "Let's talk."

CHAPTER THIRTY-ONE

Guests are arriving. When I have a shot, I'll take it.

No. Not until the announcement.

Announcement won't matter if she's dead.

I said no. Wait for my go.

Copy?

COPY?

Dylan, yes or no, copy?

—Text messages between two prepaid mobiles,
5 October 2024, 1:47 p.m.

AT EXACTLY TWO O'CLOCK ON the dot, Prince Benedict of York arrives at St. George's Chapel—which is really more of a giant Gothic cathedral—on the grounds of Windsor Castle, dressed in a morning suit with a tiny red daisy pinned to his lapel. His hair is slicked back, and he greets several people on the steps amidst the pageantry, making a point of ignoring the cameras and shouts from the press who are stationed at the bottom of the stairs. He is, by all accounts, the epitome of princely composure, and at his first appearance on English soil in more than a year, it would be easy to mistake him for the heir to the throne.

I see none of it in person. Instead, I watch on a tablet as Ben disappears inside the open doors, and then the feed switches to a series of security cameras strategically positioned within the chapel and surrounding buildings throughout the Lower Ward. A footman speaks privately to Ben, who nods and, rather than joining the other guests in the pews, follows him deeper into the medieval stone building.

And that's when I stop watching. Instead, I set the tablet against the stone wall and take a deep, centering breath, making sure I'm hidden just to the side of the main door of the chamber as I wait.

"Small flick knife, left breast pocket," crackles Singh's voice in my ear, a warning meant only for me. But he doesn't insist we call it off. I exhale, my fingers twitching toward the structured bodice of my high-necked violet gown before I let them fall. Everything will be fine. Everything will work out exactly like we planned.

A minute later, the door opens, the well-oiled hinges silent. "Sir," says the footman, ushering Ben inside. "Your father will be here momentarily to speak with you before the ceremony begins."

"Thank you, Percy," says Ben, and though he looks as cool and confident as ever, as soon as the door closes behind him, confusion flickers across his face. I don't blame him—the chamber has to be at least three stories tall, but the only windows are at the very top, allowing limited light inside. Long tapestries hang from high above, covering every inch of the stone walls and muffling any echo. The room is otherwise empty, save for me and my tablet, and it feels like a prison cell.

"Waiting for someone?" I say into the silence, and Ben nearly jumps out of his skin as he whirls around to face me. His palpable fear is so damn satisfying that I wish I'd planned that better, if only to maximize his reaction.

"Evangeline," he says, his breath catching and his eyes wide. He's not wearing his glasses today, and I note how much less approachable he looks without them. "What is this?"

"I'm waiting, too," I say, glancing at my wrist like I forgot I'm not wearing a watch. "Do you happen to know what time it is?"

"Er . . . two-oh-three," he says, checking his mobile. "Are you not in the wedding party? Shouldn't you be with your mother, preparing?"

"Shouldn't you be with the other guests, waiting for the wedding to start?" I counter, and I step sideways and lean against the door, as if my weight alone could stop him from getting out. Which is ridiculous. The heavy iron bolt that slides into place behind me is more than enough.

Ben's eyebrows lift, but his gaze is firmly focused on the door handle now, and I know he heard the lock, too. "I'm meeting my father here," he says distractedly. He turns, glancing around as if looking for another exit, but despite the size of the chamber—at least fifty feet by twenty—it's a dead end. "And what, exactly, are *you* waiting for?"

"You," I say casually, examining my manicured nails. They're nothing fancy—just glittery ovals—but I can feel Ben eyeing them like they're daggers. "What kind of attack are you planning this time? Another bombing? Sniper? Setting fire to the chapel? That might be a little tricky, with all this stone everywhere—"

"Attack?" he says, and it's his turn to act confused. "I'm afraid I have no idea what you're talking about."

I laugh, but it's humorless. Or maybe a little deranged. "Really, Ben? *Now* you're going to pretend like you haven't been trying to kill me and my parents for the past year?"

"Kill you?" he repeats, as if this is the most scandalous thing he's ever heard. "You're my cousin, Evan. I would never."

"Mm. Spare me the bullshit. What do you and Dylan have planned?"

"Dylan?" he says, sounding equally as clueless as before. "Evangeline, if you're feeling unwell—"

"Ben? Benny? Is that you?"

The haunting sound of Rosie's voice fills the chamber, and Ben's pupils dilate, turning his blue eyes almost entirely black.

"Benny," calls Rosie. "Please—you can't do this—you can't—"

Ben launches himself straight for the door—and straight at me. "Get out of my way," he growls, shoving me aside and yanking on the handle. But the lock is old and made of iron, and worse, it's exceptionally well maintained. And even Ben and his sudden burst of fear-induced adrenaline can't break through the thick door that stands between us and the only way out of here.

"What's wrong?" I say, as if I can't hear Rosie's voice. "I thought you were waiting for Uncle Nicholas."

"Where's the key?" he says, his breaths coming quickly now.

"I swear to God, Evangeline, if you don't let me out of here right now, I'll—"

"You'll what?" I say as he tugs on the door again, using all of his strength to no avail. "You'll kill me? Go ahead and try."

He yanks again and again on the handle, until the door rattles with his pointless efforts. "Help!" he shouts, his voice absorbed by the tapestries lining the walls. *"Help!"*

"What's going on, Ben?" I say. "Are you claustrophobic? Or—what's it called when you can't stand being locked in? Cle . . . cli . . ."

"Cleithrophobia," he says through gritted teeth before pounding on the door with his fist. *"Let me out of here!"*

"Weird thing to know off the top of your head," I say. "Unless it affects you? Maisie may have mentioned something about that. About how you don't like anyone to know, since it makes you feel vulnerable."

He doesn't reply. Instead, he continues to bang on the door until his fists are red and bleeding, and for the briefest of moments, I almost feel sorry for him. Almost.

Another ethereal voice fills the air, and this one makes my skin crawl. "Ben . . . be honest, mate," says Jasper Cunningham with a low chuckle. "You didn't actually think you'd get away with this, did you?"

"I think he did," whispers Rosie, and she giggles. "What an arrogant prick."

And then a third joins them—a deep voice with a refined accent. "You forgot one small detail, *Your Royal Highness,*" murmurs John Phillip Michaels. "Mutually assured destruction."

Ben freezes, his colorless eyes wide. "What the hell is going on?" he wheezes. "What is this?"

"What do you and Dylan have planned?" I say, all traces of amusement gone now. "Tell me, and I'll let you out of here."

"I have no idea what you're—"

"Wrong answer," I snap, stepping back out of his reach. "Drop the act, Ben. MI5 has all the evidence they need to put you away for the rest of your life."

Ben's face, which was already the color of sour milk, mottles with blotchy patches of red. "I haven't done anything wrong—"

"We have proof. Lots of it. And if you want a prayer of ever walking free again, you'll tell me where Dylan is before you also go down for whatever he's about to do next."

Despite Ben's obvious panic and unraveling composure, he actually scoffs. "I won't go down for anything, Evangeline. I'm third in line to the throne—soon to be first, in case you haven't heard."

I tilt my head. "I hadn't. How does that work, exactly?"

He manages a grin, even though it's uneven and a bit manic. "The entire world knows Maisie's illegitimate now, and Alexander's finally abdicating like he should have decades ago."

"He is?" I say, even though I'm not the least bit surprised.

Ben chuckles. "What, were you counting on the crown falling to you instead? You're not even legitimate yet. And if you don't let me out of here—"

He falters, but this is exactly the opening I've been waiting for. "You'll what?" I press. "Make sure I never am?"

Ben eyes the door again. "Whoever this Dylan character is, he sounds rather dangerous. I certainly wouldn't take my chances."

I snort. "I bet you wouldn't. What makes you think you'll be named heir? That Alexander's abdicating and Maisie's being removed from the line of succession?"

He tugs ineffectively at the handle again, then kicks the bottom of the door twice, cursing when it doesn't budge. "My mother told me," he says with strained haughtiness. "And my father. They both confirmed it separately. Why else would I be here, Evangeline? To watch the delightful union between an adulterer and his mistress? The announcement will be made immediately following the wedding, and you won't even have a chance at snagging your heirs a place in the line of succession. The crown will go straight to my father, and then to me—"

"And how long will that take?" I say. "A year? Five? Ten? How long are you willing to wait before you murder your own father?"

Ben stares at me, but he doesn't deny it. "Let me out of here," he says, panic grating his voice, "and this doesn't have to get messy, Evangeline. For any of us."

Right. Because once my parents and I are out of his way, he'll have no reason to come after us again. Unless it's out of spite and revenge. "Or," I counter, "you tell me what you and Dylan are planning, and I'll tell you a secret. Maybe even two, if you stop trying to delay things."

This catches his attention, and he eyes me up and down. "I'm not planning anything, and I've no idea who this Dylan bloke is. What secret?"

"Not good enough," I say. "Try again."

"I have nothing to give you except the tru—"

"What time is it?"

My question seems to take him by surprise, and he glances

at his mobile again. "Two-fourteen. Are you going to open the damn door or—"

"Perfect." I pick up my tablet from its spot against the wall and unlock the device. I already have it queued up to the right channel, and I angle it toward Ben. "My favorite show is about to start."

Ben blinks, bewildered. "Evangeline, what the hell are you—"

"Shh," I say, and I turn the volume up just as Venetia's face appears on the screen beside a middle-aged man in a gray suit. "This is supposed to be a good one."

"—Venetia, Duchess of York, married to the Duke of York from 2003 to 2005, has joined us today to discuss His Majesty's marriage to American Laura Bright—"

"I'm afraid what I'm here to discuss today has nothing to do with the royal wedding," says Venetia, and her usual heavy makeup is replaced by a more natural look, giving her an oddly youthful glow that's at odds with the grief in her eyes. "I, like the rest of the world, have been devastated by the recent accusations against my niece, Princess Mary, and all the turmoil my son, Prince Benedict, has caused."

"It has certainly been a difficult time for the royal family, and with the news of His Majesty's abdication and the crown passing to your former husband, the Duke of York—"

"That's precisely what I'm afraid of," says Venetia, her voice loud and clear. Even Ben's heavy breathing can't drown her out. "Because . . . well, I have a confession of my own to make. One that I'm afraid my son has figured out, which may have in turn caused him to act out against the family that has so graciously treated us as their own for his entire life."

Beside me, I feel Ben stiffen, and I don't dare look at him. I need him to keep watching. I need him to hear all of it.

"I'm afraid . . ." Venetia hesitates, and I can tell that this part, at least, isn't acting. She really doesn't want to say it. But she has to. Everything is counting on it. *Everything.* "I'm afraid that Nicholas is not the one who had the affair in our relationship. It was me."

Gasps escape from those behind the cameras—producers, makeup artists, and whoever else is waiting in the wings, watching Venetia lie her arse off. Ben's breath is hot on my neck now, and I inch away, but he only moves closer.

"That's a lie," snarls Ben. "What—"

But Venetia is talking again, obviously unable to hear him. "The timeline of our marriage isn't a secret. Benedict was born eight months after we were wed, and at the time, Nicholas and I both thought . . . well, I never gave him any reason to think otherwise, of course. But I'm afraid that shortly after his birth, I confessed that I'd had . . . a fling. That I had made a mistake, and there was a chance . . . that Benedict wasn't Nicholas's. And I fear, when Nicholas had a paternity test done . . ."

Venetia trails off, and two fat tears slide down her cheeks. Beside me, Ben is frozen yet again, and I can feel waves of horror—of sheer, uncontrollable shock and panic—rolling off him like they're real.

"What did you do?" he chokes. "Evangeline, *what did you—*"

"Nicholas and I have known for Benedict's entire life, of course, and Nicholas has been the most wonderful father to him regardless of biology," continues Venetia as she dabs her face with a tissue. "It was a terrible deception on my part, and Nicholas was only trying to protect us both. For that—for my role, for all the responsibility I carry in this hoax—I deeply, deeply apologize to the nation and the Commonwealth, and to His Majesty, Her Majesty, and Her Royal Highness. Benedict recently found out about his paternity and grew . . . upset, and rather than speaking to us, he tried to . . . project the situation onto his cousin. Which is unspeakable."

"No," says Ben, his eyes wide as he grabs the tablet. I release it without a fight. "No, no, *no*—this is a lie. It's all lies. My father is my father—I've checked myself—there was no deception—Maisie is the bastard, not me—*you're* the bastard—it wasn't me—I'm supposed to be the heir—the *real* heir—not you—not Maisie—*me*—"

"Sure about that?" I say, taking a step back. There's not much I can do if he decides to throw the tablet, but I can at least stay out of swinging range. "It's over for you, Ben. You'll never be crowned. The palace is already removing you from the line of succession—"

"No," he heaves, clutching the tablet in his fists like he plans on breaking it in half. "I'm the heir. *I'm the heir.*"

"Even if you could prove it was a lie, it wouldn't matter. Maisie's still ahead of you. And now my family line is, too."

His gaze snaps to me, and I can see the question in his eyes, even though his face is red and patchy purple.

"Oh, did no one tell you?" I say, feigning innocence. "You're about four hours late to the wedding. I was officially legitimized this morn—"

"You *bitch*!"

Ben launches himself at me, and I have no time to dodge

before he tackles me to the floor. The back of my head hits a cobblestone, but while stars explode in my vision, they quickly fade, leaving me with a slightly blurry view of Ben's twisted features only inches away.

His knees pin me to the cold ground, and he reaches into his jacket, undoubtedly for the flick knife—switchblade—that Singh warned me about. But I've been training for this exact moment for weeks. Using all of my strength, I use his body weight against him and flip us over, pinning him instead, my knee digging into his groin.

"It's *Your Royal Bitch* now," I correct as he howls in pain. "What are you going to do, Ben? Kill me in a locked room while no one else is here? How are you going to explain that one? Ghosts? A temporary loss of sanity? That didn't work for Hamlet, and it won't work for—"

A flash of metal glints between us, and suddenly Ben plunges a sharp blade directly between my ribs. The impact is enough to take my breath away, and I stare down at the hilt in his hand, my eyes wide as I weakly try to grapple the blade from him.

"I'll take my chances," he growls, and he twists the knife. But as he does so, it slips against the Kevlar beneath my violet dress, further ripping the delicate fabric, and Ben's sneer turns into a frown. "What the—"

Seizing the opportunity, I pull a small box cutter from my bodice and, with one quick jerk, stab the sharp blade into the skin between Ben's thumb and forefinger. He shrieks with pain, dropping his knife and instinctively pressing the injury to the front of his suit, no doubt ruining the expensive fabric.

"Really?" I say. *"Really?"* I press my box cutter to the base of

Ben's tanned throat, until a single bead of red wells up in the hollow. Somewhere nearby, footsteps scramble and voices shout, but I ignore them, keeping my eyes locked on Ben. "All you had to do was tell us where Dylan was, and you could've given the palace something to work with—a way to spin the story so you wouldn't come off as a mustache-twirling villain. But now you had to go and do this, and how's that going to look on the front page?"

I gesture at the slashed fabric of my dress, exposing the protective vest beneath it, and Ben glares at me, the heat of his hatred so intense that the cold chamber suddenly feels ten degrees warmer. "Do it," he hisses. "Get it over with, because I'll never stop, Evangeline. I will *never stop.*"

"Never is a very, very long time," I say as the door finally bursts open, and no fewer than half a dozen PPOs pour inside to join the MI5 agents that already form a wide circle around us. All point their firearms at Ben. "And you'll have bigger things to worry about than me for a while."

As if on cue—which, knowing Maisie's flair for drama, is absolutely intentional—the supposedly ancient tapestries drop from the ceiling, revealing nooks on the ground floor that hid the MI5 agents, as well as a narrow walkway that wraps around the room at least a full story up. And standing on that walkway are more than a dozen witnesses, all with lengthy Wikipedia pages to their names.

My father, for one, who looks ready to jump from the balcony and throttle Benedict into unconsciousness.

Maisie, who's practically preening with satisfaction.

Nicholas, who can't even look at his son.

The prime minister, who stares at Ben with his mouth slightly agape, as if he's witnessing the climax of a horror movie.

The petite blond Director General and head of MI5, who is stone-faced and deeply unamused.

Leaders of Parliament I don't recognize. A man who earlier introduced himself to me as the Commissioner of the Met, which is apparently British for the head of the London police force. Several high-ranking aristocrats. People I didn't get the chance to meet before we set everything into place, ready to bait our trap.

And at the opposite end of the room, on the biggest screen I've ever seen outside of a movie theater, is a clear image of me pinning Ben to the floor, my box cutter pressed to his throat, recording in real time.

"What—" Ben gasps, but even that's enough to make his Adam's apple press against the knife, and he tries to shrink away from me and into the hard floor.

"Choose your words carefully, Benedict," says my father. "The rest of your life depends on what you say next."

"But—I haven't done—anything—" Another drop of blood wells in Ben's throat, and Singh touches my shoulder.

"We have him from here, Your Royal Highness," he says as he picks Ben's knife up off the floor. "Thank you for your assistance."

"Anytime," I say, and after taking one more moment to savor the sheer rage and fear in Ben's eyes, I finally climb off him. Part of me expects him to grab my skirt and pull me down with him—maybe crack my head against the floor, or try to break my neck with his bare hands. But even seething hatred isn't enough for him to forfeit his own life, and for now, he stays perfectly still, as if the blade were still pressed against his delicate skin.

Immediately two PPOs step on either side of me and escort me several feet away. I don't argue, and instead I glance at the slashed fabric of my bodice, scowling. When Louis altered this violet dress to cover the vest yesterday, we knew there was a chance it wouldn't make it out in one piece, but I'm still annoyed. It was a masterpiece.

"Where," says Alexander from the walkway, his booming voice filling every corner of the chamber, "is Dylan Baxter? Answer me, Benedict, or you will not enjoy the consequences."

"I'm innocent," gasps Ben as two MI5 agents haul him to his feet, and to my enormous satisfaction, Singh cuffs his hands behind his back. "I haven't done anything. You have to believe me, Uncle Alexander—"

"You sent me poison and tried to blackmail me into killing my own sister," says Maisie, and I'm so shocked she's willing to admit this—especially in front of so many important people—that my mouth falls open. "I've already handed the evidence over to MI5."

"Hearsay," claims Ben. "You could've easily set the whole thing up to frame me—"

"With your fingerprints on the letter?" challenges Maisie. "I suppose we'll just have to let a judge work that one out, won't we? I expect it'll be a *very* public trial."

"Don't forget the SIM card that John Phillip Michaels gave me," I say, looking Ben dead in the eye. "It has all the texts you two exchanged. You slip up a few times and call him by his real name, you know, and you *definitely* say a few things you shouldn't. I guess it's easy to forget how to keep your mouth shut when you think no one will ever read your messages. Oh," I add. "You also forgot to turn your location off. Rookie mistake."

Ben is shaking now—with anger or fear, I don't know, but it doesn't matter. "Whatever's on that card can't be proven," he says, his voice trembling, and despite the chill in the room, a bead of sweat slides down his temple. "It's all circumstantial—"

"And we have everything that happened with Jasper recorded, too," says Maisie. "With your face on the video."

"That was *you*!" shouts Ben. "*You* pushed him off the balcony! Everyone will know now—everyone will know you're a murderer!"

"I acted in self-defense," says Maisie, far calmer than I expect, and I wonder how many lawyers it took to convince her to reveal that little detail in front of the head of MI5. "As you can plainly see on the video, which we've already shared with the police. It's also obvious how *you* tried to pin the murder on Evan, and considering we have security footage of you in the Cunninghams' kitchen drugging Evan's drink . . ." She tilts her head and looks at Nicholas. "Do you think Robert Cunningham would be interested in telling the world that Jasper was manipulated and set up by a member of the royal family? I think he would."

"Champing at the bit," agrees Alexander, while Nicholas continues to stare at his hands in silence. "He's in the chapel. Shall we fetch him?"

"Not yet," I say. "Since MI5's still searching Ben's hotel room and confiscating his electronics. Or is that MI6?" I add, glancing between Singh and the Director General. "They're involved now, too, right? Since Ben's fled the country multiple times."

"Indeed," says Singh, and from the walkway, the Director General dips her head in confirmation.

"I thought so," I say, locking eyes with Ben once more. "But I'm just an American. I can't be expected to understand the intricacies of how the English government works."

"You'll get there, Your Royal Highness," says Singh. "It's an impressive start regardless."

"What—what about the line of succession?" gasps Ben, as if he's forgotten how to breathe. "Father's next. If Alexander's abdicating, and the entire world knows Maisie isn't legitimate—"

"I have no intention of abdicating," announces Alexander. "I did once upon a time, and perhaps one day, once Mary is ready, I'll consider it again. But for now, my place is on the throne, not only to help guide this country and my people, but to protect my family from you."

"But—" Ben nearly chokes on the word. "She's not yours—"

"Mary is my daughter, and it is treason to say otherwise," says Alexander. Which is laying it on a bit thick, even if it is the truth. "We'll be happy to provide proof to any official present who asks, but she is my blood, and she is and will remain the heir to the throne. And as Evangeline has already pointed out, her heirs, should she choose to have any, will be next."

"I haven't decided yet," I say, staring at Ben. "But either way, *you* will never be crowned."

Ben's eyes dart around in desperation now, and at last they land on Nicholas. "Dad," he says, his voice cracking. "Tell them—I'm your son. I know I am. I did the test myself. Whatever this is, I'm sorry—they can't do this—they can't *do* this—"

"Tell them where Dylan Baxter is," says Nicholas resignedly. "That's all they're asking of you."

Ben swallows hard, once, twice, and then opens his mouth like a gaping fish for several seconds. "I—I don't know. I don't know who Dylan Baxter is—"

"You went to Eton with him," says Maisie plainly. "You, Jasper, and Kit. The four of you were friends. You really think we don't know that, Ben?"

Ben shakes his head. "I had loads of friends at school. I can't keep track of them all, or be held responsible when one decides to—"

Click.

The room goes silent, and every eye is suddenly on Singh, who holds his gun inches from Ben's forehead. No one tells him to lower it.

"Let me make this clear to you," he says. "In a moment, you and I will remain here while everyone else leaves this chamber, including the royal family. If any one of them is harmed by your not-friend Dylan, then your life is forfeit. Do you understand, Benedict?"

"I—" Ben tries to reply, but he's trembling so hard that he can barely speak. "Dad—"

"He's going to leave us, too," says Singh, and Nicholas looks away, his eyes closing. "This is your last chance, Benedict, and I mean that in every sense of the word. Where is Dylan Baxter?"

Ben's chin wobbles, and a dark spot forms on the front of his trousers.

Holy shit.

"He's—he's on the roof of a tall brick hotel two streets down," admits Ben at last. "You can see into the courtyard from there, right onto the chapel steps. He has a rifle."

One of the MI5 agents radios the description into his colleagues, and Singh's gun doesn't waver. "Who's the target?" says Singh.

Ben's teeth chatter. "Evangeline."

My face is a mask, and no one else shows any hint of surprise, either. Instead, in a whirlwind of movement, four agents take off through the doors, and two PPOs join them, as well as Victor Stephens.

"Thank you," says Singh, and the safety clicks on as he returns the gun to his holster. "You made the right decision, Benedict."

Ben sinks to the ground in a puddle of his own urine, and his entire body heaves with wretched sobs.

CHAPTER THIRTY-TWO

A FRESH START FOR OUR KING

Wedding bells rang out this afternoon for His Majesty and his bride, Laura Bright, who were married this morning at 10 o'clock in a private ceremony at St George's Chapel. Though we aren't expecting any pictures from the wedding itself, an official portrait of the wedding party taken in the autumn splendor of the East Terrace Garden at Windsor Castle was released this afternoon.

With the royal nuptials complete, Buckingham Palace has announced that His Majesty's new wife will henceforth be known as the Duchess of Lancaster, while their daughter, Evangeline Bright, 19, has now been legitimized and titled Her Royal Highness The Princess Evangeline, The Princess Royal. She is the first Princess Royal to be named in nearly a century, since Princess Mary, daughter of King George V, in 1932, and the only younger daughter to ever be officially titled as such. With her legitimization, the line of succession will be updated in the future with any legitimate heirs she might have, to be placed immediately after her elder sister Princess Mary's line.

More details to come about the ceremony and happy couple as they're released.

—*The Daily Sun*, 5 October 2024

KIT IS WAITING FOR ME at the entrance to Buckingham Palace, and even though our PPOs must have told him by now that we're all safe, his shoulders are tight and his forehead is lined with worry.

He only agreed to stay with my mother after she personally asked him to, since she didn't want to be alone while the rest of us confronted Ben, and it's taken an obvious toll on him. My breath catches in my lungs, and the moment the Range Rover slows to a near stop, I push open the door and jump out, tripping over my heels as I rush toward Kit. He's there before I can hit the ground and ruin a second dress in less than an hour, and we hug each other tightly, my cheek pressed to his.

"You're all right?" he says softly into my ear. Beside us, I hear more doors and a murmur of voices as my father greets my mother, and Maisie shrieks with excitement as she runs to update Gia on everything that happened. But it all slowly disappears, replaced by the touch and scent and warmth of Kit.

"I'm fine," I say. "He tried to stab me, but the vest did its job. And MI5 was ten feet away the whole time."

He holds me a little tighter, and I know what he's thinking. Ten feet may as well have been ten miles if that vest didn't work, or if Ben decided to go for my throat instead. But I'm okay. We're both okay. "And Dylan?"

"They got him, too," I say. "You should've seen it. Singh pointed a gun right at Ben's forehead to get him to talk, and he peed his pants, right in front of everyone."

Kit runs his fingers through my styled curls and gently lowers me down, and it's only when my heels hit the ground that I realize I was up in the air at all. "At least he has some sanity left."

Near the door, Jenkins clears his throat. "We're running on a tight schedule, Your Majesties, Your Royal Highnesses," he says, which is likely the only gentle nudge we're going to get from him. Tibby stands beside him with Poppy in her arms and Fitz at her side, and the look she gives me is anything but gentle.

"Let's get on with it, then," says Alexander, and though he still uses a cane, he offers my mother his elbow, and the two of them stroll into the palace, leading the way for the rest of us to follow.

I tuck myself beneath Kit's arm as we walk through the jaw-dropping entrance hall full of white marble, red velvet, and stunning works of art, and a memory flashes through my mind from the first time I visited Buckingham Palace over a year ago. It's still sickeningly opulent, with enough wealth displayed to solve world hunger, and while I doubt I'll ever feel like I entirely belong, I walk the halls more confidently now. I can at least pretend I know what I'm doing, even if part of me will always feel lost and like I'm scrambling to catch up to what the rest of my family knows.

Jenkins and my father lead us up the grand staircase and through a series of long hallways, until at last we reach a part of the palace I had no idea existed. By now I'm completely turned around, but everyone else is chatting comfortably as we filter into a large room with three tall floor-to-ceiling windows on the far side, and a collection of Chinese artwork—paintings, vases, and golden ornaments—decorating the room.

There, Helene and Constance are waiting for us, all perched around a dark wooden table laden with finger food. An attendant offers us drinks from a silver tray, and even though I should be used to this—even though this is the ridiculous kind of life my family leads—my skin still prickles, and awkwardness slithers through me.

"Come on," says Kit softly, leading me to a corner where a pair of mint-green armchairs stand, blending in with some of the decor. He steps away for a moment once I'm seated, speaking to another footman near the door, and somehow, miraculously, he returns with two cold bottles of water half a minute later.

"I don't know if I can do this," I say as I unscrew mine and take a sip. Maybe the adrenaline is catching up with me, or maybe my brain is finally realizing just how reckless today's plan was and how close that knife came to doing real damage, but either way, my limbs feel like concrete now, and my skin is cold and clammy.

"You just watched Ben piss himself because of your hard work and determination, and you're worried you can't handle this?" says Kit with a small smile, sitting beside me and setting his hand on my lower back. "I know for a fact you're made of tougher stuff than that."

I lean into him for a moment, resting my head on his shoulder. "Thank you for staying with my mom. That couldn't have been easy."

"It wasn't," he admits. "But it was necessary. If I'd been there, I would've blown the whole thing the moment he went after you."

"Louis knows what he's doing with silk, *and* he knows what he's doing with Kevlar," I joke. "Jenkins got himself a good one, that's for damn sure."

"I certainly did," says a low voice nearby, and when I look

up, Jenkins is standing only a few feet away, his posture rigid as he gazes out across the room, watching as my parents laugh with their heads bent together. "Evan, if I might have a word?"

Even though Kit sat down seconds ago, he's on his feet again and gives my hand a squeeze. "I'll go grab something to nibble on," he says, and before I can respond, he's halfway across the room, leaving Jenkins and me alone in the corner.

I kick my feet, my heel catching on the edge of the huge rug. "It's after the wedding, you know."

Jenkins raises an eyebrow. "It is."

"You have to forgive me by now. That was part of my deal with Alexander, remember? For being okay with this in the first place?"

He finally looks my way, though he doesn't turn his head more than an inch or two. "Oh? Do you plan on changing your mind, then?"

I watch my parents on the other side of the room, where they sit on a bench together, lost in their own little world as the rest of the family mills around them. They look happy—happier than I've ever seen either of them, and it makes almost every terrible thing that's happened over the past year and a half worth it.

"No," I say. "But none of this feels the same when you're angry with me. I miss you."

Something in his expression softens, and at last he turns to face me properly. "I am not angry with you," he says. "I am—was—still am frightened for your safety and well-being. And I do not take well to being frightened like that, especially when it comes to someone I love."

A lump forms in my throat, and I have to swallow it before

my makeup is ruined. "I'm sorry. For scaring you, and for not listening to you. I never wanted to hurt you. I never wanted any of this to happen."

He sighs, so softly that I barely register it. "But it did, and while it may have happened to you, it was not your fault, despite what some unscrupulous types may have wanted you to think. And," he adds, his blue eyes focusing on me, "I am also sorry that I brought you here and put you through this."

I manage a tiny smile. "Haven't we had this conversation before? And didn't I say that I'm not sorry at all? You're the one who gave me a family, Jenkins. A family you're part of, by the way, no matter how good you are at holding grudges."

He steps toward me and, to my surprise, crouches beside my chair, sandwiching my hand between his. "You're still as good a listener as ever, I see," he teases. "I am not angry with you, Evan. I was only ever afraid. And I will, it seems, always be afraid for your safety no matter where you are in life or what reckless decisions you're making. So please excuse me if I seem a bit . . . brusque at times. It will never mean I love you even the slightest bit less than I did before. Only that I am coming to terms with the consequences of my own actions, bringing a bull into a china shop and expecting anything to remain as it was."

"Am I the bull in this scenario?" I say. "And the royal family the china shop? Because as far as I see it, there was plenty of shattered glass here long before I arrived."

He chuckles, a low, familiar sound that fills me with warmth. "I suppose you're not wrong. Still, the damage remains—to all of you. And that is something I will have to live with."

"That's something *Ben* will have to live with," I correct him. "All you ever tried to do was give me and Alexander a chance to know each other. What happened after that was never your fault. And I'm a princess now, you know, so you have to believe me."

He shakes his head, his eyes glittering with tears. "Never thought I'd see the day, Your Royal Highness."

I make a face. I walked right into that one. "We have to lay some ground rules about titles and—whatever that is," I say. "If no one's calling my mom Your Majesty, then I deserve the right to be just Evan, too."

"Whatever you say, Your Royal Highness," says Jenkins with a bow of his head, and I huff, wrapping my arms around his shoulders and pulling him in for a tight hug.

"In spite of that," I say, low enough so only he can hear me, "I hope you know how much I love you, too. You were there for me when no one else was, and you gave me something—someone—to hold on to. You're as much my family as every other person in this room, okay? Don't ever forget it."

He hugs me back in silence, though I swear I can feel a warm splash of liquid on my bare shoulder as the seconds tick by. At last we separate, and he stands again, discreetly dabbing his face with a handkerchief. "Never, Your Royal Highness," he says, and he winks before returning to his position facing the rest of the room, his expression as stoic as ever.

Kit returns a moment later with a small plate stacked high with biscuits for us to share, and as soon as he's sitting beside me, I give him a long, lingering kiss, not caring who's watching. "Thank you."

"You're welcome," he says, a bit flushed. "Feeling better, then?"

"A little," I agree, picking up the top cookie and nibbling on it. "You'll be there the whole time, right?"

"I, er . . ." He pauses, plucking his own biscuit from the stack. "I'm not supposed to. It's just you lot, not me."

I scowl. "That's ridiculous. If Helene's coming—"

"That, I believe, was Astrid's suggestion to stave off any public relations nightmare," says Kit, amused. "I'm not Aunt Helene."

"No, but you're you," I say. "Which is even better."

"And I appreciate that very much," says Kit, kissing my cheek. "But I'm afraid you're not in charge of—"

"It's time," announces Jenkins, and all at once, everyone grows quiet. Even Helene and Nicholas, who have been talking quietly in the opposite corner, turn to focus on him, and Jenkins clears his throat. "Unlike Trooping the Colour, Your Royal Highnesses and Majesties will be going out in reverse of the usual order, with His Majesty and the Duchess of Lancaster appearing last."

As everyone gathers in the center of the room, in front of the middle floor-to-ceiling window, I take Kit's hand and lead him toward the bench, where my parents still sit. "The Duchess of Lancaster?" I say in greeting.

"It's infinitely better than the Queen of England," says my mom, and she stands to gather me in a warm embrace. "Besides, it's technically true, considering your father's also the Duke of Lancaster. I saw the footage from the chapel. You're really okay?"

"Completely fine," I promise, hugging her back. "I'm just glad we made a second dress so this one didn't get sliced and diced," I add as she lets go, and I gesture to the watercolor masterpiece I wore to the wedding. "Leave it to Ben to ruin couture."

"Oh, so *now* you care?" says another voice behind us, and Maisie appears in her own version of the watercolor dress, with Gia's hand clasped tightly in hers. "Baby steps are better than none, I suppose."

I give her a look that doesn't have much bite behind it. "Your ideas were genius. Locking him in, using voice samples to have his victims speak—"

"That bit was your doing, not mine," says Maisie, though she tosses her strawberry waves over her shoulder. "I'm happy to take the credit, though."

As always. I grin. "Dad—Kit's joining us, right?"

Alexander looks between us. "I assumed so. Kit, is that all right with you?"

Kit shakes his head as the middle set of windows—which are actually glass doors—open, and a cool breeze fills the stuffy room. Outside, a cheer rises from the gathered crowd, and my insides squirm. "I couldn't possibly leave Gia on her own. It would be terribly rude."

"I won't be alone," says Gia. "I'll have Tibby and Jenkins and Fitz—"

Maisie makes a face. "Kit, perhaps you ought to stay with her after all. I don't trust Fitz. He's been getting all of these *ideas* lately, like he's trying to be Tibby or something."

"You can't have her," I say immediately, and Maisie sniffs.

"If I want her, I'll take her. But I'll concede that she's still yours. For now."

Alexander clears his throat. "I suppose there's only one thing for it, then," he says. "Gia, you're welcome to join us, too, if you'd like."

All four of us are silent for a moment, and I quickly turn my gaze from my father to Maisie and Gia, who stand there, thunderstruck, staring at each other.

"I . . ." says Gia, uncertainty written on every feature of her gorgeous face. "I couldn't possibly—"

"Of course you can," says my mother warmly. "If you want to. If you both want to."

Maisie and Gia continue to stare at each other, until at last Maisie blinks, as if someone or something has snapped her out of it. "I—well, yes," she says, straightening her shoulders. "I'd like that. If you'd like that, Gia."

Gia swallows. "Very much so. But only if you're certain, Your Royal Highness. *Only* if you're certain."

The silence between them feels sacred somehow, as they search each other's expressions. But finally Maisie nods, and Gia does so in return.

"Then it's settled," says Alexander as he uses his cane to slowly stand. Constance, Helene, and Nicholas are stepping through the door now, and my heart starts to pound. "I believe it's your turn, girls."

My fingers dig into Kit's hand. "No excuse now," I say, but when I look at him, he's smiling down at me, and I know he has no desire to let go. And so, with Maisie on my other side, the four of us cluster together, and my sister and I step through the glass door and onto the balcony of Buckingham Palace with Kit and Gia at our heels.

The crowd of onlookers is thousands strong, and as soon as we step into view, their cries turn into roars. I cling to Kit's hand with all my might, and he grips back almost as tightly, as if this, too, is freaking him out. But when I glance at him, he looks as calm as ever, and when our eyes meet, he smiles and raises my hand to his mouth, brushing his lips to my knuckles.

The crowd below us whoops, and my cheeks burn, but I'm grinning so hard that my face hurts. There is nothing in the world like being loved by him, and the feeling of luck and enormous privilege that overwhelms me has nothing to do with the palace, or the balcony, or the new title. It's him. Every bit of it is him, and this family, and how much has changed in only a year and a half. The night I accidentally set fire to St. Edith's—the night that everything changed—I would've never believed this could've been possible. But it was. It is. And even when things aren't perfect, they'll still be a hell of a lot better than I ever dreamed they could be.

The crowd's roars, which already seem impossibly loud, now turn into a sheer wall of sound, and as I glance behind me, I see my mother and father arm in arm as they step out onto the balcony and into the spotlight as husband and wife. It's the first time the people have seen my father since the bombing—it's the first time they've seen what the ABR did to him, the scars and the lifelong injuries that are evident even in his uniform. But he stands tall, as tall as he ever has, and as he reaches the rail, he leans his cane against the stone and waves.

My mother is radiant, with eyes only for him, and on their other side, I spot Maisie and Gia, their hands clasped together. And as my parents kiss for the crowd, Maisie raises Gia's hand to her lips as well, exactly as Kit did moments ago to me. I can't see my sister's face as she kisses Gia's fingers, but Gia is beaming.

I don't know what the headlines will be tomorrow. I don't

know what the media will say about my parents, or Maisie and Gia, or about Ben's supposed bastardry or any of his crimes that leak into the public sphere. But I do know that what makes this moment incredible, even with all eyes on us, isn't the crowd or the adulation. It's that we get to be ourselves now in a way none of us have ever been before. Maisie and Gia, my parents, Kit and I—even Nicholas has his arm wrapped around Helene's shoulders on Gia's other side. They—*we*—may be royal, but that's not what defines any of us.

Not to be a total sappy cliché, but it's the love. And the scandals, fights, and familial terrorism. But mostly the love.

RAVENS RETURN TO THE TOWER

The three missing ravens residing at the Tower of London have finally all been found, according to the Ravenmaster of the Yeomen Warders, Jacob Johnston.

Mated pair Bronwen and Chester returned after nearly six months of absence, while Phillip remained missing until shortly after eleven o'clock this morning, when he was spotted on the roof of the Teapots and Treason Café.

"It's mad," said Katie Mayburn, owner of the café. "Almost like he knew His Majesty was getting married. Probably waited so he could attend the wedding, didn't he?"

With both Princess Mary and the newly styled Princess Evangeline, The Princess Royal, due to start their first term at Oxford University on 13 October, the Yeomen Warders are considering their options for keeping the ravens more secure within the Tower.

"Can't say Phillip won't get a bit of wanderlust and try to follow Their Royal Highnesses there," joked Ravenmaster Johnston. "He's always had a keen ear for the dramatic. But with any luck, he'll stay in the Tower for the time being. At least until things get interesting again."

The Ravenmaster is hoping to introduce another set of ravens in hopes that Phillip will choose to take a mate and remain nearby, even in the midst of future royal scandal.

—*The Daily Sun,* 6 October 2024

EPILOGUE

(Almost) Three Years Later

I'M ATTACHING THE LAST OF my papers in an email to my Classics professor when I hear a metallic scratching at the door.

Poppy looks up from the sofa in my off-campus flat, her fur glossy and soft thanks to Tibby's militant grooming schedule. Snickers, who lies asleep beside her, continues to snore louder than my alarm clock, oblivious to the potential mayhem in the hallway, where my PPOs should be keeping watch. It's a deal that's worked well between us for the past three years—they don't bust into my Oxford flat unannounced, and I don't scream and pretend I'm being kidnapped in order to sneak away without them noticing.

The scratching sounds again, and I frown, hitting send on my email and slowly closing my laptop. If someone's out there, either both of tonight's PPOs have taken a break at the same time or they're unconscious. My pulse quickens, and I stand, reaching for the crowbar I keep beside my desk for special occasions. Ben's been on house arrest for nearly three years now, locked up in a prison of his own making in Scotland, far from any royal residence—or anything fun at all—as he no doubt waits for a chance to exact his revenge, even though he has no power anymore. No power, no friends, no allowance, and nothing to his name but the humiliation of being known as the illegitimate son of the former Duchess of York. Even Nicholas, who married Helene two years ago and is now father to a baby daughter named Birdie, cementing Ben's expulsion from the line of succession, barely acknowledges him in private.

But because Ben is still alive, I'm always waiting for him to strike again. I'm always on guard, and I always will be to some degree, because if there's one thing royal life has taught me, it's to never underestimate anyone. Especially not someone who wants me dead.

And so, as I hear the metallic scraping sound once more, I grip the end of the crowbar in both hands, ready to strike. I take slow, cautious steps toward the door, even though my PPOs have drilled into me over and over that my best chance is to run and hide, but I refuse. If Ben is coming for me again—if he's finally slipped his gilded handcuffs—then I'll be ready for him. And this time, I won't offer him mercy.

As I raise the crowbar, the door finally swings open, revealing a dark figure on the other side. But as I aim directly for his skull, the low light from the kitchen catches his brown eyes, and icy shock cuts through me.

"Whoa!" cries Kit, ducking and throwing his hand out. "Ev! It's me! It's just me!"

I curse and use what little momentum I built up to throw my weapon into the carpeted seating area, where both dogs startle at the clank. "Kit? What are you *doing*? Where are—"

I poke my head through the door, and sure enough, my PPOs are standing on either side, stoic as can be.

Kit holds up two thin metal instruments in his right hand, while his left grips a pizza box. "I've been practicing," he explains. "Thought I'd surprise you. In hindsight, maybe I should've rung you first."

The lockpicks I gave him for his birthday. I exhale, both relieved and a little dizzy from the tension. "You scared the shit out of me," I say, pulling him in for a hug, careful not to knock the pizza away. "But you really cracked that lock on your own? In under thirty seconds?"

"Twenty-four," he says proudly. "I timed myself."

"Knew you had it in you," I say, giving him a quick kiss before letting him go. "Maisie and Gia went to the pub tonight, so I'm on Snickers duty. I thought you weren't coming this weekend."

"And miss your last two days of privacy? Never," he teases, and he sets the pizza down on the kitchen counter before pulling me into another hug. "This might be our last chance to walk the streets without photographers stalking us relentlessly."

I rest my head against his chest, and Poppy watches us from the sofa, while Snickers once again begins to snore. "I can't believe the media gave us three whole years of privacy."

"Out of the goodness of their hearts, I'm sure, and not because your father threatened to pull their reporters from the Royal Rota if they didn't behave," says Kit, running his fingers through my hair. "I missed you."

"You saw me three days ago," I say, but I kiss him again anyway, lingering this time. "I missed you, too. How's your mum?"

"Good. She says hello," he says, nuzzling the top of my head. "She's been begging me to invite you to dinner as soon as term is finished."

"Just as long as she's not the one cooking again," I say, and Kit laughs.

"She was trying to impress you. She's never tried to cook for me, you know. Which is one of the many reasons why I consider myself exceptionally lucky."

I grin into his shirt. "Yeah, of course I'll come. Will your dad be there?"

Kit's laughter quiets. "Unlikely," he admits. Even three years can't fully heal the rift between him and his father, but at least Kit can stomach a meal with him now, if the occasion calls for it. Which, considering his father is typically away on business, isn't often. "Another reason I'm lucky, I suppose."

"Very." I kiss his cheek and wrap my arm around his waist, content to watch Poppy breathe for a beat. These are the moments—the quiet ones, the ones without any pomp or circumstance, without an audience, the ones that will never make headlines—where I feel like I'm home. Even when uncomfortable subjects come up. Even when we don't have all the answers.

"I love you," I say, as if that's enough of a consolation prize to make up for the difficulties between him and his father. Kit presses another kiss to my forehead.

"I know," he teases, and I swat his backside gently, startling Poppy. He laughs again, the sound of it natural and unforced, and he reaches into the pocket of his blazer. "Before we eat, I have something for you."

"You do?" I say, releasing him from my grip. Even Poppy's ears perk up, and we both watch as Kit pulls something small from his pocket.

A black velvet box.

My heart starts to pound again, and my palms begin to sweat. No—this is a graduation present, that's all. Kit isn't exactly stingy when it comes to jewelry, and the silver bracelet I wear every single day is now filled with a classy number of charms, each one representing a milestone in our relationship, or a moment together that shifted our story in a small but seismic way. The tiara he first gave me when we started dating. The compass he left under my pillow shortly after my parents' wedding. A book, a guitar, a key, a dog—representing Poppy, of course. Each one a memory. Each one special to both of us.

But none of them came in a velvet box like this.

"Evangeline," he says, and he lowers himself onto one knee. The world around me tilts, and for a beat, I think I might end up joining him on the floor. "I could spend the rest of my life telling you how much I love you and why. Why you're my best friend, my partner, the person who brings color to my world, the choice I would—and will—make again and again, without hesitation or fear. How you and I are both whole on our own, but together, we're three-dimensional, something far greater than the sum of our parts—"

"Kit," I say, his name coming out as more of a squeak. "Are you—wait, are you really—"

He chuckles. "I will if you give me a chance," he says, and he slowly opens the box, revealing a simple, beautiful pear-shaped diamond big enough to need its own security guard. "I know you wanted to wait until after graduation, and I thought about taking you out to a flashy restaurant, or on a trip to Paris, or the Maldives, or anywhere you'd like to go. But this . . . this is one of our last few moments of privacy, and more than anything, I wanted this to be for us. Just you and me. Here, in our living room, with our fur child—"

Poppy raises her head again.

"—and every memory, both the good and the bad, that we've made together so far. You already know how much I love you, and how I always will, no matter what your answer is. So while I could spend the rest of my life telling you that you're my world, I'd rather spend the rest of our lives together showing you I'm yours. Endlessly and for eternity. Always on the good days—"

"But especially the bad," I finish for him in a whisper, my eyes filling with tears. I wipe my cheeks. "You already know what I'm going to say."

"I hope so," he says with such sincerity that my heart breaks and heals all in an instant. "But I still have to ask. Evangeline Florence Phillipa Constance Bright, will you do me the enormous privilege and honor of marrying me?"

I would go to war for this man. I would tear apart the world for him and put it back together again, just to give him a single moment of happiness. But we've already done that, and now we're here, facing the rest of our lives together, and there's nothing I want more.

"I told you I'd say yes, when the time came and you asked," I say, and despite the way the room spins, my voice is steady. I know what I want. I've known all along, from the moment I accepted that Kit was permanent. And even years later, nothing has changed. "This is it. This is my yes."

He bursts out into a wide smile, and as he plucks the ring from the box, I hold out my trembling hand. He slips it onto my finger, cold and heavier than I expect, and it feels—*right.* Not the diamond. Not the ring itself, even—not yet. But that Kit is the one putting it there.

As he rises, he catches me in his arms and lifts me up, crushing his mouth to mine in a messy, awkward, perfect kiss. I slide down his body slowly until my feet touch the ground once more, and only then do I open my eyes, gazing up at him. Despite the twists and turns and darkest hours we've had to face, I'm grateful for every road that brought us here—even Ben and all he put us through. Because if it hadn't been for him, our story wouldn't have been the same. And I can't stand the thought of our life together being anything but what it is now.

"I love you," I murmur, the tips of our noses touching.

"Mm. The biggest reason I'm exceptionally lucky." Kit kisses me again, softly this time. "I love you, too. More than anything in the entire bloody universe."

"Lucky me," I whisper, and we stay like that for the space of several heartbeats, caught in the warmth and perfection of the moment as the world moves on around us.

Until my stomach growls, and our little love bubble pops. I grin sheepishly. "Pizza?" I suggest, a hopeful note in my voice.

"Pizza," he agrees. We move toward each other at the same time, meeting in the middle for one more kiss before striding hand in hand into the kitchen. And while my life hasn't always been a fairy tale—unless we're counting Grimms'—this ending, this *beginning* is the happiest ever-after I could possibly imagine for a real-life princess.

And the best part is, it's mine.

ACKNOWLEDGMENTS

I first came up with the idea for Evan's story in 2012, with a plot that was surprisingly similar to what ended up being the first Royal Blood book, even if plenty of details changed along the way. It wasn't until 2019 that I finally sat down to write what was supposed to be a stand-alone, then a duology, and has now finished as a trilogy six years later, and to say it was a journey is a massive understatement.

First and foremost, to the team at Stimola Literary Studio, including Rosemary Stimola, Allison Remcheck, Alli Hellegers, Peter Ryan, and Nick Croce. You're all rock stars, and even after almost two decades, I cannot believe my luck in getting to work with you.

To Ro and Allison especially, for regularly talking me off the ledge, and for being there from the very beginning of this trilogy. These books wouldn't have existed without you and your sparks that grew into infernos, and I am forever grateful for your endless support.

To my editor, Kelsey Horton, and the entire team at Delacorte—especially Wendy Loggia, Christine Ma, Colleen Fellingham, Noreen Herits, Kristin Guy, Ray Shappell, Tatiana Guel, Shameiza Ally, Tamar Schwartz, and Emma Leynse—not only for taking a chance on this series, but for sticking by Evan and her story during the hurricane of the past few years and graciously allowing me the time I needed to finish telling it.

To Carli Segal, my best friend, who has been there for every page of this book and every high and low of the life I lived while writing it. I know you already know, but I'm going to say it anyway: I love you. You are the Ted Lasso to my Roy Kent, and we all know where Roy would be without Ted.

To Sara Hodgkinson, who has shown more love for this series than I could ever imagine. Thank you for taking my Americanisms and banishing them back across the Atlantic, but thank you more for your friendship and support, especially throughout the past three years.

To Becca Mix and Kristin Lord, two of the biggest cheerleaders on the planet. Speaking of highs and lows, I am so damn glad we're in this together. Thank you for loving this series from the start.

To Caitlin Straw, for the forever friendship and the universes we've created that would make sense to no one else. Thank you for understanding me and my characters better than I do sometimes.

To my friends who have (almost) nothing to do with my writing life whatsoever, yet played a vital part in holding it (me) together during the past three years, when everything was falling apart:

Ashley Oswald, there are no words. Literally, nothing I can say would even come close to describing how much you mean to me and how you held not just my fur family but my whole family together while we were losing the most important piece. You are an angel.

Angie Jacob, there may be nothing more to hack off now, and no more life to save practically every damn week, but a promise is a promise, and we're stuck with each other. Seems like a good deal to me.

Karla Bellfi, your love, your support, your steadiness—you have been a cornerstone in my life since my childhood, and I hope you know how much you mean to me. Thank you for inviting me into your family when mine began to dwindle, and thank you for being there when I need a real adult.

Malcolm Freberg, you know what you did. Or maybe you don't. But you did it anyway, and you keep doing it, and I am so glad we both loved the same band and despised the same character all those years ago.

Ashley Zajac, your enthusiasm for this series quite literally got me through the worst of writing this one. I was on the verge of leaving it unfinished, but then you started listening, and it really did mean that much to me.

To every reader who has picked up this series and given it a chance, whether it's because the premise caught your imagination, because you're into royalty, or because you love vampires (very sorry about that, hope you weren't too disappointed): Thank you for sticking around this long, and I really am sorry about the wait. Writing this trilogy has been a dream, and I don't think I could ever grow tired of these characters. I'm forever grateful for the opportunity to finish this chapter of their stories, despite how long it took to reach you.

To every doctor, nurse, physical therapist, assistant, technician, aid, and helper who has touched our lives over the past few years. Thank you for taking care of my dad and, by doing so, taking care of me. There are too many of you to name, but I remember and deeply appreciate each and every one of you, and I know he did, too.

And most of all, thank you to my dad, Richard Carter, who was there from the very beginning, and who loved me fiercely for every second of the overlap of our lives. I wish I'd told you what happens next. I wish I'd given you a draft to read. But I thought you had more time. We both did. And so, wherever you are, whatever galaxy you're exploring, I hope you're still able to read this, if you want to. (Yeah, yeah, I know you still want to. You always wanted to, no matter how busy you were or how much I still had to learn.) Even after we're gone, our stories are never finished, not while the people who love us remember us, and you touched every book I've ever written—every chapter, every page, every sentence. You left a hell of a legacy, through your own writing and all of your kindness, generosity, and the love you showed us all, from family to strangers to everyone in between. But these stories are your legacy, too. I would've never been a writer without your love, support, and encouragement, and just like your fingerprints are all over my life, they're all over the worlds and characters I create, too. The gift you gave me by believing in my dreams changed everything, but nothing is more precious to me than the time we had together, and the enormous privilege of having you as a father. I love you most.

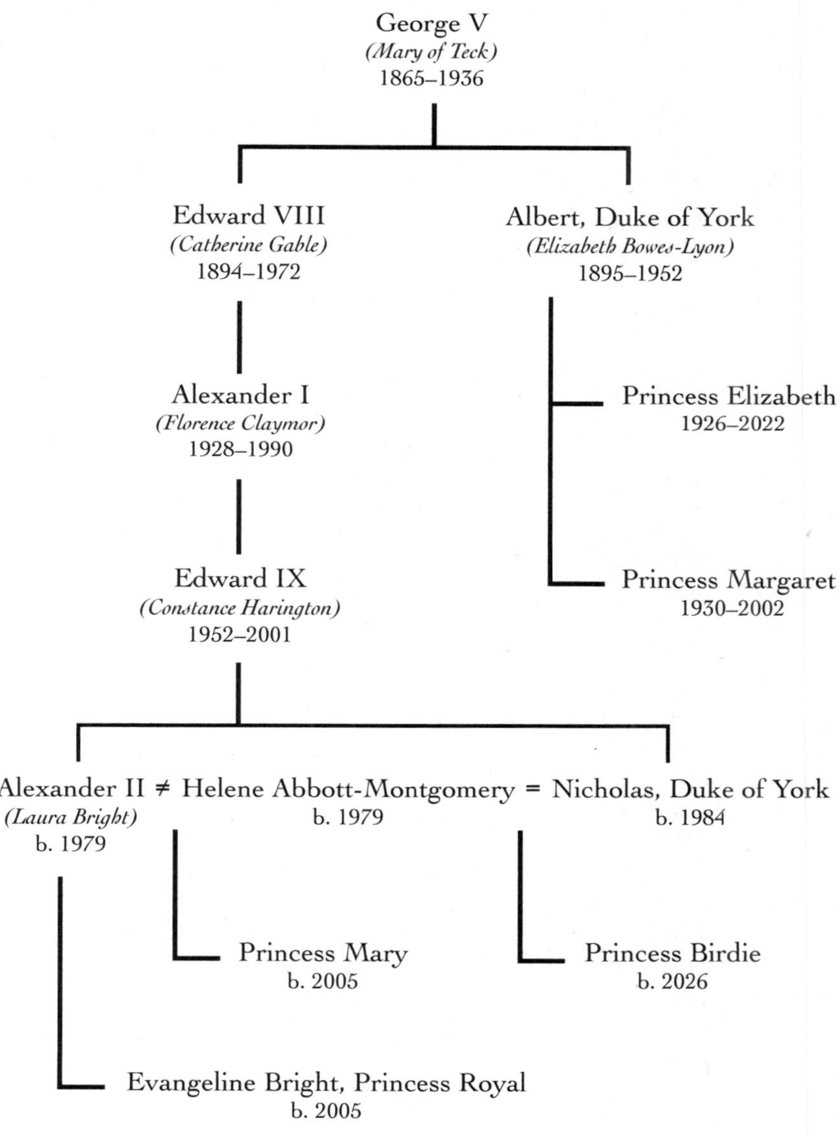
George V
(Mary of Teck)
1865–1936
Edward VIII
(Catherine Gable)
1894–1972
Albert, Duke of York
(Elizabeth Bowes-Lyon)
1895–1952
Alexander I
(Florence Claymor)
1928–1990
Princess Elizabeth
1926–2022
Edward IX
(Constance Harington)
1952–2001
Princess Margaret
1930–2002
Alexander II ≠ Helene Abbott-Montgomery = Nicholas, Duke of York
(Laura Bright)
b. 1979
b. 1979
b. 1984
Princess Mary
b. 2005
Princess Birdie
b. 2026
Evangeline Bright, Princess Royal
b. 2005

ABOUT THE AUTHOR

Aimée Carter is a graduate of the University of Michigan and the award-winning author of more than twenty books, including the series Royal Blood, the Goddess Test, and the Blackcoat Rebellion, as well as the Simon Thorn series for middle-grade readers, now a #1 internationally bestselling series under the titles Animox and Die Erben der Animox.

aimeecarter.com